Split
Verdict

Doug Booth

To those who cannot do what Wellington has done,

But for Linda, who is Madame Duvernay in every way.

Split Verdict

Friday, 13 October
Preliminaries

Maître Lefebvre swirled the amber-filled snifter slowly under his aquiline nose, intently, appreciating the richness of his favourite VSOP as he took in every word his friend and client had to say with such disconcerting earnestness.

"Yes, yes, of course. But what exactly are you not telling me, Trystan? Which I believe is the more important issue. Why this sudden urgency in such a mundane and routine matter as a will? Somehow I sense there is more you are not telling me. You are protecting me, Trystan, when I am the one who should be protecting you."

"I do not need your protection, Gaston."

"I have not seen you for several weeks, Trystan, and I see those weeks have not treated you well at all. Clearly you need something of a boost. Come," Maître Lefebvre moved slowly forward as though standing from his seat, "we shall go this very moment to my spa, enjoy a relaxing massage, a delightfully good dinner and then we'll enjoy too many of these damned expensive relaxants, as we once did before all this nonsense took over your life. Come. It's my treat, of course, and shop talk is absolutely prohibited."

His treat, of course. How Wellington despised the condescending words. How many times over the past two years had interfering and meddlesome neighbours and friends belittled him with the same demeaning phrase, at least at the beginning? They had been the primary reason behind his self-imposed seclusion, his imprisonment.

"Thank you, Gaston. Not tonight. There will be time enough when I have completed what I must do. Then I will treat you. My celebration."

"But what have you left to do? The document is prepared for your signature and, incidentally, you are greatly indebted to Madame Duvernay. Without her timely involvement I would not have had sufficient time to complete the document, given your short notice. You really are exceedingly inconsiderate at times, Trystan."

He ignored the reproach. He never called himself Trystan, not since discovering early in his youth that he was his parents' constant reminder of the couple's pre-marital trysts. Wellington took a long swallow of his cognac, placing his snifter at the edge of Lefebvre's glass desk and stretching his legs away from the leather, chrome and deceptively uncomfortable cube seat.

"My travel arrangements are complete. I leave next week for ten days. I promise we'll talk more when I return, Gaston, perhaps at the spa or over dinner. Then we'll have cause for real celebration, but not tonight."

"Yes, I know, your birthday. And why have you not alluded as to your destination, and for what reason you must leave?"

"I have a few appointments in the States, business meetings, and I did not mean for my birthday. That's all you get, so don't bother. And I expect full attorney-client privilege."

"Might I infer business opportunities?"

"You can infer appointments."

"For which you require counterfeit documents?" Lefebvre hunched over his desk, lacing his fingers together. "I am also aware of what else my dark and shady friends made available to you, Trystan. Why would you possibly want or require such a thing?"

Wellington grinned. "By "thing" you would mean?"

"I'm a criminal lawyer, my friend. I have held many of them during my career. Do not be coy with me. You are a man who feels he must apologize when others bump into you. To say this is all very uncharacteristic of you is to say nothing."

"Anyone call kill when the need exists, Maître Lefebvre. You of all people should know that. How many have you saved from injection?"

"My clients are professionals. I merely assist them with various aspects of their careers. Do not confuse them with amateurs. I was very unwise putting you in contact with such people, unwise in the extreme and I truly regret my actions."

"You worry too much, Gaston. Think of the thing as a phallic symbol, a toy. And…"

Lefebvre put up his hand quickly. "I do not want to know, not a word. Do you understand? If you are planning something foolish, I will not be able to intercede on your behalf, Trystan. I am your legal counsel, however…"

This time Wellington held up his hand, bringing the lecture to an abrupt end. He stood, his attention focused on the legal-blue document as he reached for one end of the darker blue ribbon that held the folder closed. He had to go. He had to get out and escape Gaston's judgmental superiority and inevitable questions. Despite his constant declarations that he would not pry into what did not concern him, Gaston always did.

"I have neither the time nor the desire to read the contents, Gaston. You are very certain you have followed my wishes?"

"To the letter, Trystan, as unnerving as the assignment was." Gaston stood, hesitating for a moment before he walked away from the desk. He refilled his empty glass without offering more to Wellington. "You need only sign the last page. I shall take care of the rest, as usual." Wellington unfolded the document, fanning through to the final page where he signed the first of four lines with the black Mont Blanc lying within easy reach. "Trystan, how many times have I told you about the Mont Blanc?"

Wellington ignored him, rolling his eyes, taking a deep breath and becoming serious once again. He needed to focus, to be meticulous. "He must remain here one week longer, Gaston. It is absolutely critical that he does not leave for France before the twenty-second and imperative that you succeed in your conversation with him. This document must absolutely be signed by him before my planned departure, not his. Do you understand, Gaston?"

"Your instructions are simple enough, Trystan. Yes, of course I understand. What I do not comprehend in the least is you. Though he will not like what you are asking of him, or so I am inclined to imagine. You Bartletts are what you are in more ways than one, whether you like the family resemblance or not." The lawyer grinned. "And I know you do not."

The twisted grin and arched eyebrows spoke the answer even before Wellington said: "That's of no consequence. Greed has always, and will always win out with him. Money and status come before everything else in his life, including Renée. You should be well aware of that by now. It's survival 101 and papa was an excellent teacher."

"You are not concerned that he will consider," Gaston waved his hands across the empty air in front of him for affect, "this magnanimous gesture of yours somewhat peculiar after all these years of such candid indifference towards one another?"

"No. He won't. He'll believe it's the natural order of things: his right, or my weakness. Actually, he'll think it's both."

"And, what about Mademoiselle Renée, may I ask? She has been excluded completely from your very overt generosity towards your brother, without as much as a token. From what little information I have gathered I must assume all is not well in the Bartletts' loft. She may not fair very well, Trystan."

There was nothing incomplete about the privileged information Gaston had regarding the Bartlett family. This was one of those times Wellington found himself particularly exasperated by the lawyer's feigned detachment and easy manner regarding the Bartlett family.

"She'll do fine, soon enough. Renée has always taken care of herself. She doesn't need him, she never has. And no, she gets nothing, not even honourable mention."

Gaston took the document, drumming the edges repeatedly against the top of the desk, wanting not to judge his client of so many years, though knowing from past experience that arguing would do no good. There was a single-minded determination in Wellington's eyes that made Gaston ill at ease witnessing such an uncharacteristic conviction. He sighed, reclining into his seat. "I will call him from home this evening."

"No, you won't. You'll call him now, my dear Gaston. It's four-thirty, he's there and you know what must be said. We don't need rehearsals at this eleventh hour. Do we?"

Gaston ignored the rebuke, studying the man he had come to know better than most. "You are staying for the call?"

"No. I'm not. I have my own plans to finalize and the timeline is very tight."

"Will you call before you leave?"

"There's no need. I told you. I'll call when I return and then I'll satisfy your curiosity and you can stop worrying about your implication."

Gaston nodded knowingly, not looking up as Wellington T. Bartlett made his way between the two cube seats and walked wordlessly from the private office of Gaston Lefebvre, senior partner with the law firm of Taylor, Lefebvre & Dunn. When the door closed he leaned forward, breathing deeply in an attempt to compose himself and his thoughts. Then, before he could allow himself the slightest hesitation, he pressed the cursor on his speed dial.
*

Jason Bartlett swore aloud when he viewed the caller ID. He didn't know Maître Lefebvre, though he knew of him and had always harboured an absolute and irrational dislike for his brother's attorney. He wondered why any out-of-work and borderline Account Executive like his brother would need to continue paying a retainer for legal counsel which could scarcely be needed and more scarcely afforded, especially since Geneviève had long since gone off in search of true love and happiness from the vantage of lying on her back.

Good riddance to the opportunist bitch, he thought, pressing hard on the green button to activate the hands-free mode. He answered with an abrupt and meaningful "yes", instantly compelled by a precise monologue that had been purposely scripted to make any interruption by him impossible.

"I'm afraid that's not doable, M. Lefebvre," he managed, finally. "My flights have already been booked. They have been for weeks and the conditions are replete with severe penalties."

Wellington was also aware his brother would always fly Executive Class, and always with open tickets in the event he would have to alter his plans unexpectedly, even though that almost never happened. What mattered was being seen by others and Wellington knew his brother needed status in whatever form available to him.

"As I have explained, Mr. Bartlett, the amount we are talking about is well in excess of two million dollars, and your brother has named you as sole beneficiary of his estate. His entire estate, I must add, which is no small amount, monsieur. Surely that is of interest to you, despite your brother's whim?"

Jason despised the lawyer's tone which he interpreted as more effeminate and haughty than superior, and he loathed even more anyone who didn't conform to his interpretation of normal. With arrogant lawyers the distinction was not particularly clear, especially this one.

"Of course," Gaston continued, "now that Mademoiselle Geneviève's settlement has been finalized, and she has no present or future claim on any assets, your brother is most anxious to see this very critical part of his legal affairs concluded. The one stipulation is that you present yourself at the law offices of Taylor, Lefebvre & Dunn at a time convenient to you on October 22. Do you agree to these terms, Mr. Bartlett?"

"I don't like being coerced, M. Lefebvre. He knows that. And I don't like having to alter my plans at the very last minute. My flight to Paris departs this coming Monday, the 16th, and he knows that as well. For Christ sake, this couldn't have come at a worse time. What he's doing could not be more intentional, intentionally spiteful."

"He is your brother, Mr. Bartlett. I have no doubt that forgiving a slight eccentricity on his part is well within your wide range of personal capabilities."

"He's many things, Maître Lefebvre, but it's been a very long time since he's been my brother. I suspect you might already know that. And eccentricity, I suppose so. Even you must think this whole business is exceedingly peculiar."

The silence was brief. "At what time might I expect you, Mr. Bartlett?"

"I will meet with you on the sixth, the Monday after my

return. I must also insist the meeting be brief and held after hours. I have certain commitments which I cannot alter. This matter has come very unexpectedly, as you might appreciate, and the timing is not at all acceptable. His people skills are as questionable as always and your call could not have come at a worse time."

"Your brother's stipulation is very clear, Mr. Bartlett. I am afraid any date other than the twenty-second is very much out of the question. You understand, of course." Jason needed to throw something. He needed to grab something and squeeze hard to release the pent-up energy that was quickly becoming red-faced anger. He squeezed the receiver, too angry for words, too anxious not to speak. "Mr. Bartlett? Are we still connected, Mr. Bartlett?"

Jason loathed not having the upper hand, and he despised queers or lawyers who sounded like queers. "Yes! We're still connected." The words spit from his mouth like venom. Jason often found hiding his true self difficult and this was one of those times.

"Then, Mr. Bartlett, might I suggest ten AM on the twenty-second?"

"No. The twenty-second's a Sunday for Christ sake, and will cut into my trip by a week. And, need I remind you, I would have to change my flight? I'm not even certain I can at this late date."

"That detail has already been attended to, Mr. Bartlett. I do hope no offense is taken. However, at your brother's request, I have taken the liberty of arranging alternative flights for you. He believed you might be preoccupied with other, more pressing matters. I reserved Executive Class seats in your name for late in the day, on the twenty-second. I assumed your wife, Madame de Thierry, would want to maintain the original itinerary. I do hope that is what Madame would want."

Jason knew he had no choice, and he knew he had to

make his impatience seem real, unaffected, and for the most part his impatience with his brother and Lefebvre was genuine. Of course, his wife would leave as planned; pleased she would be spending an extra week alone with her arrogant parents in her beloved Paris. He would meet her at the time-share condo in coastal Antibes a week later. He would have much to think about and do during the first week alone. Then, during his two weeks by the enticing French Riviera, he would have more time to ponder his loving brother. When he finally spoke to Gaston his tone was deliberate.

"Your concern is commendable, M. Lefebvre. Yes, Madame Bartlett will leave as planned. It would seem as though I have no choice. I will meet her the following week and we shall both be inconvenienced by your," he paused, trying hard to be civil, "my brother. I assume he will also be at your office?"

"No, sir, he will not. Unfortunately, Trystan, Mr. Bartlett, has previous commitments which will preclude his being here. He truly regrets he cannot and is equally certain you understand. In fact, he has just now left my office and will be unreachable until your return from France three weeks from now, on the second. I am certain he would be here if changing his schedule was remotely possible. Nevertheless, he has authorized me in his absence to witness the signing. I suppose somewhat irregular, although very acceptable."

"You mean acceptable to my brother, and changing my schedule, not his."

"Yes, indeed, Mr. Bartlett. That is decidedly what I mean."

The quiet over the telephone line was electric, making the tension between them and the mutual dislike more palpable. Gaston had nothing more to add to the conversation. He had followed the script perfectly, or Jason had, and Jason Bartlett had performed exactly as Wellington had predicted. He would be there, as scheduled.

"Then, may I assume you are in agreement, Mr. Bartlett?"

Jason paused, swallowing hard, trying to clear his throat. He wasn't sure himself whether he was delighted with this sudden news, or put off by the untimely disruption. "I'll be there."

"C'est très bien. Je vous attends le 22 à dix heures, Monsieur Bartlett."

Neither man heard the other disconnect. Gaston Lefebvre smiling widely as he scrolled through the speed-dial once more; Jason Bartlett poured a double JW Blue and smiled for his own reasons.

Friday, October 13, was the beginning

Sunday, 22 October
A Fait Accompli

At fifty-two, Jason Bartholomew Bartlett had occupied the office of senior vice president at IntelSanté for five years. The Directorate had approved his promotion to the position of president that would take effect in three years, the retirement date of his mentor and current president, Mr. Eric J. Bloomington. He stood a trim 1.83 metres with perfect, jet-black hair and gleaming white teeth that were naturally perfect. He didn't wear glasses; he wore Serengetis to shade his perfectly clear eyes from the harmful effects of the sun. He faithfully enhanced his tailored wardrobe twice yearly, by appointment, during his trips to France, when he would exchange one season's wardrobe with the newest fabrics and styles available from the Armanis and the Versaces of the designer world. Those who wondered at the price of his wardrobe, or whatever else he had ever acquired, couldn't afford them, and neither could he. Not to imply he didn't enjoy smiling condescendingly in response to those who were sufficiently in awe of him to ask the question.

He drank Johnnie Walker Blue, straight, from a chilled glass, no ice, and wouldn't patronize clubs that could not accommodate the prerequisite. He paid with one of three platinum cards and drove a Cadillac Escalade which he parked alongside his wife's Z4 in the underground garage of the exclusive condo building. The full-service and luxurious

15

two-tiered penthouse was ideally situated in the fashionable suburb of Outremont, complete with a sometimes colourful, sometimes bleak Montreal skyline and his brother's two million would make all the difference.

. He had always loved the feeling of being part of a class apart, although he played the part rather than being a true member of the city's elite that had struggled not to die out at the threshold of the new millennium along with his parents and the golden era they had grown into. He wasn't counted amongst the nouveau riche and never would be. He was well off and living beyond his means. Like his brother he had been reared in affluence and when their father's abrupt death preceded their mother's by one year they had both inherited five-hundred thousand dollars. The balance of the considerable estate had been bequeathed to various causes and charities, and that unexpected generosity towards the less fortunate had always been a source of irritation to Jason. If not for his father, he could have been very rich.

When the brothers had reached the age of majority their father insisted each man take out a substantial life insurance policy against the other's life. Each would remain the other's sole beneficiary until such time as either one married, so Jason was well aware of the source of Wellington's bewildering generosity. His own success and lifestyle had come to him over time and was being stretched to the limit. He had simply lost the perspective and balance long ago instilled in each of them by completely dissimilar parents and divergent philosophies about life and good living. Mr. Bartlett had been pragmatic and Jason had tended towards the man's cool objectivity and determined business manner. Wellington had not, being subtlety influenced by the humanity, goodwill and gentleness of his mother.

At some point Jason's learned condition became a state

of mind, with a predisposition for single-mindedness, a character flaw that had begun when what had been the most important element of his life began slipping away from him, seemingly so long ago. Now he only loved Renée when there was a need, when they were in public together, or when he was not with his mistress of ten years: Carmelita, the office hottie whose husband had died some years earlier.

Those deeply engrained characteristics were not the only ones differentiating Jason from his mirrored brother. Those in his social circle would browse through the Robb Report and dream, still unable to stretch the budget enough to upgrade to a better whatever, still envying those who could step up. Wellington, on the other hand, had never invested more than 500 dollars on a suit and he usually waited for sales. He never spent more than seventy-five dollars for a shirt and his usual pinch tassel loafers never cost more than three hundred. His three-year-old Honda Accord was leased and his home was simply a house he had always hated, a country-styled cottage that had come with a city-styled mortgage and boasted every amenity Geneviève had thought Renée would have wanted. He had tried his hardest to share time with her there, but being together had never seemed natural, always forced or feigned, struggling with the inner conflict when he should have said goodbye.

The house was situated at the foot of the diminutive mountain that stood watch over and gave title to Le Village-du-Mont-Saint-Hilaire and still had a mortgage he could barely afford. He drank Johnnie Walker Red as a statement of frugality over taste and more frequently than before. His billfold was always coming away from its thin collection of low-denomination bills and both his haberdasher and barber had become strangers.

Wellington was ordinary and dull when compared to his brother. In fact he dwelled on the apparent and superficial differences between them and hated himself for doing so, fully cognizant the resentment ran deeper than mere sibling envy or the debilitating disease that had taken him over.

Of course, the root cause of his ruined life wasn't exclusively Jason. He was merely a social barometer, Wellington's constant reminder of how unsuccessful he had been in life: his personalized measurement of failure. He hated so many others as much as his brother, or himself: all those who continued disparaging him for the differences between him and his brother which he had no control over, like Geneviève. Fucking whore, with all her brain-fucked boyfriends who thought they could get into shape by getting into her. Her frequent late nights at the health club had gradually become entire nights away from home and the rarely shared intimacy between them, which had never been more than a two-sided pretense, ended.

He hated her most and, strangely, had not thought of her at all over the last year. When he had, previously, he thought of a bitch in micro-fibre thongs, a loose tank top and open legs, despising her for all those wasted years. Not thinking about her had ironically been his final gift to her, a selfish gift she would never know to be thankful for.

They had first met at the health club where she worked as a trainer and the charming, tall and elegant Wellington with his European flair, poise and timid simplicity had instantly infatuated her. Not long after they had begun seeing one another, which is to say his parents' time frame, he had introduced her to Mr. and Mrs. Bartlett. She had immediately mistaken what his parents had and Jason's flamboyant lack of restraint with what she could have with Wellington, and she had anxiously said "yes" when he asked.

He had always been disinclined towards marriage, for no reason he could readily explain to those curious enough to enquire. However in his particular industry a happy spouse was requisite to the advancement everyone interpreted as success. Her wedding had not been anywhere near as grandiose as Renée's, as Jason had alluded to on several occasions in a mean-spirited attempt to diminish the brother whom he had always regarded as better suited to mediocrity. He would change with her help and her input, she knew, and he would be every bit as successful as Jason. She and Renée would be friends. They would do lunch and shop at all the best boutiques, they would play tennis at the club and they would attend tea parties together and do benefits. That was then.

Several years after their marriage, years before Geneviève had thought of leaving him, he had met Gi-Gi one day while at the juice bar of Geneviève's newly built athletics club which had been funded largely by his recent inheritance he had willingly shared with her. Gi-Gi had come through the door wearing form-fitting Spandex and had smiled at him. The timing had been right and they became instant friends. Over time the warmth and need for friendship grew into an intimacy both had been searching for, and separately they wondered why the closeness had become difficult over the past two years, uncomfortable, when they should have been so happy.

Wellington had tired of the lies and the secrecy, tired of always being the kept man and all those special evenings with Gi-Gi had become less frequent, which had put a tremendous strain on the relationship. Gi-Gi fought hard to understand why and had always wanted desperately to reach out, but Wellington had become withdrawn, distant, and now they only spoke when he had something to say.

He was an unemployed Account Executive and becoming more unemployable every day. The industry viewed him as fifty plus, unwanted and unneeded. He hated being obsolete, a has-been, and he hated himself, which wasn't the problem. Hating himself could easily be remedied, especially now with nothing left for him to lose.

And what of those others?

What he needed was to stop hating them, to unleash himself once and for all from their grasp. He needed to escape their suffocating dominance over his life and his deepest thoughts, which they controlled without culpability. He had lived the past two years in virtual seclusion, not so much shielding himself from the world as hiding from it. So who would miss him when he was gone? No one, he guessed fairly accurately. His time for freedom had come.

For the most part he had spent the last twelve months alone, thinking, formulating, putting together a plan, *the* plan, and now he had come or gone too far to concede defeat. At first the plan had been subconscious, a fleeting and incoherent thought that would come and go, a thought he had interpreted as regret and self-pity. Then, at some point, the macabre thinking had transformed into an agenda and his thinking had come to an end, a newly created agenda remaining: the plan. And the plan was perfect, his first agenda in two years: an agenda without flaws, and certainly no misgivings.

*

Neither brother wore jewelry, with the exception of identical school rings, although Jason did wear a wedding ring. Wellington had discarded his the very moment Geneviève had walked out on him after fifteen years of marriage and several years of cheating. She had left him virtually destitute after the settlement he could barely afford, now that he had been between positions for those two years. Two full years in reclusion with absolutely nothing to show for them apart from diminishing personal finances, a costly divorce and friends who had quickly become conspicuous by their absence.

His neighbours had eventually come to avoid him because they didn't know what to say, and now they openly shunned him because he had neglected the maintenance of his house on their beautiful street for so long. He hadn't done anything during his time at home. He hadn't washed the windows or swept away the cobwebs and his front lawn had become overgrown with weeds. At first he had hired a contractor to manage the snow removal and the lawns, though his real need was to avoid anyone who might have thought to ask obvious and imposing questions that were none of their damned business. Perhaps if they had known, none of them would have had the slightest interest in talking with him.

The service had stopped when the payments stopped, he was headed into another winter of neglect and to all of them he had become the house at the end of the street behind the huge twin maple trees. They had no kids, thank God. The point was moot, he thought, being that the bitch would certainly have taken them along with everything else.

He didn't miss her, he never thought of her, and he had let Gaston take charge of the divorce proceedings. Perhaps that particular decision had been a mistake; he was a trial lawyer. Though, in truth, she had been the real mistake, one he had made for all the wrong reasons and he'd be paying the price for his cowardice for a very long time. The time had come to get over her. The last time he had seen her was the night before she had walked out, the night he had told her he would be spending more time at home, again.

Two years ago, the night when she had finally realized she would never have the privileged lifestyle Renée enjoyed. She was then forty-three, youthful and attractive, smart, and tired of living in the shadows of the successful brother. She was tired of excuses, always declining invitations for ski weekends, elbow-rubbing social events or exotic vacations because the timing was never truly convenient. And never would be with Wellington.

She had never accepted the truth from Wellington that all those invitations had been a simple means for Jason to taunt and ridicule him, and her, to feel superior beside a brother who was already deeply burdened with self-recrimination for his own inadequacies. Jason would never allow them to infiltrate and dilute his influential circle of friends and associates whose relationships were founded on the understanding of mutual gain and reciprocity. They didn't fit in and they never would.

Wellington would not deny she had become successful in her own right as a businesswoman and physical trainer, albeit on her back. She had begun earning good money and had been asked out by most of her male clients. She knew men found her attractive. She enjoyed the attention which soon became a need, an obsession; though she could never enjoy her life the way she wanted, not with him, so she lived life behind his back. She could never know, could never be certain when Wellington would once again be spending more time at home. She wanted more, she deserved more and she hadn't for a second faltered before closing the door behind her.

Bitch. It wasn't as though he hadn't tried all his life.

There had been no malice in the separation. Initially her disappointment with her life had developed into a short-lived guilt, which mutual friends had eagerly reported, unwittingly adding to Wellington's already deeply rooted resentment. Now he didn't care. She had been forgotten, the emotions had quelled. He had read once that people who sincerely don't care are the most dangerous, the most unpredictable to themselves and others. When one has nothing to lose, and personal gain has no value, what then? And who really cares anyway?

He had always been measured against Jason, and he had always hated feeling second best. Since their youth they had looked the same and dressed the same, had been educated in the same schools, in the same classes and had even been sick at the same times. They had summered together each year with their parents in the south of Spain where their stock broker father owned a condo in the then untouched region of Almería, which he had put in the name of his pampered and dutiful wife. Their secondary education had been completed at a very select and private academy for the insufferably precocious children of society's well-connected. The school was located in Montpellier, south of Nîmes in the wine region of Langudoc-Roussillon on the shores of the then pristine blue Mediterranean and by their mid-teens the brothers were fluent in three languages. Their father would have accepted nothing less.

They would need French in order to realize the success in Quebec he was expecting of them, and he believed Spanish would be an important language in world affairs by the eighties and into the nineties. He wanted the boys prepared to meet the world head on and they were, differentiated by imperceptible tonal differences existing in their speech, regardless of the language, which was seldom discernible to their most intimate acquaintances whose company they seldom shared as they grew older. They had spent so much time together during their youth that in the eyes of others they had become one, and Wellington hated him.

Returning to Montreal after four years abroad, and largely due to the father's influence, they had been accepted into the McGill Faculty of Science programme and both young men had obtained their respective degrees by the age of twenty-two. As Jason went into a two-year MBA programme, followed by two years of Computer Sciences, Wellington had decided upon the labour market. By the time Jason received his advanced degrees, and with his father's input, Wellington was already into the fifth year of a promising career in the lucrative pharmaceutical industry and his first year with the Spencer Pharmaceutical Corporation.

That was then. So much had changed and so much had not.

*

Apart from a golden tan Jason maintained with frequent spa visits, which his company sponsored as a perk, and a slightly different hairstyle he maintained with weekly visits to a fashionable salon, the brothers were indistinguishable. They were identical in every way, including the monogrammed school rings neither man ever removed.

Inwardly Jason truly did believe he loved his wife with a series of learned and habitual motions they had both adapted to and performed well, though in truth, or in denial, he loved being seen with her more than being with her. They had fallen out of passion, not out of love's facsimile and the passion had been lost for too long to rekindle the burning heat of the first intimate embraces they had shared during their first summer. They had become comfortable friends and neither cared to recapture the past. So sad that such a powerful obsession for one another had been discarded, never knowing what he had done or what he had not done. And at this point, after so many years, what did it matter, he often thought? That's why he had Carmelita and occasional others: those special moments that were no longer special to Renée, or with her.

Somehow there had always been a void in the relationship which had insidiously evolved from the least likely moment and he only ever dwelled upon the hollowness when he was alone. He had never thought to ask Renée why, possibly because he had never wanted to hear the answer. If there had even been a real need for him to hear the words.

Inexplicably, the day of the wedding had altered what he and Renée had shared so intimately during their first season of untamed love and their eager exploration of one another. At first he hadn't noticed the change coming over her

24

because he was too self-absorbed in his escalating success. But a subtle nuance of disenchantment that neither one could define in the newly sanctioned marriage, particularly René, had begun to emerge. Wellington on the other hand thought he might want a wife to love again, not certain of the reason or need, and certainly not yet. As much as he wanted to dream of her, to feel her in his arms, to smell her and taste her once more, this time for more than a fleeting moment, he had pushed that thought from his mind. Until he succeeded, all that he did and all that he thought was the plan.
*

Renée Bartlett, née Renée Christine de Thierry, proud citizen of the city of Paris, France and self-declared free citizen of the world invaded Montreal during a summer long forgotten in a flurry of European flair to immediately captivate the tall, dark-haired, and athletic Jason. Her elegance, beauty and charm that somehow excused her free-thinking and joie-de-vivre attitude instantly captured and gripped his heart. She was intrigued by his unblemished fluency when he spoke her language and the casual arrogance he thought was confidence. She was twenty-one; she was beautiful, exuding a sensuality few women could.

They fell in love immediately. While she spent the summer in the world's second largest French-speaking city as a linguistics exchange student from the Université de la Sorbonne they made love and felt love as though they had been in the world's first, her city, Paris. Why not? He was twenty-seven; six years her senior, smooth in every way and a successful Account Manager with IntelSanté, a Montreal pharmaceutical firm that would soon expand their market base to include subsidiaries in Madrid, Brussels, New York and Tokyo.

They were the industry leaders and would eventually lead the industry with a new and aggressive web-based pharmacy that would adversely impact and destabilize the competition for quite some time. He would be part of it and she would be with him, always. They were a perfect couple and that summer had been a perfect summer. They had loved with the fervour and intensity possessed by all young lovers, and had planned a future rooted in that heated love.

That September Renée returned to her native France to complete her final fall and winter semesters from which she had graduated at the top of her class and, despite all the heartfelt and fearful pleas of her parents, she had immediately returned to Montreal and Jason. Monsieur and Madame de Thierry had implored her to remain in Paris where the wealth and social standing of the de Thierry name carried influence and would guarantee her a successful career in her field, heartbroken when she insisted she would work in Montreal and be with Jason.

Jason and Renée married the following spring in an excessively extravagant ceremony. Of course, her parents did attend, although their own relationship with Jason would always be cold, distant at best. The wedding would also be the one time they would see his brother Wellington.
*

The Friday night bachelor party at the elite gentleman's club, Le Millionaire, had been the beginning of the thirty-hour pre-nuptial ritual. The fathers of the bride and groom were invited, each declining for different reasons, and no one cared. In fact, most were pleased, Jason in particular. The club was restricted to members and the calibre of entertainment was always high-end with tie and jacket required and discretion was always guaranteed. By the time the last call had been served Jason had been entertained by the club's most popular girl in a more private setting, courtesy of his male entourage who had waited impatiently throughout the hour to hear his detailed account, by which time he was oblivious to his surroundings and quite unable to talk, let alone satisfy anyone's curiosity.

One of the services occasionally made available by the club to the more preferred clientele was an after-hours limousine service, which would later be added to their monthly statement and certainly never mentioned again. Jason and Wellington shared the ride to their parents' home where several guests had been invited to stay for the wedding, including the parents of the bride-to-be and the bride herself who would enjoy her privacy in the east wing, separated from the groom by two floors, several hallways and the uncertainty that doors might open at any moment.

Renée had spent the eve of her special day with her new friends who, for the most part, were the significant others of Jason's old friends. The mothers, who had been at the obligatory bridal shower a week earlier, were absent by choice when the girls had joined up at La Soirée Pour Elle for an evening of pulling at the waist bands of muscular and oily male dancers wearing fake tans and nylon g-string-banks, which the ladies eagerly filled with tens and twenties.

She had also enjoyed her own abundant share of white wine and temptation, cognizant all the while of constraints imposed by self-righteous peers or, worse, the fear of gossiping lips. They were Jason's peers, not hers, and for that reason alone much of the excitement of her evening was imaginary. Wine becomes more compelling with wine, and the most important day of her life was upon her.

The taxi ride to the Bartletts' stately home when the evening had ended was uncomfortable and ungracious, only the effect of the evening's festive excessiveness making the driver's suggestive advances seem charming. When she arrived at the home she over-tipped him, forgot him, and eased herself out from the backseat, concentrating on not falling on the four levels of imported flagstones leading to the front entrance.

Opening the double mahogany doors required leaning forward and squinting, scratching the antique bronze faceplate of the one-of-a kind English-made lock with a scrawling attempt to insert the key. She fell inward as the massive doors swung open effortlessly on ball bearing hinges. Moments later she crawled on all fours and grabbed at the ornate lever-styled handles to push the huge doors to the closed position, finding herself struggling to keep up as she was pulled awkwardly along the cold marble floors on her knees towards the portal. She would be married in less than twelve hours. This was not good. She rubbed her face hard, pushing herself up against the heavy doors and stood there, dishevelled. She had enjoyed her evening nonetheless; graduating her way past tipsy to drunk, and either didn't care or was unaware she had left her keys in the barrel of the lock.

She would never remember how she had succeeded in locating the en suite room the Bartletts had assigned to her. The bedroom area with its private bathroom was elaborate and spacious and decorated according to the elegant tastes and generous allowance of Mrs. Bartlett. The adjoining sitting room allowed guests to relax as they would in their own homes with their feet up on designer sofas and chaises-longues as they listened to their choice of music from a wide selection of cassettes, watched television, read a book or enjoyed the always full wine rack and calming muted ambiance.

The gentlemen's limousine arrived moments after Renée had barely negotiated the stairways and hallways to her private quarters. She lay sprawled on the sofa in the en suite with the door still open, the soft hue of the integrated lighting making her appear more peaceful, more inviting, more tempting in her stupor than she would have felt had she been conscious.
*

28

Wellington hated drunks, especially when they were fornicating whoremaster bastard brothers. They fell together twice, entwined and entangled as they climbed towards the same doors Renée had scarcely managed to pass through moments earlier.

Wellington swore, seeing the tear in his slacks and the searing pain told him the injury would be more serious than mere bruising. They had been raised, directed and moulded to be successful, not religious, although any swearing during their youth within earshot of their father brought swift and severe admonitions and extra-curricular writing assignments on the benefits of proper and civil communication. Bastard! How would this piece of smelly flesh be fit to marry his Renée in so few hours? The after-stench of cigars on his breath was overwhelming and, after so many, what difference could there be between his brother's Blue labeled scotch and his Red. His brother was seriously pissed when he landed unceremoniously on the polished hardwood floor of the Great Room.

Wellington stared at the keys he had pulled from the lock. His parents customarily gave houseguests monogrammed solid bronze key chains they were expected to accept as open invitations for future visits. The keys belonged to Renée. He studied at the unconscious mound on the floor that was snorting, though otherwise still, turning his attention towards the stairs as his mounting curiosity became an urgency making him both uneasy and excited. He removed his footwear and climbed slowly, one step at a time, not once thinking to hesitate. He felt no guilt because he had done nothing to feel guilty about. What he felt was disgust towards his brother who lay insensate and reeking at the bottom of the stairs. His stomach was constricting, making him want to retch as he continued up the spiral staircase and along the carpeted hallway to where the soft hue of amber lighting shone beyond its source to paint the pure white walls outside her room.

He paused, mere centimetres from the door's threshold, holding his breath, his lips pursed as his heart began palpitating to the point of rupture. He took one step closer, stopping one last time before peering into the en suite, not knowing what to expect. He was afraid, driven by the same fear. He was obsessed and more excited by the moment.

She was there, slouched on the sofa. Her head reposed sideways against the silky smooth brocade of muted yellows and greens that were the backdrop to her soft and creamy white skin. Her thighs were slightly parted and entirely bare between the edges of the deep-red linen mini-skirt flaring out across her waist and the band at the tops of her nylons attached to the pure white butterfly ribbons of her garters. He stood there, paralyzed, absorbing, memorizing, terrified his breathing would wake her. He was half in and half out of the doorway. He was spellbound by the rise and fall of her breasts and mesmerized by the stillness of her soft thighs protruding from her white silk panties so perfectly showing evidence of the moist softness that lay beneath. She was titillating, arousing.

He was transfixed, stranded between heaven and hell, and staring at her perfect body that was so peaceful, so inviting with her arms spread out like a snow angel on a perfect winter day. His body was reacting to urges he could not suppress. He wanted and needed to see more of her, to kiss her, taste her and smell her. He wanted her. He had always wanted her, to see her naked and hold her bare skin against his. He had always loved her, and always would. He stood a moment longer, memorizing the vision he would carry in his mind for a lifetime. He checked the hallway to be certain, absorbing all that he could of Renée before closing the door behind him.
*

Seeing Jason standing at the head of the aisle as she walked towards the altar with her arm entwined tightly with her father's, Renée felt an immediate difference towards the man she was about to marry. She was flushed; her heart was palpitating wildly, which all the guests attributed to girlish innocence. Not so. The cause was far from girlish and not at all innocent. She was aroused by her desire for the man who had loved her with such a heated intensity so few hours earlier, and by the warm pain still lingering deep within her. The love-making had been different, illicit and raw, and would be for the rest of their lives. She loved Jason beyond words.

"I will love him, papa."

"Oui, ma petite joie, mon cœur. Je le sais."

Although he didn't understand and said nothing more, except to the priest when he had choked on the words that would one day inexorably alter everyone's life.

The partying that followed the ceremony continued through to the very early hours of the following day until none but the very young or unconscious remained, and then with no great memory of the hours that had passed. Renée was the first to leave the reception, with Jason, who had not fully recovered from the night before, trailing closely behind her to the raunchy chorus of cheers and encouragements coming mostly from the younger male guests. Wellington took in the scene silently, unobserved and without expression from a dimly lit corner where he sat with one knee arched on the second cushion of a love seat he had commandeered some hours before.

She had glowed all evening long as she danced with each of the gentlemen and all the younger ladies, giggling and laughing, engaging each nearby guest in conversation during dinner and tossing her bouquet to create the most chatter. When she danced with Wellington he had held her close, pretending happiness for his sister-in-law, savouring her essence, the last few moments he would love her and feel her warmth. He would never again hold her as tightly. Never again would he be so close to her. Jason was everything she could ever have wanted, and she was everything he would ever want.

Wellington signalled the bartender who brought over another double JW Red, straight. He took the old-fashioned from the tray without speaking. He was in another place, another time, reliving what was already a fleeting moment in his life he would relish forever. They had gone, and she might just as well have died. He loosened his bow tie and brought the silky white softness from his breast pocket to his cheek, inhaling the pungent aroma emanating from the soft, silky folds. He ordered another Red.

*

Monsieur de Thierry had spent his time with the Bartletts studying every action, every word, and every mannerism of his soon-to-be son-in-law. He recognized what was a noticeable difference between the twins and he lamented what he saw as truly opposite natures. Jason was clearly a man driven solely by greed and ambition, with a single-minded need to succeed. He saw Wellington as introverted, a disturbing quietness disguising a deep resentment that would fester over time and eventually bring grief to the Bartlett family and his own.

That night, after M. de Thierry had given his daughter to her new husband, losing her to him, and as he lay so alone in the guest room with his wife sleeping closely against him, he gripped at the down-filled duvet and cried silently for his daughter.

*

Renée had been away from her husband for the better part of a week, visiting with her parents in France. M. de Thierry had never changed his opinion of Jason, and being alone with his daughter was a happy event for him.

As much as she and Jason had grown apart over a

twenty-four year marriage he somehow missed her, though what he missed most was her presence. There was an unmistakable and unfamiliar void in the city condo. He hadn't returned to his normal work schedule that week, though neither was he concerned with the pretense of working late to close new accounts, even though Renée had known for years. Her name was Carmelita, the office flirt and Jason's whore.

He would have to do something with the rest of his life. He was a young fifty-two, in good health and had so many years ahead of him to finally live out the dreams he had worked so hard all these past years to fulfill. And he was a few hours away from the ten AM meeting with the lawyer, realizing that he was actually reciting, rehearsing. Without knowing why.

He hadn't been alone for much of the week, though he had spent his evenings intellectually alone, contemplating the twenty-second with Gaston Lefebvre and the future that would follow in the wake of the meeting. He wondered who would be there, in his future, and who would not. He knew Renée would not, and very soon. Perhaps Carmelita would, but he shared no real connection with her beyond the physical.

She was twelve years his junior, six years younger than Renée and the relationship was no secret at IntelSanté where she worked as Executive Assistant to another VP. She wore expensive and alluring designer lingerie under décolleté silk blouses and skirts or dresses, the total look of a woman in charge of her sensuality when other women in the office milieu wore plain black skirts or perma-press slacks with plain white cotton blouses and washed-out bras. She had legs and didn't care who saw them, preferring garters over pantyhose.

They saw each other for dinner and very often he would spend time at her apartment until the early hours. She was the perfect woman, the perfect mate: a whore in bed, a lady when need be. She had often expressed her objection to formal marriages the second time around, which was not to say she would be tossed away as easily as yesterday's newspaper. Being free of her would involve a significant financial loss and possible irreparable damage to his career whenever he deemed the timing appropriate. She was already very problematic and had been for some time. Everyone knew, even though they pretended not to, and he did have the promotion to consider.

She wasn't the whore everyone thought she was. He was, and he had no doubt his reputation would give her the upper hand when she needed the upper hand the most and him the least. They were lovers, each other's corporate strategy and undoing their ten-year relationship would have catastrophic implications. She had become an important instrument within the corporate structure which he had played to his advantage on many occasions, and she had complied willingly because she saw the larger picture that included being with him and that was not good.

Renée had her own sense of the future. She no longer needed him, if she ever had, and that was a concern to him vis-à-vis his career. He would soon need to choose one woman over the other. Leaving Carmelita would be costly and he would never entirely be free of her, however for Renée to divorce him at the same time would be ruinous, leaving him without options. His personal life would not be viewed well by the Directorate or the shareholders with barely three years to go.

Though he knew Wellington was the real cause of his sleepless nights since the phone call from his ambulance-chasing lawyer, not the choice between two women. Why now? Why after all these years? And when would that two million dollar windfall be his?
*

Wellington Bartlett had always despised his fraternal double, whose predilection for hidden agendas and deceit had always conflicted with his own sense of right and wrong. Despite the sentiment, they had always been considered as one persona in the close-knit pharmaceutical world they lived in and Jason's more high-energy personality had long ago set the bar. They had always worked for competing firms, starting out as Account Executives and Wellington often remembered with regret the years of their father's overbearing influence and guidance in matters regarding their careers.

While his brother had nurtured his twenty-six year career by cheating, conniving and coercing his way to the top, leaving broken careers in the wake of his success, Wellington had struggled through five attempts to establish himself in the lucrative drug industry. Each time was the same, falling victim to his own sense of righteousness, honesty and his brother's competing sense of self, not to mention Jason's constant unscrupulous manipulations.

Wellington had had enough. He was mentally exhausted and tired of his ineffectual life. He was an image in a mirror, an image without a soul. He didn't exist. He never had. He had hated his brother then, and he hated him now; though hatred no longer mattered. There was no time left to hate.

When Wellington saw his brother on the rare occasions they were brought together by happenstance, he was exempted from the confusion others experienced when seeing the brothers together. As Jason stepped from his always-gleaming Escalade, customarily overdressed for a Sunday morning, Wellington knew exactly what and who he was seeing. At that precise moment Wellington felt an even greater distance between him and his brother. He had expected an emotion of some sort as he prepared to embark on the journey he had meticulously planned over the past year. There was none. Not the animosity he had expected to feel or the hate he had always harboured towards the look-alike that had cursed his life. He felt a sense of equality and closure. He finally felt equal to the man he had always despised and had always strived to surpass. The competing would soon be over. He would endure no more failure and he would at last enjoy the eternal peace he desperately longed for.

*

The downtown law offices of Taylor, Lefebvre & Dunn occupied most of the tenth floor of the antiquated and weather-stained Dominion Square Building: Montreal's aging monument to the legal process which local politics could never Frenchify to l'Edifice Dominion or La Maison something or other. The building was a masonry relic and ancient landmark at the core of a city that was increasingly adopting the appearance of a bombed out section of Baghdad with its decaying infrastructure the city tried tirelessly to disguise from tourists and investors. The once second largest French-speaking city in the world, its French-speaking citizens reduced to a minority amidst reckless immigration, had long ago lost any hope of greatness. The downtown core had steadily become a dismal mélange of abandoned and neglected buildings and storefronts with a burgeoning homeless population that laid claim to unclean entranceways and patches of broken sidewalks to beg for dollar coins or jeer at nervous passers-by who denied them. The framework of the year-long poverty scene was the towering steel and concrete high-rises, some notably decaying with age while others were perversely shiny and new. Together they lifelessly inter-connected daily routines and crumpled asphalt streets that concealed continuously bursting water mains that had celebrated their centenary decades earlier.

Security had been advised of his arrival, his name sufficing as a pass through to the offices which were closed to all but Jason B. Bartlett on Sunday, October 22. Gaston Lefebvre, one of the city's foremost litigation lawyers, best known for his success in criminal cases, responded to the single loud knock against the glass-plate double doors trimmed with polished brass and embossed with the plain bold letters: TL&D

"Bonjour, Monsieur Bartlett. Please, follow me. Je vous en prie. I must excuse myself for having made you wait. My assistant, Madame Duvernay, is otherwise occupied. I do apologize."

Jason sighed inwardly at the diplomatic and artificial preamble that was so much a part of Lefebvre's profession, not much different from a mortician, he thought. He didn't need or want Lefebvre's meaningless banter. He wanted out, to be at the airport and en route to France, not with Lefebvre negotiating his way through excessively polite formalities. The windfall had seemed too good to believe when he had received the call a week earlier, and still seemed altruistic if not suspiciously out of character for a ne'er-do-well brother whom he seldom saw or gave thought to.

"Monsieur Bartlett, please be seated." Maître Lefebvre waved his arm, indicating a low-back leather seat that seemed better suited to a bar lounge, not a law office.

Jason took a moment to scan the office decor. He liked what he saw: an elegant cross between sterile and chic, far removed from the traditional oak-panelled walls, dark sombre carpets and heavy furnishings with oversized seats intended to make clients appear diminutive and pitiable, though no compliment would be forthcoming. Lefebvre had obviously brought in a designer and nothing had come from a department store. Everything was high-end boutique-quality and custom-made. The pedestal desk was a sheet of smoked glass balanced on a single stainless steel post. On it were a closed laptop, a phone, a black Mont Blanc fountain pen and a closed notebook. One entire wall of resilient white laminate was a series of vertical and horizontal drawers of various sizes, also containing a wardrobe, a bar, an entertainment system and a filing system. At right angles to the wall was the discreet outline of a door leading to what must be his private washroom, Jason thought. That and the other walls were white to the point of being blinding and the dozens of miniature overhead halogen spotlights made the highly-polished white birch floors seem more like a mirror. The blinds were also white, closed to the outside and the only other pieces of furniture were the two bright red low-back cube chairs. His own executive ergonomic recliner was high-back, bright blue and had a discreet dial pad recessed into the arm for perfect comfort, or image.

"May I offer you refreshments, Monsieur Bartlett, perhaps a coffee or mineral water?"

Jason studied Lefebvre as he sat behind the desk. He was impeccably attired and Jason knew the cost of each item from the soft-leather Italian-made shoes to the pink gold Cartier that showed slightly from under the pale blue and crisply starched French cuffs extending from the gray-blue Armani sleeve to the solid gold Florentine links. His tie was of the finest silk and intricately knotted. The man was a fashion show piece and clearly paid attention to the minutest detail of his dress code. The man had style, giving credit where credit was due and that his brother could afford him was a mystery.

Maître Lefebvre had seen family photos of Jason and Wellington together, although seeing Jason sitting in the very seat, and in the same manner, as his client a week earlier was unnerving. He was expert in searching for the nuances of truth and deception, but he could see none that was physical in what he observed, save Jason's hairstyle. What identified him as a different person were the verbal and the non-verbal. There was an authority in his tone and his posture that his brother lacked. He had a presence that was inherent and Maître Lefebvre had an immediate dislike for him. He was not a man to trust or confide in.

"No. Thank you. Will this take long?" Jason glanced at his own gold and blue Rolex for affect. "I do have a flight to prepare for."

"Indeed. I have prepared the document, which is simple and straight forward, Monsieur Bartlett. Your brother saw no need to prepare a living will, nor a power of attorney, simply the last will and testament in which he has designated you as sole beneficiary."

Jason's pensiveness was exaggerated. "Did he say why?"

"Why, Monsieur Bartlett?"

"Yes, Monsieur Lefebvre," he repeated, "why? Why me, and why now? He must have told you we've barely spoken to one another since our teens."

"No, sir, he did not tell me that," he lied, "and I never thought to enquire. I am, of course, his attorney and such an invasion of privacy would be improper, undeniably inappropriate. You understand."

"No. Actually I don't understand."

"Your brother's instructions to me were explicit, Monsieur Bartlett. Family is family, after all. No children are involved and the former Mrs. Bartlett is, of course, excluded from further consideration. He made no mention of any other distant relative, so I assume that leaves you, Monsieur Bartlett."

"What do I sign?"

Jason eyed the leather bound notebook on the desk, anxious to leave. Lefebvre reached for the phone, fingering a single key before reclining. With his back to the door Jason hadn't heard her come in. The clicking of her heels resonating across the bare floor announced that she had joined them. He didn't turn, nor did he acknowledge her by standing when she passed through his peripheral vision. He wasn't accustomed to standing for secretaries and he was glad he hadn't. She had the blue tinted document in one hand and a titanium Cross pen in the other. She placed the will at the very front edge of the desk and stood there quietly, with the bottom edge of her A-line skirt challenging his attention.

"Monsieur Bartlett, this is Madame Duvernay. She is my assistant and a competent paralegal. She will be acting as the Executor of the estate, as requested by your brother. She has fulfilled that capacity on several occasions for other clients and I assure you she is very efficient in the performance of such duties."

When she glanced down in response to the introduction, she caught his eyes unabashedly taking in every inch of her and understood immediately he was visualizing her in the nude. She had heard of him, about everything he was, or thought he was, and her instant loathing for him was hard to disguise. Although the absolute resemblance of the brothers momentarily shocked her, she saw beyond the physical to someone entirely unlike the Wellington she knew.

For longer than she could remember, Jacqueline had imagined herself with him, though she had also known he was married and involved with another. He didn't need a further complication, and neither did she. He was, after all, a client, and wanting him did nothing to curtail her social life. Her life went on. She was private and discreet in all matters, including her own. She had always been particular in the selection of her partners, a requisite standard set by someone who had never been aware of her secret passion for him.

She thought of Wellington regularly, often fantasizing they were together when they were not. On one occasion she had called out his name when the timing had been the least appropriate, bringing her evening to an abrupt end and she hadn't gone into work the next day. She exuded a reserved sexuality, intimidating most men who would only chance to stare and dream the impossible, and when Wellington was expected at the office she would dress in a way she thought would turn his head, never flaunting. What she didn't know was that Wellington had often imagined himself in romantic situations with her, often times when he was with Gi-Gi or Geneviève.

That day she dressed with a purpose: to taunt, not tease the man who was eying her. Her thin smile vanished immediately. Lefebvre understood completely.

"As I have already explained, Monsieur Bartlett, you are the sole beneficiary of your brother's estate. It is not customary, nor required, that we disclose to a beneficiary the full contents of a will they are named in. Suffice it to say your brother has left you a single life insurance policy in the amount of two million dollars, his house, which is currently valued well in excess of five hundred thousand and various other assets that are listed herein. At this point he has incurred no debts, save a second mortgage on the house and his car, both of which are insured for their current values."

Jason again examined the secretary who stood clearly assessing him in a way he thought was judgmental. She made him uncomfortable. Clearly she was a woman not easily intimidated, even though she would barely reach his shoulders in her alligator pumps.

He had been thinking of her naked. Who wouldn't, he thought? Not thinking of her naked would be impossible and he was certain she was enjoying every moment of his mental imagery. Her silk blouse was sheer navy, revealing every contour of her breasts, creating the illusion of her nipples being hard, and unbuttoned precisely to where the clasps of the embroidered pale-blue-on-navy demi-bra came together.

Her skirt was winter white and two hand-widths above the knee with a side slit that opened nicely, revealing more of her thigh. There was no need to wonder how much more he would see if she sat, or whether she was wearing pantyhose or nylons. She was definitely in nylons or stay-ups and he found himself completely distracted.

She was too reserved, cold, and probably lived with her mother or sister, he thought. She was probably hungry for a good lay if she could find anyone who would want to fuck the Ice Queen and she wouldn't be his first one night stand, or his last. And doing her wouldn't be cheating on Renée. He'd been doing that for years with Carmelita whom he hadn't cheated on since Renée had moved into the guest room, unless he might have forgotten the occasional indiscretion.

"Perhaps Madame Duvernay would be more comfortable sitting."

"Thank you, no," she replied. The pig might have shown his colours, she would not be showing hers. This wasn't Wellington sitting beside her.

"If we are ready to proceed, your brother has also indicated I am to serve as witness, which is not irregular in the least." Maître Lefebvre shrugged, matter-of-factly. "Your brother has few friends and you are his remaining family. Do you have any questions, Monsieur Bartlett?"

Jason did have questions, ones he had asked himself repeatedly over the past nine days. When? When would he get the money? Was his brother ill? Was he dying, and, if so, when? Would it be within three years?

"No, not as such. It's a very generous gesture on my brother's part, given the circumstances of our past. I can't help being a little curious as to the reason and the timing."

"I don't understand, Monsieur Bartlett, what you mean by the timing." Lefebvre took up the Mont Blanc, sliding the document towards Jason who stood at the implied request. "Your brother merely chose this time to organize his affairs. There were certain other matters requiring his attention before he was able to prepare a document that would be uncontested. You understand, of course."

Jacqueline Duvernay handed Jason her more slender Cross pen. He signed on the second of four lines as silently instructed by her with a single extended finger, assigning to him an eventual two million dollars from out of the blue, which he still found incredulous as he returned the pen. She signed next, as Executor, leaning purposefully over the document and allowing her skirt to respond exactly as she had intended. Maître Lefebvre signed last, witnessing the other three signatures with a richer, blacker ink before dismissing his assistant who walked away without saying a word.

Jason resisted glancing over his shoulder. "Do I get a copy, for my own files?"

"No, Monsieur Bartlett, you do not. That would be quite irregular. However, the document will be duly registered with the proper provincial departments as required by law."

"Is it amendable?"

"By that you mean the name of the beneficiary?" Gaston saw clearly why Wellington despised the man. He was indeed motivated by greed, and his humanity was non-existent.

"Whatever."

"Yes, sir, the beneficiary is amendable, albeit extremely unlikely."

Jason hesitated, not embarrassed in the least, waiting for the door to close behind him. "My wife and I," he began, completely at ease, "are not what one would call comfortable with our current marital status. In fact, I'm in the process of initiating divorce proceedings against her, proceedings that, for one reason or another, I have temporarily put on hold."

"I take your point, sir. The outcome of your current situation would, of course, be contingent upon the interpretation of any pre-nuptial agreement, or specific clauses to a marriage contract relating to divisions of properties or assets that were acquired during your marriage. You understand, of course, I am speaking beyond my field of expertise," and that you are entirely despicable, he thought.

The meeting was over, each man standing as though drawn up by the same puppeteer. The handshake was a formality and Jason walked to the door not intending extend any further acknowledgement.

"Monsieur Bartlett," Jason hesitated for a brief moment, continuing to open the door before turning, "your brother did have one other message which he asked me to convey."

Jason showed his exasperation, as though he'd been expecting something more, a condition, a game to entertain his brother. "And that would be, monsieur?"

"You are to meet with him for a late breakfast at his residence, the morning of November 03. I believe he expects you at precisely nine AM."

Jason shook his head. "He's insane. He's lost whatever small sense of reality he might have possessed at one time. My flight lands at midnight on the second, maybe."

"Shall I tell him, Monsieur Bartlett, the next time he and I meet, that you shall join him for breakfast, or that he is insane?" He had had enough of this arrogant, self-infatuated twin.

Jason's tone acknowledged the intentional affront. "No, Monsieur Lefebvre, you shall not say anything. We are what we are, he and I. He already knows I will be there."

The door remained open as Gaston went to the phone.

Monday, 23 October
The Big Easy

They had all said not to give up hope. He was good, he was one of the best and someone would certainly pick him up in the very near future. Pick him up, they had said, like some discarded object left behind or forgotten, dropped without any thought of the consequences. No one had considered the consequences. There were always consequences and, if so for him, why not for them?

He had listened to them, sincerely wanting to believe their words while he maintained his empty agenda and daily regimen of spending his days alone in his home office, on the Internet and phoning contacts who would seldom return his calls.

Then he became aware that he was no longer part of any network, he never had been and by year's end his agenda was a useless book of blank pages: a testament to the reality that he was finished. And his brother willingly reinforced that sentiment. Alone with his empty agenda, in his empty house, he found himself filling in dates which would have been significant as well as places and times of meetings he would have attended throughout the year, had his life not been arbitrarily altered by those whom he suspected no longer remembered his name.

That was the root source of a straightforward plan that had taken control of his conscience and sub-conscience minds, a plan he had nurtured through to the moment when the theory of what might happen metamorphosed into practical application. The most complicated part of the plan had been coinciding the first week of Jason's trip to France with the first week of Bill Henderson's two-week annual vacation to the Dominican Republic. With that accomplished, he was free to concentrate on his long awaited meeting with John Roberts.

John Roberts was the Divisional VP of Sales and Marketing for the Spencer Pharmaceutical Corporation, the second largest North American manufacturer of capability and energy enhancing drugs for body builders and athletes. He was also the man directly responsible for the dismissal of the company's Northeastern Account Representative fifteen years earlier. They had been Wellington's second employer, having wooed him away from a century-old employer where promotions were rarely up for consideration unless someone quit, died or got fired. Unfortunately only one of those ever seemed to happen, and not with any convenient regularity.

Spencer Pharmaceuticals began following his success from afar as he increasingly became a competitive threat to them and, when the timing was good for them, they approached the eager Wellington with promises of everything he wanted to hear. There would be much more money, definitely promotions, paid trips and bonuses. He signed on.

The move had been good for both parties. His success over the next several years was unprecedented, as were his personal and corporate financial growths. Nothing had slowed his pace, including the hard-hitting recession of the early eighties. He simply had a knack for being in the right place at the right time, and with the right person. But the arrival of the nineties did slow him down, during the hardest financial downturn since the Great Depression of his parents' time and Roberts had been there to watch.

Brought in to replace the then National Sales Manager who had been blamed for the recession and sent home, Roberts' mandate was to staunch the sagging sales, rising costs and each of his subordinates had been given immediate notice of the planned consequence should he not increase sales and reduce his financial burden on the company. Wellington had seen the end coming since day one and could do nothing but wait. Absolutely no one was hiring and Roberts wasn't going away.

His dismissal couldn't have come at a worse time. The recession was far from over. Living costs had skyrocketed and he had spent the last four years married to a woman who had become accustomed to a very comfortable lifestyle he largely supported, a woman increasingly difficult to afford.

He had been one of the company's most successful Account Managers, one of the most talented and becoming over-qualified for his limited responsibilities. He had been promoted to District Manager, and then to Regional Manager. He was climbing the ladder at his own speed and should have been one rung away from his objective of becoming National Sales Manager, an important fact Roberts had not ignored.

The company would not be able to ride out difficult times without draconian cuts and Wellington would be a good starting point, also sending a message to Wellington's direct reports to tow the company line. Wellington was very good, Roberts had said. There was never any doubt about that, and everyone liked him. The economy had simply become a corporate inconvenience, Roberts had explained, without adding that he was feeling more threatened by a dedicated subordinate than his superiors. Wellington was gone.

Since that time the company had gone through more

mergers, more buy-outs and Roberts had very remarkably survived the turbulence. Wellington remembered the man's words as though he had heard the excuses a few hours earlier: "You're good, Wellington. It's the timing that's bad. You must understand the difficult position we're in. If it were any other time we wouldn't be having this conversation. You're young. You'll get by." He was thirty-eight and devastated.

"Get by, my ass. You screwed me over for no reason, you son of a bitch." Wellington answered again, years later, looking around to see whether anyone seated nearby had heard the brief monologue.
*

The US Immigration Officer flipped through until she found a page in the passport she seemed to prefer. He remembered the routine questions, returning a smile that precisely matched the agent's. He was going to New Orleans on business and that's all she had to know, after which he would go to Punta Cana for business and pleasure before returning to Montreal with a stopover in Savannah, Georgia.

She wished she could go with him, she commented, folding his tickets into his passport. She hated the thought of winter coming, she hated being at the airport at four AM and her rotation to a warmer climate wouldn't be for several more months. He took the documents, telling her not many women could look as good as she did at such an early hour, and that seemed to work for her.

Delta Airlines didn't know him from Adam or Abdul, so they coded his baggage tags for close inspection by the ten-dollar-an-hour wannabe commandos at security who suspect everyone and like no one. He lifted one bag onto the inspection table and was told summarily to step back, as though suddenly a risk. Then he was told to lift the other bag, once the first had been closed and stamped approved for furtherance to another checkpoint where some drippymouth hound would sniff and scratch at his luggage. And he wasn't anywhere near the gate.

Did he have a computer? No. He didn't. Did he have any metal on his person, any coins in his pockets? No. He didn't. He should take off his shoes to accelerate the scanning process, they insisted. No. He didn't think so, not until they thought to install carpets. The man asked for the boarding pass by pointing at the card with a blue latex-covered finger, airport-speak, and put it into the pocket of his shirt that at least a day late for the laundry bin. Go through, he was told with the same blue hand. Thank you, he replied. He would wait to see his briefcase go through first. Then he went through, without bells or whistles, but he had been number 189, or whatever, and the second process off to the side with everyone curiously watching was much more thorough. They went over him as though he was Abdul instead of Adam and thought he was laughing at them, ridiculing them. He wasn't. Jean-François LeTuvier was, laughing at the irony when they checked his passport once more before handing back his boarding pass.

Everyone at the gate was half asleep, waiting for the 05:30 flight to Cincinnati that would connect him to New Orleans for an expected arrival time of 10:01.
*

No one did hear, and if they did they didn't care. They were too busy being indifferent and unaware, despite the repeated subliminal messages reminding them they were all responsible for the safety of others and that they must report all suspicious actions or baggage to the nearest airport official. This as they lay facing downward, their unkempt heads or arms pressed against public seats or strolled into washrooms with coffee cups in hand, not their luggage. He had gone into sales to be by himself, a loner, and that had somehow become a contradiction.

He would board in thirty minutes and arrive at the hotel

in the Big Easy well before noon, with ample time to relax after his trip and get into the French Quarter for dinner at Mike Anderson's. He was in no hurry. He would be in town for two days and so would John Roberts.
*

Mid-August was a beautiful time along the meandering Richelieu River, joining the St. Lawrence River to Lake Champlain and the Hudson, for those who had a reason to see beauty. Mont-Saint-Hilaire was the channel's midway point, though he had no such need and hadn't missed his evening walks along the shoreline for some time

Two months earlier he had cashed in the three Treasury Bills that made up the remainder of his financial portfolio, each one redeeming twenty thousand when converted into US dollars. The first ten had gone entirely for the documents and other items delivered by Lefebvre who had effectively initiated the transaction, quickly washing his hands clean of guilt with strong words of advice to his client: that he would be wise to keep his eyes closed and his mouth shut. Twelve thousand in cash was paid out to four different travel agents for an itinerary that included several one-way First Class flight segments and four hotel reservations. Six thousand in cash went towards a new wardrobe he had promised himself, one that would better suit his agenda.

Half of what remained he left behind, certain the other sixteen thousand would see him through the next ten days. He had never had so much cash on him at one time, double what he had spent on himself over the past few years combined. There was also another bank note, the mental note the banker had made that Wellington Bartlett was literally penniless and without prospects. Sufficient funds remained for the next automatic payments on the house and the car, then nothing.

Wellington knew the bank would soon invite him in to

explore impossible payment options on his house, and the car would not be his for much longer. He was on the verge of desperate times, yet he had no sense at all of desperation. Strangely, he felt liberated. For the first time in his life he felt alive and motivated for all the right reasons, his own reasons. His time had come.

*

Leaning into the portside window as the aircraft lined up over Lake Pontchartrain for its final approach into New Orleans' Louis Armstrong International, Jean-François felt as though he had been transported to an earlier time, though without any sense of attachment to the past. For as far as the eye could see, there was only a solitary yellow shack with that same dull red speck that was probably the skeleton of an ancient rowboat in the middle of the expansive green and watery marsh at the southernmost part of the lake. He wondered who had once lived there, or who still did, and why: perhaps a deranged hermit, perhaps someone who simply preferred reptiles and rodents to their equally repugnant human counterparts.

When he stepped from the plane, through the telescopic walkway and into the concourse, nothing had changed. A surge of good and bad memories flooded his mind as suffocating heat struck him like a hammer. He had always been amazed by the locals appearing so fresh at the end of each day, when most northerners with white forearms protruding from short-sleeve shirts looked as though they had spent the day fully dressed in a sauna. And New Orleans was a sauna, a big dirty one.

Unless they were dark-skinned by virtue of their birth, the women of New Orleans were a ninety-five on the brightness scale. They seldom ventured into daylight, though, on the rare occasions they would, having a gun secreted in their purses to discourage or kill someone who had intentions of harming their dignity or pride wasn't

51

unusual. Charm, poise and graciousness were in their blood, their breeding, their thought processes as dwellers of the Swamp and the most corrupt city in the US.

Beyond the borders of the French Quarter, New Orleans possessed no more character than any other North American city, and was as French as any other American city. The toe-tapping Cajuns, who did speak French, lived to the west in Lafayette where they ate gumbo and crawfish in French, danced and sang in French. The only French in the French Quarter was in its name and on the menus in a few overpriced restaurants boasting world-famous English-speaking authors with French names who were their chefs.

The locals didn't call New Orleans the Big Easy. They lived in the Swamp: a city of one-point-three million swamp dwellers who didn't bury their dead, rather they created small cities of crypts to house them. They celebrated death with loud street bands of musicians dressed in black, playing jazz and waving brass horns in the air as they followed behind black horse-drawn carriages carrying the dearly departed behind windows curtained in black. The Swamp was a hot and sticky place whose residents believed in the black art of voodoo and hexes, death by sorcery, straw dolls and pins.

To Wellington the French Quarter by night was exciting, alive, loud and sexual where people went to do what they couldn't do at home, a place where fifty weeks led into Mardi Gras and another fifty were required to decompress from the fervor. The Quarter never slept. Women wore panties only if they wanted to and, if they did, they wouldn't necessarily keep them on. And men went to party, forgetting their wives as they gyrated over and into the sweaty bodies of liquor-filled women who would only be pretty until the sun came up.

Escaping the hookers and the pickpockets was nearly impossible. If you did, street vendors and entertainers would happily lay claim to the contents of your wallet. Every other storefront was a sex boutique, a tee-shirt shop, a strip bar or a voodoo shop where you could browse through the window or enter to buy something or other that would allow you curse, kill or cripple the person of choice.

The streets smelled of the piss of men who cared not at all if they were seen with their members in their hands, shrunken from the sticky heat of the night. Women would squat behind a curtain of drunken friends, splashing the sides of their own sandals and bare asses with the erratic jets of warm liquid hissing out from under their gathered up skirts, unimpeded by the panties they had left in their rooms. There was always a daily supply of fresh dog excrement, kept soft and pungent by the torrential midday rains that never completely washed away the fly-coated stools. Then there were the scruffy and battle-weary cats and rodents that fought one another constantly for the fetid food supply stored nightly inside bug-infested containers lying alongside darkened alleys which only the very drunk and the very hopeless would dare to enter.

The Quarter never slept, nor did first-timers who would always choose hotel rooms with balconies that were private observation decks on Bourbon Street if they could afford the exorbitant premiums for the privilege of letting the passing world see into their rooms as they felt up naked girlfriends or wives by open windows or doors. Bourbon Street was a street theatre lined with twin rows of endless balconies filled to the point of collapsing under the weight of tourists who wanted either to show bare body parts normally reserved for lovers or spouses, or see them throughout a nightly visual sex fest with free admission and free of guilt until morning.

Regular visitors to the Swamp, reluctant or willing, learned quickly to reserve courtyard rooms that were always quieter, if not private, with long communal balconies encircling lush gardens or pools. One could still be a voyeur in the comfort of his or her room, or perform for an unknown and unseen audience who might, or might not, be participating or capturing the digitalized moment for their friends at home.

The music was always loud, arguably the best jazz in the world and the restaurants were good, though certainly not the best in the world, with certain notable exceptions.

By day the Quarter was a hot and filthy part of town with stains and smells of urine and vomit from the night before and smelled like an unflushed toilet. Homeless drunks slept along the sidewalks late into the day and jobless teenagers sat cross-legged beside them with a pet or stray dog to avoid arrest for vagrancy because the cops wouldn't know what to do with the animals. They actually did know what to do with them, but doing so would upset the Animal Rights Activists; the Mayor would be pissed off with the Chief of Police and no one wanted that, especially the cops.

The pickpockets were at home counting their earnings from the night before and planning the evening to come. Hookers were applying ointments that would sooth and sanitize their reddened parts and cover the bruises left behind by inexperienced or single-minded hands. By day, the narrow city streets were home to the hordes of tourists who were either trying to forget the night before or eagerly anticipating the next. Daytime in the Big Easy was an inconvenience: twelve or more hours that separated one night from another.

Wellington had long ago done the riverboat thing. He had visited the small cities of the dead, visited the Bayou and had patiently listened to the canned speeches of plantation guides who had long ago lost interest in what they do. During his frequent visits he had always stayed at the Double Tree Lakeside in Metairie at the southern end of the 40 km long causeway crossing Lake Pontchartrain. When he was alone he preferred the hotel's modern elegance and quiet setting to the loudness and bon vivant character which was an anticipated amenity when staying at the quainter French provincial hotels in the Quarter, where he would always be required to stay for annual and bi-annual meetings.

Irrespective of the hotel's location he would always go into the Quarter for his dinner and entertainment and this time Jean-François would be staying at both, though neither hotel would recognize him as a long-ago frequent guest. When he booked his room at the Double Tree, he also booked the second night at the Maison Dupuy on Bourbon. The Double Tree had a shuttle service to their other property on Canal Street that was walking distance to the Quarter and that's what he would take.

He had known exactly where and when Roberts would be booking rooms for the annual Spencer Pharmaceuticals Sales Meeting. Some things never changed. He would stay at the Maison Dupuy at the corner of Bourbon and Toulouse, along with the company's entourage of a few key decision makers and a few dozen more adherents to those decisions. He would have his evening meal at Mike Anderson's on Bourbon Street with many of them where he would drink his whiskies and smoke his cigars. He would spend the rest of the night watching women from Idaho or Kansas show everyone their bare breasts in exchange for a couple of coloured beads they would keep forever as a reminder they had once done something daring and sexy, maybe even a little dirty in otherwise uninspired lives. Wellington had counted on it.

Darkness had fallen by the time Wellington got to Mike Anderson's for dinner, which was also as he had remembered: two floors of darkened ambiance with a sloping second floor balcony trimmed in the traditional iron lace where large numbers of male patrons would gather to drink and throw beads to those women from Idaho and Kansas, yelling at them to show their tits. Roberts would later spend his evening there, and the next, drinking and yelling to the women he thought most willing.

He gave the hostess his name. Then he saw Roberts. With him came a momentary surge of panic, even though they hadn't seen one another for fourteen years. From what he could see they had been years of plenty for the shapeless and overweight man who was now completely bald and sported a nose in the middle of his reddened face that had turned purple and grotesquely large. He seeing a man in failing health brought on by the excesses of good living and poor personal health care. Life was filled with contradictions.

Fifteen years earlier Roberts had been fighting off middle age and many of his vile habits had not yet been perfected. Wellington remembered him using liquor as a convenient means of disguising his lack of social skills. The man had been a social drunk, apparently he still was and that was a good thing for current purposes.

That was the essence of the man he had come to meet. Wellington stood there, doing his best not to stare, his concentration broken when the waitress called out his name a second time. He was so close and Roberts had no idea. His table gave him a clear view of Roberts, sitting staring at the man who had in a single moment started a chain of events which had so affected his life. He had reached the point of no return. There was no going back and Wellington was as uneasy as he was eager. His unease prompted by the possibility of failure, his eagerness borne of the anticipation of his first meeting.

The restaurant was a Bourbon Street must-do for seafood, which wasn't the main specialty on any menu du jour. That was the balcony. The eatery was one of Roberts favorite spots, always crowded, and because of that he had never liked to stand out by being alone. He would invariably press a few of his toady subordinates into service for an evening most would not remember. When they had finished their meals, and had ordered more drinks, the five or six men would all trail their boss up the stairs for the street-wide and standing room only Bourbon Street spectacle.

Wellington had barely touched his meal, though he had gone through two glasses of Merlot that had tasted particularly good, never taking his eyes from Roberts who had begun easing himself from the booth. Wellington threw down three twenties that would cover the meal and tip and did likewise, immediately close enough to the last man in the servile procession to touch him. Sweeping up the leather folder holding Roberts' itemized bill and credit card receipt, he stopped beside the waitress who had served them as his supposed colleagues trudged up the stairs.

He gave the girl seven fifties to cover the bill and the tip, with another twenty for the inconvenience of reversing the charge, explaining that Roberts had refused to let him pay and that he hadn't wanted to argue openly at the table in front of the underlings. He thanked her, told her the service was excellent and that she would see them all again. Good night.

Walking across the street he looked up, chuckling at seeing the few dozen men who were all gawking at the endless procession of female passers-by, ready to throw beads at the ones they thought would most likely respond to raunchy requests to show them something, anything: tits, or an ass, all for the prize of a beaded necklace that had cost a dollar each. Roberts squeezed right in there with them, holding a drink in his hand, a cigar wedged into the corner of his mouth, his eyes opened wide as he began yelling, jeering and throwing.

Wellington strolled away, intending to return to the shuttle bus that would return him to his hotel. He had no reason to stay longer.

*

After a little shopping at the French Market the next day for certain articles he had chosen not to bring with him and a visit to a particular voodoo shop on rue Royal, Wellington would have nothing left to do, despite feeling as though he should be doing something. The agenda had been planned, the script had been written; he was in New Orleans and he had set the stage for the first act of a five-act play that would take him to the Dominican Republic and Savannah before returning to the colorless post-autumn of Montreal for the final curtain. He would see Roberts the next evening at the same time and in the same place to confirm all was in order, then again when Roberts' evening would come to an end and they would finally meet at the Maison Dupuy.

He would need all the rest and relaxation he could manage if he were to get through the hectic agenda of the next twelve days, but he needed something, an outlet, a way to vent the pent-up energy building within him which he had to dispel. He needed balance critical to his agenda and he was beginning to feel anything but balanced. He knew he shouldn't, he tried to dissuade himself, but until the following afternoon his time was his own. He would still have ample opportunity to sleep, refocus and be on time for his appointment the next evening.

*

By night the purple, blue and pink painted façades of Bourbon Street gave way to flashing neon lights in the same gaudy tones. The interiors of bars and clubs were smoky and dimly lit, camouflaging faded walls, aged furniture, soiled carpets and patrons being openly familiar with one another. There was no code. You did what felt good, whenever you felt good about doing it.

With the exception of one early morning so many years ago in his parents' home, Wellington had never done anything he considered risqué, illicit or even remotely intriguing. There was no better time. He was in the Big Easy, a premier city of sin. If he didn't do it now, whatever it was, he never would and what would have been the purpose of the agenda.

He had grown up in the purified and sanctimonious environment created by his parents. No degree of swearing was tolerated, vacations had been creative learning events engineered by his father, his mother was more innocent than Mary and at the beginning his wife had possessed the sexual curiosity of a Mother Superior. Then, when she had developed her insatiable appetite for carnal knowledge, notwithstanding her equally insatiable appetite for fine living, she had chosen to take her inventiveness elsewhere.

His lover, Gi-Gi, was inclined towards private living and the relationship had remained a tight-lipped secret all these years. He felt out of control. He was nearing the edge, the precipice from which he would plummet into his secret thoughts and dreams and he liked the intrigue. His relationship with his lover had never been open, though he was certain, or had convinced himself, that Gi-Gi would not feel threatened by anything he would do so far from home.

He wasn't into strip bars, not even good ones. They were a tease: Touch me, feel me and then fuck off, but please come back. And why pay to simply see it when so many women out there would willingly give it up for a couple of drinks and a few well-chosen words about how pretty and young they looked? Of course, she knew and you knew it was all bullshit. She liked the words and you liked the feel of whatever part of her you were touching at the time. He wondered how far he could go with a woman, what he could do with one if he let himself go and said to hell with inhibition like he had always wanted. He hadn't been with one that way in such a long time and suddenly he needed to feel the wet heat inside one. And there they were. They were young. The bodies were mid-twenties, though the faces testified to a longer and harder existence, the innocence gone, replaced with cynicism and street smarts. They were whores and no one ever paid for the pleasure of being in an old one. He said the word aloud in a whisper they wouldn't hear. He enjoyed hearing the word as much saying it. Two young whores and they were going to hit on him. Whores.

"Hey, baby. How'd you like to taste a bit of something so, so sweet? I'm talkin' sweet, baby, like them fudge cookies your mama used to make. Uh-huh. You wanna put some nuts in my fudge, baby?"

She was black, with red hair that flickered purple in unison with the overhead strobe, and he judged about 1.77 metres in her neon stilettos that brought her eyes to just below his chin. Most of her well-padded frame was exposed to the night air. The flirt skirt she was wearing did exactly that and her tank top was a formality to satisfy the cops who had probably already been with her in some dark alleyway.

"My name's Seraphina, baby, but I can be anyone you want." She looked up at him, bringing one hand up between her legs, stopping after she had brought up the bottom of the cheap cotton skirt high enough for Wellington to see what he'd be paying for. "Y'all got a name you like, baby? You got a name for this?"

His eyes riveted to the hand she moved slowly up and down with her fingers parted so he could see her glistening lips beckoning him in response to her expert touch.

"How much?" were the first words he spoke.

"Y'all want to touch it, baby? You touch it, and you gonna know it's worth it." She was waiting, challenging him eye to eye.

"How much for the night?" He grinned, still focused on

the edge of the skirt she had pulled higher. "Let's say five, maybe six hours."

She laughed, dropping her skirt, moving her hands to her bared hips. "Baby, I ain't never been with no man who can last six hours with me. Baby, I'm Seraphina."

"Hello, Seraphina," he responded. "Now, will you answer my question?"

"That depends, baby," she smiled at her friend, "on what you want. On top is one hundred, from behind is one-fifty and in the behind is two-fifty. It'll be a much better price if you want all three."

"And how much do you charge for two... all night?"

She tilted her head. "Which two you talkin' about?"

"The two of you, together." He nodded towards the other woman who had remained at the curb with one foot on the street and the other on the sidewalk. She was showing as much of herself as she could to anyone passing by and waiting for eye contact with the one who would pay to see more of her in a room, buy her a drink and not beat the crap out of her.

She smiled. "That there's Dalila. We work together all the time. It's six hundred for à la carte. And the room, baby. We don't pay for the room."

She called over Dalila who was the complete opposite of Seraphina. She was a head shorter, thin, if not skinny, and her white skin was splattered with freckles making it difficult for him to discern whether she was white spotted with brown, or brown spotted with white. She wore white spandex shorts that showed most of her bare ass and the minutest detail of what wasn't bare. She wore white stiletto boots, a white push-up bra, and bleached hair that was more like white straw and brighter than the glare of the streetlights. She looked like a skin-tight Halloween costume.

He had to admit he was tempted, and there couldn't be anything more diametrically different than these unlikely whores. He wanted someone. He had already planned on getting laid the next night, and had intended to wait, until seeing the women lewdly displaying themselves produced an urge too strong to resist. Tomorrow could wait. His life had been the same for too long. He needed a change and two girls at once would certainly be that. Besides, hadn't he just been bitching to himself about it? Get a life. Please.

Six hundred in cash and the deal was done. There was no going back. The two women came together to walk arm in arm in front of him, leading the way. The skeletal man at the front desk had a month's worth of stubble and a singlet he might have washed once in ancient history. Wellington dropped the hundred-dollar bill in front of the cast iron grill separating them, not wanting contact with hands so yellowed and frail the man had to crumple the bill before picking it up.

Most of his dried skin was dotted with sores made worse by scratching and picking and Wellington wondered if he had stopped bathing before or after their proliferation. He'd stopped breathing immediately after the old man had opened the cracked lips of his rotting mouth to speak with the use of a tongue that was freakishly long and damaged by the remaining few chipped and blackened teeth that weren't all in the front. He could well have been a cadaver and Wellington was relieved when the corpse-like shell returned to his magazine and beer without offering a receipt. The man took a foamy gulp and belched without bothering to remove the cold cigar butt that somehow appeared permanently lodged in the mouth like another protruding black tooth.

The flight of stairs leading to the second floor was green. The walls were green and the lights were green, giving a ghastly hue to the black whore's skin and red hair. The white one was just green. There would be no romance this evening, and no eroticism for the women stripping off their clothes or for him seeing them. They pulled off their tops with the same matter-of-fact efficiency. The black one had her skirt off and tossed on the floor before her friend had a chance to push her shorts to her knees. Neither wore panties and the boots on the white one seemed more like natural extensions to her legs. She kept them on.

They lay atop the bed naked, facing each other before Wellington could even close the door. They were looking at him. He wondered what they were thinking, trying to remember the last time and, whores or not, he was going to enjoy himself. The room smelled not much differently than the girls, and the closer he got to the bed the more he realized he was probably in the girls' room, their place of business. The bed was barely wide enough for two, let alone three, and the smell grew more pungent the closer he stood to it. He wasn't fucking anyone in that bed.

He went to a set of drawers standing alone against the wall, pausing before loosening his belt, letting his pants slide to his knees. If he was going to fuck them he'd do each one standing up, or at least with his feet on the floor. He had come this far to do what he had never done before and he would do so on his feet. They were the experts. Let them find a way.

The salt and pepper whores were caressing each other's breasts and arms, showing no interest in him. Whenever he was ready, they would be. They had already been paid and they were his for the evening, with him or without him. Most men would already be slipping and sliding all over them, mauling and hurting, poking and prodding with unwashed hands and latex-wrapped members that would often unwrap as the owners strived to get the most out of the usual thirty minutes.

Wellington had begun thinking the same thing. These

women were not only whores, they were carriers: lab rats not yet captured for clinical testing before their inevitable destruction or their rabid destruction of others.

"What's wrong, baby?" Seraphina started the talking. "You already seen my sweet thing. So now let's see yours." She beckoned him with a cupped hand. "Let's go, baby. Show us what you got for us."

"First, I want to watch. I want to see the two of you together."

"You don't want some of this pink cotton candy, baby." Seraphina pushed open Dalila's thin white legs, wide, so he could see all of her. Then she laughed, bringing her hand down, blocking his view and warming her friend at the same time. She was right. Dalila's labia were bright pink, smooth, and completely bare. Against the rest of her skin her lips looked like slivers of pink meat placed neatly, precisely by a catering service,

Using Dalila's own wetness Seraphina worked her fingers slowly and expertly, showing Wellington what he could be doing with her. When she lowered her face, bringing one of the barely visible pink nipples into her mouth, the two joined in a black-on-white ballet of twisting and arching body parts and lips that opened to send and receive unwritten messages and signals. He sensed those messages were more for selfish pleasure, not his, though his own pleasure had begun. The women could have been lovers, and probably were. They needed no direction, especially his. They were natural together, not shy or hesitant. They were familiar to one another and not pretending. Neither was he.

Watching their bodies entwined, opening to each other in a way he had never seen women together was becoming too much for him. He was tired from standing and wanted badly to sit, much of his energy spent and his arms were aching. He would require more than mere visual stimulation if he were to regain the strength needed to take an active part in the evening's events.

He draped his jacket over a single wood chair and sat naked from the waist down with the exception of his socks and looking very foolish. The girls had changed position, the smaller Dalila watching him as she bent forward to kiss and caress her lover's inner thighs, her glistening face reflecting the blinking pinks and purples of Seraphina's neon shoes. He couldn't see Seraphina, though he could hear the muffled sounds of her mouth against Dalila who suddenly drew a deep breath and arched. She smiled wickedly, enjoying the hot darting sensation before crossing over the ebony body to stand, leaving Seraphina entirely exposed to Wellington's gaze. He had seen women cleaned that way before, mostly in photos, though had never felt the smooth difference or the enhancement.

Dalila's face was drenched and smelled strongly of Seraphina as she helped him off with the rest of his clothing before helping him on with his complementary sheath which was already tight-fitting. Seraphina looked up some moments later at the familiar sounds of bodies working in concert. Neither woman said much once they began. They weren't that kind of therapist.

He spent the rest of the evening doing both the girls in a way that required them to get out of bed and not him in it. They had proven themselves as the expert technicians he had expected. He liked Seraphina, preferring Dalila because she was smaller, tighter, a difference he did feel and her body was easier to work with and manoeuvre. Her breasts were a bit on the smaller side, he thought, but Seraphina's were never far away and neither woman seemed to notice when he strayed. Seraphina was busy enough with herself when she wasn't doing Dalila or being done by her and Wellington who hadn't bothered asking either of them whether he could do whatever he wanted to do at the moment. He just did and they seemed not to mind.

They didn't kiss, and Wellington didn't try. He did feel the urge as a natural part of what was happening, holding himself in check because he thought kissing would somehow be disgusting, like putting his tongue into something unclean and that would have spoiled the evening. In fact the women didn't want to kiss either, and not because their mouths were private or out of bounds or the one clean place on their public bodies they could call their own. He had done everything to them and with them he could possibly have imagined, feeling as though divine providence had delivered him to the whores and the dingy, smelly, infected room to spend the entire night fornicating and saying lewd words. He had always wanted to speak that way, each profanity making the women increasingly responsive. He loved hearing them beg for more.

At first he had wanted to experiment with Geneviève, to see and enjoy those parts of her body she had forbidden to him, eventually realizing he had wanted her that way for all the wrong reasons, part of his contrived process intended to make him forget he had made a terrible mistake. She had always been his second choice and, as he became her second choice, eventually she had become his third and now he was in a filthy room fucking filthy whores.

What would Gi-Gi think of him? He didn't think of them as whores any longer. They were bodies open and available to his. The threadbare shag carpet was hard and prickly everywhere and Wellington was making his own contribution to the crustaceous topography with several lifeless and soggy testimonials to his prowess and endurance littering the surface. He was glad he had kept his socks on. Whoever might be picking them up, he wasn't.

The women's bodies began telling them they'd had enough. Their adjacent ports of entry needed rest: *Access denied! No Exceptions! Closed for Repairs!* Their bodies ached everywhere. They had been two to service him, and even with the several more tender intervals they had enjoyed when he had preferred watching them together, the pace had not slowed. Once he had made the commitment to live out the coming weeks according to his plan, he did precisely that.

He sat watching the girls for some time, wondering how they could sleep in such a disgusting bed, despite the fact they were the ones who had made it disgusting. He was sure the sheets had not been washed in weeks, not so sure they hadn't merely been dried to save time and money, though the girls were more on each other than on the bed. Their lips were touching lightly, Seraphina's fuller breasts teasing Dalila's almost boy-like chest with each breath.

In sleep they were a curious sight. They were no longer street whores who would likely be dead within five years. They were helpless urchins without a home. Helpless innocence and he wondered why. Why did some people always do so well while others struggled all their lives to break even? Micro-latex wouldn't save them. Maybe they would both be better off dead, carried to a better place behind the black curtains of a black horse-drawn carriage and celebrated by musicians dressed in black.

More likely they'd be in the same bed the next night with another faceless fornicator with sufficient funds for the many and varied services. They were whores, though the word didn't sound as intriguing to him as it had hours before. He wanted badly to shower, but there was no way he was stepping into the single stall that had no curtain, a rusted metal floor and God knows what mixed in with the rust. Besides, the room had no door, he still had his socks on and they were staying on. Relieving himself into a bowl that had threatened to overflow after each use had been bad enough. He'd wait.

The heaviness of the women's sexuality would coat his entire body until he got to the Double Tree. His hair was matted, his skin was still slick with sweat and parts of him hadn't been as raw since he'd been a frustrated teenager. He was exhausted, drained physically and emotionally. He could not yet understand what he had done throughout the night, let alone believe. He needed rest and he needed to leave. He wanted to touch the women one more time, under the thin cover he had pulled to their waists, to touch them everywhere without waking them and without touching the cover again. He didn't want to comfort them, or even thank them. He wanted more. He needed more.

He had promised them an extra four hundred and before he left he put four bills on the chair that had been his prop for the evening.

Tuesday, 24 October
Initial Closure

The taxi ride up Causeway Boulevard to the southern shore of Lake Pontchartrain was quiet. Wellington knew the driver could smell him and he consciously rolled open the window enough to feel the slight breeze against his slightly glazed face. The taxi didn't smell much better, even with the window down, he thought. At least he had a good reason for the scent clinging to him like an aura, a badge of honour, a prize for being the best. Though the best at what, he wasn't sure. He gave specific instructions, with no intention of being helpful. More because he suspected the driver still had a few years to go before swearing allegiance to the flag as a new citizen of the US.

Three or four doormen were always on duty at the Double Tree Pontchartrain property. One of them opened the car door, greeting Wellington with a smile. The others standing at attention as he clambered from the car without tipping the driver. The man hadn't done anything to merit the extra money, not like Seraphina and Dalila. He just didn't ask for change.

Another doorman held open the heavy glass panel by its polished brass plate at the side of the revolving doors: the path of least resistance for their beleaguered guest. They liked that Jean- François spoke with them in Spanish and when they believed he wouldn't hear the young Latinos broke into smiles and nods, paying homage to one of their own who had obviously been to battle and had triumphed over overwhelming odds. He did hear "¡Qué santo varón!" and he wanted to smile at the familiar compliment, varón a varón. He did feel like a man, for the first time in a long time.

The walk through the lobby was like running the gauntlet for Wellington, albeit at a much slower pace. He hadn't expected to see as many people at such an early hour. He had misjudged the time and suddenly realized the sun had risen. The five or six hours with the girls had quickly become eight, and were well worth the extra four hundred. At the elevators, there could not have been more people flooding out towards him and around him if he had sent out invitations. Everyone politely pushing and shoving, vying for First Place at the Checkout counter, each one looking at him, smelling him, knowing what he had done and with what. Scent of a whore and everyone recognized the smell of a whore, especially the women who studied him as they walked slowly by, thinking themselves superior as they took in his dishevelled appearance and smelled him. They knew. They were probably whores themselves, at least some of the time, and, he thought, they smelled worse than he did.

Do Not Disturb! No Moleste! He stripped and left a heap of clothes on the floor. A long, hot shower brought a deep red hue to his skin. He itched uncontrollably from the invading dryness and scrubbed his scalp until he saw hair swirling at his feet, all the while bracing himself against the stinging force of the steamy liquid pellets relentlessly assailing his red-raw member. Although he had never seen the need to luxuriate in hotel bathtubs he endured for half an hour, partly for relief, partly for penance.

His meagre breakfast was two chocolate wafers laying on one of three pillows, beside them a simple note from housekeeping reminding him their primary goal was his complete satisfaction. Signed by Ophelia, the note ended up on the floor with the extra pillows and he woke past noon.

He felt rested, very relaxed and he no longer smelled. His clothes were another matter and, once he was dressed for the day and evening ahead, he called the concierge to have someone come up for his laundry. He would incur an extra charge because he had done so after the cut off time, but that was a concierge's raison d'être and good ones got the job done. He left a twenty on top of the plastic bag in his room before going out for lunch, knowing he'd be gone for a good eighteen hours.

He wore his usual oxblood-coloured loafers, navy blue dress slacks, a mock turtleneck in the same tone and a burgundy-coloured blazer with a navy blue pocket hanky. He also carried a small suitcase in order to have something in hand when he checked into the Maison Dupuy, which he would do before lunch.

He had noted the other tasks in his agenda so he wouldn't overlook any of the critical steps leading to his meeting with John Roberts that evening. He had wanted some time at poolside to tan and rejuvenate, disappointed that wouldn't be possible.

*

The hotel had been built in the familiar style of the Quarter with gabled windows, French doors and wrought iron lace balconies that lined the Bourbon Street façade and the inner wall of the courtyard. The interior was grand and refined, a relaxed pace contradicting the urgency and decadence that existed beyond the intricately carved doors of the lobby entrance.

Jean-François was always well-received by hotel staff because he approached them well. He had a casual charm that worked for him, which might possibly have been sincere, though he had never given the attribute much thought. He was who and what he was; no one else, nothing else. His name would not show in the system as one of the hotel's frequent guests from years ago, though his request for a second floor Executive courtyard room had been honoured and the view from his room would be the serene and picturesque fresco from another era he remembered.

Once in his room he went immediately onto the balcony, as he always had in the past, this time not to admire the pool or the garden. He was looking directly at the French-styled doors leading into Roberts' room two doors over on the balcony they shared. Leaving the double doors of his room open, he changed into a pair of walking shoes, Dockers, a polo shirt and a cap he had bought to wear once. He poured a JW Red from the mini-bar and went out onto the balcony.

The courtyard was a lush garden of green grass and exotic flora. A single cluster of trees with wide-reaching branches shaded a pool he remembered as always being deserted. The surrounding patio was tiled with flagstones and sparsely decorated with intricate iron tables covered with checkered linen and matching iron chairs without covers for early morning coffee or late night cognac. No one cared to notice him, nor did he look down, leaning against the railing and staring at those French doors until he finished his drink and returned inside.

He sat on the edge of the bed and pulled the phone book out from under the Gideon that had never been opened. He scanned several pages of interest, noting the most intriguing number listed under Personal Services, which he knew was a hit and miss proposition. He had no referrals to rely on, no experience to rely on. More importantly, he had a need and a desire that hadn't left him since early the same morning. The two were as distinct as they were unrelated and he made the call from the lobby.

He had liked the name, Elegant Escorts, and the swirling double EEs highlighting the advertisement. The transaction was straightforward, like ordering an all-dressed pizza with extra cheese, hold the anchovies, and that surprised him. The lady's soft southern and unhurried voice asked a few specific questions regarding his preferences before alluding to the few restrictions. Then he gave the name of the hotel, his name and room number, his credit card number and expiry date. Mission accomplished. Miss Celeste would arrive promptly at 8:00 PM.

He put Miss Celeste out of his mind for the time being. He had not eaten since his meagre pickings at Mike Anderson's the night before and he felt as though his head was about to cave in. Rue Royal was like any other in the quarter, though much cleaner and boasted excellent patio restaurants where one could relax, enjoy small portions of expensive food, and mellow under an autumn sun with the appropriate selection from a first class wine list. The meal would be a pleasurable experience enhanced by some of the most beautiful women in the state sitting nearby, and he would wait. Eating something quickly was more important than the time-consuming pleasantries of fine dining. Soon his life would be that way forever, or for as long as his forever would last. There would be time for finer clothes, courtyard restaurants and the expensive wines. Today he had an agenda that would culminate with one of the most important meetings of his life, more so for Roberts and much remained for him to do. Lunch would be a function, a means to an end.

Rue Royal was also home to the Royal Café and the best Po-boys in the Quarter. The locals never liked their prized hoagies being called subs and Wellington had always ordered them "dresseda" because saying "with lettuce and tomato" labelled the eater as a tourist. The beer was extra, and the women passing by in flowing silk skirts were free. Their silk blouses and short breezy button-front dresses were on the house, no charge. He ordered a shrimp and crab dresseda, a Corona, and leaned against the outside wall of the building to eat and remember better times.

He remembered the times he had spent with Aston in the Quarter, when they would eat beignets together with café au lait at the Café du Monde before visiting the art galleries and high-end specialty gift shops. Low-end voodoo shops were also a priority because Aston had a thing about curses, death and the after-life. There was no such thing as a high-end curse boutique.

Trespassing into the domain of Marie Leveau was serious business. The exalted voodoo queen had died years earlier and many locals believed she still lived within or beyond the vaulted gates of her darkened tomb. Not one of them he had known would ever talk of the dark priestess or her art jokingly, which had always given Wellington the creeps to think someone could be killed merely by another's determined will.

He missed Aston, as he missed many others taken from him in a corporate divorce he had no say in, nor any control over. He hadn't particularly missed New Orleans; he missed what New Orleans was: The Quarter, good memories and he wondered if that would all be expunged in the coming hours. He hoped not, not all of it.

He walked through the doorway into a world, not a shop, a musty world of curses, hexes, potions, pins and wishful thinking. Only two types of people ever walked through such doors. One, the awestruck and curious tourist from Kansas or Idaho who had nothing to fear beyond their simplemindedness; the other, anyone who wished deathly harm on others and who sought to do something about it.

He tugged at the brim of his cap as he went in, not as a polite southern greeting, and twirled the ring on his finger. The ancient woman behind the cash was dressed like a gypsy and scrutinized him from behind a leathered and sun-dried face badly decorated with creases and moles. Her hair was long, uncombed, purple, and exploding from under a skull-tight bandana she had tied into a permanent knot. Her left eye had a black wart under its lid that prevented its full aperture and gave her a sleepy, sinister appearance. Her hands were bone white with brownish-yellow nicotine stains and liver spots that made them dirty and untouchable. Her French accent was unreal and Wellington had neither the time nor the interest in making her feel more stupid than she was. They both knew, and that was enough for him. Besides, he had already found what he needed.

A chill ran down his back as he walked out, not because he had gone in, because he had gone in with a purpose and he needed that not to bother him. The next stop was a jewellery store on Rue Royal where he had frequently shopped in the day that once was. Then he went to Canal Street where he purchased the few remaining items not readily available in the Quarter.

At five PM he wondered where the day had gone. By six the sky and the city was dark.

*

His purchases lay on the turned down bed, save one, and he studied them devoid of emotion. He knew he should have been scared, yet he wasn't. He was excited and didn't care. French doors were standard. Where they came from or who made them didn't matter. What mattered were the quality of the glass and the wood. These were hotel quality with panes measuring 15 X 31.75 centimetres and that's precisely what the single patch of duct tape was cut to before he laid the adhesive-side-up on the bed. Any and all wrappings and waste were put meticulously into the newly purchased suitcase, the one item he had carried through the lobby.

He had hoped the tape would not be necessary, but when he had returned from his shopping spree he'd tried to open his own set of balcony doors from the outside by wedging his new mini-crowbar into the crevice and had failed. Plan two was in effect, not what he had hoped for, but he would make do if the bar failed him twice.

By six PM the warming sun had already disappeared behind the west wall, creating a haloed effect over the enclosed and deserted courtyard. Wellington was dressed in business casual attire, leaning on the cast iron railing outside his room and focused on Roberts' doors and a single line of light escaping between the curtains. Leave for Christ sake, he wanted to yell. Leave.

The lights remained on. Nothing felt right. Something was going wrong. Roberts should have left and this was no time to screw up his first meeting. Just fucking leave! Then the reality hit Wellington like a bolt. Roberts was a frequent traveller, an experienced hotel occupant and that was one serious oversight on his part. Shit! Wellington would give him credit for that small amount of intelligence at least. He would have left the room with the lights on in Corruption City and probably the television. Shit!

Wellington ran to the lobby, waited ten minutes that seemed like sixty and walked as quickly as he could to Mike Anderson's without attracting attention, as though anyone would have noticed. The newcomers were already on the hunt for tits, or getting seriously psyched up to show them. When he did get there, Roberts wasn't, and that was a major brain-fuck as most every New Orleanian who wasn't brain-fucked would say.

He declined a table, telling the hostess he was looking for friends who were probably at the second floor bar or on the balcony and he hurried up the stairs, royally pissed off. No Roberts. He went to the bar, dropped a ten for a double JW Red and walked out onto the balcony that was practically empty because there wouldn't be anything worth ogling, begging for or laughing at until ten or eleven at the earliest. Where in the hell was Roberts? Already six-thirty and his plan was going to shit.

What reached Wellington long before any visual contact was Roberts' loud and effusive manner. John Roberts was the man of the hour and would be for as many hours as he could keep his enlisted cronies around him. There he was, walking along Bourbon Street at the head of his litter. There was a God. Yes, there was, or a voodoo queen, and there was Roberts who was on the threshold of meeting one of them that evening.

Wellington waited a moment before ordering one more Red, making his way to the main level where he suddenly found himself standing beside Roberts. The Johnnie Walker allowed him to remain calm and not implode from the effort as the Roberts party was seated. He was next and he left as quickly as he could, offering no excuse to the hostess who would never see him again and wouldn't care less if she did. He'd be at the hotel and in his room by seven, voodoo queen willing, one hour before Miss Celeste was expected to arrive. The timeline was too tight and his feigned composure was costing him untold years. He arrived on the hour.

He showered out of consideration for her, paid particular attention to his hair and dressed in the same business casual as earlier in the day. He took another miniature JW Red from the mini-bar, drained the contents in a single gulp and filled his pounding chest with as much air as he could before closing the lights and stepping onto the balcony and into the solitary darkness of night.

Good for him, and bad for those who had opted for the raunchiness of Bourbon Street over the true romance of a secluded and sculptured garden, subtly lit by the calm turquoise of an untouched pool and the incandescent amber glow emanating from surrounding courtyard rooms. That was true sensuality. He hadn't expected to see the entire area abandoned and the few guests who were still preparing for the evening would see only darkness beyond their

lighted rooms.
*

He hadn't practiced. Perhaps he should have, though the speed and agility with which he worked would have surprised him had he not been so intent on the task at hand. Even the unusually warm evening air had no effect on him. He was driven. He was focused and the next few seconds were crucial; a fact he subconsciously forced from his mind.

The tape fit perfectly over the plate glass. He had made an allowance for a tab that would hang from the top horizontal cross section of the small frame, intended as the back-up he didn't want to use. Recovering the hundreds of minute glass particles not adhering to the tape and flying between the portal and rubberized backing of the curtains would be impossible.

He immediately forgot the issue. He reached for the crowbar, jamming the wedged end upward and partly into the barely visible joint between the doors that weren't budging, neither was the crowbar. He forced upward, his gloves making the job all the more difficult and the reflection staring at him from within the glass was disturbing in the extreme. The steel tip penetrated a few millimetres and he was astonished when he twisted the iron bar to the side and one of the two doors moved imperceptibly inward.

He was in, the weight of the curtains against his back giving him an immediate sense of what he had accomplished. He was filled with a terror he hadn't anticipated, hadn't allowed for and he gasped not realizing he had been holding his breath. Don't panic. For Christ sake, don't panic. Just get on with the plan.

Roberts' Executive suite was as large as his own, though the motif was modern American, not traditional French provincial. The decor was highly polished mahogany set against deep crimson walls and the black glossy frames accessorizing the walls complemented the production pieces of graceful figurines in lustrous black and maroon-coloured ceramic.

The bed had a slatted low-rise headboard, a cherry-on-black brocade cover and matching pillow shams of a softer, silkier fabric. An unknown artist's rendition of a southern belle reclining by the edge of a trickling brook amidst pastel colours was the only artwork not framed in black. The frame was as long as the king bed was wide and perfectly matched the headboard.

He drew back the curtains, opened the patio doors and went to the main door. He knew Roberts would have requested the turn-down service usually performed between eight and nine. He opened the door and inserted the laminated Do Not Disturb card into the electronic lock, debarring housekeeping. He pulled back the bedcover and top sheet in a single motion, exposing the freshly laundered bottom sheet fitted to the mattress which he covered with the one he had taken from his own room before remaking the bed to its original condition. He left his own top sheet in the suitcase, should he require it later in the evening.

The carpet was a pale cerise to balance the darker tones of the room. As he bent over to lay out the bottle of Premier Cru Château Margaux'87 and matching long-stem wine glasses on the glass-covered coffee table, he made a mental note that his footsteps were being recorded in its plush cross weave.

She would arrive in twenty minutes and he would need every one of them to control his breathing. He was surprised the hotel had not installed dead bolts on the patio doors, but then the doors were intended more for appearance than security. What little security he had seen were cameras in the lobby and at the elevators on each of the three floors. There was nothing at all in the courtyard or hallways of concern to him.

He had badly scratched the brass strike plates between the patio doors with the crowbar and the last few items on his to-do list were to replace those with the ones he had removed from the twin doors in his room, remove the tape from the plate glass, remove his gloves and verify he had returned all tools and accessories to the suitcase he then put alongside Roberts'.

Like most seasoned travellers, Roberts kept his clothing and personal belongings in a suitcase with the exception of a few shirts for the next day, his slacks and shoes. His closed briefcase leaned against the wall beside it. The few personal items Wellington could see were the toiletries in the bathroom, a travel clock and a half-full bottle of Jack Daniels. What Wellington really wanted was a JW Red which would come later. Instead he a poured a glass of Château Margaux, taking extreme care not to spill a single drop on the luscious cerise carpeting.
*

The soft knock at the door announced 8:00 PM as precisely as any Swiss timepiece. He wanted the full impact of seeing her and avoided the temptation to first peer through the fish-eye peephole. He pushed against the brass lever with the Italian-silk pocket hanky that stayed in his hand as the door swung open between them.

"Mr. Roberts, my name is Celeste. I do believe you were expecting me."

He forced himself not to ogle her. She was stunningly gorgeous. She stood eye to eye with him, dressed entirely in black and she was truly the most elegant vision he had seen in a good while. She wore a wide-brimmed silk fedora accented in ruby-red with a discreet vintage broach showing against its wide black satin band. A delicate lattice of black mesh draped over its wide brim, not fully concealing her perfect white teeth behind full raspberry lips and her piercing brown eyes. A satin wrap loosely covered her shoulders.

"Please come in, Miss Celeste." He stepped aside, holding the door open with the back of his hand as she passed through, letting it close on its own with a final tap of his elbow. His heart was pounding.

"I love the way they have decorated your room, Mr. Roberts. Is this your first time at the Maison Dupuy?"

"No. It's not." He came close to asking if it was hers. "Actually, I come here often for meetings and conventions."

She walked through, pirouetting in a full circle before stopping in the centre of the bedroom area. "The décor is so charming, so relaxing. I understand why you would enjoy coming here."

"After a while they all look alike."

She smiled at that. "Yes, I do suppose they do, after a while." She removed her fedora uncovering hair so black, more like deep midnight blue and worked into a sophisticated French braid. She placed the hat casually on the sofa and rested her patent leather evening purse against it, smiling at seeing the wine. "May I, Mr. Roberts."

She went towards the patio doors, opening them, not waiting for his answer.

"Please do. May I pour you a glass of wine, Miss Celeste? I hope red is to your liking. I wasn't certain. Or may I order something more to your taste?"

Shut your mouth, and for Christ sake stop your babbling, you idiot.

"Red will do very nicely. Thank you, Mr. Roberts."

She stepped onto the balcony where he joined her after a moment and several more deep breaths.

"Now that we're enjoying our first drink together, perhaps we can be less formal? Would you mind calling me John?"

"The wine is excellent, John. Thank you." She gazed out over the garden. "The setting is so lovely and so peaceful."

"And deserted," he added, "which I find particularly strange. Don't you?"

"Yes. I do indeed, a beautiful backdrop from a bygone era that will certainly be taken from us one day. And so few of us will know to miss the romance."

"How so?"

"Elegant ladies once sat in petticoats and under parasols, fanning themselves with embroidered handkerchiefs as their gentlemen callers stood by their sides in spats, tails, neckties with ruby pins and satin-covered top hats. It's not at all the same as faded jeans, bare feet in open sandals and tank tops."

"You're a romantic, Celeste."

Her lips curled in a wide smile. "In my business a touch of romanticism does most certainly help. Shall we go inside?"

No response was needed. He followed, closing the doors behind him and setting his glass on coffee table with hers.

"Would you prefer that I close the drapes?"

"That is entirely up to you, John. Suit yourself. The evening belongs to you, after all. Though don't you think not knowing can be very exciting…dare I say stimulating."

"Not knowing?"

"Not knowing who might be watching you, or not."

She closed her purse, placing the strip of paper beside his glass.

"A beautiful romantic with a touch of wild abandon. I agree." He paused. "Why not?"

She lounged into the plush sofa, "and I much prefer getting business out of the way first. This is your receipt and you will notice we appear as a restaurant, not as an agency. I believe Madame Sainte-Marie has explained the limitations."

"Yes. She did very clearly." He sipped at his wine. "This is actually my first time doing this sort of thing, inviting a lovely woman to my room."

"Why, thank you, John, and I hope not your last. Our business is bringing pleasure to our clients or perhaps an experience they cannot enjoy at home for whatever reason. We do not cast aspersions or question."

She looked over to the bed, then at him with a raised eye brow and a coquettish pout.

"I wasn't sure whether I should wait or not." He went to get up. "I'll do it now."

"As I said, the night belongs to you."

He nodded, trying not to appear like a nervous schoolboy working hard at his first erection. "I'll prepare the bed."

Celeste eased herself to the edge of the sofa, letting her wrap fall from her shoulders. She took a sip of wine as she watched him put aside the pillows and neatly fold back the sheets. He had not yet removed his jacket, or his shoes, and was somehow more ill at ease than she would have believed of a man of his years and obvious experience. She possibly was his first paid experience, surprisingly. That would not last for long, she thought. What most of them needed was a first time with someone different, someone good and then they were hooked, so to speak. What came after was easy. She went to him from behind, pulling his jacket from his shoulders, guiding it down his back and onto the edge of the bed before easing him into a sitting position near the pillows.

She lifted his one foot, then the other, removing the oxblood loafers. Then she told him to do the rest, she didn't do socks. She stepped away to let him appraise the goods he had requested as she took one final sip before beginning what she had come to do. She wore a shimmering black décolleté evening dress tied at the waist, wrapped snugly around a perfectly proportioned and sculpted body. She helped the waist-high ruffled butterfly slit fall open as she reclined once again into the sofa, revealing the laced tops of her dark nylons and narrow bands of black-laced garters stretching to where the tops of her bare and slightly tanned thighs became bare hips.

She stood slowly, positioning herself between him and the French doors, slowly working at the loosely knotted silk fabric that held the chic and flimsy dress together, letting it float to the plush carpet as though in slow motion. Her skin was perfect and he believed she would be thirty-something, heading towards a perfect forty, which meant he would at least be able to talk with her. Her stomach was flat and tight, without being hard and her legs were slender with the firmness of someone who took care of herself. Her pure black demi-balconet bra was embroidered with black lace, worn for effect with a black silk-feathered ribbon that connected the space between each of her rounded and firm breasts. Her panties were a matching black silk V-string thong with a tiny embroidered mesh front. Discreet pull-away ribbons sat high on her hips connecting to a hand-sized V that disappeared into the centre of buttocks sculpted to delicious perfection at the base of a perfectly curved back.

He couldn't take his eyes from her, completely unabashed by his own body's immediate response to hers. He wondered who else was watching and hoped someone was. He stood and went closer to her. Her hands caressed her sides gliding slowly upwards towards her breasts that she cupped and squeezed ever so slightly with her eyes closed and her head slightly tilted. The sound of his own heart was all he heard and she was soliciting no help from him as her delicate fingers worked deftly and mischievously at the ribbon he wanted to tear at. His eyes went immediately to the breast she bared first. Working her shoulder away from the loosened strap she freed the second of her magnificently firm and pale breasts, each with its tiny dark crown giving evidence of the pleasure she had already brought to her evening's work.

She left the dress and bra where they fell, taking a few steps to where Wellington stood, slightly thrusting out a hip for him to tug at the shiny tell-all ribbons. He shook his head, no. He wanted to watch and she stepped back, scolding him with a smile and feeling pleased her client was so visibly responsive to the first ribbon separating and falling away. She pressed her hand firmly into the moistened V between her legs, holding the flimsy material in place. He was losing his mind, watching her pull at the other side. He never would have believed he'd be sitting in a hotel room watching an absolutely beautiful woman strip for him, or that he'd be so aroused by her, by any woman.

She stood with her feet wide apart. One side of her panties hung down, one hand working easily at her own arousal as the other side fell away and two of the ribbons came together from behind her open legs. She was smiling at him, teasing him, breathing deeply, waiting, seeing his eyes focused on her hand that was feeling her increasing moistness. She pulled her hand away, bringing her red-tipped fingers to her glossy lips. She inhaled deeply with her eyes closed, her head tilted back, exposing the smooth lines of her neck. The thong refused to fall away and he was mere seconds from pulling Celeste to the bed, throwing her onto the sheets and forcing her legs apart so he could push his firm and pulsating member deep inside her.

"You are still dressed, John. Must I assume you are not enjoying what you see?"

She was both smiling and inquisitive. His heart was racing. She wasn't at all what he had expected. His mouth was dry, all the moisture in his trembling body converging to where the need was most urgent.

"I'm sorry. I ...."

Children with fully functional penises, she thought.

"John, must I assume you would prefer to watch me alone this evening, in bed by myself, perhaps from outside on the balcony? That would be very naughty."

She looked down as her panties fell away and Wellington finally saw all of her.

"No. Thank you. I think I'll be staying in tonight with someone very special."

He ripped at his socks that he thought stretched too much before snapping from his ankles. He hadn't cared that Seraphina and Dalila had seen him in his socks all night, even watching him while he urinated, not this one, not Celeste. His sweater came off over his head in one fluid motion and his slacks followed. He would find his belt later.

He hoped he had sounded witty, which was secondary. What he wanted was right there, right between her legs and he could tell even with the distance between them that she was ready. She had almost no hair and what little she did have was trimmed short and shaped in a dark, narrow V. The skin around her slightly darker outer folds was smooth, the more delicate lips they protected were paler, glistening with moisture which would soon be his to taste and breathe.

His member was throbbing painfully, forcing with a mind of its own against silk underwear the French would call a slip and everyone else would call French, or European, or too small or queer. Her clitoris was just as hard with two fingers rubbing urgently along either side of its bright pink length and she cried out when she touched its glossy and sensitive tip.

"Celeste, I haven't seen anything that sexy in a long time" he said. "Now, let me see if I can do as good a job."

"In a moment, John, please. No lady wants a run in her nylons that cost as much as these do."

"Hurry," he urged. "I'm dying here."

"John, go to the bed, right now. Lay back and watch a while longer. Go," she insisted, firmly, with a giggle. "I'll get to you in a moment, bad boy."

She was drop-dead gorgeous in a way Wellington had never before thought of women. She was tall, slim, perfect and very naked, wearing nylons with garters and a ruby-studded choker matching the single ankle strap of her stilettos.

"Leave them on, my treat. I'll buy you ten pairs. Please leave them on."

She had one foot on the arm of the sofa, facing away from him, pushing out her taut and inviting buttocks so they were ever so slightly open to him and he fought the urge to go behind her the way he had with Dalila. But Celeste was not a whore, not to him, or not yet.

"I want you that way."

"Which way would that be, John?" She ran a hand fully over the bare curvatures of her ass, probing, taunting him.

"Just like that, they way you are, with the nylons and garters. Don't change a damn thing. You're so sexy."

She swivelled from her hips, with a smile that became a laugh. "Ten pairs and you lose those panties. Deal?"

"They're not panties," he argued. "They're briefs, the finest Italian silk." He thought for a moment, for no reason. "Okay, they're gone."

They were, in a flash and Celeste placed the two hundred-dollar bills in her purse before pulling out a foil wrap.

"I brought a few as well."

"If you don't mind, John, I truly do prefer mine. Not that they are particularly extra special… they're mine. Do you understand?"

"Yes, I understand."

He didn't understand, nor did he care. All he wanted was to put the thing on and ram it deep inside her, and she knew as much. There couldn't be very many anatomically correct men who wouldn't want to get inside her, forgiving queers and feeling sorry for eunuchs. She knew that as well and her knowledge allowed for a very lucrative career. Wellington held out his hand for the condom.

"John, how should I put this?" She kept the foil in one hand, placed the other hand on a curved hip. "My gentlemen friends do not service me. I service them. That is what I do, sir."

"I'm not into dominatrix."

"Neither am I, John. I simply do what I do better than most men. Actually, I should have said all men and most women. Now, lie down."

"You do women?"

"Yes, John, I do women, on my own time, lovely, sexy and hot women. Now, lie back."

He obeyed subserviently, jumping backwards onto the king size mattress like a little boy waiting to hear a bedtime story and looking absolutely ridiculous when the purple rod protruding from his centre began swaying to and fro like a phallic pendulum.

She didn't mind at all as she straddled his thighs, taking his member between the outer edges of her palms and sliding the latex sheath downward in one fluid motion, held between her thumbs and forefingers. No woman had ever done that for him, Wellington straining his neck to watch, fixated by the folds of her lips coming apart as she gently pushed him back so that she might move up and over him.
*

When Roberts' clock showed ten, the sex Wellington had thought of as lovemaking was over and he hadn't wanted that part of his evening to end. Being with Celeste was different, more refined than Seraphina and Dalila, more perfected; Celeste making their time together seem anything other than her way of making a living. The evening had been about quality rather than quantity and, if not as depleted as the previous night, he was certainly as satisfied.

He had watched her from outside on the balcony in his silk slip and with a JWR as she dressed. She joined him for a final glass of wine before saying good-bye. He had wanted to kiss her raspberry lips, to taste them, but no. That was not to be. She had allowed other forms of kissing throughout the evening they had mutually enjoyed, intoxicating kisses that made him drunk for more and he hadn't stopped, possibly adding to the pleasure of anonymous others beyond the darkness, but never on the mouth. She was what she was. She enjoyed her life and her work. She enjoyed the tingling excitement of having a new and different dalliance every evening. Even so, those gentlemen weren't her lovers and kissing was for lovers. Sorry, John. That's for her, not for you.

The time was 10:15 and she was off the clock. Wellington brought her in close against him, not to kiss her. His hands went boldly to the open slit in her dress he slowly and smoothly made wider as he brought his hands up to her hips and pulled at the silken black ribbons. They both looked down as he put a hand to her warm centre, pressing gently, letting his fingertips savour her wetness before coming away with the moistened silk trophy. He wanted more of her. He had not finished his exploration of her, being one with her and knowing she was going home to another woman excited him even more. He brought another hand to a breast, gently pulling away the dress. He fit another hundred into her bra, careful not to scratch the tender skin beneath, which moments before he had been caressing and fondling. He went to feel her, to enclose a breast in his hands one more time. He wanted more, Celeste didn't. She knew better.

Guiding his hand away from her breast, she smiled at him and hugged him dispassionately before stepping into the room, leaving her glass and walking to the door. There was nothing any client could say, ask or do that would surprise her. She was well aware of the signs. She blew him a friendly kiss and was gone. Good-bye, John, and that's exactly what he was. As much has Wellington hated that her portion of his evening had come to an end, he had much to do and when she disappeared into the hallway he forgot her and stepped into Roberts' room with his hanky in hand.

She would doubtlessly be identified as soon as the police traced Roberts' credit card expense, but Wellington would delay that as long as possible. In the meantime she wouldn't be recognized by anyone reviewing surveillance tapes taken from the cameras in the lobby or at the elevators. She had been a woman in black, possibly a hooker, possibly not. From which one of the few dozen rooms on the second floor would she have come, from which agency and how long would anyone take to clue into that? Even when they eventually would, the tapes would show she had left before Roberts had returned to his room. If nothing more the clue would be a piece of a puzzle that would never fit. He would make certain, later.

He laid the open suitcase in the middle of the floor, pulling away the bottom fitted sheet he had stretched over Roberts' bed, fixing the covers and pillow shams exactly as housekeeping would, although much more quickly. He had no need to replace the top sheet, though he did check the toilet because Celeste had peed in a way he would never forget. He checked that under the seat was dry and folded the paper in the wall dispenser according to hotel protocol.

Next were the wine bottle, the long-stem glasses, the corkscrew and the lead wrapping from the bottleneck that all went carefully into the suitcase on top of the tools and soiled sheet. That's when he noticed the coagulating blotch on the desk he had lifted Celeste onto at some point over the previous two hours. He had lost count of her orgasms. She was a veritable vending machine of viscous juices and being on the desk wasn't the first time she had cried out. He had simply forgotten how much of her heated fluid had spilled from her.

He had positioned her there with her back against the wall so she was facing him with her legs draped over his arms at the elbows, with his hands grabbing her firmly at her knees that allowed him a perfect view of her parted buttocks. He had needed no help guiding himself past her well-lubricated and heated lips he had helped to make a deeper shade of pink, neither one taking their eyes from her folds fluttering in and out in concert with the sometimes slow, sometimes urgent thrusts of the glistening and pulsating appendage ramming into her. So much for her doing him. They had been so intent on making the explosion happen that when the climax did happen simultaneously they burst out laughing when she began slipping and sliding from the desk in her own viscous puddle. And once again he had carried her to the bed to lay her gently onto the crumple sheets and change his latex sleeve.

Her fluids were irrelevant. What he might possibly have left was the larger issue and the clean-up had taken longer than he had wanted at the cost of two hand towels needed to remove most of Celeste and buff the remaining traces of their love-making to a high gloss that matched the rest of the glass-top desk. Next the bed was made ready and the towels were added to the suitcase which he closed and carried to the door. Expelling a deep breath he began dragging it repeatedly across the room until the entire surface had been covered and he was satisfied he had approximated the appearance of a freshly vacuumed carpet. He left a few dozen footprints that would have been Roberts' and went to his own room to drop off the luggage,

relieve himself and return with two fresh towels and the requisite item he had not needed earlier.
*

Wellington's eyes were too out of focus to read the luminous dial on his wristwatch. He had no idea how long he'd been sitting with his legs stretched out in the semidarkness behind the louvre doors of the second and empty closet in Roberts' room. His feet were cramped at uncomfortable angles to avoid touching the noisy metal legs of the ironing board and he prayed Roberts would not choose to press any of his clothes when he returned to the room.

One shoulder was firmly pressed against the rear wall and the other wanted to rub against the flimsy slatted doors. Sitting at an angle to avoid inadvertently causing them to spring open made his backache. The alternative would have been hiding behind the curtains, leaving him exposed, vulnerable to possible detection by others standing on the balconies. Someone watching him enjoying Celeste was one thing, the more the merrier. Being seen concealing himself behind hotel drapes would be quite another and not good. He wanted terribly to stand upright or stretch, unable to do either, a very moot point if Roberts did decide to press his clothes and pull open one of the doors. Then they'd both be dead of heart failure.

His bowels were channels of agitated water and he regretted not eating before beginning his nightlong escapade. He asked himself in a whisper whether he would have time to run to the mini-bar for a snack, knowing better, answering he had come too far to be caught with his hand in the proverbial cookie jar by the man he had come to kill. He held up his wrist against the slats crossing the frail door, hoping for even a weak beam of light that would make his watch clearer to him. Instead, his mouth went instantly dry and his heart constricted in a way he thought would kill him when he heard two long and dull double clicks of Roberts swiping his magnetic card through the electronic lock.

Roberts was inside the room, centimetres from Wellington who saw clearly as his quarry immediately hurried into the bathroom. Wellington was witnessing an event, not merely a man pulling himself out from his pants, leaning forward, bracing himself with both hands against the wall in front of him and pissing away his evening to the drawn out chorus of vile and liquid farts that would reach Wellington long before the sounds ended in sporadic and strained spurts.

Roberts was a pig. He always had been a pig and Wellington suddenly felt reassured his prey would not be using the hotel iron at such a late hour. His thoughts drifted to an earlier time, remembering how Roberts wore stains as accessories the way most people wore jewellry and had always been unkempt. From what he could see nothing had changed, Wellington believing he would vomit over himself as Roberts' stale air infused his secret place.

Roberts hit the doorframe of the bathroom hard with his shoulder as he staggered from the bathroom, then back in, teetering a moment too long for Wellington who thought his prey was seconds away from crashing drunkenly into the louvre doors and onto him. Though somehow Roberts steadied himself, somewhat, disappearing into the bedroom area to deprive Wellington of all but his bodily noises and curses intended for no one, including when he turned on the television and could find nothing of interest. The television was good, Wellington thought. The noise would serve in two ways: keeping the old fart preoccupied and, once turned off, Wellington would know Roberts was ready for bed and peace everlasting.

Wellington was oblivious to the grunts and groans of a man who was too out of shape to pull off his own socks without the threat of bursting a blood vessel and he recognized the sounds of shoes being kicked off, a belt being unthreaded through its loops, zippers coming down, and clothes being tossed into a corner. He hadn't much longer to wait, he thought, until Roberts passed by once more.

This time he was naked and by the time Wellington opened his eyes again his unknowing host was bent over with his knees in the forward position, leaning against the side of the tub. His pimpled and stringy mauve-coloured scrotum dangled behind him, holding marble-size testicles even with neighbouring ankles lined with the red-purple scratches of broken blood vessels.

Wellington had never seen anything so flaccid and troll-like in his life. Roberts' stomach was a series of fatty and mole covered rolls, one overlaying the other and his hairless chest looked more like two white chicken fillets tenderized by pounding them with a wooden mallet. The skin covering him so droopily possessed a translucent quality that showcased a vertical thoroughfare of swollen and crooked purple veins. His arms had absolutely no tone, skin sagged at his armpits and his elbows, and his hairless and spotted legs seemed disproportionately spindly for the purpose of carrying their distorted burden. The network of lumpy veins extended to feet and toes Wellington could smell. They were long and tipped with thick yellow nails curling downward. The man had jowls and the purple tint of his face had deepened from bending over the tub, seeming freakish against the rest of his pallid body parts when he stood. The room was filling with steam and Wellington lowered his line of vision as Roberts leaned forward and away from him to first lift one leg and then the other over and into the tub.

Roberts was even more ridiculous clambering out from the shower. His hair was wet, stuck to one side of his head and Wellington thought to pass the time by counting the numerous irritated blemishes and sores decorating the man's body from his shoulders to his feet. Then he thought he wouldn't. The end was coming near with Wellington on the verge of opening the doors, standing to apologize for being there to kill him and going to his own room for a JW Red. The man's loose skin was moving in every possible way with each tug of the towel. His chest was rocking to and fro, opposite to his balls that had become less controllable because of the hot shower and his penis was a shrivelled purple grape peeking out from under its excessive skin to stare at Wellington eye to eye.

The job was finally done, Wellington grimacing at the man's inattention to his personal grooming. He hadn't completely dried his hair, nor had he bothered to comb over the rogue strands. He hadn't brushed his teeth, nor had he used a deodorant, and those toenails. Christ, those toenails: thick, yellow and irreparable shards packed with white matter no cream could penetrate, nor would anything his company manufactured save him. Wellington took a deep and silent breath as the bathroom lights flicked off and the troll stepped out and into the bedroom.

There was an easy fart, then another sounding forced. Then the sound of sheets being tugged, the television clicking off and the sound of drapes pulled along the track before the mini-bar opened and closed which was followed by sounds of two miniature caps being twisted from bottle necks and tossed into the wastepaper basket.

Darkness came shortly after, followed by the sounds of a weakened body collapsing onto the sofa and Wellington lowered his head to his chest in an attempt to relax. Perhaps Roberts was going to fall asleep on the sofa while he downed his last drink of the night and his first one of the day. No matter. Then the stomach-wrenching coughing fit reverberated through the quiet room accompanied by the heavy clank of glass on glass. Then finally the bed made the cushioned noise Wellington had been waiting interminably to hear.

Eventually the farts, the heavy breathing and the nauseating coughing spells subsided, replaced by the constant drone of Roberts' erratic snoring. There was no rush, no panic, no concern as the night belonged once again to Wellington. And he was ready. He took the time necessary to open the closet's twin doors silently, first opening one side with a hand firmly gripping and guiding the bottom edge, then leaning forward and doing the same on the other side. When he stood he did so slowly, unfolding himself one joint at a time, letting his blood circulate and stretching to regain his mobility.

The curtains had closed out most of the moonlight, though the room was bright enough to move around and the pale carpet immediately showed him everything Roberts had cast aside. Even with his shoes on Wellington could make no noise on the carpet unless he tripped over something. His path was clear to the corner, allowing him to peer across to Roberts lying spread-eagle with the top sheet pulled up as far as his waist. The room smelled like an abattoir and the pig was in bed with the stench of liquor, smoke and bad living emanating from him. Wellington waited. The time was 01:15. There was no hurry.
*

Seeing Roberts snoring loudly and coughing involuntarily in his sleep, Wellington stood for a moment considering the incongruous imagery, seeing the troll lying where three hours earlier he had been with Celeste. How he had savoured gazing between her open legs at the source of her feminine fragrance as he titillated the responsive tips of her firm breasts with his fingertips, lingering there before tracing them slowly, teasingly over the warmth and smoothness of her belly as she arched her back to give him access to more of her.

Wellington eased himself gently onto the bed alongside Roberts, straddling the soft fleshy mass in one fluid and slow motion. When he sank his full weight heavily onto Roberts' spongy abdominal area the stinking drunk woke.

"Good morning, John."

The man had infused his system with two more shots of Jack Daniel and was more numbed by drunkenness than when he had returned to his room. His yellowed and blood-shot eyes were dull from years of drinking and bleary from the evening's events. Sleep had just begun to carry him away from reality when bewilderment came before realization and terror.

"What the fu--!"

Roberts' eyes opened wide with fear as Wellington's gloved hand clamped hard on the wide-open and speechless mouth like a steel jaw.

"John." Roberts' head was jerking, trying to free itself. "No, John. I need for you to stay perfectly still. Do you understand? You must be still or things won't go well for either of us." The head, ghastly in the low light, slowed slightly, trying hard to wind its way from under Wellington's oppressive grip. His nostrils were flared wide open, leaving wet residue on the edge of Wellington's glove, his chest heaving in rhythm to his erratic heartbeat. "I need a yes to that, John. Please." His hand stayed firmly affixed to the contorted face. "Just nod a yes. Can you do that for me, John? Can you?" Wellington relaxed his grip barely enough for Roberts to acquiesce. "Thank you. Now I need you to close your eyes for a moment, John. And John, please, when you open them stay very still." Roberts did as he was told. Wellington removed one hand, bringing the other up to where the tip of the twenty-centimetre silver pin was introduced well into Roberts' right flaring nostril. "Now we can talk, John. You don't remember me, do you?"

"How the fuck would I know who you are?"

97

His eyes were rivetted to the metallic streak. He was terrified, frozen, seeming to want to pull his head into his torso.

"It's a silver pin, John, with a black pearl at the end. Any old hat pin certainly wouldn't do, not for you John. I wanted the best for you, and twenty centimetres long. That would be eight inches to you. So, please stay as still as you are right now. I have no idea how big your brain is, or how far it is from your nose, but I'm sure it's less than eight inches."

"Fuck. I can't even see you. What do you want, money?"

"Don't swear, John. Swearing is for the under educated, the socially under privileged, not successful corporate icons, Mr. John Roberts. Don't you agree?" Wellington waved a finger. "The question was rhetorical, John. There's no need to answer."

"What do you want?" Roberts' eyes were crossed, staring at the pin.

"My name is Wellington Trystan Bartlett, John. Do you remember me now? I was one of the best Account Executives Spencer ever had. You even said so," he rotated the pin between his forefinger and thumb, "the day you got rid of me, John, the day you fired me without just cause."

Wellington could see in the man's eyes the journey Roberts was taking fifteen years back in time, searching for the impossible right words.

"That wasn't my decision. I only carried out a decision from the top floor. I had no choice."

Wellington put an admonishing finger to his lips.

"You mustn't speak so loudly, John. Now, what were you saying?"

"I wasn't responsible. The decision came from the top, not me. I did what I was told."

"John, you were pretty close to the top. We both know you didn't make a decision that would benefit Spencer. You made one you thought would most benefit you. You needed me out of the way because I was one step away from coming to the Swamp, ahead of you. Instead of you."

"No, you're wrong. That would never have happened."

"You were a fool then and you're a worse fool now. You screwed me over, big time. Tell me, John. Were you always this vile and smelly? My god, you're absolutely fetid. You knew then, John, and you know now that I was one of the best, one of the most successful. I was also a serious threat to someone who had, by some wasted miracle, been promoted to manager, to his level of incompetence. That's you, John, incompetent, and you were looking where there was no need to look. You didn't have to do what you did. How'd you do it, John? How did you get there? Who did you fuck, John. Or should I ask who you saw fucking? Your kind don't get anywhere without help. Who helped you, John? Who did you see and what were they doing?"

"I was following instructions." Sweat was oozing from Roberts' entire body; he began shivering violently. "What happened came from the top. You know as well as I do."

"No, I don't. John, you never called me Wellington. You never acknowledged what I had done and you despised me for what I would have accomplished... had I stayed, of course. Or, better said, had you not terminated me."

"No. It's not true. I was doing my job. They wanted you gone, not me." He needed to cough badly and was close to choking on his own fowl-smelling phlegm that filled the space between his half-open mouth and the glove. "I never had anything against you. Never. Not once. I did everything I could to maintain the team, to keep you, but we were in bad times."

"Non, non. Ce n'est pas vraie, mon petit Jean. You were always pissed with foreigners, weren't you? I was first, then

Manuel, ¿no es verdad, Juanito? Hell you even thought the rep in BC was French, you racist prick."

"Maybe I can do something now, something to make things better." Roberts wasn't breathing, he was gulping at the air around him, his sweat mingling with tears, making his eyes all the redder and swollen. "We can meet later. We can talk this over. Please. We can talk right now. We can arrange something, talk. We can make up for the past."

"You wanted me out, John. Why not admit it and feel so much better about yourself?"

"No. It wasn't like that. I swear it wasn't. I was given specific instructions to reduce personnel and costs."

"John, you ruined my life. I must admit, other opportunities did come after Spencer, no thanks to you. But shit happens. You should be familiar with the routine: first one in, first one out. Life was never the same, John. You turned my career into a game of catch-up I could never win …and I never did." Wellington chortled. "There's one thing we have to say about shit…once we step in it, it never goes away. And tonight you're the one in shit, really deep shit."

"Please. I have a wife and family. Don't! For Christ sake, don't! We can talk."

"I had a wife, John. She left me, not strictly because of you, but you're in there. You're certainly right in there. Do you know I'm losing my house and my car, John?" Wellington's hand pressed against the head, forcing it up and down ever so slightly as though nodding in agreement. "I don't believe you, John. How could you possibly know and not want to do something to help?" He paused. "Do you really want to help me, John?"

"Yes. Yes, I do." This time the head moved without help, the answer muffled. "I can make calls, right now. There is something I can do. I know I can."

"You wouldn't even give me a letter of recommendation, John."

"I don't remember what happened years ago for Christ sake. Why wouldn't I? I can give you one now. I've got contacts, serious contacts." Roberts was on the verge of madness. He was about to step across the threshold of death's dark door into a world that terrified him, a juncture where the wretched and the pitiable first surrender to the cowardice befitting their final moment of desperation and terror, when they plead for even the briefest continuance of their worthless existence. Wellington could not have hoped or prayed for a better conclusion to his first meeting. Roberts was crying, and sobbing, or choking. He was so pathetic, and so perfect. "Please let me try. Please let me do something to help. I'm begging you."

"There you go again, John, thinking about yourself. I would have thought you would have learned your lesson. You know, being more concerned about the welfare of others. You don't want to help me, John. You want to wake up and find yourself alone."

Wellington reached into the breast pocket of his jacket, pulling out Celeste's black silk panties, whispering an order to Roberts to open his mouth, slowly bringing the hand that had kept Roberts' head still to his wildly palpitating chest in a slow, massaging manner while concentrating on the alignment of the silver pin centred in the flaring nostril.

"It's okay, John. It's alright … really." Wellington was gently rubbing Roberts' soft bare chest. "You know, John, I was in here earlier this evening, in this very room. I was fucking one of the most beautiful women I've seen in a very long time. I even did her on the desk and the sofa. Those are her panties in your mouth. True, she might be a whore, albeit top notch, but a whore nonetheless. And she's what I'll remember most about this evening. I won't remember you at all, John, the same way you didn't remember me."

Roberts was whimpering uncontrollably. His entire face was covered with sweat, viscous fluids flowing from his eyes and nose beginning to seep onto his chin from the drenched panties in his mouth. His torso was jerking involuntarily from the convulsive panic.

"John, we both need to relax." With a speed that was not alarming to Roberts who lay somewhere between terror and hope, Wellington brought the lethal pin in line with the gloved finger that had come to rest between two ribs "Can you do that for me, John? Can you take a deep breath and relax?"

Roberts had hope in his sickly yellow eyes for the first time and he tried frantically to find air for his struggling lungs and to please Wellington, erupting once more in a spasm of coughing and spewing, trying desperately to spit the sodden silk from his mouth.

"Don't kill me, please. I don't want to die. I'm sorry. I have a wife. Please. Is that what you're trying to say, John? Did I understand you correctly?" The frantic head nodded. "I thought so, but you're not listening to me, John. I asked for one more, so give me one more... a deep one."

The delirious head nodded yes, sputtering what sounded like "we can talk this out. Together we can find a way."

Roberts filled his lungs through his nose, abruptly choking on his own mucous, gasping one short breath of air into his crowded mouth, sucking the panties deeper into his throat and cutting off any hope of breathing. Wellington could feel the mounting pressure. He saw the bulging eyes, preoccupied wondering whether Roberts was about to die on his own. He couldn't let that happen and was caught off guard by the unexpected onslaught of putrid flecks of sputum hurling from Roberts' gaping mouth, leaving the man's face grotesquely covered with twisted black ribbons. He made a subconscious notation to get rid of the clothes shielding him.

"Okay, John. I guess that one was deep enough. No shit." Roberts wanted to say more, but couldn't. "Are you afraid of the dark, John?" Wellington's question was not rhetorical, waiting for the reply as the paralyzed head pressed hard into the pillow, so desperately wanting to signal no for Wellington, but it couldn't find the mobility needed to respond. "Never mind, John, it doesn't matter. Nothing matters anymore. There is no difference between peaceful darkness and sleep, between peaceful sleep eternal darkness. I envy you. Absolutely nothing matters anymore."

A sudden long blast of muffled air spread from under Roberts, the air in the room filling quickly with the foulness of his wet and loose excrement. Wellington winced. There was no question he wouldn't be wearing those clothes again.

"Whew! John, you've been eating that Cajun shit again. Listen, don't be embarrassed. You're nervous, which is understandable. Anyone would be. Why not think of our meeting as a new beginning, John, a chance to start over, like the chance you gave me to start over?"

Wellington repositioned himself for strength and precision while Roberts struggled to suck a few precious centilitres of air through the silky wad covering his mouth and into his congested airways, grateful for any chance to start over as the tiny rapier plunged smoothly through a reddened sore on his blotched epidermis, past yielding flesh, and into his frantically beating heart.

"Good night, John Roberts. Rest in peace."

The meeting was over and Wellington sat exhausted, wondering whether he should have expected more. The needle had penetrated as Roberts struggled for breath, in effect stifling his own scream, producing a few wet sputters, a few restrained convulsive kicks from under the sheets and a single spastic twitch from each of the useless arms. Perhaps he shouldn't have wasted the panties. He had expected more pain, more flinching and more blood. Wellington had screwed up and would not do so again. He

had wanted Roberts to suffer. He wanted them all to suffer and the others would. He promised. Anyone can die or go to sleep. He wanted them all in hell first.
*

Wellington stepped into the hallway, letting the door close behind him. Then he went back in using Roberts' card. He walked past the corpse, stopped at the mini-bar before opening the French doors into the room and walked out onto the narrow balcony to lean against the iron rails. Holding the miniature JW Red out towards Roberts he whispered, "To your health, Mr. Roberts, to our successful meeting and your restless eternity in a place where you need not be concerned about being a good human being."

A pillow would have been too easy. The CSI people would have much more fun working a case with a black pearl and silver pin in the chest than they would with contusions to the face. Celeste was all he had touched in the room with bare hands. He had removed all other traces, except for the pin, and retraced each and every step in his mind as he sipped from the miniature JW Red. Closing the doors, he went to his room through his patio doors and put the tiny bottle in the suitcase before opening another from his mini-bar. All that was left for him to do was replace the strike plates, remake the bed as though he had slept in it, use the toilet, leave the seat up, unroll and flush some of the toilet paper from an unused roll and take a shower before returning to Roberts' room for the last time.

Wednesday, 25 October
Final Denial

Wellington stood peering out from his room at 3:30. All the other hotel guests who had gone out to party, fornicate or cheat had come back to sleep off the excesses of the evening or pass out. The courtyard was black, enveloped in an eerie stillness.

He was tired, exhausted, yet somehow he felt invigorated and vibrant, more alive than he had felt in over two years. Despite not having finished the Roberts portion of his plan, he needed a breather, a little balance. He would go back. In fact, he had no choice. Doing so was a critical part of the plan, his agenda.

The room was rancid with Roberts' now historical farts, his bad living and the foul-smelling fluids that continued seeping from his loosened orifices that had relaxed that much more with his transition into eternal peace. Roberts hadn't moved and the black silk ribbons were the focal point of the repulsive still-life that had begun losing its colour, save the random collection of sores, bruises and the yellow of its lifeless open eyes. Wellington was mutually and completely indifferent to the naked corpse in the bed as he went to the front door to repeat the process of opening it with the magnetic card. That done, he methodically filled Roberts' briefcase with the cadaver's two rings, a Seiko, his wallet and a cluster of bills, leaving the charger for the laptop in the side compartment. When he had finished with the cell phone he needed to satisfy his curiosity about one other piece of information before leaving Roberts' temporary resting place and was pleased when he found what he needed in the leather-bound agenda. Roberts' presentation was scheduled for 10:45 AM, after the break, by which time Wellington would be moments away from boarding US Airways flight 567 that would put him in Punta Cana by 2:54 PM.

The first flight segment would depart at 7:20 and would take him to Charlotte, North Carolina, leaving him adequate time for a fast-paced walk to Canal Street where he could get a cab to take him to the intersection of Veterans and Causeway Boulevards where he could grab a quick bite at a twenty-four hour before grabbing another taxi to the Double Tree. The magnetic door card was used one last time, the patio doors were closed in the locked position and Wellington returned to his own room congratulating himself on a successful workday. He had set a goal for himself and had accomplished what he had set out to do.

Roberts would have said he had achieved results. Good work, Wellington.

*

He gave himself an extra half-hour at the Maison Dupuy, sufficient time to shower, change his clothes and prepare a short list of priorities which would include the time and whereabouts to dispose of certain of his effects that would no longer be useful.

He neatly compacted and bagged the clothes Roberts had ruined. He would take them with him as carry-on and discard them in one of the men's rooms in Charlotte, including the shoes he had been wearing. The paper contents of the wallet were flushed and the few hundred dollars would replace a few of his soiled clothes. The tape went far into the first alley he passed and the utility knife went into the second. The two rings and watch were tossed into separate sewers on Bourbon, the empty wallet went into a sewer on Canal Street and the ID and credit cards dropped into a drain on Veterans along with the screwdriver. Everything had been disposed of beginning five blocks from the hotel, remembering he had once heard most cops regard the fifth block as the demarcation point of any crime scene. The gloves were shoved into a large cardboard coffee cup at the airport and tossed away before passing through security.

Roberts' cell, computer and briefcase were bonuses he had not considered and would keep all three a while longer. He bought a box of ten CDs at the airport and spent his in-flight time to Charlotte analyzing the data, bringing himself up-to-date, burning those files he considered pertinent. At a later time he would upload the photo that would have its date and time automatically imprinted, once he was certain the computer would not be checked by the TSA.

*

The one unlikely item to be found in a trash can in any airport men's room is a bare human hand: as secure a hiding place as any safety deposit box and Wellington had completed the more mundane tasks outlined on his list, including the list itself which he had written on toilet tissue.

He had been in the air en route to Punta Cana from Charlotte for about an hour, which would have made Roberts not only late for his own portion of the meeting, but for lunch. More likely, the police had already been called in by horrified hoteliers who no doubt were still trying their best to calm some jolly-faced, happy-go-lucky Cajun maid turned hysterical witness to the sinister Black Art she had intruded upon and that would certainly cause grief and pestilence to befall them all and curse their remaining days. Meanwhile, the cops would stand around grinning as they waited for CSI technicians to arrive and extricate the black-pearl stud firmly affixed to Roberts' chest as a prelude to exploring the various possibilities.

He thought they would probably assume a pissed-off girlfriend at first, or a belligerent unpaid hooker, an unhappy employee, a break-in or a novice voodoo practitioner who saw no harm in borrowing Roberts to practice on. They might think to get the credit card number from the hotel file, though he had often heard from locals that New Orleans police were better known for corruption than intelligence. Celeste would undoubtedly be implicated, though he had accounted for such an eventuality with two simple amendments to the agenda and was certain the necessary inconvenience to her would be short-lived.

The more confusing he could make the crime appear, the better. He had no great concern for Celeste, not even if the cops were to find her DNA by some fluke. Being in any hotel room was her sole raison d'être and she might have been in that particular room any number of nights. She had been all about sex, though she had left unaware she had been all about the plan as well. He wondered whether he would remember her, and for how long. Then he forgot her, stretched out and slept for the
*
The A319 banked steeply into its final approach over the shallow and breaking turquoise waters of the Atlantic that relentlessly caressed and enfolded the sandy white shores of Punta Cana, incessantly replacing what they swept away, perpetually redesigning and shaping the slopes, contours and romance of the island retreat. Wellington had no particular desire to gaze out from the porthole. He knew. For a few years the island had been a vacation destination for Geneviève and him when they weren't in Spain. The last time had been four years earlier as Hurricane Jeanne prepared to batter and devastate the island and Geneviève prepared to devastate him.

"Ladies and gentlemen, we are into our final approach," the voice announced. "Please discontinue the use of all electronic devices immediately and bring your chair backs and your tray tops to their upright positions. Please check that your seat belts are securely fastened and that all carry-on luggage has been stored under your feet or securely placed in one of the overhead bins. We remind you to please use caution when opening the overhead bins as contents may have shifted during flight."

The A319 banked again, slowing abruptly to a speed that would allow a comfortable and smooth landing at two-hundred kilometres onto the narrow strip of white concrete extending from surrounding lush, green foliage. The airbus dropped much like an amusement park ride, provoking a chorus of oohs and aahs. Those beside him and others were craning their necks to see the aesthetic platter of changing greens with white and turquoise porcelain borders in a setting of aqua blue, their place in paradise for however long they would be staying: some for a week, while others were coming home. Those like Jean-François would participate in business meetings and depart soon thereafter. He had a clearly defined goal with a singular objective whose success would depend fully on a series of specific actions, some of which he hadn't yet fully pre-determined. In short, Jean-François would necessarily wing three elements of his plan.

He knew what he could accomplish based on information he had previously gathered. Once in place he would collect new requisite information that would permit him to create and progress through a series of actions, determining appropriate times and places to successfully implement those actions in order to successfully attain his objective. Not the perfect sales cycle, he thought, however specifically designed to achieve a given end.

The jet touched down at 2:54 as scheduled, likely as a

result of no one onboard necessarily having to arrive on time. The air flooding into the cabin was abusively hot, laden with moisture and only then did most passengers decide thick wool sweaters and leather jackets might be inappropriate for a climate averaging 30° C. Those who weren't stripping for comfort were on their cell phones calling home, telling mommy they had made it, or the wife, saying he'd be home as soon as possible, while others were haphazardly retrieving camera bags, plastic bags and Duty Free liquor from the stuffed overhead bins.

The sun glared to the point of blindness after the four plus hours in the cramped quarters of the front cabin. He had purchased First Class thinking of the reserved washroom, larger seats and better service with better meals and free drinks. The meal was adequate, the drinks were free and the washroom had constantly been invaded by the less fortunate in coach. He wondered why those herded into coach always seemed compelled to acknowledge the pilot's success by clapping and cheering when the man might well have screwed up or fallen asleep and they would never have been the wiser.

The first of the clappers to disembark seemed not to know where they should go, nor have any understanding of what the ground personnel were saying to them. He exited last and didn't suffer that inconvenience. He quickly by-passed the masses and headed towards the one terminal entrance that wouldn't cause an outbreak of brown flailing arms and scurrying feet.

He'd been on the island previously, though for Jean-François LeTuvier the stopover would be his first and last. He knew to come in quickly from an angle, making it difficult for the reception committee of two young girls dressed in folkloric dress to grab him by the arms and frame him for the requisite welcome photo. His Spanish was flawless and he cut in behind them, slightly pushing them over, with a polite apology young and impressionable Latinas would appreciate. They giggled and smiled sweetly at the innocent repartee as the camera clicked a blurred shot of Wellington's back.

As always the customs agents were politely indifferent to what was just another European visitor who responded with the expected muted smiles of unilingual and xenophobic travellers who were mostly German and French. Silent smiles were exchanged. Papers were exchanged, stamped and returned to another pale tourist whom they soon forgot.

He would have preferred taking a taxi, but climbing onto the number 35 bus destined for the Bambu Club would at least allow him a modicum of anonymity. Not that he cared. He simply knew the men who manned the guard houses at the entrances to each complex within the walled resort took note of each person leaving or entering. He saw no reason to tempt fate.

The Bambu Club was known for its excellent service, though some people are more adept at commanding attention than others. Jean-François' passport profiled a worldly traveller and he carried himself with a sophistication he very often ignored when others didn't. He had nothing to prove. He was gracious to everyone and when he spoke he did so in a manner compelling those nearby to listen: a family trait, a benefit of being a Bartlett or a LeTuvier.

He signed in and his bags were delivered to his room while others still sucked rose-coloured welcome cocktails through straws, looking geeky, lost, doing whatever they were told and going wherever they were directed. By 5:30 he had selected the first sitting for dinner. He poured a two-fingered brandy because the label said brandy and what was in the bottle was at least the colour of scotch. Then he choked, bolted to the patio doors not a moment too soon, and the bellhop rushed back thinking something had gone wrong.

Jean-François gave him an American hundred and wrote "Johnnie Walker Rojo, o, Negro" on the scratch pad by the phone.

"¿Comprendes, amigo? Quiero dos botellas de rojo o negro antes de esta noche. ¿Puedes hacerlo para mí?"

Of course he could. Someone, a brother, a sister, an aunt or an uncle would know where the kid could pick up a couple of bottles for the Frenchman in 2619.

"Sí, señor. Lo antes posible."

"Amigo, I hope as quickly as possible. If not, this stuff will certainly kill me." He pulled out another twenty. "When the deal is done, hombre."

There was nothing more to say. Wellington would have his bar set up by the time he returned from dinner at the restaurant which would open in less than an hour, giving him time to press his clothes that had been steam pressed in his suitcase since his arrival, have a shower and dress.

The dress code was casual. He had purchased new clothes for the tropics before leaving home, though he would buy more that evening after dinner as part of those specific actions he had listed. Casual dress didn't necessarily mean the same to everyone. For Wellington relaxed dining meant dress slacks with proper shoes, a silk or cotton shirt, preferably with sleeves and a button or two opened at the neck, and socks. Socks were a must by any standard, particularly with cuffed pants.

Looking around he saw the Haves and the Have-nots: Have-not men with bare legs and arms, and some with bare armpits who either didn't have money, brains, decency, awareness, or any combination thereof. Their have-not bare-bellied women wore pants that showed too much ass and tee-shirts intended to draw the eye to inappropriate amounts of their mostly junior-sized bare breasts for the social setting they were in. Most of them were young, pierced and unaware brain-dead newlyweds who had spent several thousand dollars on wedding dresses and rented tuxes all in the name of bullshit. The ceremony finished, they reverted to their primal and natural instincts of scavengers flocking to the food source, fearful others would grab up the last remaining morsel of victuals in one of the most plentiful buffets one could envision.

The others, the Haves, were exactly the way they should be. The ladies dressed in simple, yet elegant summer dresses, none with nylons and most with heeled evening sandals. The men had chosen more or less what he himself had selected to wear. They were the ones enjoying, despite the need to dodge erratic two-way processions of frantic, foraging feeders who perfunctorily consumed sustenance while on irreverent hunts for more as part of their need to balance value with cost at the all-inclusive club while displaying bad upbringing and bad manners at their finest, en masse.

He loved being in the tropics. He loved the feel of a silk shirt, except the two in combination didn't like him and moments after stepping into the main lobby of the hotel he was drenched in his own sweat, making a mental note to replace his silk shirts with cotton during his in-town shopping spree. He wouldn't be leaving until late Sunday afternoon and, even though he didn't feel rushed, he knew the next few hours would be wasted if he didn't accomplish at least some specific actions based on what he already knew.

He had begun his quest for relative information on Henderson several weeks earlier. He knew the Hendersons spent four of their six vacation weeks on that part of the island and in which hotel. On the twenty-second he had simply called the five-star hotel to confirm Henderson had arrived at the Bambu. Beyond that he knew the Hendersons were staying at the resort until November 05. They had selected the 9:00 PM sitting for dinner, Henderson enjoyed gambling a little too much and, if Wellington left right away by taxi, he would be back by the time the couple would be heading to the casino. He also knew Henderson enjoyed participating in aquatic activities available at the club and, in particular, he enjoyed boating. At any rate he had during a sales meeting twelve years earlier and Wellington was gambling that some things never change.

He would have preferred the wider variety of stores in Santo Domingo, but the capital was halfway between him and Haiti and time didn't allow the luxury of a hundred-kilometre taxi ride on uneven and pot-holed roads in a twenty-year-old rusted-out Ford with no air, no shocks and no treads. Not to mention that being alone in Santo Domingo at night wasn't a smart idea. The city was impoverished in a still poorer country, though nowhere as poor as Haiti where the social and economic aftershocks of hurricane Jeanne continued. In any event, such a long trip would mean missing the Hendersons, depriving him of an opportunity to gather information that would bring him closer to his goal.

The taxi was much better than he had imagined, equipped with air and Higüey was fifty kilometres closer. So, all in all, the ride was bearable. He asked the driver to wait outside the men's boutique where he bought a few cotton dress shirts, slacks and a pair of shoes paid for by Roberts. Then they went to the only dive shop in the fishing village and the driver waited again.

He was a certified diver, had been one, and even though the certification remained in effect it had essentially become proof of his ability to drown himself. He hadn't thought of scuba diving for so many years he wondered how awkward he would feel or how awkward he would appear to them as he went through the list of equipment he would purchase, though he wasn't intimidated in the least. He had been trained by one of the best marine biologists and ecologists in North America and had dived in waters, currents and conditions at home that these Dominican hotshot gigolos could never imagine.

Stepping into the shop Wellington was instantly familiar with the smells of neoprene and silicone, the equipment, the colours and the cost. When asked by the disinterested clerk if he required assistance, Wellington answered no. He knew what he wanted. He knew the quality, the colour and the specifications. He was buying, not renting, which meant the requisite ID was green and produced in the United States.

The mask was low-volume, the fins were closed-foot, long-blades for high performance and speed, the snorkel was a pro model with an accelerated draining feature, the gloves were lightweight for increased dexterity, the vest was standard marine quality and the binoculars were 7X50 affording him a thousand-metre field of vision. That was all fairly mundane and ordinary, albeit top quality, as were the 5-kilo self-orienting Bruce anchor, the two metres of chrome-plated marine chain, the two cotter pins, the sports bag and two bungee cords.

What he really took pleasure in was the stainless steel mini-knife with its rubber grip and seven-centimetre blade, the titanium dive knife with its fourteen-centimetre serrated blade and the slim-line forty-centimetre high-performance pneumatic spear gun. With the exception of the vest and the spear gun, each item was coloured inconspicuous black and the transaction was completed with cash. All he needed was a ride back, and all he wanted was a scotch.

The two bottles of Johnnie Walker Black were on the bureau and the twenty was gone. The time was 9:30 and he knew Henderson well enough to know he didn't rush his meals. He had time to get over to la calle Carabeña and purchase whatever else he needed. The small tiendas lining one side of the street were strictly for the impulse buyer, strolling couples or window shoppers. The quaint shopping avenue was also the main thoroughfare used by guests to access the casino and if he missed Henderson at the club, he wouldn't miss him there.

What he needed he could get at the hotel boutique and be in his room to prepare for the rest of the night before the Hendersons finished their meal. He didn't particularly feel the need for a disguise; Henderson wouldn't recognize him right away, if at all. Ten years had passed since their last encounter; all the same, he would err on the side of caution.

Daytime on a wide exotic beach populated with deep-tanned and topless European women who strolled or lazed around in miniscule backless thongs the size of Band-Aids would render him unnoticeable in his uncharacteristic beach shirt, his new baseball cap, a zinc oxide-coated nose and sport sunglasses meant for those who wanted to look cool. He'd be one more American geek on the beach thinking the women couldn't tell he was drooling over their naked bodies from behind his cool shades. Good, because that's how Henderson would dress and act. That was the plan, though the longer his primary persona could put off being recognized by Henderson, the better. The suave Jean-François LeTuvier, however, would be visible most of the time.

*

The Bambu was well-equipped for the afterhours of their clientele. The Have-not zombies would not be dancing in the discotheque for another two hours and were slowly disappearing into their rooms to recharge themselves for the night ahead. The Haves from both settings were everywhere, lost in their own intimacy and romance. The outside bars were filled with couples holding hands, kissing or playing cards. The protected patio bar was being set for the nightly show while Wellington sat alone waiting for Henderson with full visual access of both exits off the main dining room, waiting in the new cotton shirt thoughtfully paid for by John. And there he was.

He was Wellington's junior by three years and the same height, though he carried several extra kilos and looked several years older. Much of his blond hair had gone. What little remained was swept over and his face glowed with the deep red of excess, not the healthy afterglow of a day under the sun. His chest-to-stomach ratio had reversed in proportion to the excesses of good living and for some reason he was walking like Charlie Chaplin. His wife, Pat, was a year or two either side of forty and came to his rounded shoulders. Wellington remembered her pretty much as he saw her at that moment. She walked without any air of confidence whatsoever, and he noted very little effort would be required on his part to interact with her.

His mind raced, giving free rein to his many uncontrolled thoughts until he had time to sort them all out. She was lacking in a very real way, through no fault of her own. The fault was Henderson's. For some time Wellington had made a point of keeping abreast of the abundant rumours revolving around the couple and he knew a good deal about Patricia Henderson.

He stayed well behind them. The secure compound was not designed for the procurement of women, the string of one-night-stands other Caribbean resorts offered unofficially; nor was the retreat designed for those with unrealistic hopes of matching up with the perfect mate. This resort was for couples in love or trying to be, of whatever description and orientation and singles would instantly be singled out.

They walked alongside one another, not talking. Henderson finally succeeding in lighting his cigar against the prevailing sea breeze without thinking to change sides and let his wife walk on the healthier windward side.

Wellington stayed well behind them. He felt no threat of being seen or losing them. He was protected by the darkened pathway, dimly lit by occasional globe-shaped lamps and the glow of the moon adding more romance than illumination for the two-way traffic of new lovers and old enjoying the sounds of breaking waves and the wind's gentle caress.

The one night of the week la calle Carabeña came alive was the vibrant and lively Thursday night Caribbean festival, the rest of the week the pedestrian avenue reflected the relaxed pace of the island. Rushing in any form was incongruous. They walked slowly enough and Wellington could tell not a word had been exchanged between them by the time they arrived at the end of Carabeña and the Palace. The final fifty metres to the casino were on the sedate grounds of the Palace, sombre more than dark and he was close enough to hear them, had they been speaking. Not a word was said. They climbed the stairs to the entrance and Wellington continued on to the Palace where he could select a perfect Cuban to smoke at the casino bar while he watched and formulated.

Henderson was dressed like someone who had the money to dress well, while possessing neither the interest nor the flair to carry it off. Wellington observed that no one paid any real attention to him, except the croupiers who repeatedly accepted his money in decidedly one-sided transactions. Pat was wearing an excessively ordinary pink coral jersey wrap halter. Her Capri pants were dark beige, giving her the look of someone who had grabbed the first thing in the closet and her sandals had wooden bottoms with white leather straps that went with nothing including her woven straw purse. He wondered what she was wearing underneath. He imagined a plain white brassiere with sensible white, all-occasion full briefs with a reinforced panel for the more mature woman who still had those moments and would never have to worry about undressing for a real lover, or a real man.

No one was paying attention to her either, which he thought was sad, although he understood. Her mousy blonde hair was tied in a ponytail with a rubber band. Her lipstick was red, too dark, and her eye shadow was green and too light. Her fingernails and toenails were uncoloured and he doubted they were lacquered. She wasn't unattractive, quite the opposite. She could probably be very attractive if she had someone to be attractive for, herself mostly.

Henderson was fully focused on losing his money and hadn't once cared to see how the wife was, or what she was doing. Jean-François ordered another JW Black. He drew in deep-grey smoke from the twenty-centimetre Cuban, smiling inwardly. Good people believe that eventually good things happen to good people, the ultimate urban myth, a factoid propagated by the hopeful and Pat was probably a good person. He ground the grey ember into a crystal ashtray.

"Be patient, Pat. I'll do my best for you, for both of us," he whispered. The Dominican bargirl thought he had spoken to her, turning expectantly to see him stepping from his barstool and walking away. "Pardonnez-moi, mademoiselle," he ventured, "This seat is taken, yes?"

She glanced up, at once startled and surprised the handsome foreigner had stopped and was talking to her. With the typical cool aloofness of unilingual travellers, and the uneasiness of a woman unaccustomed to attention, she nodded a no and turned away to look at anything that couldn't look back.

"Thank you, mademoiselle. The barstools are so uncomfortable, are they not?" There was no reply, and none was sought. Pat kept her head facing away and Jean-François knew exactly what she was thinking. "You are

American, no?" Now she would have to answer, or he would have to leave. One, two, three, four, he would walk away at ten, then five, six…

"No. Actually I'm Canadian, from Toronto. That's in Canada."

He smiled, gallantly. "You are here to take your vacation with your parents, perhaps, and they will not let you play at the tables because you are too young, no?"

Now she had to smile, wanting desperately to avoid his eyes. "No." She drew out the word which, if coloured, would have been blush. She adjusted her position and put her hands into her lap.

"Allow me to present myself, mademoiselle. My name is Jean-François LeTuvier and I place myself at your service."

He dipped his head slightly in a modified bow, waiting, and she could see his smile all too clearly from the side.

"Pat Henderson."

He sat, reclining with a casually elegant air.

"Pat," he mused. "Pat. This name is coming from Scotland, no? Did you know, Pat, that this is, comment dirais-je," Jean-François took a moment, "this is the name of the granddaughter of your Queen Victoria. Oui, c'est ça, Patricia, her granddaughter."

"I did not know that. Thank you." Her lap was the best alternative to his eyes. "We don't have a queen any longer, not really. Well, we do, formally, although most of us don't see the need."

"Royalty is a thing of the past, Pat, no? We Frenchmen, we have known this very well since 1793. This was not the first time the English refused to learn from us."

"I'd love to visit France, one day. It's so romantic, so European."

Jean-François chuckled. "That is because France is in Europe, Pat. In fact, without France there is no Europe."

She misinterpreted the remark, frowning and looking away. He knew at once she thought herself ridiculous for having said such a thing. He touched her hand quickly, pressing lightly. "I am joking, of course, Pat. Sometimes we confuse rudeness with humour, no? Please do not be angry with me for my careless words. I will feel so bad. D'accord, ma belle fille?"

"I don't know what that means."

"It means everything... and also it means too little. It means that I am so sorry. It means that you are so pretty. May I call you Patricia? To say Pat is too quickly over, no? Is it not so much better to take pleasure in a name that is, hmm, how to say, so pleasing?"

Now she truly was blushing. "When I said European, I meant the way you all enjoy life much more than we do. I guess this is the closest I'll ever get."

"Why do you say such a thing, Patricia? We are all free to do whatever we wish, n'est pas? When you want something so much you must search for a way until you do find what will make you happy. Then you will be free and feel free also." She shrugged, not answering. What a sad woman she was, and Jean-François was sensing a deep regret he had not anticipated. "You must not be so sad, Patricia. Be patient. You will be happy soon. This I know." He leaned very slightly forward. "Your eyes are much too green and much too beautiful to hold such sadness."

"How would you know that?" She turned half smiling. Jean-François had no idea where the words had come from or how he had spoken them. "How do you know I will soon be happy and what makes you think I'm sad?"

"You are sad. I see this in your eyes and one day soon you will discover what happiness is. This I do know, tout simplement," he sighed, easing himself partly off the sofa. "I regret that I must now leave, Patricia. I hope that I will see you again. Might I hope for tomorrow evening?"

She shook her head. "I'm married."

"Yet, I see no husband." He smiled, raising his eyebrows discreetly. "I am French, Patricia. We pay little regard to these formal matters. Perhaps we will meet, how do I say," he toyed, "par accident, no? Yes, by accident, à la plage, no?"

"I don't understand," however much she wanted to. They had been together for a mere five minutes and he had given her the most attention she had received all week from anyone. Of course, she wanted more.

"I will be at the beach tomorrow, yes? I hope you will be there also." He gently drew up her hand and kissed her lightly at the very moment her heart skipped a beat.

Jean-François returned to the bar. He ordered one last Johnnie Walker Black and walked out nonchalantly with the snifter in hand. He bought another twenty-dollar Cuban at the cigar store and waited outside in the darkness of the manicured and floral grounds, hoping that what he couldn't see couldn't see him and he wasn't referring to the Hendersons.

One long hour ticked by before Pat Henderson walked out unescorted from the casino. She unhappy, forlorn, and he wondered whether she was thinking of Jean-François LeTuvier. He was very certain she was and he gave her a one-minute lead before following, wondering as he strolled behind her how she would look squirming under his naked and sweating body, being so romantic, so European and so seduced.

She had had no choice but to return along la calle Carabeña and the main pedestrian artery between the hotels in the compound. There were uniformed guards everywhere and she had no reason to feel unsafe. She walked slowly, going nowhere and he matched her pace, wondering how easily he could walk into her life and influence her in the short time he would be on the island. They weren't so different from one another, not that she would ever know.

She turned with a start when he whispered her name above the distant murmur of endless crashing waves. "Patricia, it is I, Jean-François. Do not be afraid." He read her expression. "I was enjoying a night hat at the Taino, ma belle fille."

She smiled. "I know what that means now: everything and too little. And that I'm pretty."

"I lied about that, Patricia. I should have said beautiful, not pretty. My English is so poor at times, unfortunately the best or the worst times. Pretty is for little girls and you are clearly a woman."

She giggled. "Nightcap."

"Pardon?"

"The word is nightcap, not night hat."

She giggled again, walking away from him.

"Nightcap, nightcap. Yes, of course. I will remember these words." He hurried, stepping up beside her. "Perhaps we should have one, n'est pas, so that I do not forget these words, Patricia?"

"No, really, I can't. My husband will be here very shortly. Thank you anyway."

They turned into the final entranceway leading into the main lobby of the Bambu, slowing intuitively as the romantic ambiance of the deserted path yielded to the bright lights of the atrium.

"I am also at the Bambu, Patricia. I know now that I will certainly see you tomorrow. How happy this makes me. Adieu, chérie, on se voit demain." He kissed her hand, turning towards the outside bar-terrace. "Adieu."

"Yes!" she shouted, causing nearby heads to pivot. She cleared her throat. "I mean...yes" He swivelled from the hip in mid-stride, beaming. "Yes. I would like to." She looked like a schoolgirl and Jean-François saw something in her eyes that had changed in a blink. "One," she emphasized, "then I must go."

She hesitatingly took the hand he held out as he walked towards her. "Entendu, chérie. I do promise, if such is your wish."

Thursday, 26 October
Dual Deception

They later compromised on two, and had spent the warm evening oblivious to the untouched second round of drinks and the passage of time as they both talked and both listened. She was more interesting than he would have ever imagined and as the evening went on he was all the more convinced that after some initial confusion soon to befall her she would do very well for herself. He knew then his impact on her would be significant.

She and Henderson had no children together and his daughter, who had never accepted Pat, was away at school. She worked as Chief Administrator and Head Librarian of the Peel Regional Library. She had a Masters in English lit and was on her second of two two-week annual vacations they had begun spending exclusively on the Dominican island. Her husband took an additional two weeks by himself, which she was neither privy to, nor invited to take part in. She would spend that time alone, working. He was the National Sales Manager in the Sales Division of Circadian, a Toronto-based pharmaceutical firm specializing in generic over-the-counter drugs and his work kept him away from home on a regular basis. After nearly twenty years with the company, he had been passed over for a promotion that would have made him a junior VP, a promotion he had bragged about getting. When he didn't, he began staying out of town more regularly, drinking more and changing towards her and her own success. Not that they had ever been the perfect couple.

She was thirty-nine, a true blonde, and was too career-minded to think of having a family, not that she would with him, apart from the intimidating mental images of the medical implications that haunted her. Jean-François was forty-five and the Directeur des Comptes Internationaux Stratigiques for a French firm manufacturing diagnostic equipment specifically for sports related medicine. Though he worked for the most part in Europe, he did make occasional trips to the US. He had taken the opportunity to visit Punta Cana between scheduled meetings in New Orleans and Savannah.

The second round of meetings would be as mentally demanding as the first and he hoped that enjoying a few days of rest and relaxation under the sun would have a positive effect on the outcome, particularly now that he had met the most beautiful woman on the island. No. He was not with his wife. They had divorced two years earlier and he had no children. He often visited Montreal, which he understood was not far from Toronto, though he had never been there. He had been educated in France, he spoke fluent Spanish and he adored women with emerald green eyes, chérie.

She had not shied away as he more frequently floated his hand over hers and eventually she stopped feeling guilty, giving their time together all her attention. By three AM he had draped his jacket across her shoulders, even though the temperature hadn't dropped. Their conversation had not slowed once, however the casino would close at four and explaining to her husband she had spent all that time alone would be difficult.

"I can't tell you how much I have enjoyed my evening, Jean-François. It will be the best part of my vacation, but I must go. I won't be able to explain this."

"I understand, chérie." He released her hand and stood, moving to the back of her chair. "I will escort you to your villa."

"No. Please. I'll be alright."

"But I must insist. Darkness does conceal many dangers and a woman alone is very dangerous, no?"

"No," she giggled, "a woman alone is fine. Thank you."

"You are welcome, chérie. And now we go."

She demurred, a little, giving into his smile but not taking his extended arm. They walked silently through the labyrinth of darkened walkways, each wondering what the other was thinking. He wanted very much to take her hand, understanding her reluctance more than he cared about being seen by Henderson. 2010-2018 was her villa address and he had learned another piece of significant information.

"I'm home."

This was the uncomfortable moment of the evening. She was married. She had enjoyed one evening with a stranger more than she ever had with her husband and she wanted the stranger to wrap his arms around her, to bring her in tightly and kiss her deeply before she could say no.

"I will wait until I see a light, a sign to me that you are safe."

"That's not necessary, Jean-François."

"Must you always argue chérie?" He grinned, remaining steadfast. "How will I know you tomorrow?"

"No, no. You mustn't. That's not possible. The evening was wonderful, but I can't see you tomorrow."

"I must, if only from a distance. Please do not make me sadder than I already am to leave you."

She rolled her eyes, smiling. "Let me go in. The patio, up there, that's mine." She pointed up, and before he could think to kiss her she tiptoed and kissed him on the cheek. "You can wait if you want. I think I would like that."

"I will wait." He cupped his hands around her bare shoulders, stepping in towards her, tilting her chin upwards as he brought his lips to hers. Pressing ever so lightly against the soft warmth he could feel the searing heat radiating from her face. When he pulled away he held her steady a moment longer, letting her regain her composure.

"Je t'attends, chérie. Dors bien."

Sunrise was two hours away and the few minutes seemed like an eternity until light burst through the patio doors and she stepped onto the balcony, standing by the railing as he would see her in a very few hours. He bowed deeply, smiled and walked away.

*

He had learned a great deal from Pat about what would happen over the next three critical days. Henderson normally arrived back from the casino around four-thirty and would sleep until nine, when they would go for breakfast. He would spend one prepaid hour on a beachfront massage table from 10:00 to 11:00 before going to the pool bar for a few cold ones and meeting up with her for lunch at twelve. Then he would take out a Jet Ski or a five-metre cruiser on alternate days for two hours at a time. Thursday was the boat, Friday was the Jet Ski and Saturday would be the boat again, after which he would order a few drinks from the pool bar and remain there until the sun lined up with the horizon. He would end each day at the villa apartment for a few hours' sleep before dinner, the casino and starting the process over again. She had never been invited along and she had forgotten when that last bothered her.

Pat would begin her day walking along the beach before breakfast and spend the rest of her time alone either at the pool, on the beach or taking a break from the sun in the villa. He had always insisted that he join her for lunch, not for her company, rather because he preferred being waited on and lunch was always buffet-style. She never went into town and seldom strolled along la calle Carabeña, often beginning her evening in the casino and ending her day as it had begun, alone.

Wellington's day would begin well before Henderson's and he sensed Pat would be at the beach earlier than usual. Some twenty-eight hours had elapsed since his meeting with Roberts and he had only slept those few hours on the plane. He still had much to do and didn't want to put off what could be done during his so-called off hours at the risk of not doing them at all. He assigned himself one last task before waking at six-thirty to meet her at the pool entrance to the beach.

After their walk together he would grab a fast breakfast while she went to change for her breakfast with Henderson and he reserved a masseuse for 10:00 – 10:30. At six-thirty he was still awake, just having finished his work. He had read through all the files in Roberts' computer, using all but three of the CDs to complete the download. The wallpaper image of Roberts lying in bed would shock the first person to open the computer, and he placed the NOPD icon in the centre of the screen. While en route to Savannah, Monday, he would mail the computer and cell phone to the New Orleans Police with a one-day service.
*

To the NOPD

Good day to the Criminal Investigation Unit.

Early yesterday morning, Wednesday, October 25, shortly after 1:00 AM, I was killed as I lay naked in my room at the Maison Dupuy. As you are already aware, my death came unexpectedly and in a very unpleasant way, though the event was relatively painless and very quickly accomplished once the process began, if one can forgive the preceding interview with my killer and the rather humiliating condition of my person both before and after my passing. I apologize for having soiled myself and for any physical discomfort I might have caused your personnel.

During that interview I came to realize and understand it was not so much that my death was necessary, as it was my life that had been unnecessary. I have done little in my life that will make me proud in death, and I am grateful for his truthfulness and his insight regarding that matter. The silver pin was merely his way to awaken my senses, to prick at my sensibilities before sending me on my final journey into eternity and a fuller understanding of self.

I presume you will persist in your efforts to locate my killer, and you should. Though, I warn you. Do not be deceived by the obvious. Do not take the easy road for I am certain you possess the skills to uncover the truth, if, indeed, you possess a capacity for patience. By way of example, you may have noticed the scarring on the inside of my left nostril where he first positioned the pin. I must say I am relieved he finally did put it through my chest and not my brain, for I likely would have survived to finish my half-filled bottle of Jack Daniels which we did not share and that he placed on the floor at the centre of the bed.

By now he is also fully aware of the contents of my briefcase, though I no longer have any interest in that particular aspect of our meeting, except for the cell phone he employed for the express purpose of recording my humiliation.

Dated in death, Thursday, October 26
New Orleans, LA
John Roberts (deceased), most sincerely
*

He cleaned them both completely and from then on would handle them with gloves. He showered, changed into white linen beach pants with a draw string and threw a tee shirt over his shoulders. The time was six-thirty, and he had learned one other interesting piece of information from Pat: Her husband had brought his computer with him.

*

He did not take his eyes from her for the full two minutes she took to walk to where he leaned against a palm tree whose trunk sloped lazily along the sand before curving upwards to block out the early morning sun. She was smiling like a schoolgirl on a first date and he noticed how different her stride was, and her hair. There was something within her, about her; something basic enveloping her: an aura he hadn't seen the evening before. Her hair fell loosely onto her shoulders and was full and lustrous.

Her sandals were low-heeled fashion slides with a single white patent strap that gave a new dimension to her slim legs. The loosely fitting white satin sleepshirt opened and closed playfully against her belly and upper thighs as she came closer. He smiled widely, showing his appreciation for the way she had dressed for him and he could not help but pay respectful attention to the tiny yellow V she had intended would tease him.

"I was hoping you would be here," she said in a whisper.

"I was hoping so much that you would not change your mind."

"I didn't sleep very much."

"There was not much time for sleep, chérie; and, really, what have we done that would tire us?" He brought her hand to his lips. "Shall we walk?"

He held out a hand so she would give him her sandals. Then she laced her fingers into his, jerking him towards the water as she began running.

"This is so, so bad, and I don't feel bad at all," she shouted excitedly, still ahead of him.

"Being with you is not bad, Patricia. Not to share a few moments together would be much worse, chérie."

"I dreamt without sleeping, Jean-François. I lay dreaming of this moment, wondering how I would feel."

The cool water foamed across their feet, erasing their shallow prints as they turned into lovers strolling hand-in-hand with their pale elongated shadows following behind them.

"I must kiss you, Patricia, this very moment. I must."

"Chérie."

"Pardon?"

"Call me chérie."

In a fluid motion he released her hand and tossed her shoes away from the water as he stepped in front of her, blocking her way, bringing his hands up to undo the single button she had decided would both hold her sleep shirt together, and not. Instinctively her hands went to her breasts, cupping the petite mounds into the warm satin of her shirt as she gazed up at him, making him pause long enough to gently pull her in closer by the shoulders and kiss her the way she had dreamt he would.

"I must see you, chérie. Why do you tease me this way?"

She released her breasts, slowly, bringing her hands to the protective button and letting her shirt fall open. Her skin was perfect, the slightest roundness at her abdomen accentuating her femininity, her breasts barely covered by tiny triangles he could not ignore. He slid his hands around her bare hips, drawing her closer, kissing her eagerly as she let him explore the small of her back and buttocks with one hand as he kept her close with the other.

"We will spend the day together, and the night."

"No! That's impossible. No. How could you even think such a thing?"

"Last night you told me that this would not be possible." He eased the shirt from her shoulders, guiding the satin smoothness along her arms and the contours of her back before letting it flutter to the sand. "You are beautiful, chérie. I must see all of you. I must know all of you." He gazed at her breasts, mesmerized, then into her face before frowning at seeing her nod a firm no. He smiled. "I am not a very excellent negotiator, chérie. So my final offer is that we spend the evening together, no?"

She hesitated. "Perhaps, after dinner…and only for a little while."

"This is a yes, no?" he said, feeling content. He smiled even more and hugged her tightly. "Good, very good. I will come for you after dinner."

"What can I call you?" His eyebrows squeezed together, uncertain. "You know, like your chérie. What can I call you, like chérie?"

"Certainly not chéri, chérie. This, of course, would not do very well at all." He sincerely considered the question he had never been asked before, and neither had Wellington. The best he ever got was a generic "dear", and this new situation was comical to him. "Not for a man. Really, no one has ever before called me by a special name."

"No one has, not ever?"

"No one, not ever." She retreated a single step, studying him. "I don't believe you. Look at you, better yet, look at me: Miss plain Jane."

"I do not know what you mean by this plain Jane."

She lowered her chin, "never mind," and shook her head. "If someone like me from Hicksville can be a chérie to someone like you, you can be something to me." She punched him. "Understand? So what are you? You're too slim, so hunk is out of the question, and too French, so honey won't work."

"What are these words you are saying, chérie? And the world thinks we Frenchmen speak so quickly," he laughed. "What are these hunks and these plain Janes who live in this Hickeyville? Where is this strange place where you live?"

She took his hand and began walking. "Sorry, too much, too soon. My fault. I suppose I'm a little too excited and a little nervous. I'll be quiet. I'm sorry."

"Do not ever be." He squeezed her hand and swung her into his arms. "Your voice is too lovely not to hear."

"You're a babe…a real babe."

He was taken aback by the strength in her arms as she wrapped them around his waist.

"You like this appellation for a man, this babe?"

"Yes. I like this appellation for a man, this babe, as long as he's mine."

"I am yours, chérie," he kissed the top of her head, inhaling its freshness. "Is it not so wonderful to be so uncertain, a little afraid," he kissed her again, "of what our lives should be like always?"

"So your life is always like this?" part of her really wanting to know. "I don't think you're one who's afraid."

"We men, even Frenchmen, are more afraid than you might think, chérie, in the presence of beautiful women. As good as we believe ourselves to be, we are never good enough."

She hesitated, her weak smile contradicting what he saw in her eyes. "Some men are better than others, babe." She took his hand, chortling, realizing she had never spoken truer words.

No one would doubt they were lovers, and their two hours alone seemed more like minutes to them. When the time came to part, her eyes moistened and he kissed away their sadness.

*

He had learned more and he felt all the more anxious to meet privately with Henderson. Pat was very certain he'd be throwing her out in the very near future, though she would actually welcome a divorce that would end the mental and physical abuse. At a point she had stopped talking, wanting

134

to walk quietly and be alone with Jean-François. They had lain in the warming sand for what seemed the longest time, holding one another, not talking, and listening to the ocean. Their kisses were sensual whispers, the closeness and intimate warmth strange to him, though he absorbed the sensations willingly and then, too suddenly, the time came to part and he missed her.

Throughout his meal Wellington had forced himself not to gulp his food. By the time he watched the two of them walk into the restaurant like virtual strangers she had reverted to the woman he'd seen the night before, not the excited and sensual girl they had discovered together moments earlier. He finished his meal too quickly and his ten AM massage was purely a function of basic necessity, although the instincts that are native to all men demanded he be there. His sunglasses were narrow dark slits that produced a somewhat sinister appearance that conflicted with his clownish shorts and his shirt that was a tie-dye nightmare from the seventies. His cap was pulled down over his ears and his nose was coated with white zinc oxide against harmful UV rays.

He was lounging on a beach chair three or four metres behind them, listening and processing each word in his mind, Henderson's voice reigniting vivid memories of every meeting they had ever had together. The man hadn't changed beyond the physical, and neither he nor Pat had a clue Wellington was there. Henderson was leaving everything with her and she would meet him at the outside snack bar for lunch in two hours. Could she manage that, he asked? She nodded. She wasn't wearing the satin sleepshirt. Instead she wore a plain and shapeless cotton pullover cinched at the waist. He could tell she was no longer wearing the little yellow Rio with delicate side ties and virtually no back that had allowed him to feel her so freely and so intimately.

Henderson left her without saying another word, making his way to the massage tables as though he had been by himself, not thinking he was leaving Pat alone once again. She made no attempt to look around and no attempt to remove her cover-up. She simply sat staring out to sea. When she did finally scan the beach on either side and behind her, and found she was alone, she stood and walked away.

*

His table was one over from Henderson's with the one between them unoccupied. Henderson lay on his back, much to the young masajista's amazement and overtly comical reaction to his huge gut sloping downward over heavy knee-length swim trunks pushed up by the girl to reveal legs that were pasty white to his +knees and seemingly too weak to offer any real support. Wellington had experienced the process several times during previous vacations. He knew the girls enjoyed pushing and pulling men's swimsuits for maximum exposure or untying women's bikini bottoms as a means of attracting more men to their tables.

He had never before seen Henderson without his shirt and could easily have waited longer for the event. His front was matted with hair and the girl was chattering away in Spanish with her co-workers about how she wouldn't be able to get her oils to his skin without getting her fingernails stuck. Henderson looked over at Wellington who joined in on the conversation while removing his shirt, cap, and glasses, causing them to stop talking when they realized his fluency in their language. Their silence turned to giggles when he suggested that the bigger the man, the better the lover.

"Es verdad, señoritas, créanme. You must not laugh at this seemingly huge and lethargic man for he is most certainly a virile and vigorous lover."

They burst into uproarious chatter as his girl smacked the vinyl tabletop indicating for him to lie on his back, when she summarily pushed his swimsuit to the most extreme limit of modesty. They knew most men enjoyed the innocent brashness, and they didn't care much about those who didn't. Henderson had no such luck. Wellington's session lasted thirty minutes, Henderson's was one hour so that before the latter rolled onto his stomach Wellington had been in that position for fifteen minutes of rubbing, slapping, pulling and stretching.

His ass was red, his body slick with oil and his swimsuit served no real purpose other than making the slippery contact with the girl's fingers and palms all the more sensual as he fought off thoughts of Pat he knew would create an embarrassing physical reaction and more giggling.

"Yes, tomorrow at the same time, definitely. Sí, señorita, por cierto, contigo," he promised her, thanking all of them. "Hasta luego, señoritas, y muchas gracias."

Henderson looked over at the clown with the white nose in the crazy shirt and baseball cap. Jerk. And what's with the glasses, asshole?

Wellington noticed him staring. "Hey, man, how ya doin'?"

The eye contact was direct, as Wellington intended. Henderson said nothing in return and buried his face into the vinyl-lined space intended for spinal alignment and comfort. Wellington shrugged with a smirk, more for the girls to see, and walked away. They waved good-bye, called him cariño and he heard them giggle some more, either at his nose or Henderson.

*

The hotel's mostly European clientele were still in bed, fondly remembering or desperately trying to forget the night before. The beach, for the most part, was American territory.

She had intentionally moved beyond view of the

massage tables, waiting and hoping. She had changed her swimsuit as well and was wearing the yellow string Rio. She lay on her front with her top straps undone, most of her nicely rounded buttocks glistening with lotion under the sun. He took a deep breath and paused for a moment. She hadn't seen him. He could still walk away and be free of an unneeded complication, but if he went forward there would be no going back. He knew that, and he continued. She was tempting beyond words lying so innocently that he nearly forgot to remove his clothing, change his swimsuit and wipe off his white nose in one of the nearby beach cabanas.

He came to her from the front, not seeing her smile from under her sun hat as she brought up her hand, passing him the lotion, her torso remaining still so her breasts wouldn't show. She had been scanning for him, watching, waiting, and he went inwardly cold for the sake of his own preservation. He knelt beside her, silently, applying gentle pressure to the inside of her legs so she would ease them apart. She did, arching her back to accentuate the firm contours of her nearly naked body. He took a deep breath, pulling at the side ties of her bikini, wondering, letting it fall away from the top curve of her buttocks with no resistance.

"I am glad to see that you did change chérie." He could scarcely swallow, seeing his hand purposefully pushing away the skimpy material as he worked in the lotion, mesmerized by the feel and look of her skin undulating under his touch."

"Are all Frenchmen so forward, babe?"

"Yes, chérie, which is the reason we are always seen with the most beautiful women while others must be satisfied with whatever is left."

"That's horrible, and I do have legs and shoulders, you know." His other hand worked at pushing away the loosened straps of her top and laying a thin cable of lotion from the nape of her neck to where his other hand was happily at work. "Your hands feel so good, babe." She moaned under the pressure of the impromptu massage and penetrating warmth of the sun. "God, I would love being French, being so sexy like this all the time."

"But you are sexy, chérie, very much. What are you talking about? Why would you think that you are not? We will be sexy together, when we are together, and you will be sexy when we are not. You must promise me."

She squirmed abruptly, sending the appropriate response. His watch read 10:55. He had conceived what he believed was an excellent plan to accomplish his meeting with Henderson, one that did not include being caught in the act of massaging cream into his half-naked wife. He tied her strings, albeit as loosely as he could.

"Roll over, chérie."

"I don't want to. I like this."

Women, he thought. "I want to feel your body against me, chérie. I want to touch you and squeeze you, but not here, and not now. Come, we shall go to the pool."

"Jean-François, we can't. He'll be there, drinking."

"Not here, my love, at the Taino. Even with one hundred people, one thousand people, we will be alone together."

She turned and sat up so hastily that her breasts came away from her top. All too late she brought her hands up to cover them.

"I will hear no arguments from you, chérie. This time," he insisted, "it is you who will carry the shoes. I will carry this," and he took up the tiny pile of strings and triangles."

"Jean-François don't be so mean. Give me that, right now!"

"But, darling, have you not told me that you want to be French and that we are lovers. Is this not so? What better place, what better time, my darling?" He stood, smiling. "Perhaps at the pool, no?"

She was as nervous as she had ever been. Other than a few experiences with clumsy boyfriends, impersonal doctors and Henderson, no one had ever seen her bare breasts. She dropped her hands quickly, before she could change her mind and stood facing him directly, raising her hands quickly in response to his smirk.

"They're not perfect. I know." She put her head into his chest.

"Not perfect? Chérie, how gorgeous they are, as you are. I love them. They are perfect. They are in need of some colour, of course, and we shall attend to this small matter. I cannot wait to feel their warmth and their softness against my chest, my mouth."

"Then why are you laughing? You're so cruel."

"I am a man, chérie. That is what we do, when we do not know how to act in front of our women. Forgive me, and come with me."

He held out his hand and smiled.

She followed his downward glance, instantly forgetting her breasts. He had tied her Rio bottom so loosely that the tiny V front had worked its way below the V of her natural and lustrous blonde curls. He stood and watched, enjoying what he was seeing and smiling widely as she tried too hard to right the wrong. Then he stooped, sweeping up her towel and beach bag before walking away, leaving the shoes for her. She was beautiful, and before the week was done she would be gorgeous, and not just her breasts, her whole person, and she would be the first one to see the real Patricia. The partiers from the night before were migrating with lethargic slowness to the beach and the pool areas, most of them backless, many of them topless and Pat quickly forgot her nudity until they arrived at the pool entrance to the Taino.

"Monsieur," which sounded more like moan-sewer, "would you please return my modesty?"

"Chérie, please, do not make me sad. You are so natural and so beautiful."

She held out her hand, moving her cupped fingers as a directive and he stood back as she expertly went through the gyrations and contortions that ended in a final bowknot. They were alone, essentially. The other guests at the pool were living their own romantic agendas in secret worlds far away from anyone else, their reverie briefly broken. The scream was loud, the landing awkward and the ensuing smiles were friendly and knowing. Being in love was wonderful, if only the whole world could be so in love.

Whatever was wrong with the rest of the world wasn't their problem. They were in love and he wanted her to believe that for as long as he was able to love her. The wall of hectic water she splashed his way did nothing to deter him. He gripped her as he would a mere reflection of herself, lifting her straight out of the water, holding her high before letting her slide against him, feeling all of her, bringing her in close against his skin the pool water had quickly cooled. Their kiss was passionate, suffocating, Jean-François once again gaining control of her strings as he carried her around the chest-deep pool. She clung to him, tolerating the subtle movements she could neither prevent nor deny.

Her bare breasts pressed hard against him and he wondered what she was thinking about the hardness he could feel pressing against the softness of her thighs. He had not anticipated this. Christ, not in a million years would he have thought this possible. She was weightless. Her skin was naked and warm under his touch in the cool water, smooth with the oiliness of the lotion. He wanted badly to seduce her, to be inside her and feel that special feminine warmth once again. He wanted her bare breasts against his lips, to kiss them and feel her bare legs around him.

The aura encasing them was sensual and sexual, and now there were people everywhere. He was oblivious to them, alone with her, aroused by the feel of her skin and her lips as she moved to put hers on his, not to kiss him. She wanted him closer, to be one with him. She loosened her hold on him slightly, letting her body drop a few centimetres before locking her legs around his hips where there was no mistaking whether she had noticed his firm reaction to their closeness. He pulled easily at her side ties, pushing her away and then back to him. They were together. The first time she had been so completely protected and so completely naked in public.

Her nipples were dark pink against their surrounding whiteness and had become smaller, pointed and shrivelled with the freshness of the water. Seeing soft contours shimmering with beaded oil and feeling their petite hardness against his chest was too unbearable for him and she knew it. He had to understand what was happening to him, to her, with them, and why so quickly. What was happening hadn't been factored into his plan. She hadn't been factored in and the whole Pat thing was major faux-pas, a worrisome brain-fuck. She was on vacation, he wasn't. She was enjoying a flirtation and he was very confused.

"Chérie, darling, you must go now. Soon it will be noon."

"No."

"Yes, you must, if only that we might be together later, for the rest of the day and evening."

"No." She pulled herself against him and he felt the hardness of her pelvis as much as his own. "Not now."

"Chérie," He kissed her hard, tasting the sweetness of her tongue behind the sharp ridge of her teeth, lingering there for a long moment, "you must. May I tell you something?"

"What?" She wasn't looking at him.

"I want you. I want you badly and I cannot explain to myself why. I want so much to have you today, tonight, chérie, the very way that I want you again, right now, right here. You must think of this when we are apart for so short a time, which for me will be an éternité." He squeezed her hard before putting her down, facing her towards the ladder and handing her the twin triangles. "I will find you, chérie. Do not worry. I will find you. Do not think that I will not."

She walked against the water to the ladder, dipping to her shoulders to replace her bottoms and fix her top before climbing out; her face glowing with a pink flush at what she had done. She glistened like white gold under the sun and he stared unashamedly at her two very bare cheeks as they played against each other. Jean-François made a mental note that her body would be evenly tanned by week's end without the markings of the tiny Rio he watched her free from between her beautiful full cheeks before bending and stretching to put on her satin cover. She walked away, most likely satisfied she had tormented him.

He smiled widely, thinking goodbye Rio, hello thong, hello to the new Patricia. Women, he thought. What was he doing? Why hadn't he met Patricia twenty years earlier instead of the bitch? Why hadn't he seduced his boss' wife during one of the company parties? He dived into the water, not wanting to think.

*

Jean-François needed sleep. The ninety minutes Henderson would take to eat and get to the beach concession overseeing boat rentals and other aquatic activities would be better than no sleep at all. She had strutted away as though grief stricken as he stayed immobile in the pool feeling infected with guilt. As much as he thought himself impervious to what was happening, he wasn't. Like it or not, they had made love, heated or tempered, and that was a human connection for as long as he remained on the island.

At that instant, making the rest of her day special for her became as important as continuing the preparations for his meeting with Henderson. To-date that encounter had no defined timeframe, though Saturday seemed appropriate: double duty. He had eaten nothing, though he had taken the time to enjoy two hits of JW Black on his balcony before falling into a light twenty-minute catnap. The time was 1:25 and Henderson was proving himself a creature of habit and that was good. Pat was nowhere in sight and he suddenly felt worse than he had when he had made her go. She would never know how unwillingly.

He had changed into the geek outfit he had worn to the massage station, including full-size cargo trunks that felt horrible against the skin. He could have put twenty of his usual micro-fibre Frenessis into each of the six zippered pockets, settling for the one he wore underneath in the event he would have to swim any great distance.

The five-metre Pro Line sped away from the floating orange mooring buoy too quickly, with the trim tabs fully in the down position. The white foam caused by the wake was impressive to those walking along the beach who were probably unaware the agitated water was a true sign the person at the helm had more money than brains. The boat travelled the better part of a kilometre off shore before its rocking motion stabilized and the wake became less aggressive.

With the paperwork completed, Jean-François was off. He wasn't new to the water. He had completed several boating courses over the years and had once owned a nine-metre Sea Ray. The Jet Ski was set to go and he did. He learned Henderson always booked his time one day ahead for the boat and that he always went out from 1:30 to 3:30, when everyone else was content to sit, sleep or float.

The seas were calm and his new Navigator Pros caught him up to Henderson in a matter of seconds. From a thousand metres away, and with his back to the sun, Henderson had no idea he was being observed. For Wellington, he might have been sitting in the boat with Henderson who had kept his hat and shorts on, stripped off his shirt and life vest and was propped against the centre console drinking beer and urinating over the wrong side. Wellington stowed the binoculars and started doing figure eights as he made his way closer to the boat without being more obvious than the usual vacationer who didn't care much about what he was doing. He waved once, did another eight, waved again before stopping and then he took off full throttle towards the shore with four minutes left in the hour.

He walked well away from the concession before changing out of his disguise, not that he appeared any different from most North American tourists; though in his Frenessi he fit in more with the Europeans. The heated sand gave way under his feet, making walking difficult. Most men lounging around were reading or watching what he was watching, while the women being watched lounged this way or that to their best advantage while pretending they weren't.

The beach vender was British and her wares were the smallest and most colourful bikinis on the island. Her sales pitch was entertaining for the men and enticing for the women who gathered around her to try one after the other, taking on and off their bras, pushing or pulling at bottoms judged by each other as either too small or not small enough. He walked slowly, enjoying the show, and then he heard:

"Shopping around for a new model, monsieur?"

He twisted from his hip, following her voice downward and smiling widely. "You are so beautiful." He fell onto his knees beside her, pressing his hands into the small of her back, not allowing her to turn. "When you left me this morning you could not hear, chérie, when my heart cried out for you. Can you forgive me?"

"Have you eaten?"

"How could I eat, seeing you with another? No. I slept a little, though not very well."

"You made me leave so you could sleep?"

"No. I did not." His hands glided from her ankles to her buttocks where they rested, kneading the soft supple flesh before moving up to her shoulders where they massaged her briefly before moving back down. "Not to sleep, chérie, to energize myself. I want you tonight as I pray that you want me."

"You like bums."

"Pardon, chérie, bums?" He kept rubbing. "Je ne te comprends pas. Of course I do like homeless people."

"No, silly. I meant bums," she stretched out, raising and wiggling hers for emphasis, "these… bums."

"Ah, you mean asses," he placed a hand on each side, following her rhythm. "But, yes, I adore asses, women's asses. I am French, chérie. We live for women's beautiful asses."

"Bums, please…bum is nice, ass is rude."

"They are both very nice, no?" He slapped her bum and he kissed her ass before he took a little bite out of each. She jumped up, seeing his smile and fell into his open arms.

They walked the entire stretch of beach, eventually slowing to a stop. She let him undo her top and hold it for her, feeling shy at first when some men gawked, gradually feeling good about herself when she knew others enjoyed what they were seeing; especially her Frenchman and very soon she forgot completely her breasts were bare.

He told her how beautiful she was in her Rio bottoms, if she had to wear something. She pulled lightly at both side strings.

"I've had this for two years and this morning is the first time I've worn it, for you…my sleep shirt, too. The first time was for you, babe." She reached for his hand, pressing

146

it hard against her cheek and against her lips. "Just once I wore something much bigger than this, right here in Punta Cana," she smiled, "you know, trying to be European with my straps loose across the back and showing a bit of bum. When he finally returned from his macho boat ride he told me to go to the room and stop acting like a slut. Later, when he came to the room he slapped me and ranted on for the rest of the evening. I never did it again. I don't know why I even brought this thing."

"For me, my darling, and for everyone." He brought her into his arms, peering deep into her eyes with a gleam she could not yet define or understand. "Come, our day is young. We will play, no?"

She was also part of a test. He wanted to know whether young Dominicans at the concession would recognize him as the geek in the Midwest backyard barbeque outfit. They didn't, but they did enjoy watching Pat slip into her vest before climbing onto the Jet Ski. The water was calm and turquoise and Wellington ran at about 600 RPM, the perfect speed to make minimal headway. There was no direction and no rush. She told him she wanted to feel him close and he stopped, facing her with a litheness and agility that didn't surprise her. Her open vest perfectly framed her breasts. He let her unbuckle his and lean into him; their jackets taking on a comical look of yellow and red wings that would not let them fly or do anything else she thought possible.

Her watch had become the focal point of her day and she hated each hour more than the one before. She wanted one more hour and threatened to jump off when he shook his head. Fine, if that's what she wanted, though she had to understand that no meant no. If she wanted to jump in and stay a while longer he was in full agreement. He swept his arm gently and firmly back until she was no longer there, anticipating a happy scream, not the unhappiness in her voice and in her eyes.

"Come, chérie. Let me help you, or do you prefer to swim to the shore? I can wait for you there."

"You're a horrible man," she sputtered, sneezing salt water from her nose, spitting out the water she didn't swallow. "Completely horrible," she gulped.

"Ah, I see. You are, in fact, resigned to swimming to shore." He pushed the electric start.

"Jean-François don't you dare! You get me out of here, right now!"

He cupped a hand behind his ear, straining to hear, straining even more not to laugh.

"Will you love me if I do chérie, really love me?"

"I already do love you, stupid!"

She shouted out the words before hearing them and the sea became a peaceful, quiet place. Neither knew what to do or say. For either one to smile would be ridiculous and speaking would break the gentle calm, their barrier. She hung there for a long moment, suspended from her vest, swaying like a drenched pendulum. Someone had to make the first move.

She splashed like a child learning to swim when she began building the needed momentum. She refused his hand, lunging upward and grabbing at the saddle, twisting herself into a sitting position behind where he stood with his legs astride. The silence between them was more deafening than the roar of any ocean, though not having her arms wrapped tightly around him as he steered the PWC to the beach was worse, so he slowed the craft and reached behind, taking her hands and encircling himself. The beach boys automatically ran down, securing the craft to its mooring line as the couple jumped into the waist-high water. She swam away as soon as she tossed him her vest, Jean-François walking behind her, catching her firmly as the first large wave swept her against him.

"You're not stupid. I'm sorry."

"No. Possibly I am not, chérie. However I do feel that I am very stupid. I have a beautiful girl in my arms, one who says that she loves me, and I am doing nothing."

"I don't know you at all. Sometimes I can't even understand what you're saying, but I know I love you. I really love you."

"You are sad, Patricia, and you feel alone. This should not be when we are together, as we are now."

"No. Not now." She looked at her wrist. "I hate this watch. I hate this watch!"

He set her onto the sandy bottom, holding her by a wrist, knowing full-well she was struggling to stand on her tiptoes with each new wave.

"Patricia, my darling, we can no more hate time than we can this wind and these waters, no?" He smiled, undoing the metal band. "But, at least, we can throw away the watch, n'est pas?"

"It's time for dinner. I guess we should go."

Being with him was becoming hard to take. He was leaving her again, though she tried hard to smile.

"Your dinner, and how do you know this without a watch to tell you so?" He shook his head slowly, not taking his eyes from hers. "Not my dinner, or yours. The festival, chérie, is tonight. What I propose is that you have dinner at six-thirty this evening at table number 48. Of course, the gentleman at this table is a stupid man, I hear. He is too stupid to find his way alone to la calle Carabeña. However, he is so easy to love."

"Jean-François are you serious?" She knocked her forehead into his with help from the wave that slammed into her back. "Please say you're serious."

"Yes, though I regret that we must be apart to prepare ourselves for our evening ahead. Had we our proper clothes, I would not let you leave. Will you be alright by yourself, until we meet?"

"Yes, yes. He'll be sleeping or working. I'll say I'm too hungry and can't wait. I'll say I've made arrangements for a table alone during the first setting."

"I hope he does not see you, chérie." He lifted her. "Like this, I mean. I am becoming more jealous by the moment."

"He hasn't seen me like this for a very long time, babe, and he won't tonight. I promise."

The contours of his face and what she saw in his eyes both mesmerized and frightened her. "Patricia, remember this day when you at last declared yourself a free person. Never be afraid again. Promise me. Never. And I promise you that I will be there when you need me. Always."

The tepid water and the humid late afternoon air together had not caused her to shiver so suddenly and violently. She knew what he had said could not be true, although at that very moment his words were very true and very believable. They kissed, and she believed every word.
*

Henderson had been sleeping, allowing her to shower and change without him knowing she had even been in the room. She walked out, leaving a note explaining she had decided on an earlier dinner before browsing the street venders at the festival and that she would probably meet him later in the evening at the casino, knowing he wouldn't care. He would have more time to himself for drinking, albeit with one less person to yell at and berate.

She had chosen a dress and sandals she thought Jean-François would like the most. She tore the price tag from a pair of panties she had never worn and left the room without even taking the time to adjust them properly, not wanting to make any noise. Her hair fell to the nape of her neck, still wet from the shower and swept back, held in place with a large barrette decorated with in-laid coloured shells that matched her midnight blue linen summer dress. Pearl buttons trailed from her waist to the centre of her breasts where she had left the top two open, the fabric folding away, held teasingly in place by delicate spaghetti straps not for him but rather to show him she was also proud of her breasts and of becoming a different woman.

She had never gone out for an evening without wearing a bra, not to mention wearing sheer panties for the first time under a loose fitting skirt that fell to her knees and daringly unbuttoned to her upper thighs. Her slip-on sandals had low heels, matching the colour of her dress and satin-covered clutch purse. She wore no jewellery. Nothing she had was good enough and she hadn't dressed to please a man in ages. When she had arrived on the island she hadn't needed any new clothes, now she did badly.

He thought she was stunning as he walked behind her. He wondered how any woman could wear those plastic fangs against their heads and not scream out in extreme agony. Her dress was more cocktail style than evening casual and he loved the look which perfectly complemented his own slacks and jacket. Together they would be the perfect couple.

"Bonsoir, chérie."

She turned, smiling, not stopping, making him walk faster to catch up. She certainly wasn't the same woman from twenty-four hours earlier.

"I knew you would be behind me."

"And how did you know this? Are you a sorceress casting a speel over me?"

"Spell, not speel, and no, I'm not a sorceress. I knew… that's all." She twirled. "Do you like?"

"You are a sorceress. How could I be so enchanted by you otherwise? I am the most proud of all the men here tonight."

Her happy giggle sounded good to him in a way he could not explain and he took her hand, unexpectedly jerked as she abruptly stopped.

"Babe, would you do something for me?"

"Anything, you know that I would."

"This evening, will you pretend I'm yours?"

The words had scarcely passed her lips when he kissed her more passionately than he had all that day. "Chérie, you are mine, as I am yours." Her chin felt soft, vulnerable against his fingertips that raised her head towards him. "But why do you say only this evening, chérie. Come, they wait for us."

"Who?"

"Everyone, my darling, everyone waits for us, for you."

*

The Haves and Have-nots did not exist in their world. He and Patricia were alone in the garden of their own Eden. Who was the man with the French accent sitting in front of her speaking fluent Spanish to the maître d' who had come to welcome them? Jean-François had pulled out her seat, he stood when she stood, he had helped her with her plate at the extravagant buffet and he had an excellent sense of style. He was soft-spoken, well-travelled, well-educated, completely self-assured and completely unpretentious. Who would divorce such a man, she wondered? Why was she guiltlessly letting him be so ardently familiar with her, why was she dining with him and why did she love him? She knew she deserved what was happening, that's why. He had been perfectly right earlier in the day. The day was hers to remember and she would.

He reached across the table for her hand. She was sitting silently, barely touching her meal. He wondered what could possibly be going through her mind, and what the hell was he doing. This would not end well, not for her, at least not in the short term. Then she would get over the illicit dalliance and she would get over him. Jean-François and Henderson would soon vanish from her mind as a single memory: Henderson for his brutality and neglect towards her, Jean-François for the brevity of their time alone. He was on the island for the sole purpose of killing her husband and now he was fighting off emotions he had once believed he would never feel again. Shit! I am sorry, Patricia, I truly am. Merde!

"May I refill your wine?"

"No, babe, no more wine. I would rather go. I want to walk with you along the shore like the other lovers. I want them to see us the way I see them."

"Then, that is where we shall go." He took her chair as she stood.

"You are very handsome tonight, Jean-François."

"You say my name well, Patricia, like none other. Though I fear, chérie, that I feel very naked before all these people who surround us. In my haste I have carelessly forgotten my mouchoir. All of them, in fact." She smiled with a frown, not understanding. "Mouchoir, mouchoir, chérie." He put both his hands to his face as though blowing his nose. "My silk mouchoir, chérie, expensive silk for this pocket."

He pointed to his jacket.

"You mean a pocket hanky, silly… pocket hanky."

Then he said something he instantly regretted, completely unable to blame his carelessness on the wine. "I will take you to France, chérie, if that is what I must do to stop you laughing at me."

"I am not laughing at you, Jean-François. However I would like to know more than moan-sewer," she fought with the word, "and chérie. And, you know what? I will."

Everyone watched the elegant couple walk by arm in arm, smiling happiness for them or frowning envy. The sun and the moon had crossed paths. The sand was cool to the touch and twilight cloaked the intimacy and romance of couples strolling while others splashed and danced in the ocean's white froth. Not a single word was spoken, not a single sound was heard beyond the silence of the ocean and the intimacy of one's thoughts or the romance of one's hopes.

La calle Carabeña changed the quiet mood in a blink, no longer the quaint little calleja lined with aquarelle and pastel coloured storefronts. The avenue was alive with musicians, performers from all the hotels, vendors with tables of their wares set up outside and a single madman with what Jean-François estimated was a fifteen-metre boa or python curled around his neck and shoulders. Pat giggled again. The hideous thing was less than a third of Jean-François' estimation. So much for her brave Frenchman and she changed sides with him.

The colours of the costumes were as vibrant as the dancers who wore them and no one was sad. The atmosphere was pure agitation and excitement, transporting everyone to another time, another place, to wherever they had to be or wanted to be. The music was loud and cheerful and the din of voices even louder. Couples posed for couples, flashes flashed, humble vendors emanated poverty and affluent onlookers pretended not to see or understand. Or truly didn't.

He kissed her hand with a smirk, and was gone, returning in a hurry with two plastic goblets filled with something far less drinkable than a fine Paulliac, but in the humid tropical heat even a Paulliac would insult the palate.

"Thank you. It's the one alcohol that doesn't make me drunk."

"Then we must find something else for you, chérie."

He pulled her in closely with a tight hug.

"My day has been intoxicating enough, monsieur. Thank you."

"À votre service, madame. Je t'adore."

"Can you say that again, more slowly?"

"The French do not understand the meaning of slow, chérie. You understand or you do not, tout simplement." He hugged her even more closely as he spoke, kissing the side of her head. "Come, let us sit down, par là, and I will tell you of our agenda and also teach you more words." He began to walk, Patricia freezing as she realized they were going in the direction of the casino. "Do not be afraid, my darling. Remember my promise to you, and yours to me," and they walked through the grounds of the Palace, past the lobby and into the pool area where the only company was seductive lighting and tranquility.

"Tell me about our evening." She was trying hard to appear calm, despite her heart racing from anticipation, not fear.

"Tonight we shall finish with these tourist obligations and go to the discothèque where you must promise to not make me look too bad. Then we shall return to the Bambu with our hands and hearts together as one, like the young lovers that we are. What do you think?"

"Sure, dancing is nice," she paused. "That's it? That's our evening? And, by the way, I never dance. I haven't danced for years."

He ignored her. "Yes! Is it not perfect, chérie? We shall dance in each other's arms all evening."

She smiled, softly, though not as well as any mediocre actress. He wanted right then to take her, lift her onto his lap, squeeze her tightly and speak the words he knew he never could. "I am not finished, chérie. Later, we will return to my villa if we must." He took a sip of the heated wine, grimacing and looking at the glass without seeing it. That's when she punched him. "We shall drink champagne on the terrace as we slowly undress one another before we make love all night long, until the morning sun does arouse us all the more."

Her visible skin fluctuated from tan, to pink, to red, and then to purple in an instant, the wine in her mouth spraying from her nose across her dress before she could react.

"I'm sorry, Jean-François. I'm sorry. I didn't mean to. Did I get any on you?" He smiled, passing her his napkin and shaking his head no. "I hate dancing."

He grinned. "As much as I do hate festivals with the loud noises and ugly man-eaters?"

"God, I hope so."

*

The moon somehow knew not to shine too brightly and shadowed his apartment. The birds were still and the rustling leaves at the tops of tall palm trees were their serenade. They had said nothing returning along the path to the club. Those who passed them might have thought an emergency had presented itself and they would have been correct in assuming a mounting urgency that could not be enhanced with words. His apartment was a four-room suite and much more elegant than her single standard room. The champagne had been chilled, as he had requested, the fresh fruit and cheese plate had been arranged with flair on the white linen table cloth, the bed had been turned down and fresh orchids had been scattered across the bed and tiled floor. She was stunned. She had been intrigued by the thought of being with him in his room for the entire evening, perhaps nursing a drink from the in-room bar or a glass of wine, yet she had not imagined anything like this. What would living with such a man possibly be like, being with him all the time, loving him every day? He poured wine into her glass before his and tapped the crystal together in a silent toast. He kissed her hand and she tiptoed to kiss away the solitary tear threatening to dampen his cheek.

"You know how I feel, and I feel how you do, babe. Make love with me."

She put a hand against his chest, for him not to move and backed in past the sliding patio doors. One button at a time, with agonizing slowness from top to bottom until her straps loosened and she seductively pulled at the front of her dress, letting it fall past her shoulders onto the floor. Her panties were snow-white with a cire band fitted perfectly against her slightly tanned and soft skin. Through the darkness he saw the slightly darker wedge of curls showing through the front of the sheer mesh fabric.

He put his hands together in prayer, sending a silent message that was returned to sender. She nodded no and stepped out from the crumpled linen encircling her feet, protecting her breasts until his embrace covered them. He kissed her and she kissed him as their mouths became glued. Holding her close to him became increasingly impossible as he tore at her panties. She ripped at his shirt, tearing the fabric. She jerked at his buckle and tugged at his pants with equal success, not realizing or not caring she was completely naked and being put on the bed with her heeled feet high in the air, framing her new lover.

His clothes came off by virtue of their excited gyrations and hungry lust, by which time they were a moist heap of soiled fabrics. Ten o'clock surrendered to eleven as lust surrendered to passion. One AM followed midnight too quickly and the next hour went unnoticed. By three they smelled of sex, his bed was soaked and their mouths were swollen. He was chafed raw and she didn't recognize the unfamiliar tingling pulsating inside her. Their urgency had dismissed the primary need, the requisite precaution, though secretly the thought had crossed his mind in a flash. Perhaps Pat had been too shy to ask, and if she didn't care why should he? What did one careless moment matter when your primary mandate was your own death?

She could barely pad her way to the shower. She was gorgeous. Her skin exuded a scent that was sensual, her breath intoxicatingly sweet. She didn't like ass, she liked bum and her breasts were not tits, he surmised. She liked to fuck, just not the word. And he knew better than to challenge the moment; not even with a French accent. He stood transfixed, watching her shower with the curtain drawn back. The vision too much to bear, seeing the curves of her body arching to a silent rhythm as the luster of her blonde hair darkened and straightened under the weight of its wetness, conforming to the curvature of her neck. He cupped a hand, filling his palm with scented liquid soap and stepped in beside her to cleanse and soothe what she had not yet touched, quickly drawing back his hand when she winced at the stinging sensation. Her eyes closed tight, her teeth clenched against the searing pain. She held her breath, grimacing, exhaling a loud gasp. He had absolutely no idea what he should do to help her, stepping behind her and wrapping her in his arms as the hot stream of water splashed against her belly, trickling in gentle rivulets to soothe her.

To touch her, to feel her against him as the cascade of steaming water ran down her perfectly sculpted form into her crevices and past her contours was too much for him. He splashed himself with the soap and stepped out, not caring about rinsing himself.

"What is it, babe? What's wrong?"

He was naked and he felt vulnerable, not because of his nudity, because of his sensibility. "I'm sorry. I wanted simply to soothe you, to hold you there one more time. I am sorry, chérie, for hurting you this way."

"Don't be sorry, you silly boy. Have you ever been sorry for having a massive erection?" She shut off the water, reaching for his towel. "Though, perhaps a little less soap next time would be better, monsieur."

His true regret extended beyond simple indelicacy. Men instinctively knew the danger of other men, women did not. Despite their other qualities and so-called intuition, women were often blind to obvious threats.

"Remember my promise, chérie, and yours to me. I am afraid for you."

He turned and walked silently away. When she came out from the bathroom, wrapped in the towel and running a comb through her hair she glowed. She let the towel drop and smiled when she saw him looking in at her. He wasn't smiling. He was dressed and leaning moodily against the balcony railing, not ready to see her go.

She was seeing an unfamiliar side of him, another dimension, another anomaly for her to define beyond the man who made her feel good, safe and protected. She went to him before dressing. Neither was she ready.

Friday, 27 October
Dining Out

He had insisted. He would escort her to her room as a precaution. He opened the door, taking time to scrutinize the small moonlit space as she squeezed in between him and the frame. She was nervous, for him more than herself and, as much as she wanted him near, she was anxious to close the door and for him to leave.

She stayed with her ear against the mahogany barrier until the echo of his footsteps on the tile floor faded entirely. Then she replaced her wedding band before running the shower to completely moisten one of her towels. She changed into an ordinary ankle-length cotton nightgown, pulled on a pair of sensible underwear and stepped out onto the second story balcony. She knew he was somewhere out there. She blew a kiss into the heated night air and waited a long moment before going in and leaving the doors open as he had asked her.

Concealed on the steps of the adjoining villa he felt no recognizable emotion seeing her standing so perfectly in the moonlight. He felt no envy, nor did he sense the slightest fear. If anything, what he felt was a newfound duty towards her though he would never phrase the sentiment quite that way. Drunks on vacation could be happy and boisterous or sad and melancholic, sometimes even excessively rude or excessively polite, but drunken losers were always belligerent and Henderson would be coming from the casino in one hour or less. He would wait, and he would listen. There would be no hesitation if he felt in any way that she was threatened. He had already told her what she should do.

. He tried to relax, waiting with her room key in one hand and her pungent panties in the other, wondering what she was even doing in there. Then suddenly a dishevelled and unstable Henderson was muttering curses into the early morning air as he tripped unceremoniously on the first step and landed knees first on the second. Had the railing not been there to grab onto he would have stayed sprawled face downward. As it was he managed after several failed attempts to literally pull himself up to the second floor landing. When he disappeared into the corridor Jean-François pocketed the keys and panties and crossed to where he would be closer and better able to hear.

The first light was dim, probably coming from the bathroom where Henderson was spilling his night's liquor from one of two ends, or both. The patio doors turned black, followed suddenly by another brighter light that absorbed the moonlight and the doors closed with an eerie scraping sound and a bang. Wellington climbed the steps three at time, walking silently on the sides of his shoes to Pat's room. This time he was the one putting his ear to the door, hearing a foreboding quiet. He knew she was wide awake, feigning sleep to avoid confrontation or being hit. She knew to open the door in the event of trouble, she knew where to go and she knew not to hesitate. He waited a while longer, half hoping, and then he left. She would be with him again in two hours.

*

Raspberry permeated the air. The fragrance was strong enough to taste. Half opening his eyes his head jerked, slamming against the pastel pink stucco, startled by the two closed eyes so close to his own.

"Shhh," she whispered, putting a finger to his lips. "My poor darling, you look absolutely horrible."

"I fell asleep, however not before I was certain, chérie." He leaned forward, rubbing his head. "You are fine? Nothing bad has happened to you?"

"No, nothing at all, except that I missed you. I would have run to you right away, like you told me. I would have come to you."

She wore her satin nightshirt without her sandals, his roaming hands quickly discovering she hadn't bothered with panties or a bra.

"You have become quite brush, chérie. I do hope that you have something more for yourself in that bag. I have made you a wicked woman, no?"

"You have made me a woman, period, and I hope I have more to learn, babe. I know there is." She stood, trying to pull him up. "And it's brash, not brush."

"And this? What is this?"

He kissed her where her shirt had opened, his hands pressing into her bare buttocks.

"Okay, okay, I'm not that wicked. Stop that." She pulled at his hair, twirling around, hoping no one had seen.

"Tell me first, what is this?"

She turned away, starting down the steps. "It's what you won't get if you don't follow me."

No more encouragement was needed. He did look terrible and he would have his clothes cleaned before wearing them again. He was exhausted, they both were, and a walk on the beach seemed too challenging. Yet staying inside brought the inherent danger of falling asleep and wasting too much of the exotic day ahead. She watched him change and whistled when he pulled on the Frenessi. She was slightly darker than the day before and, when she came over to him he lifted the bottom of her shirt to see the tan line from the yellow Rio. He had expected at least a pretend slap, but she simply held out her hand to him.

"Do you still have my panties from last night, babe?"

"Yes. Why?" He went into his jacket pocket, pulling them out.

"I can't wear this old lady thing anymore, and the yellow one is still damp from yesterday." She emptied her beach bag onto the spare bed and threw the larger paisley tankini into the wastepaper basket. "I thought I'd wear my panties on the beach before breakfast, if you don't mind. There won't be too many people."

He chuckled. "It is too bad for them."

"He thought I was asleep. But I wasn't, and apparently I'm no better than a," she paused, trying to force a smile, her lips quivering too much, "you know, that word, and a whore."

He unbuttoned her shirt, holding the two sides apart.

"You are not a whore, Patricia. You are beautiful, exciting and recently alive. You are, chérie, and be proud that you have discovered yourself at last. What we see is such a small part. The rest of you, and what is ahead of you, is so much more important." He grinned. "Still, I do not mind to keep looking."

They went to the beach as though they belonged together as lovers. They lay side by side on a single chaise-longue, he in a red Frenessi, she in white mesh panties he had shaped into a micro bikini bottom and whose usefulness was highly debateable. He enjoyed the weight of her leg across his front; she forgot the dimensions of time and place, letting the sun warm her. The shirt lay in the sand by their side. They woke past nine o'clock, stretching, kissing and clambering from the beach chair. From the corner of her eye she noticed two men eyeing her approvingly as she stooped to gather the shirt and she wondered how long they had been watching her with her leg draped provocatively over her lover. She had never been so naked in such a public place. She liked the feeling and wanted more.

Jean-François had been right. She was going through a metamorphosis and the old Patricia would never return. The new Pat was more than a woman being risqué for the first time, discovering she actually took pleasure in her new freedom and the attention she deserved. The transformation was still too new, too dream-like to think of being so analytical. And why should she be?

They ate at the Taino, though neither was interested in the array of fresh foods prepared and laid out every morning in the pre-dawn hours in preparation for the first wave of the Haves and Have-nots. She remained in the most secluded corner of the outside terrace, feeling somewhat less dressed in her satin shirt than she had at the beach in her sheer panties and suntan. There would be hell to pay when she would eventually go back to change, but she had been in hell for so long already. What was another day or two, or even a week? Jean-François would be leaving in two days. As she lay against him she dreamt of being with him all the time, being with him in France and Spain or anywhere he would take her. No one could pretend the feelings she felt emanating from him. He was real. No one could pretend that much. How could that be possible?

She had also discovered that, as elegantly as he spoke, he was very often a man of few words and she would have to become more adept at reading his eyes and interpreting his frowns and his smiles. But how could she do that in the two days left to her. What did it matter? Where would he go and what would he be doing as she struggled through her last week alone? Who would he be with? Who would be in his thoughts? Not her, she knew that much and she cried. Not from sadness or self-pity, from her new self-assurance that had been too long in coming.

Her time had come, and she was thankful for what those few minutes without him had given her. The decision was final and irrevocable, arrived at without Jean-François' input or his knowledge. He had come into her life like a spontaneous bolt of lightning, with the same overwhelming effect. Still, her life was her own, not his, not anyone's and that same bolt would carry him away.

Jean-François came to their little table for two with a tray of biscuits and fruits, fresh orange juice and a carafe of coffee that would be full when they left.

"What are your plans for the day, chérie? What would you like to do?"

"I'm going into Higüey. There are some things, many things, I want to buy. I'll go by myself if you would rather stay here."

"I will accompany you, chérie, of course. Why do you say such unkind words to me? May I ask what exactly you wish to buy?"

"Everything, babe. Will you help me, when I have trouble deciding?"

"Yes, of course. Why do you even ask me? And what is it that we are buying, chérie?"

"A new me."

"I do like the old one."

"I don't, and you have no choice in the matter. So stand back or step aside." She reached out quickly for his hand, to balance the retort that had come out badly. "But not too far. I still need and want your help."
*

He could not have been more thrilled. They agreed she would gather the few clothes required for a trip into town, leave a note explaining she'd be back later in the day and that she had eaten earlier. Then she would go to Jean-François' apartment to dress for dinner. Exactly what he had planned, though saying so would have been anti-climactic. He had one errand to run and he would see her at 10:45 at the very latest, which would give him time to revert to an American geek with a nose painted white. Henderson showed precisely at ten.

Jean-François arrived a few moments late, observing requisite protocol. "Discúlpame, señorita, por haber llegar tarde. Lo siento," he lied, clasping his hands together and appearing unconvincingly pathetic.

Time was money. She slapped the table, telling him to lie on his back. Henderson jerked his head see what all the fuss was about with the usual phobic apprehension common to his sort when excluded from conversations by their own narrow and self-taught limitations.

"Hey, man, how ya doin'? Never hurts starting the day getting a little one-on-one rub, eh? You were here yesterday, weren't ya?" Henderson turned away from him without answering and the girls exchanged shrugs. "Es un gilipollas, yo creo, señoritas. ¿Qué creen ustedes?"

Henderson was a jerk the girls agreed by giggling as they often did while watching and commenting on the various shapes and sizes of various non-Latino guests walking past their workstation. He jumped onto the table and within a few minutes was wondering why he'd bothered wearing a swimsuit. She had flipped him over sooner than he had expected, or wanted, and after a few fleeting moments she smacked his mostly bare ass as a sign he could sit for a final once over, up and down and across his shoulders: a perk for those clients who tipped her and had no hair on their backs.

He didn't rush to the apartment. Nothing she might happen to see would lead to complications. He had securely locked everything of a questionable nature in the room safe or his sports bag. He had one more errand before going to her and he called his room hoping she would answer. She didn't, and his priority was a fast dip in the ocean to remove the zinc oxide and superfluous layers of massage oils before stepping into a cabana and changing from geek-American into micro-Italian.

She was sitting on his balcony sipping from an old-fashioned glass and stayed as she was as she watched him come closer. He had no idea what was in her mind and he wasn't about to ask. Something had come over her and his instincts, which most men of intelligence keep in reserve for those occasions when they might possibly be confronted with the female condition, self-activated.

He had a fast shower and as he dressed for a casual afternoon he noticed her panties and satin nightshirt were crumpled together in the wastepaper basket. He joined her on the balcony.

"You are fabulous, chérie, absolutely fabulous."

"If you lie to me now, I will always think you're lying to me, Jean-François." There was no smile. "I look like a Midwest farmwife and you know it. All I'm missing is a brat on my hip and sagging teats."

"You are not such a thing at all, chérie. Or I would not be here. You are radiant, more so than the sun itself."

"Oh, puke." She stood abruptly, kissing him without warning. "Save that for tonight."

"What is puke?"

"What's in the bag?"

Neither one answered.

*

It was one of those times when everything fell nicely into place, particularly silence, as long as he could be nearby to see Henderson returning the PWC and make some sort of contact with him. He suggested lunch, as much for himself as for Pat who probably could have done without her double shot of JW Black, but she was a lady on a mission and even the most daring male was smart to quietly acquiesce.

Her first purchase was a short, flame-coloured wrap

dress with metallic trim and a matching wide brimmed hat, which is what she wore out of the store. Her second purchase was a vivid pink mini-dress with a ruffled bottom and bra top he carried with the two shoe boxes. The second tienda increased his load by one yellow and orange floral halter dress designed to highlight the swell of her breasts which she decided would be bare, and a white linen shirt dress with fewer buttons than needed. When she tried it on they both saw in the mirror the need for one more purchase. The third tienda was for lingerie and her strict criterion were tiny and sexy. What she expected of him was to nod one way or the other, nothing more. She chose what she needed at the moment: a bright white bow-back string with a tiny embroidered front in the shape and size of a butterfly. She had nothing to discard. Then new sunglasses followed new purses, sandals and she let him take her for lunch before she began again. When she sat, she fussed with the hem of her dress making sure he caught a long glimpse of her panties.

"You are amazing, chérie, absolutely amazing."

"I'm starved." She stared blindly at the menu. "Please forgive me, babe. I feel as though I've awakened from a terrible nightmare I've been living for too long. Will you forgive me? Can you understand and forgive me?"

She looked at her bare wrist out of habit and he chuckled.

"Perhaps there is a good watch store in town, chérie. However, I do know of one on la Carabeña."

"It's not a watch I want. It's a new me, and I'm long overdue."

"I have a surprise for you, chérie. To discover what exactly you must come with me to la Carabeña. Had I known of your plans," he shrugged, "but I did not."

"But I'm not finished, not by a long shot."

"My darling, you must learn French for me. These

expressions of yours are so crazy. Misère!"

"My expressions!" she countered.

He ignored her, signalling for the waiter. "We have two hours, not more, and then we must go. Entendu?"

"Now you're telling me what to do."

"Yes. There are times when a man must tell a woman. You will understand, believe me."

She stuck out her tongue as he ordered, crossing her arms.

Despite the excellent food and the cool refreshing wine, neither one could pretend they wanted to stay any longer. They left, and by the end of those two hours Jean-François was more of a lackey than a lover. He could barely be distinguished behind all the shopping bags filling the sub-compact taxi that brought them to the juncture of the Palace and la calle Carabeña. The street was abandoned under the oppressive midday sun and the gaily-coloured shops, so muted and charming at night, were brilliant and blinding.

"So monsieur, what's this big surprise?"

"This, my darling." He opened the door to the spa, indicating she should walk through. "I shall return for the new you in three hours."

He spoke to the ladies in rapid Spanish. She already knew he could, still amazed at how easily languages came to him. He was clearly giving them instructions because they all nodded in unison and when they looked over to her they giggled. Who was he, what was he and what was he doing with her? She had treated him badly and loved him deeply without knowing why. She only knew for how long and that he understood the turmoil she was struggling with. The senior attendant at the spa took the bags for safekeeping, except his own, the one he had held for the past few hours since leaving the apartment.

"Tomorrow morning, chérie, you will wear this for me, for everyone, no?"

He gave her the bag and kissed her before walking out.

*

He couldn't help thinking the sooner he killed Henderson the sooner he could stop wearing that ridiculous outfit, and she was worried about anyone thinking she was a farmwife. Henderson had come back on the Jet Ski and was being controlled in the waves by the beach boys as he belly-flopped into the water. Wellington sat on his rental, watching, waiting, and when Henderson glanced his way he waved a greeting and called out something that was muffled by the breaking waves.

Sixty minutes later he was back. He would have liked to dog Henderson a bit, but being with Pat was better. Being seen by Henderson and recognized would suffice. Now he had to change into his street clothes and finish off one more bit of shopping before being at the spa to meet with the new Patricia. Keeping her waiting would not do, not this time.

At five minutes shy of 6:00 PM the sun was weakening and the quaint pedestrian avenue was filling with window shoppers and strollers whose feet flip-flopped along the irregular narrow sidewalk. American tourists wore thick cover-ups that outlined still wet bikinis; Europeans wore satin or silk cover-ups outlining only the wetness.

When he stepped through the double doors she wasn't there, and that was good, though apparently he triggered an alert as the place became abuzz with girlish excitement and they all disappeared behind the curtain leading to the restricted inner sanctum.

First, a single brown head with gleaming white eyes and a beaming white smile stuck out from behind the curtain, then a second, then they all burst through and the curtain stayed open for their latest creation to walk through. Jean-François couldn't believe his eyes. He couldn't have feigned more surprise than he felt at that moment. He knew instantly all those adjectives like beautiful, gorgeous, and stunning would all seem trite and not appropriate for such an astonishing transformation of an already beautiful woman. He suddenly felt strangely intimidated, and if she hadn't broken the silence they all would have stood there quite some time.

"The farm's been sold, cariño," she said, easily. "Do you like?"

He nodded dumbly. Awaking from his trance he went to the girls who were as eager for his reaction as Pat, hugging and kissing each one. Her skin glowed naturally. Her eyes were thinly lined with black mascara, her lips highlighted with liquid reddish-purple and her fingernails were painted the same tone with a French trim. Her hair was pulled into a single braid interlaced with a row of colourful coral beads adorning the nape of her neck. The turquoise chiffon sheath dress he hadn't seen was décolleté and the open back displayed the smoothness of her skin entirely. A narrow belt separated the flared skirt that was mid-thigh when she stood, allowing a discernible glimpse of aqua blue high-rise panties as she sat or unabashedly crossed her bare legs. Her untried ankle-wrap leather sandals were semi-stilettos, turquoise, and her toenails were lacquered to match the clear lustre of her fingers. The swell of her breasts drew attention to a simple diamond locket suspended from a chain so delicate as to be imagined more than seen and the tiny lobes of her ears sparkled with twin diamond studs.

The spa's manager had a boyfriend working at Harrison's who had willingly made two trips to show Pat pieces of jewellery according to what Pat suggested as her budget and described as her wardrobe. She had been pampered with a full massage and herbal shower, a facial, manicure, pedicure and new hair-style, acquiescing and undergoing the final treatment once the metallic blue slingshot bikini had been stretched to show her what she'd be in for if she didn't.

Her fingers were fidgeting nervously with the straps of her pale blue evening purse and his attention was drawn to them. He had taken care of the ladies in advance and he had no regrets as he watched Pat hugging and kissing them all and hearing their admonishments she didn't understand about her tears. Now he had a very big problem. How could he possibly walk by her side along a sandy path to the Bambu when she was so enchanting? He was dressed well enough, but by her side he'd seem like a beggar which would not do at all. The Palace was accessible from la Carabeña and off limits. He opted for the Taino even though it would mean an extra ten minutes of humiliation for him. He couldn't wait.

Most of the guests were playing pool volleyball, drinking in the pool or learning to dance by the pool. The lobby bar was abandoned, which suited his mood perfectly and he ordered two glasses of Chardonnay. The dress, mid-thigh when she was standing or walking, was much more mischievous when she sat and he made no excuses for sitting all the closer to her. He would not allow others to see what he could not and he found himself not wanting to leave. He had to change for dinner which meant leaving her, but he couldn't, and she knew. She luxuriated in his misery and her elation, and he knew that.

"Go, cariño. I'll be safe alone for at least thirty minutes. Any longer and I can't promise you won't find me in the arms of another more devoted gentleman."

"Chérie, I would die. Promise me that you'll will not."

"Promise me you'll hurry." She shooed him with the very fingers he had been reaching for. "Go," and then she called out, "Cariño, wait." He jerked to a stop. "The bags, darling, don't forget the bags."

She was truly enjoying her new self.

He had noticed her ring was missing. She hadn't once asked about dinner plans and she seemed not the least bit

anxious. In fact she was extremely relaxed. What the hell was happening? What the hell had he done? He wasn't sure, though at the moment he was too busy running, and not at all gracefully.
*

He made reservations at el restaurante Mama Juana, specifying he must have their most romantic and secluded table for a very special lady. He also specified a view of the ocean, the moon and a bottle of Grande Marque champagne. The maître d' assured him of his closest personal attention to their evening and an even closer handshake finalized those arrangements.
*

She hadn't moved, though her Chardonnay had been replaced with another. The hem of her dress teased at the very limits of a newly defined modesty with not a square centimetre of her bare legs left to imagine. She crossed them slowly, seductively, when she knew he could see. Just as well they were in a public place, he thought. Had they been alone, he would necessarily have cancelled the reservation.

"You're very handsome, once again, cariño. What a couple we make." She rubbed one leg seductively along the other. "I asked the barman to bring you a Johnnie Walker Black, not chilled."

She didn't ask him if that was alright.

"I have planned an evening, chérie, a special evening for you. I hope that I have done well." He leaned forward, reaching for a hand to kiss at the moment the scotch arrived, and both men grinned knowingly. "We may linger only a short while with our cocktails, and then we must make our way to the restaurant where we are expected by eight."

"I want you to do something for me, cariño."

"Anything at all, and I notice that your time with the ladies this afternoon was also instructional."

"I love my new word: cariño. It means…"

He smiled. "I know what it means, chérie."

"I was going to say it means everything."

He conceded his error of interjecting too quickly. "What do you wish of me, chérie?"

"I know what I asked of you last night… this is different for me. Tonight I want you to be in love with me, not just love me. Be in love with me, for the entire night. Can you do that?"

"There is no one here who does doubt how I feel, chérie, nor will they when they see us together and feel deep envy."

He rubbed her ring finger in search of an answer to an unspoken question.

"It's not missing, darling," she said. "It is gone forever. I've had much to think about these past two days. Thank you."

"Thank you?"

"Yes, thank you, for this, thank you for me." She ran her hands along her thighs to her knees. "I could never have done this on my own."

"At some point, chérie, we all do what we must. True…sometimes we are frightened by what we do, and you are no exception. You would have found your freedom one day very soon. You would have become who you are now becoming." He stood, gazing at her. "Our evening awaits us, madame. I do hope that you feel rested and that you are in love. You will need both qualities, I do assure you."

The good with the bad, he thought. Some people admire, others stare and Jean-François didn't feel the need to whisper what he deemed an adequate response to those around him in terms of silk and polyester: "The Polies stare, chérie, while the Silks admire. You need only care about the Silks."

A glistening moonbeam carpeted the sea. The breeze

was warm against her fragrant skin, the champagne was chilled and musicians sang and played the most soothing and romantic songs from their repertoire. They were in a world apart as they spoke about everything, mostly about her, and about nothing, mostly about him. How could he speak of his dreams, his future, when his future might never be? He had created a parallel world, one half of which would completely self-destruct in seven days.

She had written a note to her husband as Jean-François had suggested, though not the words he had suggested. She wrote that she was leaving and, in fact, she had left forever. He should not expect to see her again. She had made arrangements for separate accommodations during her second week. She would send a maletero for her belongings at a time she knew he would not be there, and would he be kind enough to comply for reasons of proper decorum? She would file her papers during her first week at home and would go to her sister's from the airport.

She felt not the least bit sad or remorseful. She was eager and intentionally made no comment as to what part Jean-François should play in her future. He, everything, she knew, was too new and he was going in less than forty hours to somewhere she had no idea about. He would be lost to her and she had begun steeling herself against the inevitable and fast approaching moment. Whether she would succeed or not, she had no idea. He could always find her. If he wanted her badly enough he would, but it wasn't the moment to dwell on the unknown.

The gastronomy was superb. They danced as they ate, they kissed as they danced and Jean-François struggled to conceal his sudden concern. He was becoming peeved with the other guests who seemed to want to admire them as he tried to force from his mind the images of Henderson scouring the compound for his lost wife and the two together soured his mood.

He wished she hadn't done it, albeit innocently. She didn't realize that within sixteen hours her husband would be missing and that some might consider an impromptu separation at that particular crossroad of his life somewhat curious.

"I am happy, for you, chérie. That you have made such a decision."

"So why don't you sound happy? What's happened to change your mood?"

"I am sad that I will not be with you next week. I fear for you. I am jealous of what I will not know."

"What you will not know, darling?"

"You are very beautiful, very tempting and whether you know or not you are very vulnerable. I am jealous that I will not be the one to see you in all your lovely new dresses."

She kissed her fingertips and brought them to his lips to silence him. "Hearing you say those words makes me happy, Jean-François, which is why I am spending the night with you. I've made you unhappy with my letter. I'm sorry, really I am. But I am no longer afraid and won't be ever again because of you."

"I now begin to lament my enthusiasm, chérie," he returned, modulating reality with fiction, truth with falsehood.

Her napkin dabbed at the corners of her mouth. "The dinner was great, darling. Now I need you to hold me, to make me feel safe. Let's get out of here and go dancing."

"I had planned the discothèque, chérie, but now I believe the noise will be disturbing to us," he frowned, "to me."

"I said dancing. I didn't say where."

She swung her legs out from under the table and stood, smoothing her dress under the watchful and envious eyes of the Polies and walked out, leaving him to follow very closely behind, sneering at those he passed.

*

His second floor apartment was near enough to the outside terrace for them to hear the more melancholic music emanating from strategically positioned speakers, secluded enough for them to feel alone. Good. She could feel the emotion welling inside her, seeking release. Good for anyone watching or who happened to see. So many strangers had seen her virtually naked during the past two days, especially the ladies at the spa. What hadn't they seen, and what was one or two more? She liked how she felt. She liked the new Pat and she wouldn't go back, not ever. Though much of how she felt was being with him. Everything she felt was because of him.

She pulled the PVC armchair over. "Sit, monsieur. May I offer you a digestive?"

"Digestif, chérie?"

"Shut up. Is that a yes, or no."

"It is yes... and a big one also."

She was gone a few moments before returning with his double Johnnie Walker Black, not chilled, and her iced double vodka, giving him one before sipping from the other. He was so tired she doubted if he could even talk, although the air was still and their most subtle whispers would be carried away into the night air. She leaned over, loosening two more buttons at the top of his shirt, kissing him, pausing to take another sip of the iced vodka which two days earlier she would have watered to the point of tastelessness before adding ice.

She brought her hands to the nape of her neck, twisting them one way, then the other, and guided the two wide straps that were the daring front of her dress to her waist, bringing her hands against the flatter smoothness of her stomach to the softer more malleable roundness of her breasts. Her nipples were firm when she leaned forward, teasingly, not letting him kiss them, and more erect when

177

she pulled away. Unfolding the wide satin belt she pulled it completely from its loops and held both ends as she ran it crossways against her bared skin and to and fro across her breasts that moved tauntingly for their special voyeur. Clear lacquered thumbs hid beneath the body-hugging waistline, taking hold before joining with slowly moving fingers, together pushing down the short, flared skirt, first showing one thin aqua-blue band of her panties. She waited teasingly before showing other. She turned so the slender lines of her perfect back glowed with the muted light of the moon and he could see the bands of her panties and the sheer V that became nothing at all between supple mounds as she moved to the music he had forgotten.

She pushed all the way with both hands, straightening slowly, leaning against the railing with one hand as she raised the opposite leg away from the dress and kicked it away from her ankles with the other, standing before him in butterfly wings and stilettos. She bent from the waist, reaching with tantalizing slowness for her drink, taking a long swallow. He went to do the same, missing the glass completely and she reached down again, reaching for his and brought it to him, facing away, sitting in his lap so he could feel and see the full roundness of her bare buttocks against him. He went to touch, but she slapped him away and stood once more with an admonishing finger.

Her thumbs went to work, locking into the bands of the panties he had been trying so hard to see through and she pushed them enough to tease, not enough to satisfy. She couldn't think of her pounding heart. She was thinking of his, her lover. One hip went out and the first band came down, then the other hip and the second band followed. She turned, pushing with both hands as she bowed her body out and back, slowly releasing what little was trapped in the warm shelter of her soft flesh.

She leaned against the rail, peering over her shoulder,

throwing him the moistened silk he caught and breathed in deeply. She waited, teasingly, turning slowly, stopping halfway and raising her foot to the small table so he could see only her profile. She leaned forward for one more sip. Her body was perfect, to him and anyone watching. Her nipples were more erect than he had ever seen them, accented against the moonlight. Her skin was perfect. She glowed, looking as smooth as he knew she was to his touch. Her expression spoke a million words. The lady would no longer be told what to do, or how. The dormant Patricia, the real Patricia, had been unleashed: The world beware.

Sitting had become uncomfortable and he couldn't afford for her to sit in his lap again. Turn. Please turn, he wished. She did, their eyes locked, blowing him a kiss before stretching her nude body, arching herself over the railing, running her hands lightly across her breasts before resting the one closest to him on the railing and placing the other where her raised leg blocked his view.

"You were very bad, my darling, very bad. Saying what you did to those ladies at the spa this afternoon. You have no idea what they did to me." Christ was anybody hearing this. Had anybody seen her? He said nothing. He couldn't swallow, too immobilized to reach for the drink that would soothe his arid throat. "The night is so warm, darling, yet I feel so cool, down there, as though you were blowing your cool breath into me." Her voice was a purr, a quiet groan not meant for him. He was merely a happy bystander. Holy shit! Turn! Turn, he screamed to himself. "It hurt less than I imagined and was really erotic. At first I was afraid, shy, and then I simply enjoyed. Oh, did I simply enjoy." She paused, thinking of what she had said. "I never imagined. No woman has ever seen me or touched me so intimately. The feeling was so good I'm beginning to wonder about myself, about what I might have missed." Jean-François was passing the point of self-control, his hands threatening rebellion. "Do you know, darling, how many herbs and soothing lotions can be applied to you when you're lying there feeling so," she suddenly jerked forward, catching even herself off-guard by the spasm, "not bare, not even vulnerable …desirable, yes, desirable. I hope you like what you will see, darling, what everyone will see tomorrow, you bad boy," the leg came down slowly as she turned to face him, "when I wear that very little thing you bought me."

Her blonde pubic curls were gone. The ladies had turned her into a living, breathing sculpture of sensuality and desire. The pale pink and undulating petals of her lips seemed darker. They glistened in the moonlight and the uneven line between them seemed smaller and innocent.

"Patricia…"

"You've created a monster, darling. No one has ever seen me so entirely bare, so naked, no one. Yet a man I have known less than forty-eight hours does and he wants to touch me there, caress me there with kisses and make love to me. Do I have that about right, cariño?"

"I do believe that is correct, chérie, yes, and much, much more."

She stood with her stilettos far apart, waiting, with her locket and studs sparkling in the moonlight. "But, first, we're going to dance. You did say we would dance, didn't you?"

"Chérie, I fear that would be rather comical at this point, at my very great cost."

"Expense, not cost, expense, you poor sad man. You can't even stand, can you?"

He could stand, though not without considerable difficultly that would be well beyond the empathy of most women. She was adamant. She was going to dance, and she did. Women don't need men for everything. Actually they don't need men for anything, not even for that. Something else she had learned.

The air was warm, the night was bright, her man loved her, she was naked in the moonlight and the music was perfect. Sleep could wait, everything could wait. She danced.

Saturday, 28 October
Slingshots and Spears

Her nude body lay diagonally across his and she stared at him, dreaming of truly being his.

"You did not keep your promise to me last night, monsieur." she whispered, poking at his side until he stirred. "Did you love me last night?"

"Yes, I loved you, chérie." He opened his eyes one at a time, reluctantly. "Now go to sleep, please. If you are not tired, I am."

"I don't think that was lovemaking. I think there is another word for what we did, monsieur. Did you love me?" she insisted, thinking she was being coy.

He eased her away. He was exhausted. "That you ask me such a question hurts me so much. Did I not show what I feel for you, both in public with those voyeurs who would not leave us alone and with my gentle kisses when I thought I had hurt you with the ardour of our lovemaking? Call it what you want. Before I could speak the words to you that would have come easily, our evening, our lovemaking, surrendered to darkness so that I might dream of you and love you all the more."

She jumped up, sitting on her knees and on the verge of hysterical laughter, not completely attuned to his use of English syntax. However her light-heartedness came to an abrupt halt when he swung his legs over the side, stood to pull on a pair of slacks and throw on a clean shirt before walking to the door, closing it quietly behind him. Pat had lived for so long in the faded fields of grey, black and white that any colour in her life was very foreign to her, though she knew the colour would disappear along with him in so few hours. She knelt in the centre of the bed in stunned silence and burst into a flood of tears, too preoccupied with her own anxiety to rationalize. He sat at the end of the walkway leading from his apartment to the beach, massaging his elbow that had turned slightly blue-black. It, or rather she, hadn't been in the agenda. She had not been in the plan. Damn her to hell. Having a flirtatious evening with someone's wife was one thing, having a full blown affair with the wife of the man he would kill in the next seven hours was something else. That many hours earlier she had danced until falling exhausted and naked into his waiting arms.

He had not told her the complete truth when they woke together. What was the manipulation of a few inconsequential lovemaking details considering the full depth of his raison d'être for being there? He needed a reality check. He was losing his sense of balance and he couldn't let that happen for any reason. Play the game, just don't lose. Winner takes all, loser dies. She was the fourth woman in almost as many nights, so what, and his nights weren't finished. What made her so different? If he allowed himself to mismanage his focus now all would go for naught. He'd be screwed, royally screwed. He would have wasted his time, his money and his considerable hard work, and for what, a little bit of pussy, tits, babe, cariño and chérie.

He couldn't have been asleep more than a few restless minutes before she was on him, accusing him, sticking her finger into his chest that irritating way. A moment later he had left her behind the closed door.

When her lap dance had finished he'd carried her to the bed, positioning her with some difficulty because she hadn't wanted to release her hold on him. When she finally understood that what she wanted would be much easier if he was also naked, she tucked the pillow under her breasts to watch him undress, whispering to him to be very bad as she ground herself into the sheets. He felt uncomfortable, as though she was starting without him after a romantic evening of handholding, dancing and laughing. Anything other than romantic love would have spoiled the evening, despite their mutual readiness.

If he hadn't set any records, she certainly did. On several occasions he had no choice but to muffle her cries with hard and ardent kisses and she had taken a full two hours to fall asleep. He watched her for several long moments, lying beside him in total innocence and serenity, oblivious to his hands sweeping lightly over her body and to the sheets he drew over her before leaving the room with the stealth of a cat, leaving her to dream

Her letter to Henderson had been uppermost on his mind from the very moment she told him what she had written, words that would certainly be incriminating. She should have listened to him, goddammit. If discovered, the letter would undoubtedly implicate her in her husband's disappearance and he along with her. The Dominican police would love that kind of three-way kinky shit. One way or another he would have to get the letter before leaving the island paradise. And he would.
*

He had gone directly to the bar at the casino and had ordered a drink, even though he had already seen Henderson as he came in through the Palace entrance connecting from the inside. He was leaning over a gaming table with one arm and holding his near empty glass with the other. By Wellington's watch the time was three-fifteen.

184

He doubted such a small casino would have much in the way of a sophisticated video surveillance system, but as a precaution he kept his head as low as he could and casually walked around dropping in a few quarters. He sat inconspicuously within sight of Henderson, finishing his drink. When he did he left through the Palace entrance and walked as slowly as he could to the apartment to which Pat had kept the key.

The living area was clean except for clothing Henderson had strewn across the room after housekeeping had been in to clean. Three of the four complementary liquor bottles were empty, as were the six beer bottles; the only liquor remaining on the modified speed rail was gin. And, from what he had seen, Henderson was already drunk enough to start on that.

On the davenport there was a computer, a briefcase, a stained glass and all manner of note pads and papers held in place by a cell phone, chargers and a gaudy gold-rimmed pen with the letters BH etched into its titanium casing. His search was meticulous and memories of John Roberts began invading his mind, though he would have no closet to hide in and Henderson would defend himself. If ever he would curse Pat, there would be no better time.

The one closet was filled mostly with Henderson's clothes and he searched through each pocket of every pant, shirt and jacket he could see. The bathroom turned up nothing, nor did the trash basket. Perhaps he had thrown it out. No. Henderson wouldn't have done that. He would have kept it to use against her in court. She'd called him stupid when she had yelled out that she loved him. Who's stupid now, he thought?

The letter wouldn't be under the pillows. What she had written wasn't a love note and Henderson wasn't exactly the tooth fairy. The radio clock read four and the deserted husband might have to die sooner rather than later. Under the bed was spotless and the letter wasn't something anyone would leave lying around. No camera bag also meant no camera and who would bring a gorgeous woman like her on vacation without a camera? Henderson must have kept the letter with him. Bitch!

At four-ten he would have preferred being in New Orleans, sitting on Roberts. Hell, at this point, he'd rather be kissing the old fart back to life. He had checked all the shoes, the empty suitcases, even hers which had been carelessly crammed with clothing she had left behind. He had gone through all the drawers, even the ones jammed tight with a week's worth of their soiled clothing. He found nothing, with no choice but to turn off the lights with too few moments remaining before he would hear the thud of a body falling against the door followed by the sound of a key being forced carelessly into the barrel of the lock. His mind flickered with ludicrous logic, a race against reason. Why would Henderson change his clothes and put a letter like that into, where, his shirt pocket, or his pant pocket? He hadn't been wearing a sports jacket and there were two hanging in the closet. The note was in the room, like a piece of vile trash hidden from view, like dirty laundry hidden from the neighbours. The letter was in the dresser.

A blur of colours passed through his hands, muted by darkness and a confusion of textures as his hands pulled and pushed at the male and female contents of the first, second and third drawers. Nothing. Then he saw the night table, the damned night table, he thought, with a solitary light for reading and a solitary drawer for whatever one would have put away to read at a later time. The slovenly thump against the door came as expected. His heart was palpitating wildly and he tried his utmost to calm himself, convincing himself what might follow didn't matter. He had always known the risks and the consequences and neither had ever mattered to him. What did matter in a very large way was completion, finally seeing something through, closing the deal without external interference.

There was no alternative, short of pre-mature murder. He hadn't jumped from such a height since his brother had kicked him from the leading edge of the high board at the community pool: a time in their lives when their parents had deemed it appropriate for them to experience and mingle with "those other children" as a necessary part of their rounded and more privileged education. That was forty years ago. The light had gone on forty seconds ago and his money was on the luckless gambler coming out onto the balcony with a gin in hand for a late night fart, a peculiar moment for Wellington to remember northern trees and shrubbery were strong with fibre that allowed them to endure their harsh climate. Their southern counterparts lacked fibre and were less strong so they might sway easily under the constant tropical winds when they weren't shading lackadaisical dark-skinned natives who sipped milk from coconuts and waited for their nets to fill.

All men hesitate when hesitation is least admired and being discovered hanging by his fingers from Henderson's railing by Henderson, or by the night watchman who could be seconds or minutes away, were not options. He cursed her and released his grip.

*

"Buenos días, señor. Me llamo Karl."

"Sí, Karl. Ya lo sé. ¿Como vas, amigo mío?"

"Muy bien, Señor LeTuvier. Muy bien, gracias, ¿y usted?"

He had completely forgotten. Karl was the last person he would have wanted to see, with his happy smile and cheerful voice. Karl had problems too, he must have, but no one would have guessed. Why he had even thought to plan an intimate breakfast on the beach that would surely exacerbate the already excessive complication was beyond his own comprehension.

"No muy bien, amigo." He imitated a smile. "Anoche, amigo, ¿comprendes?"

Karl nodded knowingly, not slowing to set the blanket, the plates, and the serving dishes. "Sí señor, comprendo. Hablamos del amor, ¿no? !Qué bueno!"

"Veremos Karl, veremos."

"No, señor, vemos. Vemos ahora mismo." He pointed, forcing Jean-François to turn, still favouring his elbow.

She was a dishevelled mess, no less gorgeous to him than the night before. She was standing there, still, her hands tightly clasped at arm's length. He studied her body as an easy excuse to avoid her eyes. The yellow silk robe seemed oddly pale against the intense morning sun and her face was streaked with blue liquid veins flowing from her bloodshot eyes to the quickly spreading stain on the wide lapels. An uncomfortable moment, but he knew she would not stay there much longer dripping tears before turning away from him.

"Am I as cruel as I appear?" She shook her head with an imperceptible no, focused on the breakfast spread Karl had just completed. "I lament that I have come to my breakfast with less than I need to create a perfect experience."

He seemed annoyed as he stood, still avoiding her eyes as he extended his arm.

She remained still. "What did you forget?"

"You, Patricia, I forgot you. Will you join me?" He reached out to her, forcing a sheepish grin. "Will you at least let me wipe your eyes?"

The impact landed them both on the sand and Jean-François thought he had crushed his own teeth with the acute pain shooting from his elbow.

"I'm so sorry, Jean-François." She ran her hands over and around his head, feeling the large bump. She was alarmed. "I've hurt you."

"Is this what we have come to so quickly, chérie, you and me? Not babe or cariño, simply Patricia and Jean-François, like a brother and his sister? You have not hurt me in any way, chérie. My slight injuries are of my own doing. However you are scaring me very much with your face. Mardi Gras is not for another three months and you have ruined your beautiful new robe with these coloured tears that are certainly my fault."

She examined herself, seeing how much her tears had spread across her front. "Oh, shit!"

The shadow advanced towards them, slowly, blocking out the sun and seemingly uncertain. Karl leaned forward and handed Jean-François a fistful of napkins, whispering "buena suerte," hombre a hombre. Then he broke into song and danced away from them with an impossibly wide smile.

"What does this mean "oh, shit", chérie?"

"Bullshit."

He cocked his head, not understanding.

"You don't know?" she pressed. "You really don't know?" He shrugged. "It means nothing. It's an expression people use when they're angry with themselves. It's not very nice."

"Better that you are angry with me, chérie, for being the stupid one that I am."

"That can never be, babe, absolutely never." She kissed him full on the mouth, peering directly into his eyes. "Never."

She pulled away, easing herself first to her knees, standing upright into the sun for full affect as she loosened the silk belt to her robe.

"Chérie, I do hope that you are very naked under there. I must tell you, however, that even for this place that would be too European."

"I was hoping you would like me in silver-blue, not really thinking of it all over my face. Actually, I was hoping

189

you still liked me."

Would she always take his breath away, he wondered? Would she always steal his senses and make him blind to reality? The two narrow bands of silver-blue joined as one at the newly sensitive apexes of her legs, each scarcely covering the tiny peak of each breast as they travelled separately over her shoulders to join together again where the curve at the small of her back transformed into the firm roundness of her fully tanned buttocks.

"I know I acted like a slut last night and I'm sorry. I told myself I never would again and then I went ahead and ruined the evening. This is all so new for me. I guess I got carried away. Can we start over? I'll try so hard not to scare you away."

"No, Patricia, we cannot start over, and you ruined nothing. We will continue from the very second we opened our eyes so early this morning, when our newness with each other made us unsure and possibly afraid, no? You were not a slut last night. Do not ever think that you were, not ever again, and I did love you, and not because I said that I would. You were delicious in every way, a real woman, and do not ever do that again. Not now, not ever."

"What, babe? Don't do what?"

"Do not ever be tempted to return to what you once were, not for me, not for anyone."

He held out both arms and she saw the pain.

"I did hurt you, darling," she squealed.

"No, you did not. I have told you my wounds are of my own doing and will heal nicely. Now, come to me quickly so that I might hold you."

"No," she smiled playfully, "not quickly, babe... eagerly, always eagerly, but not quickly, not ever again. If you want me quickly, then you must come to me." She ran her hands along the silver-blue bands, drawing them away from her body. "You haven't told me how much you like your gift to me, cariño. I can change if you don't."

He wanted to tell her to never leave him again, and how ridiculous was that? "Yes, chérie, you will have to change." He filled their glasses with orange juice and champagne, and then he stood, exactly what she hadn't expected and her face flickered with frowns and uncertain smiles. "As alluring and as beautiful as you are, chérie, you will certainly distract each man who will see you, and all their women will hate you too much."

"So what? They're all wearing something skimpy, and what about the little thing you wear?" she pouted, beginning to feel angry.

"Yes, darling, unfortunately neither one will be inappropriate for our moonlight cruise this evening." He held out the glass to her. "I wish to toast the most beautiful woman on the beach, the island, and also the most naked."

Anyone passing would have stopped and wondered at the two of them to determine whether he was being mauled by a madwoman and in desperate need of help, or loved by a woman set free and very much in need of privacy. From not too far away the silver-blue bands would have appeared to the casual observer as two glittering streaks reflected by the sun.
*

He hadn't told her. Somehow what he had to say hadn't fit the mood he had created and he wondered as he floated her around the Taino's pool whether he had subconsciously avoided the issue. He wondered why he was even thinking about it. The answer was clear: Of course, he had.

He had been right about one thing. Everyone was looking, even the French women who were topless at the pool with the skimpiest bottoms. She wore the micro tell-all bikini well and no one would have believed the metamorphosis which had transformed her over the past few days. She would have to know and there was no better

191

time. She lay face down on the rubber float, physically exposed and emotionally vulnerable. What were a few tears, or a look of hatred? She was a woman. She'd get over it.

"Chérie, please. I need a moment of your time."

"Darling, you're the one with the watch. Remember?"

"Yes, I remember. There is something that I must tell you, which I cannot do while seeing you this way." He waved an arm across the chlorinated beads accentuating her nudity. "Please."

Transfixed as she climbed the chromed ladder, he was at once in awe of her and disgusted with himself. He could not tell himself he had done what he had for her, nor would he. Her implication would be his downfall, which was motive enough. Why should he care with six days remaining until Friday? That was his real resolve, his true purpose. That's why he had to care so much. Everything else was a means to that end, a prop, a convenient camouflage in a make believe world, a ruse.

She draped the silk robe over her shoulders. "What's the matter, my darling?"

"This morning when I left you, I did not do so to walk without purpose. I admit that the timing was not very appropriate, however very necessary nevertheless." He paused. "The reason for my leaving was, in fact, also the reason I hurt my arm and my poor head."

She leaned forward on the chaise-longue, beaming. "Do I have to know how you did that?"

"I fear so, chérie." He unfolded the letter, hesitating for as long as she needed to absorb the reality of what she was seeing. "This was wrong of you." He was unapologetic. "You should never have done such a thing. Do you understand, chérie, not ever?" She stared disbelievingly at his hand and the letter, her face expressionless. "This would have been a mistake, Patricia, a very big mistake for you. Such a letter could be used against you in a court and might possibly have finished you."

"How did you get that?"

"When I left you this morning, I did so not for the first time. Much of the time you slept, cariño, you did sleep alone. I went to the casino to see that he was still there, and he was. I went to his villa to search for the note. Finally I did succeed and jumped from the balcony as he was coming in."

He rubbed his arm in a feeble attempt to make light of the drama.

She showed utter disbelief. "That was stupid, Jean-François, plain stupid. You have no idea how angry he can get. How could you?"

"Do I care, chérie? A man who will physically display his anger against a woman is no danger to another man, even though he believes himself superior." He looked at the crumpled paper. "This has never existed."

He folded the letter and struck the match he had plucked from the folder in the nearby ashtray.

"He used to call me a slut and a whore. That's why I was crying this morning. I thought you thought I was a slut for doing what I did on the balcony. The one time I tried being sexy, something I'm obviously not, for a rare evening alone, he laughed at me and called me bad names, especially the two worst ones. You know the ones I mean."

"Yes, I do know the ones."

"So I stopped. I guess I'm out of practice," she shrugged, trying to laugh.

"Chérie, what I saw, what you did for me alone was erotic and exotic and natural. You could not have been more sensual and arousing. Remembering makes me want you more. You are not out of practice." She suddenly laughed uncontrollably. "What is so amusing, chérie?"

"You, jumping from a balcony in the middle of the night with your lover's letter clutched in your hand and then bumping your head and almost breaking your arm. Some Don Juan you are."

"And this is so funny, that I almost was killed to protect you?"

"Yes, darling, I'm sorry."

"You are the bad one, I think. Come, I want everyone to see this bad woman that my fate has forced upon me."

"Forced?"

"Yes, my darling, forced. What else could it be? Your magic has made me too weak to protect myself against your very charms. I must make everyone aware of how evil you are."

She kissed him. "You are the one who makes me weak, darling." She pulled at him. "And I can still be weaker than I am."

"I must leave you for a little while, chérie." He pulled a crisp hundred from his pocket. "I want you to go to the market and buy another new bikini, your choice, and surprise me this afternoon. Also, you must wear your robe while I am gone so that they may not see how beautiful such an evil woman can be."

"Where are you going? Can't I come?"

"How can I surprise you if you are with me, chérie? No. You must do your thing for me, and I will do mine for you."

Oh Christ, even he had trouble believing that one, managing to catch the crumpled bill she threw at him as she stood and rushed off. At least she had blown him a kiss and was laughing as she left, not to mention turning heads.
*

"Hola, señoritas, ¿y cómo van ustedes?"

They all stopped to acknowledge him, and giggled, causing each of their clients to strain their necks to see him, including Henderson who saw the geek in the shirt staring at him.

"My last day, man. Might as well make the best of it.

How 'bout you? When you goin` home?"

Henderson lowered his head, not answering, and Wellington wondered if he even had one tiny muscle hidden under that sloppy and toneless gut. The thirty minutes flew by so quickly that he was completely taken by surprise when the masajista smacked his nearly bare ass as a sign for him to get up for a fast once-over before making room for another client. She would not have guessed he was staring fixedly at the man whose death he had been contemplating for the past thirty minutes as she manipulated and massaged the knots from his back, knots due in great part to the shapeless man on the adjoining table.

Enjoy your rub, Bill. I'll see you later. He tipped the girl, smiled and left. He had one errand to run before returning to his villa to change and get the dive bag. He also wanted to make sure she wouldn't be there. He walked the beach alone, scanning. She would be easy to spot and he had guessed correctly that he could walk right past her and she wouldn't notice him. That's exactly what she did on her way from the open-air market with several plastic bags swinging in opposite directions in obvious rhythm to some tune being sung in her head. She had kept on her robe, making her strangely more desirable. He sat with mounting expectation as she stepped into a beach cabana at the Bambu and closed the door behind her. He stared at her feet moving up and down, one at a time, and then up and down once again after a brief pause and before stepping out.

What barely rated as an eye patch, much less a bikini bottom, was a deep coral colour. She wore no matching top and when she stepped so matter-of-factly under the outdoor shower by the cabana all eyes were watching as her whole body burst into one glittering silhouette of perfect curves, her nipples reacting tauntingly to the freshness of the water. She'd been right, after all. He had created a monster in her. Still she didn't see him and for the better. Even though he wanted to be with her, to let her live her dream to the fullest, to prepare her for a new life that was days away, business came first and one little item remained to address.

With that half done, he went to the villa to change and verify the contents of the black bag. He took a deep swallow of JW Black, neat, at room temperature, the liquor burning his mouth more as a salute to himself, he thought, than fortification. Who cared? He needed no fortification. His resolve was unbroken. She was laying on her front and facing the ocean, away from him. He dropped the bag in the sand where he could see it, some distance from her feet. He knelt by her side, taking both halves of her very tempting ass in his hands, massaging and kneading them apart and together to his own advantage.

"What are you doing, you bad man?"

"I am being bad. Is that not what you want of me?"

"God, yes. Be bad and don't stop."

He threw himself forward into the sand, stretching out alongside her on his good elbow. "I must leave you for a little while longer, not very long. Nevertheless I must, and then I shall come to you. Will you be fine by yourself in this little thing that covers nothing of you?"

"Yes, darling, of course. If not, I'm sure one of these young men around me will want to help me. Don't you think so?"

"You are potting, chérie. I will not be very long. I will miss you for lunch, but do not pot, I beg of you."

"Pout. The word is pout, and I'm not pouting. Why can't I come with you?"

"Because I must go into Higüey, darling, and having you with me would be too great a distraction. I would fail miserably in what I must do and have only myself to blame."

"You won't tell me why."

"I will tonight, my darling, when we are fully satiated

with our love making."

"Go, then. Do your thing, if you have to. But I need you to bring me something."

"Anything you wish chérie. Tell what you need?"

"I'd like a Spanish dictionary. I see they treat their women much better than you Frenchmen."

"That, my darling, is because they learn their lessons from our French books. Believe me. You would quickly be disappointed with any one of them. I will come to you before you know that I am gone. Why do we not meet in the room at, let me say, four o'clock. D'accord?"

"Four!" Her expression showed total shock. "I might be there, though I wouldn't count on it. Those Spaniards are looking better the more I see at them. You'd better knock first when you come back."

She turned her head, lifting her buttocks off the chaise longue for a second soft smack and a long squeeze.

He whispered. "Spanish men are children, chérie. They smell of their mother's milk. Wait for a real man who will love you the way you must be loved."

He commanded all his will power not to touch her when she flipped over, covering her face with a towel and not saying a word. He had lied to her about Higüey and felt no guilt. He had actually been expected at la calle Carabeña and had taken his time walking there and back. The remaining hour until one-thirty was spent a few dozen metres away from her, watching her, wanting her and praying he would have her again if only one more time.

When he stood to leave he walked directly behind her and stopped, though she never would have recognized him. All those around her thought he was a voyeur and they either openly pointed at him or shook their heads in disgust.
*

The Jet Ski was moored, waiting for him. Henderson had been gone thirty minutes and had just disappeared from the

197

field of view allowed by Wellington's binoculars. The sea was calm enough with half-metre rolling waves and the ten-kilo bag made no difference whatsoever to the performance or balance of the PWC. He had mounted and secured the bag with bungee cords without the slightest intervention or interest on the part of the beach boys. The adrenalin rush had kicked in. There was no self-doubt, no sober second thoughts. Not now. He was gone at full throttle. He whispered what, in essence, was a hope more than an inappropriate prayer and peered over his shoulder scanning the beach, resisting the urge to isolate her with the binoculars.

*

Locating Henderson could not have been easier. He was at the exact location he went to each day, either with the boat or a PWC. He was a creature of habit and they were well beyond sight of anyone with a camcorder or binoculars. From Henderson's perspective the PWC had been coming his way at full throttle, then nothing, suddenly dead in the water, then suddenly lurching ahead at full throttle and then nothing. What the hell? What was the idiot doing, Henderson wondered as he watched the show, putting on his baseball cap to reduce the surface glare so he could get a better view of the geek's problems?

The Pro Line wasn't too much farther ahead of Wellington and he waved, hoping the person in the boat would help him, or at least let him onboard where he would feel safe. A few minutes more and he would be able to yell for help. Maybe the boat had VHF? Shit! Something else he hadn't thought about. Idiot! Shit! He began waving as a friend would.

"Hey! Hi!" He waved some more, then he played with the throttle lurching the craft forward and coming close to colliding with the day-cruiser. "Hey, man. I thought I recognized you. How ya doin'? Man, am I happy to see you.

Don't know what happened. The thing just quit, stopped running the way it's supposed to. It's the salt water, I guess." He paused, appearing confused. "Think so?" Henderson stayed as he was, watching the multi-coloured freak holding onto his gunwale and letting the two crafts smash together. "Hey, man, if you can help me out for minute or two, I got the perfect thing for two buds on a no-broads outing." Out came the bottle of JW Black. "Not bad, eh? We've got to get away from the bitches somehow. Massages, yeah, but a little booze out here is the perfect way. The wife won't let me drink. She says I can't handle it. Fuck her. What she doesn't know, eh? Damn straight."

"Grab the line and tie off. Climb over. We'll get you fixed up in a little bit."

Henderson removed the team cap and wiped his brow. He tossed the cap onto a pile of empty beers cans, not far from the few still unopened. The geek, Wellington mused, had come along just in time. Wellington passed Henderson the black bag before straddling the gunwale to climb into the boat. "Thanks, man." He grabbed at the loose end, securing the two crafts together.

"What do you have in this thing? It weighs a ton."

"Booze for one thing, and some snorkeling gear." He opened a side pocket, retrieving the JW Black. "Can't say I brought glasses." He uncapped the bottle. "I wasn't exactly expecting to visit with anyone."

Henderson reached for an empty can, making sure the contents had completely drained before holding it out to the geek. "Don't be shy, captain's prerogative."

What do you know about captain's prerogative you half-drunken fool? "Here, man, take the bottle." Henderson did, and poured until the scotch began spilling. "Hey, man, don't forget your guests. Got another can?" Henderson kicked one over, ignorant son of a bitch. "Thanks, man." Wellington poured a healthy portion over the lid, cleaning it, looking straight into Henderson's eyes. "No insult, man. We can't be too careful these days, especially here. Know what I mean? Here's to good living, getting laid and getting pissed."

They both raised the cans.

"Down the hatch." Henderson belched. Then he downed enough to make him cough.

"That a radio? Hey, can I call for them to come get me?" Wellington suggested.

"Yeah, in a bit, but first things first." Henderson put the can again to his mouth. "We can call in the troops later if the thing still doesn't work. We don't want anyone seeing the evidence, right? The paperwork for this piece of shit reads like a fucking insurance policy."

"Good point," Wellington agreed, smiling widely at the one-sided irony, "not to mention the wife. All she'd do is bitch that I shouldn't be out here alone in the first place."

"Tell her where to get off."

"Easier said than done. We don't always get to say or do what we want."

"Yeah, we do, especially with them. What you need is to get back to the basics. The way it used to be, in our parents' day. Know what I mean? Man and wife and less of this liberal bullshit."

"Sure do. You mean a little in-home therapy."

Henderson pointed his index finger as an adamant gesture of agreement and took a deep guzzle that made Wellington wince. He was drinking scotch like cola in 30° Celsius weather as a chaser to several beers. Go for it, asshole. Bottoms up.

"It's for their own good. I mean, really." Henderson hesitated not sure how far he should take his venting. "Hell, why not, it's not like this is going anywhere. We're leaving in a week anyway. She doesn't know yet, but I've already filed to get rid of her. She's been a real monkey on the back.

Seems every time I open my mouth it's to tell her what to do, or what not to do. Soon as I'm out of here it'll be over. The lawyer's already doing the paperwork. Finally, after twelve, fourteen years, whatever," he took a gulp, "I'm getting rid of her. She's been a wart on my dick and cold as fucking ice. Thinks I don't know she's over there showing off her ass and tits and who knows what else on the beach, while I'm out here. Got to keep them in line every so often, know what I mean?"

"Your wife?"

"Yeah the wife. Who the fuck do you think?"

"But you do like ogling the ladies, Bill. You're a gawker. I'd bet that much, don't you Bill? And what about your slut girlfriend? Think she's not going down on someone when you're here ignoring your wife?"

Henderson dropped the half-full can to his knee and pivoting his head for no apparent reason. "How'd you know my fucking name?"

"The same way you should know mine, Bill."

Wellington took off his cap and glasses, leaving on his gloves and zinc oxide.

"What's this, fucking show and tell? Am I supposed to know you, shit ass?"

"Well it's been ten years, Bill. We were both much younger then. I'm Wellington Bartlett, Eastern Division, and now very defunct, at your service."

"Small world. So how come you didn't say so at the massage place? I thought you were some sort of asshole."

"And what did you think I was when you fired me for no good reason?"

Henderson drank again. "There was nothing to think about. You know as well as anyone, sales guys come and go. Let them work, get the gain, get rich off them, then hire someone else for less pay and more work to start the cycle over again. No big deal. You did okay."

"Think so?"

Henderson shrugged, unaffected. "You could always have gone to your brother. Is that why you came out here," he chuckled, "to cry about the past?"

His laugh was cut short.

"No, my working days are over, Bill. I came out here because I couldn't do this anywhere else. I couldn't just reach into my bag for this." He pulled out the fully charged spear gun and the near empty can dropped to the fibreglass deck, spilling what little was left.

"What the fuck!"

"I don't have a lot of time, Bill. I thought for the longest time I had perfect justification for killing you." He smiled. "Yes. I am going to kill you. You were one of those people who, for some fluky twist of fate, had control over my career for as long as you needed to do a real fine job destroying my life. Long story short, Bill, you fucked me for no reason. You got rid of me with no regard for the impact of your decision. I was at the top. You knew I was at the top and you didn't even think to mention options, nothing, not once. You just told me to go… fuck off."

"That sounds like a real fine idea. Why don't you just fuck off back to your wife?"

"Because she left me."

"So now here you are, you saw me, and you came begging for a job." He wavered. "You thought you'd get something by getting the old boss drunk." He reached for another can, peeling off the tear-drop seal. "Shit happens. What can I say?"

"Any shit I've ever seen has come from an asshole." Wellington tilted his head for affect. "Are you an asshole, Bill?"

"You weren't alone. There were others and they all survived. It' not my fault you couldn't cut it. We were cost-cutting, being efficient. You know all that shit. What happened had squat to do with you. So why don't you just fuck off before you get into some serious shit you'll be sorry for." He hesitated. "This never happened."

"Sorry, Bill? Get into serious shit for what, killing you? For the longest time I believed I had one good reason, one reason alone, but the real reason became apparent to me a few days ago."

"And that would be?"

"Patricia... your wife. You've never appreciated what a jewel you have in her, Bill. Tell me, I'm curious. Why does everyone in pharma have a proclivity towards scotch and whores?"

Henderson went ghostly white. "You fucker."

"How did you know?" He smiled. "Yes, Bill, I fuck her. I have for a while and I will again in about two hours and again before dinner, and again when you're supposedly losing at the tables. She's at the beach right now and all she's wearing is a tiny thong, Bill, no top. The difference between you and me is that I see her as exciting and sexy, you see her as a slut. That's reason enough to kill you, but, really, the situation is a little more complicated. Here's the thing, Bill, and I need you to listen up." Henderson took another swig, scanning an empty sea. "Don't bother, Bill. I've already calculated the helicopter tours, the glass-bottom boat tours and that whole tourist thing. It's just you and me." Wellington took a sip of scotch and passed the bottle to Henderson who took it mechanically. "She knows you're divorcing her. Now that's a good thing and what you planned to do after really doesn't matter worth a shit. However I do need to know you've properly provided for her. Have you, Bill? Have you provided for her?"

"Fuck you."

"You're not going anywhere, Bill. The faster you realize that the easier all this will be and I don't have a lot of time. So listen up. Please. This is very important. You have a daughter who means the world to you, she's nineteen and how well you treat Patricia will determine how well I will treat your daughter. Now, once more, have you provided for Patricia?"

"She gets to leave. That should be enough for her."

"Normally, I would agree. Unfortunately you're dead, or will be in a few minutes. So what we're talking about is the house, some insurance, investments, that sort of thing. Is she still the executor of the will and primary beneficiary?"

"Yes."

"Yes?"

"I said yes. What else do you want?"

"It's not what I want, Bill. It's what I need. I need proof. First I need a signature on each of these four blank sheets that will be filled in by me and sent to Stuart. That is his name, isn't it? Here's how I get that proof I was talking about. If, when all is said and done, I discover you've cheated her and lied to me, I'll find your daughter and fuck her ten different ways before I cut her throat." A slight adjustment to the angle of the spear was enough to make Henderson sit back and keep his mouth shut. "Do you have your lawyer's number on your cell?"

"No."

"No? Then, do you have your daughter's address?"

Henderson's new colour had nothing to do with the blistering sun. "What if I do have the number?"

"Call him."

"It's Saturday."

"Call him, and I'll tell you exactly what you're going to say. When you're done, you'll call your house and leave the same message for Pat. Now sign those sheets and dial."

Within moments Avery Stuart was advised by his client to disregard any and all recent discussions, transactions and proceedings regarding his client's marital and joint affairs. A letter to that effect would be e-mailed to his law office and dated Saturday, October 28. A signed hard copy would follow.

"Thank you, Bill. I'll write the letter for you before dinner. Do you have the e-mail address noted, or should I call your daughter? I do hope that's the signature Stuart has on file."

"Suppose now you want me to beg? You can have her if you want her. I could give a shit either way."

"I give a shit, Bill. This is nothing personal, you understand. It's a business decision, like the company's decision not to promote you to junior V.P. after twenty years of sucking up and licking your boss' balls. That must have really hurt your bullshit ego. It's business. In fact, I'll even give you a choice: spear, or chain?" He reached into the bag for the five-kilo Bruce anchor. "Now the spear is pretty much instant, but I bet it hurts like hell. On the other hand, this way will take about three minutes and is supposedly euphoric, though that's third-party information. I can't say for sure."

"Are you out of your fucking mind? You think they won't catch you? What about the boat? If I'm not back in a few minutes they'll come looking for me."

"Not a few minutes, Bill, seventy-five minutes." Wellington touched the spearhead with a fingertip and winced. "No, I don't believe I'm out of my mind. Yes, they will go looking for you, by which time I'll be off the island and, guess what, Bill? For all intents and purposes, particularly this one, I don't exist. Wellington Bartlett is in Montreal as we speak."

Henderson lunged forward at the very instant the burst of air from the chamber sounded simultaneously with the ripping hiss as the serrated spear head pierced his distended abdomen dead centre, striking hard against his slightly bowed spinal column and jerking him against the prow.

He was staring at his own two hands clutching the black

hardened-steel shaft when the second spear struck his chest and went in half as far. What had he been talking about? He didn't remember. The spears didn't hurt. They scared him; they felt very hot and were uncomfortable, but not painful. He wasn't dying. He could tell that much, although he couldn't understand why he was actually allowing Bartlett to wrap the chain around his neck and why was he being jostled so much. The sun was hot and breathing was difficult. How could he be expected to concentrate on that and follow instructions at the same time? He felt a cold tightness grip at his throat and couldn't understand why. If he had already been killed, why was he being choked? Why was he thinking of the time his father had first taught him to knot his tie. His mouth tasted of blood, but he couldn't see any, and why was he being told to jump overboard? Why would he do that, and why was the day suddenly so dark? He felt he had to scream, to clear his throat. The hand at his shoulder felt warm and reassuring as though the man was helping him to sit on the narrow edge and that felt good, but he felt he had to scream. He had once heard how the expectation of one's death was far worse than death itself, but dying wasn't so bad, not if that's what he was doing. There were no angels and probably wouldn't be. The unexpected suddenness of the jolt sealed his oesophagus. He was suddenly cold and shivering. His nostrils burned and he couldn't scream. As much as he wanted he knew he could not and nothing around him was clear. His eyes burned and everything was suddenly quiet, calm and serene.

Henderson's descent into the warm turquoise depth was more rapid than Wellington had imagined. He was disappointed. All that remained of Henderson were the millions of ascending translucent and glittering air bubbles bursting silently into extinction at the surface. Plan your dive and dive your plan, or deal with Murphy's Law. How many times had that motto been drilled into his head? He checked the depth sounder: sixty feet.

There would be a note left behind from the deceased, albeit somewhat different from the one he had planned to compose and mail from Savannah. This one would be a business letter, not a confession of wrongdoing or an admission of guilt. Pat would be fine, and so would the daughter.

The meeting had come to an end. He took a healthy swig of the scotch and put the remainder in the black bag along with his own hat, shirt and glasses as he stripped them off. The full and empty beer cans went into Henderson's insulated cooler and he put on the dead man's shirt, glasses and hat, leaving the dull-red and limp-looking life jacket in the corner by the transom. This was the part where not caring played a very significant role in the scheme of things.

Had time allowed he would have free-dived to wave bye-bye to Henderson, but he was satisfied with what he had accomplished and had no reason to push his luck in the name of vanity or self-satisfaction. This time there could be no suicide note because he had no idea of the various clauses in Henderson's insurance policy and he didn't want to jeopardize Pat's chance to live well after the fact, though there would be a note.

Ideally he should have simply raised the trim tabs after positioning the bow for a compass heading of 140° and hang something like the insulated beer bag onto the bottom of the stainless steel wheel so the craft wouldn't turn on its own. Had he done that, and had he adjusted the throttle to twenty-five hundred rpm, he would have had at least and hour's grace before anyone would have become suspicious or worried, either about Henderson or the boat. The beach boys would have gone out themselves first, probably searching closer to shore before notifying the authorities, by which time the tiny white fibreglass dot would have been some seventy-five or eighty kilometres offshore and camouflaged in a very large ocean by the glitter of what everyone on shore would be calling a beautiful sunset. Case closed. An unfortunate vacationer would have been presumed missing as the result of a rare boating incident.

The downside to that scenario would have been the inescapable contact with the police and most likely having to explain how he fit into the lives of Mr. and Mrs. Henderson as he and Pat would be leaving for dinner. This way was cleaner, albeit somewhat less prudent. Henderson would be considered missing and his absence wouldn't be discovered until Wellington had left.

He purposely tied the PWC off to the port side of the Pro Line so anyone on shore would see only the boat as he came in from the east. He had about twenty minutes remaining on his rental. Henderson had about forty, so forty was the primary objective. He had always hated the word, and schedule, though never as much as he had over the past six days.

Wellington made his way to shore and brought the crafts to where an open air market was the focus of attention and not him. He threw out the anchor, waded onto the blistering sand and made his way to the concessions whose façades were covered with brightly coloured cover-ups, tee shirts and bikinis from the local artisans who each had the best price. He negotiated an over-priced bottle of cheap island rum while complimenting the apparently dim-witted dependiente on his English skills and bragging about Toronto, Canada. He looked back, waving as he made his way to the boat and tripped.

The purchase was left onboard the boat that was left rolling with the waves, the PWC was untethered, and he was gone, waiting until he was halfway to the rental concession to idle in neutral and change clothes once again. He felt good getting out of those death-defying cargo swim trunks, not surprised so many people drown in them each year, and headed straight into shore. By the time he jumped off into the ankle-deep water he had gotten rid of the two knives he had carried for back-up along with the empty spear gun. He ditched them all widely apart, where they would never be found, due largely to the depth and the lack of anything interesting enough to constitute a dive sight. The rest of the lighter gear he would drop off along his way to the boat.

He avoided the beach entirely, choosing instead the level flagstone path connecting the various hotels of the compound. Doing so provided him with both the speed he needed to get back to the open-air market and the ability to recognize and steer clear of Pat from any distance. By the time he was once again wading in waist-high water he had changed for the last time into Henderson's clothing and his own long swim trunks, keeping his own vest on under Henderson's buttoned shirt to give the appearance of being much heavier.

The Pro Line cut through the calm sea like a knife and he came in at 3500 rpm, simulating Henderson's lack of respect for bathers and other boaters. He cut the engine, dropping the anchor that would dig deeply and neatly into the sand well before the cresting wave would have thrown him onto shore. Henderson would never have done that, but there was a limit to how boorish Wellington would allow himself to appear, even with a disguise. What he did do in order to authenticate his characterization was stand with his arms outstretched as he bowed to the small audience of beach boys who had already slowed their pace to assist the old fool in anchoring. He slid over the gunwale and laboured at a forty-five degree angle away from them, yelling: "Mañana, One-thirty. Mañana."

They returned the wave and yelled, "Sí, mañana. Adios, señor," while thinking "Es loco, éste, y borracho." He did seem drunk. Weren't most tourists crazy, they agreed? It didn't matter. They didn't like him.

*

"Hans, good morning, this is Bill Henderson. We're Saturday PM and I'm leaving for the airport. I wanted to call to say I'm excited about our meeting in Savannah and how much I'm looking forward to meeting with you. See you then." He closed the phone.

Wellington sat on Henderson's balcony sipping warm Presidente brandy from a warm glass. He had removed the sunglasses, the hat and shirt, leaving all three articles strewn over two chairs before finding another of the dead man's swim trunks, soaking them in the shower and leaving them in the tub. He still had a little while before meeting with Pat and wanted to compose the letter when he knew he had the allowable time. He wrote it as an attachment addressed to Avery Stuart, Attorney: Avery, per my voice mail to you this AM, Saturday, October 28, I wish you to immediately terminate all actions and proceedings previously discussed by us concerning my wife, Patricia. Since our last meeting in your office, certain reconciliatory agreements and conditions have been arrived at amicably by Patricia and me that make my previous intentions unnecessary. She is to remain as executor and primary beneficiary of my estate, and the status of my daughter, Penelope, is to remain unchanged, which is to say she will receive one single sum of fifty thousand dollars disbursed at the convenience of the executor. A signed copy of this statement will be provided at my earliest convenience.

Then he wrote Monday's Meeting in the subject line. The date would show as October 28:

Hans, good afternoon, I'm writing this moments before I take off for Savannah. I have sent documents under separate cover and you should expect them at your hotel by five PM Monday. Why don't we eat dinner first and have the rest of the evening to discuss this cross border arrangement.

Best regards,
Bill Henderson
*

When he completed the second letter with the address he pressed send/receive, sending it to the Out box before the computer screen came down hard and snapped shut. He had read through some of Henderson's letters to get a feel for his writing style before authoring the list of instructions to Avery Stuart to guarantee Pat's future comfort and to make his daughter always despise him. The phone call had been for Wiernknoff's benefit. The e-mails were for Pat's and the Savannah police, respectively. All he needed was a high-speed connection and a printer.

Pouring another brandy he filled the black bag with clothes Henderson would likely have worn that evening to dinner and the casino, including a jacket, shirt, slacks, socks and shoes. The hair spray can was put on its side, the toothbrush was wetted after the paste had been applied and rubbed in using the inside of the sink, the shower was run once more, and the floor mat was dampened so it would be wet through to the next morning. He would print out two copies of the letter on the pre-signed sheets at the data centre on la calle Carabeña, keep one, and send the e-mails to Stuart's and Pat's addresses. He would also download certain interesting information onto CDs before making one last stop to pick up what would be waiting for him.

Pat expected him at four and wouldn't see him until five. She would understand. She was sensitive and vulnerable which meant she would understand even if she didn't. He left the computer absolutely clean and took only the Circadian's confidential corporate information he had downloaded. Taking the computer was neither an option nor necessary. Henderson would remain missing and eventually be forgotten, automatically converted into a death benefit file of one or more insurance companies who would have no choice but to concede the deceased was, in actual fact, dead. He took the cell phone.

Pat had become X the unknown and Wellington prayed there would be no other serious oversight he had not anticipated. The three days had been difficult and deceitful. He was grateful to have shared them with her, sharing which had made their intimacy deceitful and he was happy his time on the island was coming to an end. There had never been a question of choosing between her and the plan. He was sure she would adapt well to her newfound freedom. Feel the pain now or later. There was no difference to him. No one had ever felt his pain and no one would feel hers. Such was life.

Certainly she would be in for a few trying days of questions and possibly self-reproach, but that was part of the female condition. He wouldn't be there to help her and he didn't want to be. So what? What mattered most was being free of Henderson and his abuse, although she probably wouldn't realize the significance for quite some time and she would never realize who her real benefactor was. She'd get on with her life, or begin her life. She'd hate Jean-François for a while, but he wouldn't be around to know or care. He was a physical representation of all she had missed in life, and of all good things to come. She would have more men in her life and would either remember him as her first or forget him along with those who would follow.

What he had come to realize over the past week was how he had changed in the way he would view life, his life; not in terms of his mortality, rather his relationships. He would land in Charlotte in thirty hours and had decided to phone Gi-Gi. The time had come for him, for the two of them to be honest with one another once and for all.
*

He had no doubt she'd be pissed with him, but, as he had

learned throughout his career, bullshit baffles brains and she was a smart lady. He slowed his pace, knowing she would forgive him. They would share one last night alone, enjoying one another and she wouldn't want to ruin precious moments with female sullenness. Besides, concealing part of a man's wardrobe in small garbage receptacles along the way took time, making sure nothing had been overlooked. Not everyone could just idly soak up the sun, not to mention that he knew he had the upper hand with her.

As he strolled once again along the sand-covered path leading to la calle Carabeña he was involuntarily searching the sparsely populated beach for the tiny splash of coral that had been the only adornment covering the sexiest and most adorable lady on the island earlier in the day. She was nowhere in sight. His ETA was twenty minutes. Even the prettiest woman turned ugly when made to wait too long. The fear was irrational, tantamount to being afraid of a Pekinese, which most honest men would readily admit with reservation.

At a moment past five the patio doors to the balcony were closed. BEWARE OF PISSED-OFF WOMAN! He listened with his ear against the door before entering, hearing nothing. He wasn't very good at this. The key went into the barrel, turning as slowly as he could possibly manage, thinking she might be sleeping and that he would slip into bed beside her.

The shower was running. There was no escape for him. His one defence would be taking command of the situation. He stepped out onto the balcony and saw the shiny and twisted splash of coral hanging from the miniature telescopic clothesline, barely recognizable as a bikini and the silver-blue slingshot had wrapped itself into a braided glitter. Stay or go? Stay outside and fake it, or go in and accept what was coming his way? He went in.

The heap of clothing grew at the bottom of the closed door and his breath that was deeper than he had anticipated propelled him through the doorway into the bathroom. He had intended to step in nonchalantly and take her in his arms, smothering her objections with kisses and a crushing embrace. That all evaporated when he saw her. He stood frozen and openly stared at her.

She admonished him with a finger, either for spying on her, for catching her, or for being late. Did he care? Not more than her. She was nymph-like and bathed in the sunlight coming through the slatted windows as much as she was by the million water droplets happily ending their existence against the smooth silkiness of her nakedness. She signalled him in as she stepped aside, giving him access to the tepid, cascading water. Then she suddenly seemed bored, uninterested in him, and sat on the inside edge of the tub ignoring him completely. He rested his hand on the side of her head, his fingers massaging her matted ringlets until she stood, seeming to pose, or so he thought before she stepped out leaving him standing alone, wet and grimacing. When he finally joined her, she was on the balcony, wearing a sheer full-length robe in Mediterranean blue. He was wearing what most Americans would call fancy pants.

"I hate you. Go away."

"You do not. You love me."

"No. I don't. I thought I did, but now I don't."

"What has changed, chérie, that you hate me so?"

"I have learned how to say mi amor. That's what's changed. I have a Spanish lover, so there. I've spent the entire day making love to a wonderful Latin lover."

"But I am a Latin lover, darling. Can you forgive me?"

"You're a man, and that makes you a jerk."

"So is your Latin lover a man, and therefore a jerk, no?"

"I spent my day shopping and dreaming about Latin lovers, and not necessarily you. You, I hate very much."

She stood, and the Italian slip he was wearing was suddenly tested.

"I like what I see," he tried.

"You should, it cost a fortune."

"I do, but it hides too much of you from my eyes. I feel so deprived."

She looked down. "Too much of what? God, I couldn't be more naked. Get me a drink, mi amor, please. Vodka, neat."

"I am your eager servant, madame."

"Don't push it, Frenchie. You're this close to the Bastille." She pinched her index finger and thumb together. "Go." She hadn't moved during the few minutes he was gone. Her silhouette was beautiful and captivating to him and when he returned he leaned against the metal doorframe for a long moment to admire her and she let him. "I bought it for you, to remember me. I wanted you to see it in the light."

"I am so happy that I was not later than I was."

"I feel as though I don't know what to say to you anymore, that I can't say what I feel."

"Then that is what you must say, darling."

"Where were you, Jean-François? My day seemed like ten. I missed you so much, but I knew I shouldn't, that I can't, but we have so little time left together."

He hesitated in a way he hoped was conducive to their mood, her mood. "There is nothing wrong with missing someone, chérie, my darling Patricia, even if you are not so sure of the person. I cannot excuse myself enough, you know. However my absence was necessary for me to make preparations which I do not want to talk about now. I had business, chérie, tout simplement. I have told you about my meetings. I did not forget you, chérie; never would I forget you and I do have a surprise for you. One that, I must say, took more than a small part of my day. I also want very much for you to have something with which to remember me."

"What is it?" She turned like a little girl at Christmas, running to him, hugging him tightly. "Where is it? Show me!"

"Darling we have but one hour in which to dress for dinner. We must be at the main lobby for the taxi I have reserved that will take us to the dock. Come, let us dress. There will be time later for trinkets and, how do you say, goo-goo talk."

She slapped his face, softly, kissing him. "Goo-goo talk? I don't think so. Trinkets? Maybe."

He wasn't falling for it. He was already sitting on the edge of the single bed, waiting like a teenager in heat for the naughty next-door neighbour to open her blinds. The Mediterranean blue fell to the floor and she knelt completely and unabashedly naked to reach under the bed, knowing exactly where his eyes had focused. The box was flimsy and, he hoped, at least as flimsy as what was inside.

He did not exist. She was in a world of her own. The cover of the box was opened, neatly folded back, and the tissue paper was pulled out in all four directions as she stood naked, glowing and looking down, seemingly perplexed before turning in search of any solution.

"I don't know."

"Don't know what, my darling?"

"I don't know whether I should put on my panties first, or my dress, or maybe my shoes."

He threw himself backwards and flipped onto his front. "The shoes first, please, then the dress and the panties."

"Men are such horrible pigs."

"We know that, chérie. What is your point finally?"

No answer. She simply sat on the edge of the spare bed and strapped on one stiletto, then the other. She crossed her legs and snapped her fingers, indicating to him to fetch her drink. He did. Men weren't simply pigs they were sluts in their own right, and proud of the designation.

She smoothed out the material in the box and leaned forward, slowly removing the shimmering silver and gold tube dress with a deep cowl front. From his perspective she seemed much taller and her breasts, although not large, seemed fuller and very firm. She pulled the micro-fibre material over her head and down, hearing Jean-François moan as her breasts and the barely white V highlighting the soft folds of her lips finally and teasingly disappeared from view.

"You're such a baby." She brought the hem of her dress to her hips. "I'm not finished." She reached into the box for the smallest possible pair of panties he could have imagined. "I can't decide, babe, these or these?" She reached over for another pair, holding up the two alternatives: one sheer, one not, both matching her dress. Jean-François quickly grabbed the requisite item and discarded the other that somehow seemed too big, even though they were identical. "Thank you, darling. Now I know why you've come into my life."

The silver and gold thongs were sheer and matched the dress perfectly, barely meeting the minimum values of propriety. If her pulse wasn't racing, his was, but women being women that wouldn't matter. Once they were dressed they would stay dressed.

His heart was palpitating as she sat there coolly and crossed-legged, watching the anti-climax of him getting dressed. If he had forgotten any accessory she would be to blame, no doubt about that. All he wanted was for the meal, the cruise, and the dancing to be over so they could be where they were right then, together with her the way he knew she wanted to be with him.

*

The private charter yacht accommodated eighteen dinner guests and an equal number of crew members. Most everyone onboard had the same idea, which was either to escape those who had befriended them out of fear of spending a week or two alone with the person they had come with or to have a change from the seemingly choreographed nightly ritual of the Haves and Have-nots.

The vivid white and pale grey contours of the moon shone brightly against a black backdrop flickering with millions of distant and silvery specks. The beam widened, carpeting the calm sea and bathing the yacht's main deck with a soft white incandescent glow that was the perfect romantic accompaniment to the twisted strings of dim lights decorating the decks and handrails of the ship. The dining was intimate, tables were arranged so that quiet prevailed and the service was discreet. The waiter serving them barely spoke a word. He asked el señor to approve the choice of wine, half-filled the two glasses and left.

Jean-François spoke of his villa in Spain: the one he dreamt of having one day, the one he would share with her, where they would never tire of watching the fiery sun sink into the blue of the Mediterranean. A dream that now would never seem real without her. She reached over and gently pressed a finger to his lips. Their time together was too near the end for them to speak of fantasies and dreams. They held hands or danced between courses, when their feelings took the place of words and nothing else seemed to matter. The meal was exotic and succulent, the wine perfectly chilled and superb, and dessert was graciously acknowledged and firmly declined. Easy-listening Latin music played softly from a dozen hidden speakers and the forward deck was abandoned and waiting for them.

She wore her hair loosely and had not combed or dried it to achieve the desired look. Her dress was the main attraction for the other women and main distraction for the other men. She was beautiful and sexy, self-assured and confident, then not, becoming suddenly unhappy and squeezing him hard before taking him by the hand to lead him from where they had been moving slowly in tight small circles to the soft melancholic cries of a faceless Latin girl who was pleading with her lover not to leave her for another.

"Why did you tell me that?"

"Tell you what, chérie?"

"About her," she buried her head into his chest, "losing her lover. Why don't men ever think before they talk?"

He saw the conversation turning into one best had between two women. "You asked me, chérie. They are but words, a simple song. She got paid for singing it, also." His smile had little or no effect. The mood had changed from romantic to pensive. He took her hand.

The bench followed the full contour to the ship's bow and was cushioned for comfort. Jean-François removed his jacket. He threw it down before he sat, indicating for her to sit to one side so she could lean into his arms. She did the opposite. She swirled his jacket over her shoulders and leaned against the vertical cushions, raising one leg at a time over his.

"I didn't wear this for those old married fogies to gawk at." She paused, considering the hem of her dress that had ridden nicely, making her bare legs seem endlessly long. "Something about my legs you don't like, monsieur? Would you prefer I turn away from you?"

"I adore what I see. You know that I do. Do not play games with me, not at this late hour, my darling. We must now savour our time together, not waste our final hours with childish games. You know that I want you. You also know that I must leave you very soon." His eyes lingered over every square centimetre of her body, the silver and gold V meriting the most attention. "You were wrong, my darling Patricia, when you said what you did about how I feel. You were wrong. In fact, my darling, you were very wrong." He sighed plaintively for the effect. "When we slept together last night and you fell asleep in my arms, I did kiss you everywhere that my lips could travel across the moist warmth of your skin before whispering what you wanted so much to hear. You were sleeping so deeply and did not hear my words. I did whisper them more than to say them for fear I would wake you."

"Will you say those same words to me now?"

Her expression conveyed no particular message. She had simply asked the question and was waiting for any response.

"It is so easy for me to tell you how I feel. It is not so easy for you to believe me, perhaps" He paused. "Darling, my life is complicated at this point."

"When you told me you weren't married any longer, that you're divorced, were you telling me the truth?"

"Yes, I did tell you the truth, chérie. I may not tell you everything, but I will never lie to you."

The sun had set some hours earlier and his skin would not feel much more of it before Friday. The new ring had served its purpose. He slowly removed the plain gold band with a shrug, throwing it over his shoulders into the black sea.

"I'm seeing my own lawyer about the divorce as soon as I get home. I've made up my mind and I'm moving out. I can't be in the same house with him, not after these past nights with you. Tomorrow I'll get the front desk to move me to another room. How can I possibly sleep beside him after all this, even in separate beds?" He let her talk, unconsciously massaging the length of her legs. "Would you come to me then? Could I come to you?" There was no answer because he couldn't think of one that would sound sincere. "I'll never see it, will I?" His blank expression asked the question. "Your villa, I'll never see it and we'll never watch the sun set together."

"You speak of my dream, chérie. Dreams are so much

kinder than life. There is no pain in them, merely the perception of pain. Our pain is in living."

"To be with you, I would never feel pain again."

"Then our life together would be a dream."

"My life has already become a dream. Not even you can take that from me, not ever."

"At this juncture," he breathed in deeply, "my life is…"

"Complicated?"

"Not complicated, my darling. At this moment I would say my existence is more surreal."

"Isn't that like a dream?"

"No. It is what I, myself, have created and this is not the time for me to easily extricate myself from the tight grip that it has upon me."

She swung her legs out, straightened what there was of her dress to straighten and leaned into his arms, guiding his hand that lay across her to the top of her bare thigh. "What about my life?" The question was rhetorical. She stared at his hand and her bare legs. The old Pat Henderson would never have flaunted so much of her body in public and how easily had she adapted to being so "European" at the pool and on the beach. "These past three nights have been like another lifetime, another person's lifetime, not mine."

He pinched her chin.

"Do you not mean a lifetime in four nights, my darling? We have the evening before us, and I do believe the other lifetime was not yours. This one is yours, embrace it."

They had commandeered the bow of yacht with their aura. Passengers who were already ensconced around the aft lounge were happily enjoying their private spaces, others against the port and starboard rails. Pat squirmed against him, pulling his jacket closer to her. Neither one spoke another word until the soft impact of the yacht's fenders against the dock's nitrile rub rail stirred them.

He lowered his face to kiss her eyes open. Her face was wet. "We must now disembark chérie." She shook her head no, vehemently. "We must, Patricia." He stroked her face dry with his palms for the second time in one day, forcing himself to feel nothing. He squeezed her tightly while nodding an acknowledgment to the crew who thought they understood. They didn't.

"They'll all be able to talk together about their night together, about what they wore, what they dreamed about. I won't. I don't even have anything to remember you by."

"Yes, you do." It dawned on him she had not called him by any name all evening. "You will always remember me, chérie, as I will remember you."

"That's the nicest good-bye any girl could ever want." She tried to laugh. "I know this is good-bye. I'll never see you again. It's silly, I know, but knowing that scares me."

"When you look into yourself, as deeply as you can, you will know that I am there with you and you will never be afraid again."

"I've been afraid all evening."

"Of what, chérie? I am here with you."

"Of not seeing you after tonight, of not knowing what to say to you when you say good-bye to me and walk away, of being here alone. I can't do that."

"How can anyone know what is written in the future for them, chérie? The future is not for us to control. Our choices are to accept or to fear what lies before us. You must believe that you will never be afraid again. If I thought so, I would not leave you, not for any reason."

"But you are leaving."

He tugged at the side of his jacket she had let slip from her hip and reached into the pocket. She was completely encircled in his arms when he brought his hands together to open the slim and elongated felt box. There would be no more talking. That part of their romance had come to an end.

The eighteen-karat bracelet with delicate twin link chains held together two miniature gold rectangular wafers. On one were the words: Dreams are forever, chérie; and on the other, simply: Until.

She could barely see through the torrent of her tears. She turned, looking up at him, unable to speak through lips that were quivering uncontrollably.

He swept away the tears, cupping her face in his hands. "Until, chérie, until we can dream forever."

He said nothing more.

Sunday, 29 October
Out of Sight, Out of Mind

By the time she had finished kissing him his face was as wet as hers, literally a work of modernist art with lipstick and eye shadow as the medium. The taxi ride to the compound was quiet and Jean-François couldn't understand why the driver chuckled each time they exchanged glances through the rear view mirror. Perhaps, he thought, because each time he looked over to Pat she found yet another angle to better admire her new trinket.

The only words she spoke before falling asleep on him were: "I want you to love me as though you'll never see me again, never have me again."

She said nothing else for the remainder of their last evening together.

The previous night she had wanted him to do bad things. She had wanted wild abandon, unyielding heated passion and when he asked her mischievously what exactly he should do to make her hot and wild she answered that he'd been bad longer than she had. So why was he asking her? But he hadn't been bad, not that he could remember. He couldn't be, though he did concede secretly he would never be with her again. She was insatiable and quickly became anything but passive, moulding her body and his into whatever pose or attitude would sustain each new and bold technique she had never imagined. At one point her tears splashed onto him so freely that, as much as she tried, her hands couldn't wipe them away fast enough. Despite the distraction he didn't move. His hands were clenched firmly to her sides, not holding her in place but feeling her, his passion heightened by every one of her electric shock waves. They were joined tightly in love, even the briefest interlude excessively long. He thought of Celeste, Seraphina and Dalila for the first time since meeting her and wondered what Pat would think to discover he had been with three different whores less than a week earlier and that she had become the beneficiary of the those encounters.

That first night was a response to spontaneous lust, the second with Celeste he had planned. This, however he chose to define what happened between them, was something akin to passion or an interpretation of passion. Earlier in the day, trying to change his flight to facilitate getting away easily from Pat without the awkwardness neither one would manage well, had proven impossible and, in retrospect, probably for the best. Avoidance of any opportunity for unneeded attention was primordial.

As he readied himself to leave the room Pat was spread face-down across the wet bed. She hadn't budged when he suggested using the second bed for sleeping. She just lay there, silently, her face buried in the pillow until her sadness changed to the contentment that comes with deep sleep. He dressed and moved around the room as stealthily as he could. Her new clothes draped easily over one arm and her shoes dangled from a single hand. Her intimate items and bikinis fit easily into his pockets. What remained were a pair of panties, her silk robe, a pair of sandals and the outfit she had worn for their evening on the yacht. When he left, he did so with absolute quiet.

He was devoid of emotion when he casually walked into Henderson's room. There was no need for undue concern or haste. He arranged her clothes neatly in the closet and poured himself a generous brandy that he drank while he sat looking through Henderson's briefcase once more, satisfied he had already downloaded the more important files. He left it.

Now that Pat was intent on changing villas to avoid Henderson, as well as her seating assignment for dinner, he had much less reason to be concerned. If all went well for her she wouldn't realize her dead husband was missing until she boarded or disembarked the plane the following Saturday, at which time absolutely nothing would matter.

By the time he returned her pillow had fallen onto the floor and Pat had rolled onto her back with her legs parted so that he saw every part of her. He barely resisted hurling himself between them, struggling for long moments not to ruin all he had accomplished for the sake of a few fleeting moments which would later have no particular distinction from the rest of their evening together. He hoped he would never forget the way she looked at that very moment, bathed in diffused moonlight and exuding so much vulnerable innocence.

His suitcase was by the door. Nothing of his remained in the room and all that remained of hers were the robe, sandals and her panties. He poured a JW Black, moving quietly onto the balcony to savour the cleansing burning sensation on his tongue, the aroma, and to relish his final moments with her as he absorbed every small detail of her body. Naturally she would hate him, a sentiment she would probably replace in time with a feeling of resentment at having been used by him. She'd get over it. Maybe she would cherish the note, keeping the hate alive. Or maybe she would extinguish any memory of him. Possibly one day another lover would discover his words and hurt her for having kept the memory of him alive, possibly not. She loved him, or so she thought, confused by a whirlwind dalliance of explosive lust and intrigue. And maybe he loved her, maybe not. They had been each other's much needed release. They had not found each other, they had discovered themselves.

*

Chérie, my darling, so short a time has passed since we first met and too long since my last kiss upon your naked skin. What we shared during our few days together will be ours alone to remember, and forever cherish. JFL must be for you a fiction, as he must also be for me.

I was for you a dream and you, for me, a dream from which I awoke for you alone and for no other. For in those dreams I did love you, as I do now love you in life without the need to pretend.

Do not be angry with me, chérie. I beg of you and entreat you to forgive me. My reality as I watch you sleep is unreal, an aberration of what I once was and who I may yet become when I might once more breathe your sweet breath, caress the softness of your skin and kiss the warmth of your lips.

Until,
Tu cariño

*

He hung the No Moleste sign from the door handle so she would not be disturbed. She slept until noon, at least that's when she came out from the room wearing her tightly belted robe and carrying her sandals in one hand. He could see she was rubbing her bracelet with the other. She could have looked right at him and would never have seen him as he brought her in closer, following her through the Navigator Pros.

He had left her apartment key on the robe he had laid out on the other bed. The note he put into her hand when he kissed her one last time. He smiled, thinking she hadn't the slightest idea of what lay ahead of her. He could feel her uncertainty and her fear as her face moved in and out of his field of view. He also recognized a new resolve, a vital determination he hadn't seen before. He envied her new adventure. He knew she would never be afraid again, content he hadn't lied to her about that.

Good-bye, Patricia.

*

The overhead fans did nothing to cool the human cargo that seemed unperturbed at being crammed together in the open-air lounge and gate area of the Punta Cana airport. Everyone around him either looked rested and tanned after their island paradise vacation, or hung over. Regardless, within a day they would all look the same, feel the same and be ready for another vacation. Many of the younger women, and a few of the older ones, seemed to think they were still at the beach or the pool and had more of their thongs showing than not. So accustomed were they to strangers seeing their bare breasts, they apparently didn't mind how much they showed on the way home, until possibly sensitive parents or shocked friends would meet them at the airport.

Wellington wondered when and where his next vacation would be, and with whom. He judged the phone's battery would be good for the few precious minutes he would need, which was as long as he wanted the conversation to last. The obvious need to make the call had grown over the past few days and as much as he tried pushing the urgency from his mind he could not ignore the need. It wasn't that so much in his life had recently changed, more importantly he had begun envisioning his future and who would, or should, be part of that future.

He detested public phones, the close proximity of strangers during a personal conversation even more. However Henderson's phone served another purpose. He had no idea what he would say, he simply knew he would be non-committal and resolute.

"Oui?"

"C'est moi, c'est Wellington."

"I was just on my way out to the Plateau for an early meal. I am so glad that I move more slowly on the weekends. Where are you? I wanted to call your home, hoping you would be there, until I remembered my promise about giving you space. Are you still in the States? Can we finish the weekend together? We can order in your favourite."

"No, we can't. I am in South Beach." He hesitated, even though he knew what he'd be saying and gave Gi-Gi no chance to cut in. "I'll be home by mid-week. The Chinese can wait until then, which is the reason I'm calling. I've done a lot of thinking over the past week. Getting away from what I could no longer see or appreciate allowed me to refocus and understand what I let slip away. Recently we haven't enjoyed the quality time we need, which is my fault, I know...I know. What I propose is for you to take the week off and I'll come directly to you when I arrive on Wednesday. We can talk like we used to. I'm ready now and I have so much to tell you."

"My goodness, you're talking so very quickly. Yes, yes, but not the week, I cannot. I will arrange for Thursday and Friday and I will make reservations at the Bonne Entente for the four days. Now I must also find time to go shopping. My fall wardrobe is far too drab for such a special weekend. I am so happy. At first I was adamantly against your going. I suppose I was jealous. But now I am so happy you went, and that you are coming home. I have been afraid for you for the longest time, Trystan. I am no longer. Thank you."

"I'll see you Wednesday. I must go now."

"I will plan a special evening. All you need is to arrive safely for me. Je t'aime."

"Je le sais. À bientôt, Gi-Gi. The time will pass quickly. I'll be home before you know it."

The conversation had gone well, even though he had

taken longer and had used more words than he intended. He knew Gi-Gi loved him and he should have felt much better than he did for what he had said. But he felt strangely guilty as though he had cheated, had been cheating, and what surprised him most was the loneliness suddenly consuming him.

He had much to think about, yet he forced himself not to think. His physical and mental weariness had reached a high point, making him vulnerable to costly, casual blunders and the temptation to second-guess his well thought out and documented plan. He needed uninterrupted rest in his own bed and that would not happen before Tuesday night, or perhaps Wednesday.

*

The original venue for his meeting with Wiernknoff had changed from Atlanta, for the better. The location would have no impact on the final outcome, though far less complicated for him and less hurtful for Mrs. Wiernknoff.

He had known for some time that Wiernknoff's wife suffered from an illness that kept her confined to their home. What he didn't know was whether she was confined to her bed, a wheelchair or simply withdrawn from the mainstream due to a debilitating neurosis her despotic husband had likely nurtured over time.

How he might have included Mrs. Wiernknoff into the meeting had preoccupied Wellington for some time and he was very happy that she would now be excluded. The 3:50 departure would get him into Charlotte for a connecting flight that would land in Savannah at 10:40 Sunday evening, a lost day as far as further preparation for the meeting with Hans Wiernknoff was concerned. The preliminaries were complete. He had even called to confirm the meeting. Of course the meeting would go through. Phoning was a matter of courtesy, which he hadn't extended to Roberts or Henderson.

Hotel lobbies between midnight and six AM are lonely places. Even those designed to be warm and inviting exude no more than stark functionality and the Savannah Marriott River Front was no exception, particularly at one AM when he hadn't slept in more than forty-two hours.

He didn't set the alarm. Instead he opened the mini-bar. Morning would come soon enough, in its own time, and the day would begin with a list of strategically planned errands that would culminate with the Hans Wiernknoff dinner meeting.

Monday, 30 October
German Night

Monday began promptly at nine-thirty when he first realized the darkness that filled the room belied the hour. By 10:30 he was gone from the hotel, still wondering what he had eaten that was worth twenty-two dollars. The sky was painted with black and grey ominous clouds swirling and rolling one against the other and the resulting thunder was felt as much as heard. He waved away the doorman's apparently sincere gesture of protecting him with the umbrella he had not yet opened. He hated being wet. Anytime, anywhere, he hated being wet and the hotel's canvas overhang struggling against the wind's relentless onslaught from the doors to the curb did nothing to prevent his slacks, shoes and socks from becoming soaked. The wind carried the rain more like winter's cutting sleet against his exposed skin and any reminder of home was ill-timed. He was drenched through and his temperament was under review by his sense of rational thought and determination.

He had never seen Savannah in the rain, but this was more than a light early morning rain and would do nothing to make his visit more memorable, despite being a memory that need not last long. The driver looked back without seeing him, said good morning and turned into the traffic before hearing where they were going. Wellington was sufficiently familiar with the historic city to give the cabbie immediate and specific directions to the second address as clearly as any resident. The dry cleaner, less than a block from the hotel, was the first stop and the driver waited as a practical arrangement for both passenger and driver.

Before he left the hotel he had gathered all his tropical clothing, along with what remained of Henderson's eveningwear which he would drop off for a two-day service that would probably turn into several months before the store owner would eventually make a charitable donation to the men's mission. He wouldn't be conspicuous by wearing darker clothing at the end of October. While still warm, Savannah's autumn temperatures were moderate, more so than the oppressive summer heat that would cause most residents to remain indoors. The cooler climate also meant he could conveniently dispose of his larger suitcase which would factor greatly into his plans for the upcoming flight from Savannah to Montreal.

No one had to tell him they weren't in the best part of town, certainly nowhere for stray tourists to stroll by day or by night, especially by night, but that wasn't how Wellington was thinking of himself. His previous two meetings had changed him from the inside out. Roberts and Henderson had given him a revitalized sense of self, a new perspective and not one he was struggling with. He was good with it, with everything, merely accepting the new and improved Wellington as inherent and long overdue.

Abercorn Street was indifferently one-part historic, one-part slum and one-part commercial. Much of its length was lined on either side with gnarled and imposing centuries-old Live Oaks that never allowed sunlight to pass through the thick and overcharging Spanish moss-laden branches. The normally shaded and pleasantly cool main artery seemed cold and damp, the gloomy darkness casting a macabre and unfriendly aura particularly appropriate to the task at hand. He had located the hobby and sports store in the yellow pages that would best suit his needs and had called to confirm they stocked what he needed. The taxi pulled over and stopped where the division between slum and commercial was as questionable as it was problematic.

The gun was fashioned after the Walther PPK/S semiautomatic. As a specific action that would respond to a specific need, his specific need, he had only required a pellet gun this time. The thing certainly appeared real enough, the clerk jokingly assuring him the closer he would put it to anyone's nose the less conversation there would be about the fact the thing wasn't real: a single CO-2 cartridge would deliver all fifteen .177 rounds at eighty meters per second and the weight felt good in his hands. The need for extra cartridges and pellets brought no reaction from the clerk who chuckled when Wellington returned to the counter with the stuffed bear.

The third stop was an uptown men's store for a raincoat and hat. At first he debated whether or not to wear something that might make him stand out, as much as conceal him. As it turned out, the rain was a blessing. The final stop was an office supply store for a computer case, a second box of CDs, a utility knife, vinyl gloves, a box of opaque plastic bags, one roll of wide adhesive tape and one roll of narrow tape. He paid the fare with a tip that wasn't generous, but one he felt obliged to leave and the cabbie took the bills without counting them. When he climbed out, he left Henderson's shoes behind the driver's seat.

By two thirty he had fired off more than a hundred rounds into the tattered bear that was now blind in both eyes and he was sitting in the deserted hotel restaurant neglecting a glass of Chardonnay. Waiting for his lunch, he read through and downloaded the last of the confidential data from John Roberts' laptop onto a growing pile of discs.

His supposed rendezvous wasn't until 7:00, though he had promised Wiernknoff details pertinent to the dinner meeting with Henderson would be delivered by courier to his hotel no later than five PM. He was the courier, which gave him thirty minutes and a bit, not much time to enjoy another glass of wine, finish his work and finish off the bear.

*

Four-thirty was the perfect time for Wellington to walk from the Marriott River Front to the Hyatt Regency where Wiernknoff was staying for the other meeting that had called the German away from Atlanta. The late afternoon had turned brighter and windless. The rain had abated, leaving a disagreeably dank air to permeate the entire historic area, though cool enough so that his coat and hat did not attract attention from the few tourists and locals he passed along the kilometer-long walk along Bay Street.

His pretext for the meeting was a proposal of mutual advantage, revolving around the cross-border issue which was currently uppermost on the agendas of all pharmaceutical firms, irrespective of what side of the border they were on or the products they produced. American firms felt they were being deprived of the ability to bilk the sick and elderly by an additional six to eight-hundred dollars a year in inflated drug costs, a 30 percent loss to their coffers. Canadians were equally upset that, despite the US House of Representatives having already passed legislation legalizing the use of cross-border drugs, the FDA continued confiscating those drugs.

A division of IntelSanté, newly headed by Jason Bartlett, was about to launch another initiative that would virtually guarantee exclusive control of the mail order and Internet markets. However, Henderson had inside information that both Circadian and Integra could use in a combined effort against the fast growing IntelSanté if, indeed, he and Wiernknoff could arrive at an agreement.

The hotel was a low-rise, full service hotel, but for Wellington low-rise meant fewer rooms and more attention, which, in his case, was not good. No one paid much attention as he went through the main doors at a pace conveying confidence more than self-importance, carrying himself in a manner that left no doubt he was a man who signed off on his own expenses. He fit perfectly with the rest of the clientele: those who dictate rather than explain.

The hour was too early for dinner and the restaurant was empty. The bar area and atrium were filled to capacity with the hopeful, the pursued and the politely refused. Those who wanted to smoke couldn't and they were the ones who drank more, the most disappointed in their plans for the perfect evening. The bell captain was casually preoccupied with the standard and trivial worries of late departures claiming their luggage, optional restaurant choices and weather. The reception counter was assigning one room at a time with an unhurried efficiency exuding a blend of southern charm and northern aloofness.

The lobby was a haughty crisscross pedestrian highway of showy elegance and Wellington revealed not the slightest interest in the many women who allowed an obvious and alluring second glance at the tall and tanned gentleman in the olive-coloured trench coat and fedora. Perhaps later he would entertain the idea of some company, after business, not now. Work hard, play hard. Those were the rules. They always had been. He could play later if he cared to, but he doubted very much he would. He already had and, he thought, possibly a little too much.

He hated cell phones, everyone did, but they never said so. They were cowards, all of them, all those supplicating freaks in a world that would never be better because of them. Why was he the only one who said so, or thought so? No one had balls. That's why. Yes, sir, yes, ma'am. I'll be connected 24/7 and the tumor in my ear be damned because your annual sales are more important than my health. What was that? I can't hear you because of my tumor. Fuck you! Fuck you all. Hear that, fuckers, and dad, my precious daddy?

He studied the beige lobby phones closely, taking his time, selecting the one he thought was the cleanest and the least used. He gripped the receiver lightly, trying not to breathe in the sickly smell or coat his hand with the stickiness of sanitizing agents used to mask the inevitable hybrid aroma whose origin was the mélange of so many preceding secret whispers, inflated boasts and exasperated coughs constantly supplying the moisture required for the receptor to cultivate its invisible crop.

Wellington was careful to avoid contacting the receiver even remotely with his lips. Try as they might, even the best hotels could not keep up with his standards, or, better said, with the personal habits of most others. At the very moment he was connected with the hotel operator he held the receiver away from his ear, ignoring the receptionist who sounded more huffy than impatient at having to wait for his response.

She was waltzing through the lobby as though God had intended for all to see her and admire her. Judging by the looks she was getting from the men standing behind her, he concluded that what he couldn't see was as perfectly formed as what he was seeing from the front. How much could he teach her in one night, he wondered? How much could any man teach her in one night, or learn? How many had tried?

She had come in from the outside without a coat or umbrella, wearing a very short bra top dress that flared out at the hem and danced around her thighs. She exuded a definite air of "better have money." She enjoyed being seen. She enjoyed men appraising her, and he wondered whether seeing more was strictly pay-per-view, irrespective of which, he wanted to see. He would see.

Wiernknoff answered within moments of the hotel operator transferring the call. "Good afternoon, sir. I'm an associate of Mr. Henderson. I have a package he asked me to deliver before five o'clock. I believe you're expecting me."

She came right up to him before stopping, searching her purse for a quarter and unhooking the receiver of the phone next to his. Her dress could not have been shorter and teased upwards even more when she reached for the phone. He considered delaying his meeting a few moments longer, just to watch her sit and cross her legs.

"Yes, indeed. Thank you," he said distractedly into the phone.

He smiled at her as he replaced the receiver and she smiled. She wasn't on the house phone. She had an outside line and for some reason he thought that was good. She dialled a number, but she wasn't saying anything and he wondered whether she would. Maybe she had dialled a wrong number, a voice-mail or no number. Or had she merely been dialling his number?

He decided if she were still in the lobby when he completed his meeting with the German, he would invite her to dinner and spend the night with her. She would be a welcome release from the tension about to invade him. Stooping for the computer case resting on the floor between them he allowed himself a closer inspection of her legs and she seemed not to mind. He glanced at his watch, then at her with a smile before turning towards the elevator, paying no attention to the exiting horde before climbing alone with irritating slowness to the seventh floor.

He knew the room number. The thickly carpeted hallway was deserted and the noise of the zipper sliding along the top of his case annoyed him for no reason. He pulled on the gloves without slowing his pace, closed one zipper and opened another. There was no question that he didn't look like a messenger, but then he didn't intend allowing Wiernknoff much time to think about it. A steady hand gripped the fake gun still completely hidden in the side pocket of the foam-lined case. He hadn't missed the bear more than a few times and was both surprised and proud of his achievement and accuracy.

The other hand knocked twice on the door. Wiernknoff stood a head shorter than Wellington and was older, a year or two away from retirement. They had never met, though Wellington had attended several meetings chaired by the old man. He was not a mingler and had never stayed after meetings to socialize, at least not with anyone less than a VP. He was poorly regarded by most and truly feared by those who had climbed the corporate ladder, made instantly vulnerable by their own successes.

He wore a dark blue suit with a white shirt and red tie. He wore them like a uniform; the only one Wellington had ever seen him wear. He was fit enough for an age that his face gave away, lined with deep fissures and too white for the solid black hair he wore in a brush cut. He spoke with the unrefined gruffness of his race that was all the more pronounced amidst the soft-spoken southern ambiance that surrounded him daily. He studied the case, then Wellington who remained expressionless. The unspoken question was obvious.

"I am an associate of Mr. Henderson. He asked that I personally deliver his package to you, rather than through a service."

"This is the package?" Wiernknoff extended a hand. "Give it to me."

"Not quite. The files are inside. May I step inside for a moment?"

"No, you may not. Simply give me what you have and leave. Henderson is expected shortly and I am already left with very little time to review the information."

His hand remained extended, even as Wellington swept out the gun, pushing the barrel against Wiernknoff's nose with more force than he intended. The suddenness of the impact drove the old man backwards involuntarily. His mind was racing in a futile attempt to rationalize what was happening. Henderson had called him personally, telling him to expect a delivery. The man in front of him was well-dressed and certainly no common thief. Whether as a result of the expectation of reasonable security at the hotel, or a naïve disbelief that such an event could happen to him, his verbal response was automatic, as though talking to a member of the hotel staff or his own.

"What is this stupidity? What is it you think you are doing?" He reached for the phone. "Leave, now!" he bellowed. He was furious. "You'll be fortunate to avoid security before you reach the street. Go, now."

"Don't touch the phone, Hans, and I'm not leaving." Wellington levelled the gun. "Please, do not do that. What I've come for won't take long and it's not about thinking. It's about doing."

Wiernknoff took his hand away from the phone and stared at the gun. His eyes squinted and he leaned slightly forward. Then he began laughing loudly.

"This is a joke, a very stupid joke, just like this gun you are holding like such a brave man." He leaned against the inadequate work station littered with his own papers and crossed his arms.

"Not exactly the reaction I was planning on, Hans."

"Who are you? Who are you doing this stupid thing for?" He pointed at the gun. "This thing is a toy, an imitation. Mr. Henderson, or whoever he is, did not take the time to find out I am an owner of several handguns, a member of the NRA and a gun club in Atlanta. This pea shooter you are waving at me is good for nothing."

Wellington returned the smile. "That's very astute of

you. I suppose most men would have thrown me their wallets and promised not to tell anyone. I should probably feel stupid. Yet, for some reason, I don't."

"Go. Leave me and tell your friend Henderson to go with you."

"I can't do that. He died in a boating accident. However what I do need is for you to sit in that chair and relax."

Wiernknoff's body language spoke involuntary and silent volumes as clearly as though he had screamed them, as Wellington nonchalantly levelled the gun. The action caused his reluctant host to hesitate just long enough for the single .177 lead pellet to find its target, shattering the mirror over the desk. The discharge was silent, not the result. The second impact an instant later is what shocked both men at once. The German's entire body reacted instantly to the invasive projectile jerking him violently upwards and against the period-styled desk, his own hands muffling his scream. Wellington's brow furrowed and his eyebrows arched as he tried concealing his amazement at the effectiveness of the pellet gun.

"You're right about this being a pea shooter, but when the pea is lead and travels at eighty metres per second, well, that must hurt like a bitch. Was that a tooth I heard?" he chortled.

Wiernknoff's cheek was swelling, turning an ugly purple from the epicentre of the attack outward and blood was flowing from inside his mouth through trembling lips. The entry wound had self-sealed with the swelling. When he tried speaking a yellow and red tooth spilled out onto his chest, splattering his white shirt and hands with rose-coloured spittle that sprayed out with the decayed premolar. He stared at the abstract canvas wordlessly and afraid, as though seeing an ancient artifact.

"The gentleman who sold me this toy said it worked very well by holding it at an upward angle just under the nose. So please sit. I don't have much time. There's a very beautiful lady with legs to die for who's waiting for me to join her in the lobby. She's anxious for a romantic dinner, so you can imagine I don't want to disappoint her."

"You cannot kill me with this silly thing you are pointing so bravely. What is it you want? Money, information?"

"I suppose what I want is job satisfaction. You're not sitting." He waved with the gun. "This thing has thirteen more shots, but then you must already know that. Spit it out." There was no response. "The pellet, I need it. Spit it out."

Wiernknoff tried hard to make his grimace seem like a grin or a defiant smirk as his tongue searched for the lead ball. His eyes told Wellington he'd found it, and he held out a gloved hand. Wiernknoff inhaled deeply through his nose, closed his eyes and swallowed hard.

"No, no, no. That's not what I wanted you to do. Now they'll know, goddamnit, once they dissect you."

The silence was pervasive. Wellington heard nothing beyond Wiernknoff's frequent swallowing in an attempt to keep his mouth free of blood. Wellington waved the gun again and shrugged, indicating he wanted Wiernknoff to sit. And Wiernknoff did, wisely not flinching as Wellington moved behind him with the gun in one hand and the computer case in the other. He reached around with the roll of duct tape, the starter tab pulled back, telling Wiernknoff to hold the tab while he pulled at the roll. After the first complete wrap Wellington put down the gun and continued wrapping Wiernknoff's torso several times. With that done he bound the German's ankles and sat on the bed.

"I was your North Eastern rep until eight years ago, when you fired me, if you care. You want to know why I'm here. That's why. I want to know why you fired me."

"I have no idea why. Until now I have never seen you before, so how would you expect me to remember one person being sent home?"

"I can't believe you said that."

The German grunted. "Believe it, whoever you are. You would probably prefer that I say something to make you feel better, to placate you? I send dozens of workers home each year, for just as many reasons."

"And my reason," Wellington persisted with a smile.

"Would you possibly expect me to remember, let alone care? You should be satisfied your superiors had sufficient reason at the time. If you were sent home, there was a reason. If you did not ask at the time, why should you ask now?"

"You're not putting much effort into this for me, Hans."

"Your dismissal happened years ago and not without reason. Is that what this is all about, getting your little revenge by embarrassing me, knocking out a dead tooth? Extortion I would say. Is that what you are doing?"

"You might say something like that, though I doubt you'll have to worry much about being embarrassed."

"This little game you are playing will change nothing. What do you hope to achieve?"

"I've already told you: satisfaction."

"This will turn out badly for you."

"Yes, I know, and for you. Actually you should be grateful for this meeting."

Wiernknoff showed no curiosity watching Wellington reach under his trench coat, pull the silk pocket hanky from his suit jacket and stuff it into Wiernknoff's half-open mouth that hadn't stopped dripping blood.

"Grateful for what, you ask?"

Wiernknoff remained stoic, believing Wellington would have his fun by humiliating him and leave, keeping him bound to the chair for the housekeeping to find him in the morning. He barely twitched when the green opaque plastic bag went over his head.

"Grateful I was thoughtful enough not to kill you in front of your wife. Until recently I was very concerned about involving her, believe me or not. When I discovered you'd be in Savannah and not Atlanta, I was very pleased knowing I wouldn't have to kill her."

The two top corners of the inverted bag were pinched together, held in place with two-centimetre duct tape. The wider five centimetre tape went over where the silk-filled mouth would be and continued tightly around the head.

"It's too late, Hans, but you haven't even asked my name, or how I made out. Wellington Bartlett, at your service." He smiled. "I suppose that would be room service."

The solitary reaction came when the taped body went rigid as a length of the narrow tape was finally wrapped tightly around the neck, effectively blocking any available new air. Wellington continued with his work, ignoring the sound of the bag responding to his ex-boss' shallow breathing. He was convulsing less than Wellington had imagined and the jerking wasn't what bothered him as much as the intermittent, muffled sucking sounds lending an eerie rhythm to the German's breathing. Wiernknoff was extending his life mere seconds by conserving his breath. More power to him, but that was tantamount to holding one's breath in a gas chamber. An eventual deep breath was inevitable and the blackness existing inside the bag would be forever.

He felt as though he wanted to speed the process and shoot, strangle or beat the German to death. The gun was a fake; he had no idea where or how to apply lethal pressure and cutting his throat was simply out of the question for aesthetic reasons as much as for humanity. Inherently, he was not a violent man, though perhaps he had become somewhat vindictive, he allowed.

Wellington checked to see that Henderson's meeting had been logged into Wiernknoff's agenda and computer, pleased to see the notation. He also saw the next scheduled meeting was a luncheon at 12:30, about the time Wellington would board a Northwest flight in Atlanta. There was a good possibility the body would not be discovered until early or mid-afternoon, by which time Wellington would board a Detroit to Montreal flight that would get him home by seven. He had no time to begin the process of downloading or reading data that would be useful to the final stage of his plan. He thought of going to the lobby for a few minutes to see whether the woman had decided to wait for him, but he couldn't trust Wiernknoff to stay still and decided he would wait. If she had waited the fifteen minutes another five or ten wouldn't make a difference.

Wellington was impressed. Wiernknoff was living up to his stolid and thoroughly despicable persona. His breaths were being measured, slowly converting the precious little oxygen that remained inside the bag to carbon dioxide that would send him to a peaceful, sleep-like death. Wellington wondered whether his eyes were open behind the green plastic veil. His hands were positioned palms down against his thighs and were still. The thinnest trickle of crimson red began seeping through from under the bag and under the collar of his white shirt. The blood was darker than his previous spittle, though the stain would likely not spread far. How much longer would Wiernknoff make him wait, he wondered? He had already been patient for twenty minutes, and how much longer would she wait patiently?

The head began wobbling ever so slightly, showing Wiernknoff was in the final stages of his life and probably thinking about Mrs. Wiernknoff, their children, past vacations, sex with his secretary or anything else that would take his mind off the threshold he was passing through. The bag fell forward with a subsequent effort that was too weak to raise it back up. The worst was over. There would be no more fear, no more pain, merely a peaceful and well-deserved transition.

Wellington was free to move about the room without disturbing Wiernknoff's concentration. He had gone out bravely, defiantly, and as much as Wellington wanted them all to suffer, he did admit to a certain newfound respect for the old German. He wondered whether would be as brave during his own final moments.

His part of the meeting had all but concluded. The hotel operator would certainly be able to tell the authorities about the 4:55 P.M. call from the lobby and the five-minute call originating from Henderson's cell phone at 5:25 confirming the conversation had been logged on both phones a few days earlier. He started easing off the two rings that had become undersized for their meaty fingers over the years and stopped, though he did remove the several hundred dollars in cash from the German's wallet by the computer. The bag had not come away from Wiernknoff's head as easily as the tape that bound his torso and ankles. Those had come away without difficulty, but removing the duct tape from around the mouth and neck caused the limp head to pivot and flop in every possible direction as the plastic was stretched and pulled out of shape.

His eyes had not been closed in prayer or desperate hope. They were wide open and glaring accusations at their unseen killer. The silk pocket hanky had not absorbed the blood at all, seeming more like an expensive tie-dye square of sticky red on blue which Wellington managed to place in his bag without spilling a drop. Not that he cared. He wasn't sure whether the thud came first, though the eerie cracking sound was what made him turn. Wiernknoff had been positioned too far forward and now he lay crumpled on the floor with his head at a peculiar angle that allowed him one last exchange with Wellington who studied him indifferently.

He added the computer and cell phone to everything he had brought with him, accounting for each item before returning them to his own case, checked and double checked. He draped his computer case over a shoulder, twisted the Do Not Disturb sign from the door handle and closed the door behind him, leaving Wiernknoff awkwardly alone and at peace.

*

She hadn't gone. Good. She was sitting in one of the several plain and genderless fabric-covered love seats scattered around the lobby. She faced the bar with a half-full glass of red wine in front of her on a low-rise marble coffee table. She was coquettishly ignoring the attention she was attracting from the men standing closest to the bar's lobby entrance and, following their lines of vision, Wellington could see what interested them most. The laced edges of her clear stay-ups were an open invitation to all but the legally blind. The more attractive ladies in the bar paid her no attention and the less attractive ones were doubtlessly anxious for her to leave, and maybe she would, with him.

What would he say to her? What would she say to him? That was more critical to the evening ahead. He had never been very comfortable approaching women, especially very attractive ones, though as he walked towards her he reinforced his thinking with his successes of the past week. True, three of the four had been paid for in advance for services rendered, but they counted nevertheless, he thought. They had all been money well-spent. He wanted to take a deep breath, deciding not to at the last second. She would see him and he wanted to appear nonchalant and self-assured.

She smiled up at him as she reached forward for her glass.

Gentlemen first: "Good evening. My name is Bill Henderson and I would be the luckiest man in Savannah if you would allow me to join you, if only for a moment."

"I'm waiting for someone. Thank you for asking."

"I apologize for bothering you. But I'm happy that I did." He smiled and bowed his head slightly.

"However," she continued, as he turned away, "it seems as though she has forgotten me."

When he halted, their eyes connecting, he was gleaming. She was patting the empty cushion beside her as she repositioned herself. Life was good.

"Please sit, Mr. Henderson."

"Bill."

Wellington grinned at seeing the expressions of the winners and losers he had designated as their money changed hands at the bar; the waiter also acknowledging his newest success, signalling that he would be with them momentarily. Her accent was southern, with unidentifiable trace accents that come from travel and not unabashedly consuming her body was surprisingly easy. He knew now that by evening's end he'd be seeing and feeling much more of her.

"Felicity." She held out her hand.

"A very charming name for a very charming lady. I was disappointed my dinner appointment fell through, though fate seems to have intervened to my advantage and my very great delight."

"Do you believe in fate, Bill?"

"I believe we all have a final one."

He took up his glass after the waiter set it down, touching the rim against hers.

"Then, to fate, though not a final one."

The two glasses clinked.

She worked as private secretary to the General Manager of the Georgia Port Authority and her accent had indeed been affected by travel and interaction with visitors and clients from around the world. She hated cars and lived in the historic quarter for the easy access it allowed to her office. She came to the Hyatt on Mondays for Happy Hour because everyone else at the port went there on Thursdays or Fridays and she liked to escape shop talk.

He wanted her alone in some quiet place without the congratulatory or envious glances of the other male predators, or the obvious side glances of jealous women or their leashed husbands. Her favourite was seafood. They were in Savannah, the second largest port on the east coast. Seafood was everyone's favourite and she knew one of the best places. By the time they arrived at the restaurant his arm was already comfortably attached to the far side of her waist and one question had been answered. They were neither sensible, nor made of cotton.

She wore low-heeled pumps and that surprised him. He thought she would have worn higher heels to enhance her perfect legs, and he said so in the form of a question. A woman would not have enquired, though for a man the equation normally taken for granted was simple: the shorter the skirt, the higher the heels, which was not so for women and she pointed at the cobble stone street: one of many that had been laid two centuries earlier by black slaves. The cargo being transported from Europe and Africa at the time would often be too light to use as ballast and the cargo holds of the wooden ships would be filled with cobble stones for that purpose. Arriving in the States the ships' holds would then be emptied of the lighter cargo and the extra ballast off-loaded, replaced with heavier payloads such as minerals.

The supply of stones was endless, and the solution was using them to build durable roadways and streets, though the few that remained were in the historic quarter helping preserve a small part of history, a partial semblance of how daily life once was, when longer skirts and dresses would conceal the damaged heels and toes of a lady's slippers.

She had expected he would stop and stare at the huge thing. They all did when seeing one for the first time. How many times had she overheard ego-driven male tourists telling impressionable female companions what they were and what they carried? Of course, they were all wrong, all the time, but the women would never know, nor would they ever care that the information was inaccurate. The vessel was a Ro-Ro, she explained, one of the largest ships afloat for the transport of all manner of rolling stock. The term was short for Roll-on-Roll off and everyone watching the massive hull glide by them towards a designated berth wondered how the floatation of such an impossibly huge ship was remotely possible.

The restaurant was less than a quarter full; they commandeered one of two window booths. He wanted to sit beside her, taking the side that gave him the view he enjoyed most, barely noticing the busy pedestrian traffic. He put the computer case under the table as he always did when in airports, placing a foot inside the shoulder strap as a memory aid and prevention against any other kind of unfortunate loss.

She lived alone. She had a cat and refused all alimony payments as long as he promised to stay away. At thirty-five she didn't have many friends. The few girlfriends she did have were married and either envious or matchmakers. She had no one serious in her life. Actually, she had no man, period. Her job demanded too much of her time.

He had once worked in pharmaceuticals, a career he had given up to become an independent contractor, which had been the best decision of his life. He was making a killing. He was divorced with no woman in his life because he wouldn't make the same mistake twice. Next time he'd be sure, and besides, he was beginning to particularly appreciate life in the South and everything the South had to offer. He kissed her hand, appreciating the bare skin peeking out between her dress and the lace of her nylons. They would definitely be sleeping together tonight, but where? Would she invite a stranger to her home, or could he get her to reserve a room at one of the hotels that was not his or Wiernknoff's? She crossed her legs, not adjusting the bottom of her dress. Why wear lace to hide it? She didn't, the distraction increasingly painful to ignore, though he knew as much as he could about the obviously expensive lingerie under the dress.

Dinner had become a ruse for him, a delay, and he wanted badly for her to intuit what he was thinking. Time would tell; each course brought by the waiter an inconvenience eclipsing a gastronomic experience. He wanted her badly. As the evening progressed he looked at her more closely, measuring her words and her expressions, gauging her reactions to his.

Should he say the words, admit he wanted her naked in bed with him, that he wanted to make love with her, to have sex with her. He imagined pulling the dress over her head. He saw her standing before him in her pumps and nylons, tempting him in the tiniest pull-away panties possible that he would push past her hips before eagerly cupping her perfect bare breasts, taunting him. He hadn't heard, brought back to real time by her hand waving in front of his face.

"I'm sorry. I was in another place, another time," he smiled.

She smiled. She probably knew, he thought. "Am I that boring? No wonder I don't have a man in my life."

"I was there," he paused, "with you. I can't apologize for being there, though I suppose I should for what I was thinking."

"And where exactly is there, and what exactly were you thinking, sir?" She grinned, widely. "I do declare, sir. I believe you are giving me cause to blush."

"I believe so. I also believe that particular hint of colour would suit you."

The waiter came with the check at last. Wellington gave the chit a cursory glance, reaching into his pocket for the clip. He pulled away the first two bills that he knew were hundreds without looking, tucking them into the leather folder.

"Thank you, Bill. That was excellent. I truly enjoyed the evening."

"Enjoyed? Past tense?"

"Only if you have work to do and can't join me at home for a nightcap."

"At your place, truly?"

"Yes, my place, Bill. We're in Savannah, not in a remake of Gone with the Wind."

"I have an early flight. I wish I didn't." He didn't.

"I have an early ship, so what?" she answered, sliding out from the booth and he offered no more pretence.

"Then, dear Felicity, may I have the pleasure of escorting you home?"

"Sir, you are excessively forward."

They hurried.

Tuesday, 31 October
Say What You Mean

The fourth-floor apartment had once been a warehouse, long ago used for storing or hiding everything legal and illegal from salt, liquor, guns and broken young black men stolen from faraway homes to inherit the horrible misfortune of surviving the ordeal.

The building had no elevator. The stairway was dark, lit by a single skylight and surprisingly fresh, he thought. The steep oak steps were well-worn from centuries of use. They creaked loudly under his weight and Wellington was certain that heavier loads would make them move under foot. More importantly, his attention was focused on the hem of her dress swaying barely above eye-level, allowing him a teasing preview of the firm curves of her buttocks that were mostly bare and so close. He'd been wrong about the panties.

The first thing she said as he followed her through the door to her apartment was "don't tell me you love me. Tell me I'm good," she said, "because that won't be a lie. I am good, but don't say anything because you're caught up in the moment when a grunt or two will do equally well. Understood?" Yes, he did, and the deal was done.

Once the door closed behind them she casually tugged at the zipper at the back of her dress. She let it fall, kicking it aside. He had, indeed, been wrong about her panties, not that he cared. They were crossed-dyed, scalloped cream-coloured boy shorts she was pushing down as she walked away from him, telling him to find a wine he liked and two glasses. He was anxious to see more, chiding himself for his juvenile excitement.

Like most southern women, her skin was creamy white without the slightest trace of a tan. Her nipples were pink and proportionate to her breasts which he decided were 34s and in their original condition. She certainly lacked the overall firmness and tone of Celeste's more professional body, but her abdomen was flat and everything else was feminine and appealing in the extreme.

The apartment was completely refurbished and the cat was nowhere in sight. She had renovated the condo from top to bottom creating a modern and private place overlooking the harbour and River Street, an atelier loft lined with brightly painted pipes and drains replacing rusted and leaking predecessors from centuries or decades past. The furnishings in each room were eclectically feminine and the paintings and photographs on the walls were artistically sensual or sexually arousing, which did nothing to diminish his mounting craving for her. He made a note to ask her whether the woman who had stood her up would have been invited back.

Dusk had long since darkened into late evening blackness and the panoramic view through her undraped windows was an imposing silver disk filling the screen-like grid work of wrought iron and glass, inching its way across a curtain of distant flickering galaxies. The living tableau was magnificent to distraction and for a moment as fleeting as the flickering of each distant star, and for reasons unknown to him, he drifted into a future that would not belong to him.

The early morning sun that would wake her was hours away, he thought, as he uncorked the wine. He'd be gone by then and neither one would think much more about the other. Live for the day, and vive la différence. Felicity was too new to him to think of her as an enigma. She was a moment in time, but he had been right to make the first move. He followed the sound of running water to her bathroom with two high-stemmed glasses in-hand where he found her leaning over the tub, adjusting the flow from two separated and ornate period brass faucets. She had not removed her nylons or her shoes and cared not at all that he stood behind her, watching, his breathing telling her all she needed to know.

The pure white tub was Victorian and stood on a ceramic-tiled pedestal that served as a step. She smiled inwardly as she raised a foot onto the pedestal, causing her buttocks to extend backwards. The water pouring out was erratic and noisy, masking the hard clinking sound as he set the glasses on the matching pedestal sink. He positioned himself behind her, cupping an inviting cheek slightly more raised than its twin, letting his hand travel slowly between her legs to her front.

Being with her was like being with Celeste all over again and he wondered whether she would place restrictions on him. Why would any man divorce such a woman? Or had she divorced whoever he was: possibly a cheat, probably a loser. If Geneviève had ever moved like that, had she ever responded the way Felicity was responding, he'd still be married to the bitch, Gi-Gi would never have happened and possibly his current agenda would be much different.

He reached with his free hand, fondling a breast that was warm and firm, pointing downward and telling him she was ready. Neither one could wait. She hadn't moved from the position he had found her in and he didn't want to deprive his hands of their respective sensations. The plush towels she had laid out over the nearby wicker chair each had a gold-coloured foil square at its centre, but he waited a few minutes before reaching to open one. When he did, he did so quickly, knowing Felicity was feeling the exhaustion of pleasure and the excitement of anticipation.

"Hurry," she said, "there's no expiry date that I could see but they weren't bought yesterday."

"I'm glad," and part of him was.

"I'm not."

The point was well taken.

"I hope you have more than two."

"Yes, I do, and I plan to use them all unless you disappoint me," she answered easily, not moving. "Don't think we're staying in here all night. A girl has to go to bed sometime and I hope your day wasn't too tiring."

"No, it wasn't, but somehow I believe my night will be and don't worry about being disappointed."

"Do you always talk this much before you fuck a woman?"

No, he didn't, or maybe he did, and the next sound she made was a guttural and deep groan which came as a shock even to her, the joints of her fingers aching when she finally released their tight grip from the curved porcelain edge of the tub. She was exhausted, out of breath, throbbing nicely and when he pulled away from her she toppled lazily into the tub. The hot water rose to her shoulders, the soothing affect immediate where she most needed relief. The night would be long, she thought, she hoped, completely submerging herself, hoping he was up to her challenge with more to give her than false bravado. The last time was so long ago, too long ago to remember and she was ready for everything he had to give her.

He had been too busy to remove his clothing. In fact, he had had no chance at all. Not losing the moment seemed more important at the time and still did. Whether he was spurred by his eagerness for more of her or the thought of his pending embarrassment should she surface to see him standing like a primed and horny teenager at a peep show, he rushed to join her. That second set of waves attacked her just as she surfaced, glistening from the perfumed oils in the water and coated in the scented foam she'd been building when he had come up behind her.

She grinned mischievously, pointing towards the wine glasses. He turned, looking at them with an apologetic frown, folding his arms and sinking into the warmth. He wasn't moving, not in his current condition and comfort level. If she wanted wine, she would have to make the first move. She did, but not for the wine, and by the time they took their first sip there was as much water on the floor as in the tub and her nylons had somehow come off, snaking around both their ankles. They sensed what each other wanted or preferred, and what each other enjoyed. His dalliances throughout the week had served him well. He had never had so many women in so short a time. Hell, he had never had so many women and he loved it, them, the sensations, the warmth, the smoothness and the most intimate scents she let him savour.

Love me, love me not. Go figure. Each woman had particular reasons, he believed, her particular need which accompanied her private sense of guilt or desired sense of emancipation. If he was their elected facilitator, for however brief a time, whether paid for or gratis, for the sake of their sense of being loved more than being a lover, the distinction mattered little to him.

She held a towel for him to do the gentlemanly thing, but he declined, preferring to pour more wine as he watched her slowly caress away her wetness with the fleecy towel. Any woman, he thought, could do that infinitely better than he or any other man. Men weren't inherently gentle, not inherently sensual and that's what the evening was about: his raison d'être for being with her. Win, win.

By the time she had finished towelling, his more apparent readiness had made them both laugh, barely managing to prevent Felicity from slipping on the tiled floor they had ignored. They raced each other towards her canopied bed she had adopted from another era, draped in cotton, waist-high and covered with a rainbow of throw pillows. She arrived first with an ambitious number of foil wrappers. He came in second with the almost empty bottle of wine in one hand and two filled glasses in the other.

*

He ached nicely, and he supposed she must also. The wine stains hadn't mattered at the time. He lay beside her, naked, peering through the exotic muslin curtains encasing them. The overhead skylight was not diffused by any means and the glare of the early dawn was oppressive to him. They had barely slept and he was surprised she would actually be going to work in so few hours. Not because she was hung over, she wasn't, because he couldn't understand how she could possibly walk. She must have gone without for a quite a while. She had been insatiable, permissive and unyielding, unabashedly demonstrating a physical attribute that makes women superior to men at a time when men most seek to be superior.

She was completely uncovered, unabashed and unaware. Whether she was sleeping, or drifting into a sleep, she showed no signs of wanting to speak. Anyway, what would they say? Thank you for dinner, Bill? You're welcome, Felicity. Thank you for fucking me all night. I'm sorry you're so raw, Bill. And I'm sorry you'll burn for a week, Felicity. By the way, the next guy doesn't know how lucky he'll be and be sure to check all expiry dates.

He needed to leave, get out of there, and she wanted the same. Nice party, now everyone go home. He eased onto one elbow, studying her, wanting to touch her there, to feel her moist warmth one last time, to kiss her breasts once more, but he knew that would undo the evening or begin an anti-climactic morning. Instead he swept back the curtains and went about gathering his clothes still scattered on the still-damp bathroom floor, putting on his slacks, shirt and jacket before checking his case and leaving. Not certain how to lock the door, not caring. There was no final glance, no whisper, no pretense and no good-bye.

The walk to the Marriott was short, not more than ten minutes and he felt completely at ease, unthreatened. He walked in unnoticed, other than by the security cameras, though he wore his hat for the occasion. The time was six-fifteen on the thirty-first. He was tired, love-weary, his single-minded strength fed by the knowledge that his agenda would be completed in seventy-two hours without the need to fill in more blank pages. More importantly, before midnight, he would sleep in his own bed, alone and secure.

*

He took a fast shower to de-Felicity himself and for the most part he was dressed, though he hadn't taken his usual care. He would have preferred pulling the linen curtain around her tub and showering with her, staying with her and spending the day in bed with her, but that was a fleeting thought that evaporated as quickly as the wetness from his lonely shower.

He called for a taxi that would take him to the bus station. From there he would travel six hours to Atlanta which would put him in the city at two and signal the end of another phase. At that early hour the taxi driver would see just another lonely and tired businessman or another faceless guy who had gotten lucky the night before. Either way he wouldn't care that Wellington was five for five, or that she had been the lucky one.

He disposed of all his accessories piece-meal, including much of his clothing. Some items were dropped off between

Felicity's and the hotel, others at the bus station and some were left on the bus. He saved the fake Walther for a garbage can in a men's room at the Atlanta Hartsfield airport, the busiest airport in the world and no better place to enjoy anonymity for those who had something to hide.

His prize, his pièce de résistance, was Roberts' computer which he had sent collect to the New Orleans police by FedEx, courtesy of Roberts. His two flights would get him into Montreal by seven, he hoped. From there a two-hour drive on pothole-dented roads would put him at home in Mont-St-Hilaire after a fast stop at a province-run Société des Alcools for a bottle of JW Red. His last one, the last red, he thought, and the lady standing beside him at the gate thought he was smiling at her. She smiled.

How easy she would be, he thought, rebuking himself. Very easy, but the timing was wrong and so was she, but part of him was in denial, resisting. He took all of her into view and she knew he was seeing her naked. She let him, with that inherent female need for appreciation, if not superiority under the always-changing guidelines of dream all you want, but don't touch. Then her passport that was open for usual inspection by the robot-like gate agent came into view and he let her go ahead of him, seeing the familiar gold-embossed crest he had always thought belonged more to Mother England than Canada. He sighed. She would have been fun.

*

Autumn in Montreal never followed the calendar, always beginning too soon and never really ending, always monochromatic grey and gritty, barren, and the end of the artificially flavoured joie-de-vivre that carried the failing city through the summer months.

Thirty days hath September, and summer ends on the twenty-first when golden leaves turn brown and die, cool summer evenings turn bitter cold, the sun rises late in the morning and dusk brings darkness that will last too long. It's a time when legions of homeless begin searching for empty and private doorways or sidewalk grates that will give them warmth from the coldness of man and the weather. Such were the autumn months he knew in Montreal, the ones he had always known through to December 21st when life in the deficient city became much worse.

The last day of October, his last day of October lived up to its reputation. The brown dormant grass carpeting his front lawn was layered with a cold white frost and the paver stones tiling his driveway were coated with a thick, opaque ice crunching loudly under the wheels of the Honda. So what made this fall? Winter had arrived early, again, pure and simple, and he hated it. He hated everything about winter, especially that house. How he hated that house and how he hated being inside, trapped between walls that had been his exclusive prison for so long.

Darkness had prevailed for hours, the amber lights inside were barely visible behind the tightly closed blinds at the front of the French-colonial cottage. The broken porch light was a dark warning not to infringe upon the privacy of the owner. The delivery of local papers and advertisements had been made across the whole expanse of the front yard, as expected, and not one neighbour would have thought anything about it. No one ever had, nor would they ever.

At first, what seemed ages ago, he thought he would need a secure and impenetrable insulation against his emotions for what he was about to endure, about to continue, a barrier he had worried would not be there for him during his time of need. Not because this was home to him and more dangerous than some distant, remote place. No. He worried about the agenda and the lack of experience he had prior to meeting with people at such a level. That all changed. He had acquired the experience he once feared

261

would be lacking in order to complete the agenda. Now, for whatever the reason, he was confident that what was to come would be rewarding. He was prepared. He felt at peace. His time had finally come and he embraced the moment.

The groan of the motor, filtered by the night air, ceased when the four panels of the door had been fully pulled up into the garage as he drove in without slowing, thumbing the same remote switch for the door to close when he had cleared the electric eyes. His secret passage into the cold home he so detested took less the twenty seconds. No one saw him arrive, no one ever did. They didn't care and neither did he. He switched off the light. At nine o'clock he was alone in the darkness of a stark black garage compelling him to remain where he was, comforted by the quiet and darkness. All that remained for him to do was in his head, committed to memory, till death do we part, though the list was long and the agenda was far from complete.

He drank from the bottle.

Wednesday, 01 November
Coming Home

If October was a transitional interlude from the bright warm colours and sunny days of summer to the monochromatic gloom and permeating cold darkness that would last through March, November was much worse, the most barren of the twelve months. November was hostile, completely devoid of any redeeming character with violent winds and harsh rainy weather serving as cruel reminders of yet another bitter winter that would be greyish-brown more than postcard white, slushy more than crisp and completely unlike any digitally enhanced postcard he had ever seen. At least in recent history.

He hadn't fallen asleep. He had passed out on the sofa and woke to the discomfort of stale, twisted clothing and the tightness of swollen feet still in the shoes he had worn for too many hours. For as much as he thought about it, he couldn't remember carrying himself from the car into the living room. He hadn't been drunk, unfortunately, though he didn't know why he thought that. Self-pity, he supposed, and that made him angrier at himself than at the malicious weather noisily molesting the house from all-four corners.

He didn't see the familiar bottle with its rounded corners, though the air was permeated with invasive fumes coming from the half-full glass lying on the floor by the couch. Then he studied the swaying brass pendulum inside the grandmother clock that had begun counting off the seventh hour. Perpetual motion, she had said; a perpetual reminder more like it. He brought up the glass, drained the remaining warm scotch and hurled the empty glass at the clock he knew the cold bitch had left behind to piss him off. A grandfather would have been bad enough, but a fucking antique grandmother. Bitch.

Still coughing through his nose, he climbed the white birch staircase to the upstairs bathroom. He still had much to do. He had planned a full day and a hot shower was first.
*

He went over the plans stored in his mind, time after time, as though practicing for one of his long-forgotten school recitals he had always been coerced into performing: the socially correct thing to do...for his parents, his father, another step towards success. They had been, after all, his formative years. He hated his father. He hadn't neglected a single detail. He was ready.

He felt somehow guilty he had once envied the collectors, now he hated them and had for the past two years, particularly the last twelve months. They worked hard. So had he, so what? Some win, some lose. Luck of the draw. He had never before factored garbage day into any of his plans. Why would he? Most times simply remembering he had garbage to put out was difficult enough. But today he had garbage, absolutely every article and piece of paper that had returned with him. The suitcase would be emptied into a plastic garbage bag along with what he had worn home and all papers and documents would be double-shredded and put into another, particularly the papers relating to the recent and extensive travels of one Jean-François LeTuvier.

He felt relaxed, if not at home. He felt fresh, if not invigorated, until his hand swept along the elasticized compartment of his suitcase for a final check. It should have been empty, but it wasn't. He shivered, standing still, gripping the little box covered in blue velveteen. He shuddered to his core. Feeling the texture made his fingers constrict, as though compelled to destroy it. What was past was past, he cursed, putting the box in the pocket of his pants to avoid a costly error. The unexpected had deceived him once again, he mused, breathing in deeply to clear his mind.

The garbage was put out and all of it would be converted into minute air-borne particulate by the end of the two days remaining. Anything brought into the house from that point would be acceptable, not at all questionable. His watch showed eight-thirty, the stores opened at ten, which gave him one hour to complete his work with Wiernknoff's computer, destroy the hard disc, package the CDs and mail them.

He had promised Gi-Gi they would spend time together, quality time. Now he questioned whether he could devote any of his attention elsewhere before his nine PM meeting with Marcotte, the most complicated meeting in terms of timing and the choreography of planned events. With everything else he had to do, would he have time for the kind of intimacy Gi-Gi would expect of him after so long a time? No. There would not be time. Gi-Gi could and would wait, again. Though he would call, asking to borrow the flashy titanium-coloured Acura RL for his meeting with Marcotte and, hopefully, if all went well with that meeting, he would attend a second meeting on Thursday, one he had recently pencilled in out of necessity.

Wellington opened the little blue box without emotion, half knowing what lay inside. The inscription on the face of the 18kt signet ring was a simple *JF.* The inside read: Babe, que je t'aime. So, he mused, she had found someone who at least could write that much French, or she had bought a French dictionary and not a Spanish one. He pushed the

18kt reminder of another era into the white velveteen slot, snapped the box shut and returned it to his pocket, smiling at the idea she had unwittingly given him. Thank you, chérie, et merci beaucoup. You will never know how much.
*

What he had thought would be his one stop of the morning became six, taking much more time than previously planned. Apparently garages and home supply stores considered gas cans as summer stock and very few remained on the shelves. The trunk and backseat of the Honda were full, the computer would never be found in the Richelieu River, not even by chance, and the rain was falling with a ferocity that would dampen the deepest recesses of hell.

By the time he had finished unloading his purchases and storing them alongside the car in the garage the time was twelve o'clock and the heavy, relentless rain had turned his patio windows into mirrors. The person staring at him appeared anxious and he stopped short of asking the image why. Stepping away, he toasted the receding reflection with the final few millilitres of scotch that remained in the glass.

He showered again and changed before leaving at just past one. He would be home late. The weather wasn't fit for man or beast and the hour he'd spent grooming himself to where he was satisfied with the result had gone for naught the moment he stepped from the protection of the Honda.

His first PM stop was at a high-end haberdasher on the once-elegant rue Sherbrooke. A hundred years past the avenue had been the home of the carriage trade, the who's who of society and the long-forgotten Easter parade. Now all that remained were broken rows of clothing boutiques and art galleries, some high-end, all expensive and all housed behind drab grey stone façades.

The boutique was one he knew, but who didn't know him, and he was there for off the rack apparel he knew would be available. The boutique was one Gi-Gi had always insisted he should patronize, never understanding how much Wellington despised the arrogance of the clerks who put on airs while working in a store whose merchandise they themselves could never afford, not even off the rack. Gi-Gi maintained the polished reception and service from the staff was all part of the total experience and that they were catering to him as they would any of their more refined clientele, whatever that meant. Some arguments weren't worth the effort.

The coat fit perfectly well, the hat fit well enough and the gloves and scarf would have been out of season any other day. He still didn't like the clerk, forcing a modicum of pleasantness which he attributed to an irony he alone would appreciate. He bought a suede and leather jacket that came with a matching baseball cap, as though on a whim; he paid cash and left, completely ignoring the clerk who had finalized the transaction with equal interest.

Gi-Gi had given up the RL reluctantly, acquiescing when Wellington insisted that being seen in it would help his image for the interview, the first one in how long. The keys would be on the sofa table in the foyer Gi-Gi promised, reiterating that Wellington was to drive the Honda and not the Acura if the weather worsened, he was not to park outside under any circumstances and he was to stay in proper areas. He thanked Gi-Gi profusely. They would see each other the following evening, late, he promised, about ten, and, yes, I love you, he promised in the same breath.

He parked the Honda in the underground parking of the Hilton Downtown, a Montreal landmark which had lost its modern elegance years earlier. Most locals ignored what had once been an architectural gem, no longer a centre-piece in an otherwise historic French city with high-end boutiques and expensive restaurants. They had become blind to the lacklustre and dark brown weather-stained cube, a barren metro station that even high-pressure sandblasting could not revive, and no one cared that it boasted the same cubic area as the Empire State Building.

Walking quickly the Hilton was five minutes from the Delta where he had made the four-night reservation. Jean-François LeTuvier would need the room until Sunday at noon, not knowing precisely how certain interim events would unfold. Though he had taken the precaution of preparing for a longer period, should the need be there. He checked-in with two travel bags. One contained clothing to get him through a full week away from home, though he hoped fervently that wouldn't be necessary. The second contained some of his new purchases which he wouldn't require until the next evening. The briefcase contained CDs, LeTuvier's papers, a signet ring and a copy of his will. Whatever he might be missing he could find at one of the hotel's many boutiques.

He took the time needed; setting himself up so that even housekeeping would believe someone had spent more than token time in the room. Then he left.
*

The doorman was stationed under the protective awning, already spreading open the umbrella as Jean-François spun through the revolving doors. Huddled together, they ran side by side to the waiting cab that would take him to one of the most exclusive high-rise condos on the island. One pushed as the other pulled just as hard at the car door, Jean-François wiped his face with cold wet hands and the doorman had already examined and pocketed the five. He was at the Delta, after all. The drive took less than twenty minutes.

The keys were where he knew they would be, the car was shiny with a recent waxing and Gi-Gi wouldn't be home for hours. He knew where to find the robe which he took from the hanger, placing it where Gi-Gi would understand he had gone to the apartment for more than keys.

Long weekends without extra work and case preparation had evolved into a thing of the past, spontaneous getaways always few and far between, eventually not happening at all. He had lived with self-denial a long time and not entirely his fault, he thought, albeit for the greater good.

He had been in the car on previous occasions, never comfortable with Gi-Gi driving him around as an unconscious act of kindness which he interpreted as another reminder of his failure, another subtle infringement on his manhood which no one but he seemed to lend any importance to. The final errand gave him the most satisfaction, when the jeweller assured the well-tailored man in the camel hair coat and matching tan fedora that the bracelet would be ready for pick-up by noon the next day. He had written out the inscription, selected a suitable script, paid cash and scribbled initials that did not resemble his own onto the order form with his left hand.

At six PM he was again at the Delta for an early dinner in the city's only revolving restaurant and sat watching the cityscape evolve into a kaleidoscope of blurred nighttime colours slowly revolving away and back to him against the early autumn blackness.
*

Michel Marcotte stood 1.8. He was extremely vain and always dressed for the job he wanted in clothes he could not afford. He owned a sherbet-orange black top Mustang convertible which he used exclusively for his frequent summer weekends at the beaches of Cape Cod, notably Provincetown. He lived alone in a third-floor apartment on the trendy rue Prince Arthur and always dined out. He travelled alone to the islands twice each year, he had no permanent relationship that anyone ever knew about and secretly frequented gay bars or those reserved for more open-minded couples.

He wore imported lamb's wool and power ties during

the day and leather with studded bracelets at night. And Wellington was the one who lost his job. Marcotte would be leaving the office and heading home, running home, if not prancing to get ready. Wednesday was his special night of the week, Queen for a Night at the hottest gay bar in town, the Oral G, and he always arrived early. Tonight so would Wellington. He ordered another Johnnie Walker Red, ready for the one meeting that would give him a particular sense of pleasure and achievement. The fact Marcotte was an overtly sexual fagot beyond his office walls wasn't one of the reasons Wellington had lost his job; it was the only reason and they both knew. His long awaited reunion with Marcotte would be the most pleasurable of his four meetings, the one he would savour with particular relish. Indeed he would.

Marcotte could not risk anyone in the conservative VitaVie Corporation discovering the details of his private life. He had gone to great lengths building an image of a work hard, play hard charmer who had no time for family or friends. He would let nothing undermine that successful comfort zone, especially a direct report who had inadvertently become privy to those personal details that would be viewed by the board as very serious character flaws.

It had happened on the Sunday afternoon of the Labour Day weekend four years earlier and the weather was perfect for everyone on the fashionable rue St-Denis to strut their stuff. Bare thighs, bare midriffs, curvaceous cheeks peeking out from high-riding shorts and panties highlighting the apexes of bare thighs under summer dresses were the rule. Women sat with women flirting at a distance with men or admiring other women, men sat with men, their demeanour smug, heterosexual couples either ignoring the spectacle or whispering indiscreetly to one another about "them."

Separately they were alone in a universe, together they

were an animated gallery of the beautiful in-crowd who wanted to see and be seen. Drinks weren't drinks, rather apéros, and food was either hors-d'oeuvres or petite something or other that sounded better than it tasted and cost more than it should. Expensive and chic was what mattered above all else to those who mattered. Polyester was definitely not in and most wide-eyed tourists walked on by, either too afraid or too intimidated to enjoy themselves.

Innocent and sexy fun was the order of the day, inherent to a street without being sexually charged and Wellington sat across from Gi-Gi facing into the sun, taking it all in. Gi-Gi hated the sun, tolerating outdoor café-terraces to indulge Wellington. They were salt and pepper, at least in the summer and Gi-Gi thought Wellington was perfectly ridiculous altering his skin colour for no reason other than vanity when he was already perfectly beautiful.

The couple sitting diagonally across from them and behind Gi-Gi had been seated just moments after they had been seated and Wellington had no particular reason to pay attention to them, other than his personal feelings about men holding hands or demonstrating affection in public. Women he could understand. They were brought up to hold hands, kiss each other and walk arm in arm. But men had a code even fags should respect.

The two men were fashion copy cats. Each wore navy blue designer baseball caps on backwards, a style fast becoming tired even for teenagers. Wellington could read the word "Queen" in white, unable to distinguish the smaller font that followed. They both wore tee-shirts with the bottom 20 cm and sleeves cut off with scissors before washing so that the edges would turn up into tight rolls and give the appearance of a tank top. Their jean shorts were very short, worked on with the same scissors for the same reason and they wore white anklet socks with two-toned running shoes that had never been worn for that specific purpose.

Wellington had long ago developed the habit of watching people in restaurants and bars, studying habits, manners and body language. These two were all show: tall, tanned, slim and sinewy more than muscular, and they switched from French to English with showy affectation. They ordered what he thought was Pernod on the rocks, swizzling them to the point of dilution.

When they stood to leave Wellington was on his second Johnnie Walker. The one who had been facing away from him threw crumpled bills onto the table before pulling at his top, and at the bottom of his jean shorts that had risen past the thin, pale-white crease of his buttocks. They were smiling, laughing, having a good time and each turned in different directions to scan the patio as they noisily slid their chairs across the art deco floor tiles the very moment Wellington locked eyes with Marcotte.

Wellington froze, and his instant loss of colour did not go unnoticed by Gi-Gi. Confronting the difficult situation would have been awkward, embarrassing. There was nothing to say. What was done was done and could not be reversed. Marcotte acknowledged Wellington with an easy grin and raised eyebrow, then he turned and signalled to his companion to walk ahead of him. At the entrance to the patio he pulled his friend by the arm so they wouldn't have to pass by the most recent member of his sales force who had already made a mental note to find out what Queen for a Night was all about, not that the implication wasn't self-explanatory.

Had it not been for that one fleeting moment in time at Le Café au Lait, the three meetings of the past week would never have taken place and the ramifications of those meetings would not now be the prime topics of nervous discussions in board rooms and offices across two countries. People unknown to him or forgotten by him would now be caught up in the vying and politicking of promotions or financially motivated lateral moves and the ensuing multiplier effect would mean stunted careers for some and more promising careers for others. If that wasn't reprisal, what was?

The café wasn't a gay and lesbian bar per se, not more than any other bar on St-Denis, but Gi-Gi knew the owner who was and the man was more than eager to talk with them about Michel and his current boy-bitch. That conversation had set the tone for the remainder of the weekend. He should have felt something beyond the overwhelming sense of gloomy defeat he could not explain. Being with Gi-Gi had meant making excuses to Geneviève who was working at her health club most of the weekend, and now he was making those same excuses to Gi-Gi and had gone home, though not to Geneviève. He was letting it happen all over again, he knew.

That Tuesday had been the first day returning to work and Wellington made a point to cross paths with Marcotte. He would sooner or later, the sooner the better; despite knowing he would soon after disappoint Geneviève one more time. This time, however, the emotion he felt was bitter sweet.

*

La Reine de la Nuit sur le boulevard Saint-Laurent
Queen for a Night on the Main
Two-for-one-drinks
Hors-d'oeuvres
Contests & Prizes

*

Bring a special friend, a lover, or someone you've just met in the men's room, Wellington thought. He hadn't been anywhere on the Main for years: the boulevard which once separated the English faction of the affluent west side from the French of the poorer east side. The street was a narrow and cluttered one-way congested street, pedestrians blindly crisscrossing at their own peril from side to side between uncertain drivers and carelessly parked delivery vans in search of fresh produce or particular ingredients from ethnic markets.

That was by day. By night a double row of amber lights dissected the entire city, illuminating what was home to hookers and johns in rooms to let for twenty-dollars or cramped in the front seats of cars for ten. The Main was also home to an increasing number of indigent runaways who panhandled or slept against the graffiti-decorated walls of strip clubs and pawn shops, too falsely proud or too stupid to phone home. Then there was the endless stream of patrons who disappeared behind the doors of gay, lesbian or fetish bars, or into swap clubs for those wanting to share their lovers' bodies but fearing the prospect of answering newspaper ads from other lonely or bored couples. Uniformed and plain clothes cops were blind or tolerant. Either way they didn't care. Nothing was left to shock or amaze them as they waited for a killing du jour and the ambulances waited with them for the umpteenth stabbing victim or bar-brawl loser.

The camel hair coat was surprisingly warm, although the hat was still not his style. He drove around the block a dozen times for two reasons: being seen in his flashy titanium car and parking in the spot he had pre-selected away from the whores and the disgruntled acne-faced teenagers who would love getting even with disinterested parents by kicking in the side of someone else's expensive car. His meeting would be a cold call and timing didn't matter, whether they met at nine or ten, eleven or later. He wanted convenient parking.

The lower doors were open and the stairs leading to the second door were steep. He thought of Dalila and Seraphina and wondered if all sleazy places needed to have steep stairways. He remembered being behind Felicity, her beautiful ass, and smiled to himself before the slotted window in the door at the top of the stairs slid open for immediate inspection and subsequent acceptance or refusal. He passed the visual once over, though he had mixed feelings about being accepted so easily. The ambiance was noisy, ear busting noisy, and the air smelled of men but not the same way he remembered the spa smelling.

He had an idea what to expect and his lack of interest in whether he stood out or fit in was sincere, reminding himself he was there to negotiate for his future. Everything else was irrelevant and unimportant. He went straight to the stand-up bar, squeezed in between two potential contest winners, ordered a double JW Red and followed the golden rule for anyone in a strange bar filled with men and their dates: Don't make eye contact. Confrontation with a man over a woman was one thing, confrontation with a queen over his queer was something else, and dangerous.

The lights were low, the ambiance secret and lewd, the conversations too muted to be real. Jealousy prevailed and any normal conversation would have seemed loud. Some were dressed in suits; most wore leather pants or chaps with matching singlets and caps with metal studs. Men held hands with men and the women holding hands looked more like men than the men. Others danced and caressed their partners' backs under tight-fitting open leather vests or bolero jackets, while others gave exaggerated kisses into each other's open mouths, oblivious to their surroundings or turned on by them, Wellington thought. Those who were obviously alone searched out potential one-night stands, those who were together searched for possible alternatives and he was very happy he had no urgent physical need to visit the men's room where the mood prevailed: Show and tell, or show and don't tell as long as you show me, he thought.

The time was 10:15, and Wellington wanted out well before the eleven o'clock contest. He wondered if they might mistake him for a cop as he stood off to the centre of the crowded hall. Slim chance, he thought. And there was Marcotte who wasn't alone and clearly the dominant one for that particular evening. He hadn't seen Marcotte since the day Marcotte had fired him for being in the wrong place at the wrong time. How this would play out he had no idea and Marcotte couldn't conceal his disbelief when he saw the man he had long since forgotten.

"Salut, Marcotte. Can we talk for a few moments?" He stepped between the man and his effeminate plaything who saw Wellington as an immediate threat to his evening. "Don't worry. I won't steal him from you, sweet cheeks. It's simply business, not more than five minutes. Do you mind?" he said in a tone that meant piss off.

Marcotte smiled. "I never imagined that I would see you in here, of all people. I suppose that one never does know, Wellington, does one?" He took a shallow sip of his Pernod. "What is this business that we have?" he continued arrogantly in French.

Wellington ignored him, stepping in close to the other man. "Do you mind, girlfriend?" he said in English.

Marcotte brought a hand to the other's shoulder, squeezing gently. "Give us five minutes, cher, and another of these in the meantime?" He clinked one glass against the other.

Wellington sat in the warm seat after the other dragged himself up and away, grimacing when he saw the man was wearing bright yellow thongs with front snaps under open-back, candy-apple vinyl chaps. He had a tattoo on one buttock that was both phallic and directional.

"You have a different bitch, Marcotte. Think he'll win?"

Marcotte's expression was dreamy. "Yes. He has a good chance. He's very animated, very popular with everyone."

"I'm not at all surprised, especially with the tattoo. Is there a matching one somewhere?" Wellington turned away. "It's been a while," he said.

"Yes, and now you are here. Why is that?"

"As I said: business."

"I understand that you are still, how shall I say, between positions. We are not hiring, if that is your purpose. Anyway, we would not re-hire a previous employee. Of course, you already know that."

"I have information that I intend selling to the highest bidder. I'm giving you first refusal and, by the way, we'll speak English. This is my deal."

Wellington's French was cultured, flawless. Marcotte's was peppered with Anglicisms despite the fact he was a nationalist and secretly wished even his best English-speaking client expulsion from his ancestral homeland.

"I'm honoured, and what information would that be?" Marcotte took up his glass, visibly upset at seeing a few drops remaining. "What could you possibly have that I could want? You were never privy to delicate information at the firm, or any other company of which I am aware." He grinned. "How many were there, four, five others? You certainly did get around, my dear Wellington. What could you possibly have for me now?"

Wellington began enjoying himself. "Let us just say certain and very interesting information concerning three of your most worrisome competitors has been made available to me and I am willing to share that information for a reasonable price."

"That's it…certain and very interesting information?"

Wellington nodded. "Yes, that's it … certain and very interesting information, specific information. More precisely, information supported by graphs and spreadsheets, categorized by state and province, detailing previous and current sales results by region and territory with sub-categories detailing the activities of specific individuals and product groups."

He waved off Marcotte's new friend who had come back, standing too close with two fresh drinks in hand. The original purpose of chaps being open in the front was for the convenience of cowboys on the range, not for thong-sporting fagots openly displaying their excitement levels. When he turned back Marcotte's expression was easily defined.

"Not enough?"

The question sounded accusatory, intended to irritate.

"It's nothing, Bartlett. The year is over. At best, it's old news, even assuming it's accurate."

"Indeed, old news you never had."

"And what do you expect from of all this, your old job? You already know the answer."

"No, not a job, I'm taking early retirement." He swallowed what was left in the glass. "I want the equivalent of one year's pay, gross."

Marcotte's abrupt laugh caught the attention of all those nearby, thinking they might be missing something. "Not a chance. Not a month, Bartlett, not even a week." He motioned with the fingers of his cupped hand in and out for his friend to bring over his drink. "Sorry, I think the time has come for you to leave, or sit somewhere else." He smiled widely, looking past Wellington, nodding into the air. "That one seems like he'd be a good fit. Don't you think? Oooh. He's been drooling since you sat down."

"Then send over your bitch," ended the taunt and Wellington leaned closer. "I also have new, in-depth product R&D information, dates and particulars for new product launches planned for the current fiscal year, and planned high-level personnel changes. Did I mention strategic planning for specific markets?"

Marcotte began listening more intently. "That might be

interesting." He conceded, pausing. "Your brother has something to do with this, I would imagine."

"He has no involvement whatsoever."

"No? You mean you have come by this information all on your own."

"All you need to know is that I have it. All I need to know is whether you're interested."

"Is IntelSanté one of the competitive companies?"

"No, it's not. Not yet."

"What does that mean, not yet?"

"It means not yet. Do we have the basis of a negotiation?"

"Do you have the information with you?"

"No. I'll bring you what I have tomorrow evening, but I'm not inclined toward wasting my time. Are you interested, or not? I know my brother would be, amongst others."

"I have no doubt he would be. The question is: why me?"

"Because we both know you're a weasel. You're a fagot and we both know that. You'll be the easiest of the potential buyers to convince. And if I can't convince you I'll ruin you, the way you ruined me. I'll make sure everyone you report to and do business with is aware, in vivid detail, of your extra-curricular activities." He looked over at the younger man who was staring at them from the bar. "They might want in, knowing he's animated. Was that not the word you used…animated?"

"What I do after hours is my own affair, besides my lifestyle is a known fact. I am very comfortable with who I am."

"I have no doubt, but no one else is, so don't bullshit me." He glanced quickly towards the bar. "Maybe I'll stay for the contest, to see whether he wins. Maybe I'll take the winning picture. What is it, wet tee-shirt, wet jockey shorts, or just wet? On the other hand I think it's time to go." He chuckled, shaking his head. Marcotte didn't see the humour. "Sorry. Really, I am. That was insensitive of me. I can see you're anxious for his little performance and I really do want to get out of here. Do we have an agreement in principle, or not?"

Marcotte hesitated, pretending to mull over a difficult decision, knowing very well what he would say. Wellington was right. He was a weasel, an opportunist, and this seemed a good fit.

"In principle, yes, but not for a year's pay, I don't think so. Ten, fifteen thousand tops would be a reasonable ceiling."

"Twenty, made out to cash." He was silent for a brief moment, pushing his chair slightly backwards. "Understand that what I show you will be a sample only. Likewise, I'll require a sample of your interest level. Shall we say one thousand?"

"Let us not get ahead of ourselves. Let us say tomorrow, same time same place."

"No, I don't think so, Marcotte. I wouldn't want to put a strain on your relationship. Your little boy-toy is already set to scratch out my eyes with his French nails, or yours."

"I usually spend Thursdays quietly at home, we could meet there." He tried sounding impassive but failed. He wanted badly for Wellington to accept. The five minutes had gone into overtime and Marcotte was becoming of two minds. What if he did come over, and what if an agreement could be reached, or not. So what? Stranger things happened. "Shall we say nine?"

"Yes, we shall." He stood.

They shared a smile for different reasons.

"I'm in the book."

"I know where you are… nine o'clock."

"Bring the information, everything."

Wellington ignored the remark, scanning the bar as he pushed in the chair. "I am not into threesomes, Marcotte. Make sure you lose Miss Sweet Cheeks. This will be strictly one on one and bring the thousand."

He also ignored the smile.

Thursday, 02 November
First the Intent, Then the Need

The rain had not relented and he laughed out loud at the ridiculous thought of all those bare-assed queers donning raincoats over scanty costumes and scurrying off in pairs to finish their evenings together, before going home to wives, boyfriends or eighth-floor private offices. He was pleased with the outcome of the preliminary meeting. He harboured no doubt he had snagged Marcotte The Weasel.

He couldn't erase images of Marcotte comforting or congratulating his boy-toy in the tiny yellow panties, or out of them. He just enjoyed snickering at the thought. The Oral G was a sweatbox with more bare asses than the shower room at the Y. He avoided thinking of the contest which would have kept him awake even longer. He needed sleep, not dreams of desperate queers parading or dancing around in pull-away pouches, red vinyl and cowboy boots with splash marks.
*

The next morning the Acura sat in the garage, still wet and heavily spotted with highway residue. He had promised Gi-Gi he would not drive if the weather worsened, but did Gi-Gi mean in order to avoid accidents or avoid spoiling the pristine appearance of the car. He wasn't certain, though he thought probably both. Perhaps he would have the thing detailed, but he didn't think so.

By the time he woke twenty-four hours remained. The Acura was by no means a workhorse and he had spent the better part of the morning completing his preparations for the following day. He made separate stops at the gas pumps of twelve different service stations, filling two containers at a time with 92 Octane before returning to his house to load and unload sets of four. As little as he cared about the car, when he finished and all the containers were lined up once again in the garage, he lowered the windows allowing the air to circulate and then he forgot about it. Morning had somehow become afternoon and he felt dirty even though he wasn't. He showered once more, changed, and by 12:30 he was crossing the Richelieu River en route to the jeweller in Montreal.

The clerk was excited. Apparently some people still enjoyed their jobs. The sterling silver bracelet was perfect, not too delicate, nor too heavy and the inscription done in the Dauphin script would adequately convey the unmistakable sentiment. He was satisfied and told the clerk so. In fact he was delighted and smiled throughout his late lunch that lasted until three. When he arrived home at four o'clock the darkness surrounding the unlit property was absolute.

He opted to leave everything untouched, though he did lower the two windows of the car once the garage door had sealed off the outside. He had very little to do beyond preparing a CD or two for Marcotte, include a few blanks and place them into his briefcase. Everything else had been laid out, including his clothes, and he did a cursory inventory more for the sake of killing time than necessity.

He selected a casual deep burgundy V-neck, navy blue cords and oxblood loafers. The light-weight wool scarf was a navy blue accessory for show and affect, and absolutely necessary. He was set, every detail had been observed. He was either ready or he wasn't. Even his hair was perfect, albeit somewhat different than Gi-Gi would remember. He poured a JW Red, a good one, and then he poured another admitting to himself in the lonely quiet that he was nervous, but not about his meeting with Marcotte. His upcoming late-night rendez-vous with Gi-Gi disturbed him. He couldn't remember the last time they had spent the night together, whether their evening had gone well or whether the hours had been fraught with tension and that worried him. What he did remember were the events of the past week. More than the planned meetings, he remembered the encounters he had not anticipated. He remembered Seraphina and Dalila, the white and black whores. He remembered Celeste who brought him to new heights in Roberts' bed, on his desk and his sofa. He remembered Pat who turned round so quickly, willingly fucking him like an eager teenager in love for the first time. Finally he remembered Felicity who virtually forced him into fucking her, fucking him as well and as hard as the professional Celeste and with as much Southern charm. And all she had cost him was a meal. Good deal, he thought, a good return on investment. How could he leave all that behind? He couldn't. He'd known for the better part of the week.

Rest for a moment was becoming a temptation difficult to resist, but he didn't dare. Rest would come soon enough. He went into each room of the house, unmoved by his lack of emotion and attachment. How he hated that house. Hadn't he always? After Geneviève's departure, not even Gi-Gi had visited. Jason always had an excuse, his neighbours kept their distance and the one time he called Renée to invite her for a dinner she had been too busy, or so she had said. He had been alone in that house for two years. What did surprise him, apart from a little recent dust, was how clean and organized the house appeared, at least on the inside, and he was hard-pressed to remember how that had been accomplished.

The remaining hours seemed more like days, with nothing to do but wait. He had no one to phone and what would he say if he did know someone. No one cared. His parents had, at least his mother did when she was alive. She'd been the one person to care and he missed her. His father on the other hand had been a presence, a tutor, a guide, a barometer of his success or failure and he felt no guilt about not missing him. In fact, he felt a sense of relief, if not happiness, that his father died before having to witness his fall from grace, the abrupt end to his once promising career. He thought of Jason, his father's pride and joy, who would bid farewell to France with Renée at any moment and he grinned involuntarily knowing his brother would be complaining to her about his early morning breakfast with her errant and ne'er-do-well brother-in-law. Who needed family, who needed anyone?

His brother was good at what he did, he granted that, but that's all he was good at. What about his wife, Renée? What about her? Did he even have a clue, had he ever had a clue? No. Wellington began laughing until the laughter became uncontrollable, mixing with tears and he was bent over grabbing at the painful constriction tearing at his stomach. Then all he could do was weep until the pain left him unnoticed.
*

There was no point in eating. He had eaten a good lunch and anything ingested now would be rejected forthwith. The wind and rain finally abated, heavy clouds blocked out the stars and the 20 highway was busy with haggard and frustrated homemakers returning home from the mall in aging vans to a mundane routine. They were visibly pitiable, pathetic and weary with life compared to the night-club set speeding past them in sportier, more expensive cars they could ill-afford. They might have been happy once, he supposed. They might have had their time, but too far in the past to revive or relive. They had all had their time, for better or worse and, worst of all, they had likely forgotten each and every moment. They deserved not to remember, they deserved no more than what they had which was nothing.

Wellington had never forgotten and he wasn't too late, though if he was so be it. Let it be, amen. C'est la vie or was his life coming to an end according to plan. There was no better time to find out. He was doing one-forty when he passed other vehicles entering the Louis-Hippolyte tunnel. As he shot from the other end the speedometre read two-hundred. He slowed

*

Meetings 101: Always arrive ten to fifteen minutes before any appointment, prepared. Walk in exuding confidence, be calm and relaxed. Be in control. Take the initiative. Be the centre of attention. Never stand down. Never be intimidated by those who feign superiority to conceal fear and, for Christ sake, avoid using "sir". Be equal to everyone and, if need be, be the superior one. Above all, be good. Be the best. That's the engine that drives everything else. Some rudiments of early learning never left you. They stayed with you as haunting reminders of what you might have been, what you might have done differently and eight-thirty became nine.

Conversely, he'd once been told that if you are always on time those who wait will think you have nothing better to do. What happened to that guy, Wellington wondered? Did his personal credo eventually hold him back or propel him forward? The man had a point. He also said that when you're the best at what you do you can manipulate any corporate edict set in place to control the minions, adding that if you're not good, then you're just a jerk.

Wellington was confident he had become adequately accomplished over the past week, considering he had no formal training to assist him in his recent endeavours. He hadn't felt that good about himself in a very long time. He took the forgotten man's advice and climbed from the car at five past the hour. He'd been watching Marcotte's vague outline pacing in front of the curtained window and how the lighting in the room had been dimmed moments before nine o'clock. Fagot.

He opened the briefcase devoid of emotion, verifying and re-verifying the contents. He reached into the left pocket of the camel hair coat, pulled out the latex gloves and put them on before the tan kid leather gloves that completed the total look. He squeezed the right-side pocket from the outside, pursing his lips. He was ready. So was Marcotte's silhouette that was framed and standing motionless in the window.

*

Access to the apartment was from the outside. The building was old, not quaint, and refurbished to where the owners could still charge excessive rents. So were all the others on the street. They were the questionably enviable homes of McGill students with affluent parents, DINK couples or people like Marcotte: queers who had the money and needed either the venue or the vanity.

The staircase was steep, the iron railing rough to the touch and speckled with rust that grabbed at his gloves. The landing that appeared freshly painted from afar was chipped and uneven; the door that seemed ornate and Victorian from street level was old and built up with thick layers of paint that barely concealed the rot. The door creaked open, invisible incense billowing out into the cold night air.

"Salut," Marcotte said, guiding the door open.

"Salut, Marcotte."

"I do prefer Michel."

"I won't be staying long enough for names to matter."

"Come in."

Marcotte closed the door behind them. He turned and squeezed past Wellington, leading him along the narrow hall into the small parlour crowded with eclectic furniture that included two love seats, a futon and too many cushions for a man's home, even Marcotte's version of a man's man. The stereo played music intended to take the edge off the day, the plasma screen showed overly vivid turquoise blue waves dissipating onto an unreal and distant island shore.

Nothing matched, other than the platinum finish of the entertainment centre and he had scatter rugs with even more pillows and cushions piled into the corners. He had wine tables instead of end tables and two re-finished trunks that served as coffee tables. The walls were decorated with black and white photos, charcoal studies of the male nude and a metre-high red glass vase housed a single white glass rose. Wellington couldn't imagine that an Eastern brothel could smell worse. The scent was spicy and feminine, too pungent, and he thought of Marcotte like a stable hand who becomes immune to the bio-degradable slop in his shovel. But that was moot. He wouldn't be staying long enough to adapt.

Marcotte was dressed on the risqué side of casual for a business meeting. He wore pale blue leather slippers without socks, his pale pink satin slacks were loose-fitting lounge pants tied with a slim-line leather belt that matched the slippers and his pullover silk shirt was a deeper shade of pink with a single deep V-cut in the front that was unlaced. He didn't have the demeanour of a man who worked hard days, though he had taken time to groom and primp himself for the meeting, for Wellington. Wasted time. Wellington couldn't help but grin at the thought which would was excessively obvious.

Marcotte smiled also. "I see you are in good spirits, Bartlett. You must be confident that this, hmm, meeting will go well."

"The meeting will go well, that I can promise you. And we'll conduct ourselves in English. I wouldn't want you to misunderstand the slightest detail."

"Whatever, may I take your coat?"

"No. As I said, I will not be staying long."

"Suit yourself." Marcotte didn't seem at all discouraged. "Wellington, sit down. Je vous en prie. Oops, I'm so sorry. I see you've come bearing gifts. But first, why don't we catch up, have some wine. I'd love to know what you've been doing."

"Catch up?"

"I hear you've recently divorced."

"Yes, I am. It's been two years, officially one year. Time does fly, as they say."

"Because of Gi-Gi, I suppose."

"No. You suppose wrongly. She didn't leave because of Gi-Gi." Wellington looked around, seemingly uninterested, and he was, at least in the conversation. "Actually you were the root cause, and bastards like you, although you were the final nail in the coffin despite the fact she was a bitch. Although I haven't worked in two years so I suppose she had a point."

"Perhaps, but you still have Gi-Gi, if what the grapevine says is true."

"Yes, I do, until later this evening. Actually, I will soon have someone else in my life." He stared straight into Marcotte's eyes. "You know your little secret would have been safe with me. We all have secrets, don't we?"

"Yes, Wellington, we all have secrets. But ..." He was cut off.

"Has the amount been approved?"

"We might manage the twenty you want and not a cent more if what you deliver is actually as good as you say. I need no one's approval."

"You won't be disappointed. And the thousand?" he

queried.

"Yes, I have the thousand. Shall we begin?"

Wellington remained standing, searching for a place to lay down his briefcase.

"Did you bring your own computer?"

"No, the CDs only." Wellington opened the briefcase, letting Marcotte see the ten discs. "They're full," he paused, smiling, "and very interesting.

Marcotte went over to one of the cluttered corners for his laptop that had been in the sleep mode. When he flipped open the lid the notebook whirred to life instantly. He held out his hand for the first CD.

"There is a good wine on the buffet in the dining room. It's the next doorway on the right. Glasses are in the hutch."

"I prefer scotch, if you have any."

"No, I do not, and I didn't think to ask. I apologize. "

The computer screen turned bright blue and Marcotte paid no attention to his guest standing and walking from the room. Each of the CDs contained enough data to keep him preoccupied for hours and Wellington felt no need to hurry with the wine. He removed his dress gloves and took up the bottle, closely examining the label. The wine was far from the worst he had drunk over the years, particularly recently, but still best described as ordinary. He knelt down, searching through the glass front of the apartment-sized cellar, opening the door to examine each of the top three rows where the best reds would normally be laid. He didn't recognize the name, though he did recognize Grand Cru de Pomerol `87 and that was good enough for him, about eighty dollars a bottle good enough. The cork came out smoothly, soundlessly. He held the glass he had selected for himself up to the light, confirming the lack of water spots and residue at the rim left by previous visitors. Marcotte's didn't matter.

Marcotte had not yet progressed to the second CD,

fixated by the information he was reading. He took up the glass Wellington had placed on the wine table beside him and took a mouthful, waiting a moment before swallowing in a single gulp. He was clearly a wine aficionado, Wellington thought, no doubt, and the more expensive the better.

Marcotte seemed not to notice that Wellington had moved behind the futon and was sitting with one leg half on the sofa table, which he assumed was strategically placed for a video camera when the futon was extended. Wellington swirled the Grand Cru before inhaling its aroma, drawing a small amount into his mouth and swishing it to all corners so the many individual flavours could be detected and appreciated. He had made the right choice. The vintage was excellent and he mouthed the name.

"The wine you selected is extremely good."

"Thank you. I thought you might enjoy it. Do you know much about wine?"

"No, I don't, not much anyway." Wellington smirked. Marcotte wasn't paying attention to him, which was very good. "Does anyone know about this meeting?"

"No, no one. I needed to see and verify the data for myself first."

"And the verdict from the judge is?"

"So far, I'm impressed.

"You're the first to see them, other than me."

"How did you come by these?" Marcotte tried.

"That's not important. Let's just say I acquired the information from those who no longer care about the loss. As I said, some personnel changes are expected in the near future."

"And you know this how, through your brother?"

"No. I've already told you he's not involved in any way."

"I find that hard to believe."

"What you may or may not believe is of no interest to me, Marcotte, as long as you have the authority to authorize a twenty-thousand dollar cheque made out to cash."

"I do."

Wellington couldn't see Marcotte's eyes to determine whether or not he was lying, certain that he was, which was of no real consequence.

"Have you heard about Roberts over at Spencer?"

"No. I've been out of country for the past few days finalizing some business."

"This business, I suppose?"

Marcotte changed the CDs. He didn't see Wellington nod as he took another sip of wine before putting down the glass and removing his dress gloves once again.

"What about Roberts?"

He eased himself off the low-rise table and reached into the pocket on the right side of his coat. He leaned casually against the table, holding the garrotte tool by one makeshift handle and letting the metre-long strand of steel wire unravel and dangle at his side, at the ready. As Marcotte continued greedily reading through the information he interpreted as another step up the corporate ladder. Wellington took up the other end.

"Apparently he's dead from a heart attack. That's the latest word." Finally Marcotte twisted at the waist, facing Wellington. "At first they thought he might have been murdered, but now they say not. His wife must be going through a difficult time, knowing he died alone in a hotel room like that." He turned his attention to the laptop, his humanity expired.

"Was anything mentioned about a hooker?"

"Are you saying Roberts could have been with a hooker? That's rich. I saw him once at a conference. Believe me. No woman could possibly need money that badly." The second CD whirred and filled the screen. "Why do you ask?"

"I was concerned the police might think she had killed him and not me."

Marcotte was an instant too late realizing the inherent consequences of not remaining attentive throughout a meeting. Being multi-functional for too many current-day managers meant the ability to perform several functions at once, not merely possessing the ability to perform those several different functions. Marcotte belonged to the first school of thought which, he was about to discover, had been a bad choice.

"What?" he questioned, half turning much too late to see Wellington's grin.

"The whore," Wellington said, "Celeste. She didn't kill Roberts, I did. Goodnight, Marcotte."

Marcotte had been all too consumed by the files. Fatally. By the time his body reacted to the sensation of the cold steel wire against his bare throat, the job was half done. Wellington reached over with a speed and agility that surprised even him. For Marcotte, whose eyes were out of focus from reading the screen so intently, the thin deadly garrotte was no more than a blur.

Wellington leaned forward, braced by the table, jerking backward with such a passion that Marcotte was lifted sideways from the futon and pinned snugly against its plush upholstery. Wellington's hands crossed one over the other and the rest was effortless, unbelievably easy, which was inconsistent with his ultimate goal. Marcotte's body stiffened into a rigid arc. His legs kicked out, repeatedly crashing the toes of his soft-soled slippers into the hard varnished wood and brass of the trunks. His arms flailed outward, knocking over the wine glass at his side and missing the wine bottle at Wellington's side by centimetres. He instinctively forced his torso harder against the unyielding futon in an attempt to break away from the constricting choker, ironically succeeding in making

Wellington's task of killing him that much easier.

Almost comically, like a skit at the local gay theatre, his hands slapped at Wellington's and then, much too late, they tried prying their way between the wire and the already sticky wet skin. He tried feverishly to dig his long manicured nails into Wellington's leather-covered hands, some folding backward and bleeding while others broke off. Wellington pulled hard and down, hard, working easily at securing Marcotte to his second to last resting place and not thinking for a moment the task of wrapping up the meeting was taking too long. The meeting with Roberts was somewhat disappointing in the sense that at the end they had become practically friendly, which was contrary to the spirit of the reunion. Henderson was a little more interactive, though not at all the challenge he had expected or wanted and Wiernknoff had chosen ancestral stoicism. Marcotte on the other hand was not disappointing in the least and whether the meeting ran into overtime, within reason, mattered not at all.

The only audible sounds came from within Marcotte: intense groaning sounds, guttural companions to severe straining. His face turned deep purple, Wellington certain the veins in his face were close to bursting under the strain, even though he couldn't appreciate that particular view from his vantage point. The groaning downgraded to whining, akin to the plaintive cries of Mommy, Mommy. That was followed by the hysteria of Marcotte understanding his mortality was imminent and his rapidly diminishing strength was no longer equal to his determination that was also beginning to ebb. He was crying. His face was wet. Wellington was smiling, pleased with a job well done, thinking Marcotte must be dead after what had to be two minutes, though he hadn't been counting and thought erring on the side of caution would be the wiser choice with one minute more and he maintained his grip.

The handles were wooden dowel rods, bought the day before and drilled to accommodate the steel wire. He would have preferred nylon, but didn't trust himself to make knots that wouldn't slip. He also knew lighter gauge steel would suffice, but the extra assurance was important to him and, at the same time, as much as he hated Marcotte, he didn't necessarily want his head falling off.

Marcotte was dead. He was pretty sure, but he exerted one last effort for the sake of clarity, which he remembered had always been one of Marcotte's pet bugaboos during meetings. There was no reaction, though the stained garrotte did not come away easily. Wellington's desire to perform well during the meeting had caused the wire to wrap too tightly, cutting deeply into the flesh, taking on the shape of Marcotte's neck and tearing away some of the softer, fleshier tissue as Wellington did his best to free the coil while holding the loose head in place. That done, he ravelled the wire around one of the handles and brought the latex glove of his right hand over the compact tool, repeating the process with the left-hand glove before reaching for a second pair and dropping the garrotte into his coat pocket.

He was exhausted. He took up the wine bottle that somehow had remained on the table, poured another glass, walked around to the front of the futon, and sat beside his ex-boss. Marcotte appeared relaxed and peaceful. They had all seemed at peace at the end and Wellington felt a twinge of jealousy. He put his glass on the trunk closest to him as he stood, facing Marcotte. He inverted the bottle over the corpse and let the remaining burgundy liquid spill out over the silk and satin lounge wear that had barely been touched by blood. When the bottle was empty, he took the still warm fingers of the lifeless hand that wasn't hanging over the side and squeezed them tightly around the slim neck. He left it that way in Marcotte's lap.

He counted off the CDs and returned them to the briefcase, then he began the process of transferring data he thought would be useful in the short term from Marcotte's notebook onto the blank CDs. Fifteen minutes later he still had not finished and the computer was put into his case along with the CDs before he went into the kitchen where he washed his wine glass, wiped out the sink, and hung the towel to dry.

He resisted the temptation to witness how the other side lives. Time did not allow, though he did take one business card from the briefcase he had seen in Marcotte's bedroom. The time was close to 10:00 and he was behind schedule. He sat once more beside Marcotte on the sofa, reaching into an inside pocket. He had discarded the box downtown and, once done, there would be no going back. He had made a promise to himself and would see the commitment through come hell or high water, and he knew hell would come first.

He slipped the sterling silver bracelet onto Marcotte's wrist without emotion. The styling and inscription were simple, perhaps the way they both would have wanted in another lifetime. The front read: Together, forever; the underside read: Michel & Gi-Gi.

He hadn't found the thousand, nor had he expected to. In lieu of the promised payment he took another Pomerol for Gi-Gi.

*

The Acura started. The street was quiet and deserted, save for one or two couples strolling home. He pulled out into the one-way street and crossed to the other side, reversing for about half the block before shifting to a forward gear and sitting straight. He took a deep breath, ignoring a couple who seemed curious, or worried, probably wondering why he had stopped alongside them. He was focused, his bearings were taken and he floored the pedal.

The car responded obediently, with most of its power still in reserve, and by the time he reached the corner he had sideswiped the driver's side of at least twenty cars leaving a trail of broken rear-view mirrors including his own.

By 10:10 he was on a high and the drive to Gi-Gi's would not be more than twenty minutes. The damage to the car was extensive on the passenger side and even if he did chance to pass a patrol car the destruction would go unnoticed. He had thought of going to the hotel first to drop off the case, but that would make him late. The timing was still just about perfect. The parking garage was well-lighted and he parked the car the way he knew Gi-Gi would have wanted, giving no thought to whoever would notice the damage as long as someone did. The entrance to the elevators on his way to the apartment was equipped with obvious video surveillance, though he suspected one or two were concealed in the elevators, if for no other reason than to entertain the concierge during his lunch hours. Either way, he kept his hat on and his head down. At some point someone would have more interest in those tapes than who was kissing whom, or the already half-naked couples challenging the time factor en route to their apartments from the pool. He tossed the home-made garrotte matter-of-factly into the receptacle that was at the door. Conveniently, Friday was another pick-up day.

Wellington regarded his relationship with Gi-Gi as a friendship that had evolved beyond what he would ever have thought possible, what he would ever have wanted. He supposed more people knew about them than he cared to think about, and he seldom gave the issue much thought. Life was too short to care and those who might know likely misunderstood his need. He wasn't ashamed of Gi-Gi, very much the opposite. He just wasn't into being as open as Gi-Gi. He hated the daily "Que je t'aime, Trystan". How he hated those words he could never repeat. He never had an appropriate or timely response when they were alone…and that handbag. How he hated the signature leather handbag. Or did he hate the handbag in lieu of Gi-Gi.

He had no idea how he would explain they were over, finished, but they were. He had no choice. The break-up would be difficult, he hoped not ugly, and dealt with quickly. He owed Gi-Gi that much. He felt naked without a tool, without a plan. He had dedicated so much time and effort over the previous twelve months to preparation that the apparent lack of planning now didn't feel right. Always arrive at a meeting prepared, and this time he was anything but.

There was no way for them to maintain what they once had, he argued, or what they once thought they had, which he thought was a reasonable counter. He had changed too much. The three whores, Pat and Felicity had awakened something within him he always prayed hadn't died, something Gi-Gi couldn't give him, and he was certain that in his new life he would be with the one person who could.
*

Soft music wafted through the cavernous apartment, an integral part of the decor that was modern and completely white under the subdued amber lighting with blue and green accents. Gi-Gi lounged across the ultra-modern and low-profile imported leather sofa. He had also dressed for the occasion, wearing creamy-white pantaloons cinched at the waist and a matching silk smoking jacket with slightly ruffled edges draped open, drawing attention to a slim and regularly pampered body.

Hidden at the top of the farthest corner a red light blinked repeatedly, reflecting short, uneven beams along the walls. He had finally arrived and Gi-Gi would be waiting anxiously for him in the living room, to begin their first night together in more than a year and everything would be perfect. The wine glasses were spotless; the wine was perfect and perfectly chilled. A second bottle had been chilling in the spa for the past hour, the bath was drawn and unscented oils had risen to the surface as minute beads that would help conserve the heat. The spacious area was warm with heat wafting from the floor, Trystan's attire had been laid out, the stereo programmed to seduce and the lighting was pre-set to romantic.

"Are you teasing me, or have you broken your leg, Trystan?" he called out from his place on the sofa, unconsciously swirling the snifter of Johnnie Walker Black in a slim, feline-like hand.

There was no answer. Wellington just appeared from around the corner and stood backlit by the brighter lighting he had opened in the hall.

"I wanted to splash some water on my face. I see you've been busy."

"Yes, I have been busy and I am so angry with you. You were expected at ten. You're forty minutes late. What if I had prepared a late dinner?"

"I thought we were having Chinese." Wellington snorted a short imitation laugh. "Anyway, you should know better," he said, coming closer, "and isn't that why they call a late dinner late?"

"Will you always be so careless about time?" Gi-Gi sat up, not hiding his surprise. "You're so tanned and handsome, Trystan, so handsome, and so new. I love your sweater and your hair. You've styled it differently, somehow. Sit," he patted the cushion beside his, "you must tell me everything." He passed Wellington the snifter. "I adore the new you. I decided that you deserve Black, something special for a special night."

"And I brought a decent Pomerol, not a bad year if memory serves."

Wellington sighed deeply, not from the pent-up stress of the past two weeks he managed not to show on his face or in his eyes. He sat on the sofa, far enough away for comfort yet close enough to avoid being prompted to sit closer. Then he swallowed all the amber liquid Gi-Gi had made too warm by excessive swirling. It burned and tasted worse than warm beer. Room temperature: he should have known better.

"How refreshing, how wonderful I feel seeing you this way." Gi-Gi put a delicate and smooth hand on Wellington's shoulder without hesitation, pressing slightly. "How I have missed you, Trystan, this past week, this past year."

"I did what I had to do. I feel good; in fact better than I have for a very long time. Revisiting this last year of my self-absorption was well worth the outcome. The end result was long in coming, but it's over. I feel very good about what I've accomplished…and myself."

"That is so good to hear. The year has been long for both of us and we have much to talk about and do. We have all weekend. We have no need to rush. I have taken the time off as you asked me." Wellington couldn't help but shirk at the light touch of the slender and manicured fingers running through his hair. Gi-Gi seemed not to mind the slight. "I love what you've done with your hair. So much more like…."

"I suppose you have a bath ready."

"Of course, have I not always?"

Wellington put the snifter by the sofa, for a moment lost in thought, pondering his on again off again lover. He reclined when he saw Gi-Gi had misunderstood. Saying goodbye would be very hard, he decided, and there was no point in delaying the inevitable.

"Why don't you go ahead? Let me join you in a few moments." He filled the wine glass. "I have one call I must make."

"There's more in the spa, already chilled. As I said, the

300

weekend is ours to enjoy."

Wellington nodded. "Good, but first I need to get out of these clothes. I've been in them all day and it began early."

Gi-Gi stood, hugging him tightly. He was happy and ecstatic Wellington had finally returned to him: their time to start over, a new beginning that would take time, he knew, but now all they had was time. They would be as they once were. They would be wonderful together, the weekend would be a wonderful time and so would their lives.
*

The designer had created the bathroom for complete after-hours comfort and relaxation. The space boasted a recessed and glassed-in shower with multiple heads, a second glass door that opened into a clear steam room, a metre-deep Roman bathtub with a clear acrylic side, two pedestal sinks, a whirlpool for four and one toilet. The single bidet was for show, used strictly for chilling wine. The massage table came from Sweden, indirect lighting allowed for any combination of the full colour spectrum and a plasma screen was part of an entertainment system which could be fully controlled and seen from any one of the extravagant amenities.

Two glass towers stood two-metres high by forty centimetres square, balanced on rotating pedestals. One held the necessary designer-name toiletries, towels, lotions and games. The other, positioned between the foot of the bath and the whirlpool, housed a DVD, a miniature stereo, a selection of CDs, the remotes and a phone. Plush, deep-violet bath robes hung from one side, Wellington had brought his from the bedroom the day before when he stopped by for the keys.

Gi-Gi had been elated upon arriving home to see the obvious gesture, pulling out all the stops and had spent all day Thursday planning menus, appropriate wines, DVDs, CDs and his wardrobe. He lifted the Chablis Grand Cru

Vaillon from the closely packed ice in the bidet, poured a full glass and began disrobing, slowly.

Wellington had always referred to whatever was drunk in the bathroom as Château Bidet, the silly boy. He could be so straight sometimes. So what? Who cared about all those little arguments and jabs? He was finally back, this time to stay and of his own volition, without any henpecking and now they could be the couple they were meant to be. Gaston George was the best trial lawyer in the city and successful enough for both of them. That they would now be together was all that mattered, nothing was more important, nothing.

*

Wellington leaned against the door of the wardrobe in Gaston's expansive bedroom. The midnight blue duvet was folded down, as were the burgundy sheets and Gaston had tossed the shams onto the carpeted floor. His two-piece silk lounge outfit lay across brocade loveseat. His head pivoted, scanning the room, though he saw nothing and he felt nothing. He wondered whether he would cry or, worse, whether he would hesitate, determined he would not. Death would come quickly. He had resolved that bothersome issue the day before, though at the time the solution had been a stopgap measure and he had thought of nothing better in the meantime.

He would be killed without question, without prejudice to what they might once have had, or to what Gi-Gi believed they still could have. Wellington had used Gaston's seedier connections in the city for his own ends, true, but that would soon become too much privileged information for a lawyer to have, irrespective of client privilege: a gun permanently held to his head, a threat that would never go away. Gi-Gi was the one person who could truly discern the imperceptible differences between the twins. Despite his loyalties, the frailties of his character mixed with the paradoxical self-righteousness of his profession were real threats. In fact, together, they were the only threat. Worse, Wellington had allowed them, albeit out of necessity. Not even his treasured Renée would know, but Gaston would.

*

Gaston's loose-fitting silk jacket disappeared into the centre of the empty whirlpool, his pantaloons followed as far as the contoured edge. He was so happy Trystan had convinced him to take the rest of the week off so they could be together. He was so anxious to hear about the job interview. The new Trystan was so rejuvenated, so revitalized. Together they would share a perfect life from now on, a renaissance at long last.

The bath was deep, see-through, special-order from Europe and designed for two adults to stretch out side by side without touching either end. The water instantly coated his skin with a pink hue. When he bathed alone, which he did often over the past year, he made regular use of the removable backrest to prevent accidental slippage and possible unenviable consequences. Tonight such a precaution would not be an issue. He sipped his wine, slipping deeper into the water. He was anxious, barely able to resist calling out to Wellington that he should hurry.

*

Gaston was a practiced interrogator, familiar with the nuances of facial and body language that would instantly label a liar. That was in court or on the street. When Wellington was involved he would believe what he wanted to believe, as he had so many times before when Wellington would make impromptu phone calls before a weekend together or when he would say how much he'd been looking forward to an evening without changing his tone. That was then. Now he was sure about what he was doing, that he was doing the right thing.

Seeing Gi-Gi stretched out naked in the tub Wellington

flashed back to the first evening so many years ago. So much had changed. Most people would have experimented with a new lifestyle while on a vacation or on a business trip, but he'd chosen to take the leap with a member of his wife's health club. By then Gaston had already made a name for himself. Despite his success he hadn't yet been able to lounge in a bathroom/spa costing more than an average couple earns in two years. Wellington remembered the first time they shared a bath, how he had tried keeping their legs from touching and the electric confusion surging through him when Gaston had leaned forward, smiling, closing the distance between them, and how their legs touching no longer mattered. He remembered how the evening had become morning and how he'd left without saying a word. He thought of Felicity, smiling through the real tears beginning to form.

Since the first time he'd been the lover Gi-Gi had hoped for on too few occasions, he knew each occasion drew more self-respect from a source already in danger of becoming severely depleted. The planning of his agenda hadn't been the sole reason keeping him away over the past year. He had tired of questions he could never answer, the possessiveness and the sense he needed to continue what had become a farce to him, an untruth in a parallel world that was normal in all ways but one.

He should have left. He should have gone his own way, but he hadn't. He stayed, choosing to alter the rules of the game to suit his own needs, using the agenda as an excuse to conveniently put off the inevitable. Tonight Gi-Gi was eyeing him with a longing and desire that was once curious expectation, what Wellington had come to forget. The water was clear with traces of colour left by the oils and foam covering most of the steaming surface. Gi-Gi was fully erect with anticipation of the evening ahead, the imagery comical through the side of the clear acrylic bathtub. His genitalia were dark against his white skin that was one shade away from being too white. He had no body hair, by choice, making the ample dark hair on his head as incongruous as the plum-coloured member he'd begun maintaining. He was slim, without much tone and the arm closest to Wellington lay by his side, slightly suspended in the tinted bathwater and giving him the appearance of a lab specimen suspended in a vat of tinted formaldehyde preservative.

Wellington waved away Gi-Gi's concern about his tears, saying he was happy, that soon all would be well and that he had come in for some Château Bidet before making his call that would take five minutes. Then he noted Gi-Gi had forgotten to turn on the stereo, which was moot. He realized Gi-Gi was absent-minded, flustered by thoughts of being with him. He would simply correct the oversight.

God, he had forgotten, Gi-Gi exclaimed, exasperated by his lack of attention to detail. Wasn't that just like him to get so excited about being with Trystan that he would absolutely neglect to set the proper mood? He sighed, miffed with himself. The remote was beyond his reach.

"Never mind, I'll do it," Wellington said, already walking to the crystal unit.

"Go do your phone calling. I think I can turn on a radio." Gaston was on his knees, barely out of the water, concentrating on not losing his footing on the slippery surface as he tried standing.

"Get back in the water, or do you want to hurt yourself falling and ruin our evening?"

Seeing that Wellington had kept moving toward the pedestal, Gaston eased onto his knees and reached for his half-full wine glass, taking a fast sip that would wet a throat already dry with nerves. He knew Trystan would turn on the stereo, but he was eager for Trystan to see him naked and to see Trystan naked after such a long time. When would he undress? How he wanted to see Trystan, be with him and enjoy his closeness once again.

Wellington brought his hands from his pants pockets, the remote in one of them and the receiver connected instantaneously. He reached for the robe hanging from the outer side of the stand with his inside hand. Bringing up his outside foot and arm to balance the hundred and fifty-kilogram glass shelving unit, he guided its path precisely over and into the tub. To Gaston the passage of time seemed like an eternity, most of which he spent wondering at his lover's actions. In real time a mere three seconds had elapsed as the glass tower toppled forward and broke apart, crashing into the seventy-five kilo nude whose arms hadn't come up to be broken under the force of the crushing impact.

Gi-Gi lay unconscious, his limp body pushed forward and onto its side. The scene was perfect. The wine glass had crashed to the floor adding to the realism and a single shard of glass protruded from the hip of the slim figure like a fin, giving the appearance of a grotesque and surreal impressionist sculpture that Gi-Gi would never have commissioned for his bathroom. But still it was there and could not be returned.

Wellington pulled the plug from the outlet and pushed the bottom half of the robe elbow-deep into the water, letting the top hang over the edge of the tub, ignoring the lifeless face staring at him as though searching for an absurd security or reality. Wellington collapsed onto the floor completely bewildered and truly alone. He had achieved his objective, Gi-Gi was gone, a fait accompli with one meeting remaining that would bring his agenda and the week to a close.

Though he doubted very much he had the strength to attend the meeting, let alone see it through. True to his word Gi-Gi had gone quickly. He had wanted the closure to be painless for Gi-Gi as well as for himself, an impromptu need borne of necessity. He didn't have the luxury of giving Gi-Gi the year-long attention he had dedicated to the others and anything like a gun or knife would have been unnecessarily cruel, out of the question. He'd done his best. The reaction had been mostly involuntary, he realized that much, but Gi-Gi had twisted and jerked in the violent water for what seemed like forever before coming to rest against the clear bottom.

Wellington sat on a wet tiled floor studying a body in the process of transitioning. He whispered good-bye, reaching out to touch the acrylic wall separating them. The water was becoming more opaque by the moment and the bubbles escaping Gaston's open mouth grew smaller and less frequent. His eyes never fully closed, remaining narrow slits, and Wellington wondered if he could still be seen through them. He smiled compassionately, hoping Gi-Gi understood the need. He hoped so. Salut, Gaston. Forgive me, mon ami. He stood, replaced the plug, and walked out.
*

Describing Gi-Gi had always been difficult. He was, at once, a confident hybrid of the effeminate and gentlemanly elegance, the authoritative and the submissive. Now, taking in the details of his depilated nude body for the last time, Wellington saw him as just another lonely and pitiable fag, a dead one. That would be how the media would see him on Monday, when Gaston George Lefebvre, Montreal's premier trial lawyer, would be revealed to the entire world.

Of course, his phone would ring near 8:00 AM when the methodical Madame Duvernay would assume he had overslept, using her terms. She would then call on the quarter hour, waiting until ten or so before calling in a favour from the local precinct that would send a patrol car to investigate. Wellington could imagine how the headline would read: Montreal Trial Lawyer Found Dead in Blood Bath: Ties to underworld not discounted by police who are investigating certain unusual circumstances. The obituary would be Gaston Lefebvre's final contact with a city that would forget him before turning the page.

Wellington poured a scotch, enjoying its strength as he roamed through the apartment. There were mementos, not many, and he left them. The time was not appropriate. Who cared about trivia? The few photographs he had ever allowed were another matter. He took them in the frames, leaving him little else to do, nowhere near as much as the post-meeting workload he had previously self-imposed. He downed the rest of the scotch and put the snifter beside the wine glass and wine bottle he had touched. He left the Pomerol standing in the kitchen.

When he finished, he thought of leaving his coat, hat and scarf in exchange for Gaston's, deciding against stupidity. The car would be sufficient and when he left he did so through the main doors of the building, wearing a baseball cap and a blue-black suede-leather combination jacket that would show up as different tones of grey on the video monitor. The nylon sports bag slung over his shoulders seemed heavier than it should and by the time he'd returned to the hotel the contents had been discarded, save Marcotte's computer, the CDs, two glasses and the framed photos.

La rue Sainte-Catherine would one day necessarily be renamed Avenue of the Homeless and another broken or empty wine bottle would be questioned by no one. Abandoned coats, scarves and gloves, especially in November, would be picked up as quickly as they were tossed aside and when he turned around moments later his were already gone; the two-hundred dollar fedora with them.

Friday, 03 November
Renaissance

He was exhausted, yet exhilarated. The time was 2:00 AM. He spent only enough time at the hotel to once again construct a sense of mild disorder: simulating a bed he had slept in, a shower he had taken, wet towels and tissue paper unravelled. Then he decompressed with a JWR from the mini bar. He left the bag locked, in the corner of the room. He would have time for that later, though he had already accepted that later had become a relative term.

Walking into his living room from the garage he was seized with a penetrating feeling of not belonging, as though he had broken in, as though he was being observed. The silence and heavy darkness were filling him with haunting unease. His brother would have arrived home from France a few hours earlier and was expected at nine. Wellington was too indifferent toward his brother to care Jason would be travel weary from the flight, and obviously so, which is what mattered most, though he would enjoy his brother's curiosity about the relevant time frame of his death. How greedy could a man become? He laughed softly at the thought, knowing one person remained to expunge, the person who was probably most responsible for his lack of success, his failure: himself.

How he yearned for his life to end and for the peace that would follow, substituting for the happiness he had sought in vain for so many years. That would be his final exoneration, his final cleansing of self and his ultimate if not singular success. His death was the real and single imperative that would bring lasting peace between the brothers. He would die easily, he had promised himself, and deservedly. What better birthday gift could he offer himself? His freedom day had arrived. What more could he ask? Life was good.

Seven hours remained and he would need every moment. His day had been particularly busy, results-oriented, yet he was numbed by the mental and physical exertion required of him. Sleep wasn't an option. Not that he wasn't extremely tired, though more than sleep he needed others to see he was run down, haggard, depressed and at his wits end. Then he could sleep for as long as he wanted, forever. In the meantime he was hungry and nothing edible remained in the house save canned soups and meats that had been frozen long enough to lose their identities. His dinner at the hotel was excellent, eight hours earlier, and he needed some sort of nourishment to sustain him through the coming hours and the important work remaining.

Until the pizza arrived at two-thirty, when he poured his second glass of wine, he spent his time in the garage arranging the twenty-four two-gallon high-density plastic jerry cans according to where he would place them throughout the house. He would do the upstairs first. The bedroom was large, well-furnished and would require three, the bathroom one, the workout room another and the TV room would easily require three. He did the finished basement next, a lower level intended as a guest-game room with a full bathroom. The laundry, storage and utility areas were all behind closed doors. In all he had allowed for five cans, factoring the wall-to-wall carpeting into his calculations.

By the time he got to the main floor the pizza was

finished and he was on his third glass of Bordeaux. He placed one can under the kitchen sink and another under the dining room table. A total of two hundred-sixteen litres of high octane fuel strategically placed to produce the most immediate results, to turn the house he hated so much into a Roman candle. Nine other cans remained capped in the garage for convenience. He wanted the best for the bitch and Gi-Gi would certainly have agreed with him, of course. Though he regretted Geneviève wouldn't be there to witness her precious home going up in flames. Bitch.

At 5:30 he opened his last bottle of wine. Then he activated the air exchanger in the utility room, not at all concerned he was standing at the base of a massive home-made fire bomb. Next he went up to the bedroom and disrobed. He tossed his clothes into the hamper in his closet; he removed his watch and spent the next twenty minutes standing under the pulsating heat of the shower. Finished, he stood naked in front of the full-length mirror and shaved. He was nicely tanned and much slimmer, he mused, the way he once was, though no one would take notice because no one had seen him over the past year to know the difference. His hair combed easily into the style he recently adopted and he dressed in a nylon jogging suit and a pair of his usual executive socks. He spent several minutes standing in each of the nine rooms, not searching inwardly for any particular emotion. Nor did he feel guilty when none had been stirred. The kitchen was the last room he went into and he poured another glass of wine before returning to his office to write the letter.

He went out to the maple tree with a hammer and a single nail to post the missive at 7:30. The sky was clear and the stars had faded into another day, though what he liked most was the noticeable increase in wind velocity. He leaned against the tree he had leaned against to read so many times before, had slept against, and had spoken to when no one else would listen. He knew he would forget the house. He never thought of the place in real time, so why would he think of it in surreal time?

The Quebecois-style had never been his choice and certainly was never a home. How often had he tried sitting with Geneviève on the white-trimmed balcony under the sloping blue-shingled roof to share time with her? If there was ever a farce, those moments undoubtedly qualified. Being with her had never felt natural, always forced or feigned, constantly struggling with his emotions when he should have said good-bye. How he had always hated the house: Geneviève's way to maintain with Jason and Renée, keeping up with a family that would never be hers and his constant reminder that one day he would have to do something about it. Bitch.
*

Even though he had another ninety minutes, and he knew his brother was never early, time now seemed very compressed for him. The agenda he had so meticulously planned, with the exception of Gi-Gi, would come to an end within two hours and he felt somehow vacant. He felt empty, without purpose. He imagined his brother being preoccupied to the point of distraction with the will Madame Duvernay had drawn up and two million dollars. He didn't think the house would soon be worth much and his car was leased. Everything else had gone to the bitch, to Geneviève, and did she ever think of him? Not frigging likely, he somehow knew.

He wondered, certain he knew the answer, whether Jason had told Renée of the two million. He laughed, putting down the glass, and began brewing a pot of coffee he wouldn't drink. He felt as though he should have a last-minute bullet list of things to do, but he had done everything. All was ready, laid out to ensure the best use of his time, beginning in the bedroom. When the doorbell rang he responded as though actually accustomed to hearing the sound, greeting people and having guests.

Opening the front door was like peeling a layer of mercury from a mirror. They had long ago become nonchalant about their shared looks, though after so long a time apart they both took a long moment absorbing each other.

"As usual," Wellington began, "never underdressed even on a Sunday. I suppose I'm the second to wish you a happy birthday."

"Actually you're the first. Renée was sleeping. You might possibly remember the effects of jetlag and, I see…never overdressed. Some things never do change, brother. Happy birthday to you."

"Come in," was all he said. Any civility between them would have been uncharacteristic.

Jason walked through the entrance and into the living room before speaking. "It's as cold as hell in here."

"Then you should feel right at home, Jason. Have a seat." He gestured to a sofa facing away from the dining room. He had thrown a bath robe over the other so Jason wouldn't sit in it. "Would you like some coffee? It's more or less fresh. Or would you like a scotch? Your body clock must still be set at 2:00 PM."

"Sure, why not? I suppose you have the usual Red? "

Wellington ignored the barb and went into the kitchen for two glasses, filling them before coming back. "I didn't think to chill your glass. It's been so long your little idiosyncrasy completely slipped my mind. Sorry."

"I prefer Blue that way."

"With my recent schedule I simply couldn't find the time to buy a gift."

They hadn't bought gifts for one another in over thirty years and Jason ignored the glib response. He was more interested in the shattered plate glass refracting short, precise beams of coloured light across the floor and wall adjacent to the grandmother clock.

"Nor I," he took the glass. "Have a bad day recently?" he taunted, part of him urgently wanting to know, though not out of any concern he might have felt.

Wellington followed his gaze as he passed Jason a snifter without a word, pushing aside the robe as he sat.

"How's Renée?"

"She's fine, and she's sleeping, as I should be. So what's this all this about?" Jason began, sniffing at the scotch. "I was called to Lefebvre's office two weeks ago, on a Sunday of all days, to sign some papers regarding your will. All I was told, though I daresay instructed would be the better word, was that I should be here today as a condition of being the sole beneficiary and I need not bother calling because you wouldn't be available. What's going on?"

"Yes, that was my condition, and I apologize for upsetting your travel plans. I had no choice. I had meetings out-of-country and seeing you at any other time would have been inconvenient."

"Inconvenient for you?"

"Yes. After all, Jason, I am the one bequeathing two million dollars to you, in addition to this place for what it's worth."

"That prompts an obvious question that's been on my mind for two weeks. Why me? Why now?" he paused. "And what were these out-of-country meetings?"

"That's three questions." He put up his hand, halting Jason's response. "To answer your first question, who else is there? No one's been here, including you, for two years," he answered. "As to why now, the answer is simply, why not? It's our birthday. We inherited some bad family traits, as well as some funds and those insurance policies were originally intended as a tontine of sorts."

Jason swirled the snifter, looking intently at his brother. "The meetings, were they job-related?"

"One could say that. I suppose, being completely honest, I would describe them as settling of accounts, outstanding severance payments I never received."

"So you're still unemployed, available, shall we say," Jason chuckled, remaining motionless, "and, after all this cloak and dagger business of phone calls and inopportune meetings with your lawyer, you're not dying. What the hell are you doing?"

"Yes, Jason, I am dying."

His brother leaned forward. "But you said..."

"I said we have some bad traits and our father wanted one of us to die rich. Remember what the old man drilled into us, Jason: Respond to specific questions with specific answers, and to general questions, generally."

"Then please be specific."

"As you wish," Wellington went on. "You are my beneficiary because the decision suits me and is appropriate due mostly to the timing which is both critical and of my own doing. Had I been able to delay the selection process to a later date, I certainly would have excluded you from any benefit. I do hate you, Jason. Leave here with no doubt of that. Calling you brother is unnatural for me and what I am doing is inconsistent with my feelings. I realize, however, once all is said and done, that what I'm doing will make a good deal of sense. So, once again, you are in the right place at the right time, brother." He swallowed, enjoying the reaction to his honesty on his brother's face. "The answer, simply put, is Wellington Trystan Bartlett will soon be dead."

"How do you mean, of your own choosing? You're not sick, and I don't believe I've ever seen you so tanned. Are we talking about what I think we're talking about?"

Wellington laughed as he stood, focusing on Jason's

empty glass. "No, Jason, we are not talking about the big A."

"You must admit the question was an obvious one."

"Based on what?" he challenged. "What you think is true is irrelevant."

"There are those who wonder. Nothing's happened since Geneviève walked out on you. You've become a recluse and secretive. You know how people are, not to mention your lawyer friend."

"No, I don't know how people are. I never see people and those I should see don't bother calling, like you, like Renée. And who would give a shit? So don't tell me anyone wonders unless you're talking about yourself."

"So, I suppose finally it comes down to me?"

"You're a fool, Jason, albeit a successful fool, I grant you. How Renée has tolerated all these years with you, I have no idea. However I didn't invite you here to talk about her. I'm having another. You?"

Jason handed him the glass. "I'll tell her you still care when we're at dinner this evening."

"How nice, a birthday party?" he asked as he walked into the kitchen. "Am I invited?"

Jason stayed as he was, peering beyond the front windows. "Another birthday dinner and another set of cufflinks, or some such trinket," he said in a monotone, "and, no, you are not invited. Neither is anyone else. Satisfied?"

"I suppose you would rather be at Carmelita's right now, instead of sucking up to me for two million."

"I don't suck up to anyone, Wellington, not one goddamn person. Understood? It's the other way around and if that's what you think you can take your two million..."

"Don't say something you don't mean, Jason, or would regret. No one turns his back on two million, and the next in line to enjoy my meagre estate is Renée who might well," Wellington paused, returning with Jason's refill, "develop a different attitude about life, possibly even more understanding towards Carmelita. Or maybe not."

"I came here with the intention of discussing your affairs, not mine. But you're not saying very much." He threw his head back, swallowing half the generous portion of scotch. "What's next? Or is this going to take all day?"

"Strange, isn't it, how we're so identical, entirely indistinguishable, yet so very opposite in every conceivable way?"

"Life makes us what we are. This genetic business is strictly for medical journals and academics hoping for fifteen minutes of fame and glory. Beyond that, who gives a real shit?" He leaned back, crossing his legs and his arms. "Don't tell me you do."

"I forgot my drink." Wellington turned slowly, walking to the kitchen. "To tell you the truth, I don't. In fact, there isn't very much I do care about now, if anything."

Jason stayed as he was contemplating what else he could say, listening absently to the background sounds of glass clinking and liquid gurgling from the bottle. He didn't want to stay a moment longer, though he wanted answers to his questions, particularly the most important one: when his brother would die. He was concerned, interested in knowing the cause insomuch as it related to the anticipated date of his death. To that extent he was interested in genetics. He had never been good at small talk that wouldn't otherwise culminate in an important deal or significant agreement in principle and the advancement of his career.

Small talk was his brother's forte. His brother was small, always the underachiever. He always would be. He had never strived for success, always settling for second best, always victimized by the whims of others rather than making them the victims. Who's the fool now?

317

The two cupped hands gripping Jason's face from behind were as tight as a vice and the incongruity of the reality of what was happening within the context of the once familiar environment invaded him milliseconds too late, depriving him of advantage. He was locked in place, his arms flailing spastically and blindly at first, his body twisting to one side and the other, unsuccessfully trying to free himself, his feet kicking out ineffectively into the empty air in front of him with the same hope. The grip tightened, forcing his head into the back of the sofa with such strength the pain from the back of his head was taking precedence over his thoughts. What was happening, who was doing this to him? Wellington! Wellington! Help me! For Christ sake, help me! Who are you? Wellington, please! Please! Mother of God!

The groans were strained and muffled by the several layers of surgical gauze filling the thin space between Jason's face and Wellington's hands that were cold with chloroform dripping steadily under the cuffs of his sweatshirt. Something Wellington hadn't considered, though immediately noted as he knelt behind the sofa with his knees suspended above the floor for definite strength advantage, with his hands raised high as though in prayer, clinging desperately to a body slowly beginning to weaken.

Jason's arms began losing strength, flopping, his legs no longer kicking, twitching aimlessly. Then his head stopped moving, his body still. Wellington could do nothing but wait. He would be more cautious than he had been with Marcotte. He knew once his fingers parted he'd be unable to put them over his brother's face. He'd wait. Three minutes elapsed, two minutes since Jason's pain had vanished and his eyes had closed. He eased his grip ever so slightly, his hands and forearms aching badly, strangely relieved Jason was oblivious to the cruel world he had proudly manipulated for so many years.

Wellington took his hands away completely, reaching quickly into a pocket for the small brown pharmaceutical bottle. He hadn't bothered reading the dosage instructions, putting as much into the gauze padding as he could before the liquid began spilling through. He pushed his brother's head and shoulders slightly forward, climbing over the sofa to prevent the limp body from falling forward on its own. He was striving for perfection, wanting to avoid the slightest sign of concussion or facial bruising, not that he thought such attention to detail would matter when all was said and done, though he had always paid attention to detail: a requisite function of professionalism and a sign he took pride in his work.

Inhaling deeply he slid his arms under Jason's, not liking the fact their faces were almost touching, guiding his unconscious brother gently onto the floor, turning him over once he had stretched Jason out completely. At 9:20 Wellington's one thought was of his mental bullet list. He had practiced the process a hundred times and would be finished by nine-twenty-five.

Within seconds he was back from the garage with the suitcase he had prepared the day before. He emptied it quickly, laying the contents to one side. He stripped off his jogging suit along with the latex gloves he had worn to protect his skin from the dehydrating effects of the chloroform, dropping everything into the suitcase with the odourless hand wipes he had used to wash his face, hands and forearms. He stretched out his brother's arms, stripping off the crewneck sweater, smelling the front and detecting no trace of chloroform, which was good. The shirt was next, put on top of the sweater. The shoes and slacks came off easily and went on top of the shirt after he removed the cell phone from the belt. Jason's socks and underwear went into the suitcase. Wellington removed his own school ring, making the change with his brother's. Then he took the ring

Renée had put on his brother's finger the afternoon so many years ago he had never forgotten. The blue and gold Rolex came off one wrist and onto the other, feeling heavy, burdensome as he sprinkled more chloroform across the gauze square he had centred over Jason's face as insurance.

There was no time to think about the nude figure on the floor as he reached for the disposable plastic painter's coveralls and the one-size stretchable booties. Another set of latex gloves were pulled on, this time over the plastic sleeves, and a white ski hood left only his eyes uncovered. He looked ridiculous passing by the hall mirror and at any other time he would have laughed. The open suitcase was in the entranceway, ready. The time was nine-twenty-five.

By nine-thirty Jason had been dressed in the bath robe which had been lying on the sofa beside Wellington and was propped sleepily in the chair behind Wellington's desk. The living room floor was bare. By nine thirty-five Wellington had removed eight more of the jerry cans from the garage and had placed them as strategically planned. Now he was in the bedroom with his heart racing. He had already closed the aluminum horizontal blinds in all the rooms of the top floor and basement. They were high-end, the way she had wanted everything in the house and when they closed absolutely zero light came in or went out.

He unscrewed both caps from each of the three containers first, emptying one onto the bed, one into the walk-in closet, and the other one he laid on its side to spill out evenly onto the hardwood floors towards the landing connecting the rooms. He did the same with the ones in the workout room and bathroom. In the TV room he emptied one onto the sofa and two others onto the floor as he had done in the bedroom. Standing on the steps at the very edge of the landing he saw the lethal flow creeping slowly towards the doors of each room, and towards him. He held four wooden matches and struck the first, throwing it into the bedroom which was entirely covered in flickering orange flames within seconds. The other three rooms went up as quickly.

The basement was next. The first match went into the laundry room, the second into the storage area and the third into the utility room. The containers were on their sides. The two remaining saturated the guest bed, the chair and sofa ensemble at two diagonally opposite corners. On his way to the main floor he turned, enjoying one final and fleeting glance before throwing the last match.

Even though daylight would help camouflage the early stages of the fire, all the metal blinds on the main floor were closed tight, as he had done with the others. He readied the container in the kitchen, leaving it there, doing the same with the one in the dining room that would merge with the two he had placed in the living room to saturate the sofas and the floors. The critical ones were the four he had set aside for the office, standing open and ready.

He saw his brother as though from afar, as though seeing someone else, a stranger. He felt no connection, no animosity or regret. He had felt so empty for so long he had forgotten how any of those emotions should feel. Jason was groggy, still slumped over. Wellington touched the side of his neck, feeling the slow pulse as he pulled at the top drawer of the desk to retrieve all that remained of the package Maître Lefebvre had given him some months earlier. Gaston had known exactly what was in the envelope, though he never would have supposed for what purpose Wellington would have wanted those certain counterfeit documents, or why he would need to defend himself. He hadn't been stupid, although he never would have supposed this. Despite being a clumsy liar around Gi-Gi, Trystan had always gotten his own way.

Wellington hadn't known at first what he would need and had followed the recommendations of the men Lefebvre had put in contact with him. When they first met they checked him out, the first payment was made and everyone went separate ways. He would never see them again and never know who they were. A few days later the package had been delivered to Maître Lefebvre's office and the lawyer had finalized the transaction.

They had suggested the nine-millimetre Berretta 92FS that now seemed so ominous by itself in the middle of the drawer. When he had asked them what a gun like that would do they had looked at each other and laughed.

"It's the preferred weapon of the American Forces." they said, "What do you think it does?"

"Is it heavy?"

"Thirty-four ounces, unloaded. It'll come with one clip, full. You need any more, that's up to you. We don't do small shit. This one's a one-time favour, and not for you. Understand?"

Yes. He understood.

He hadn't held the gun for over two weeks and it felt comfortable in his hands. The luxury of conversation he had enjoyed with everyone but Gi-Gi was not his to enjoy this morning, although remembering the ease with which he had bid Gi-Gi farewell gave him strength to attach Jason's lax fingers to the plastic grip. The effort was awkward all the same. He needed his brother to take the gun firmly in hand, to co-operate. He had one chance or the agenda would fail and all he had accomplished would be for naught. He ran to the kitchen for a glass of water, taking the gun with him. When he returned he threw the cold contents into Jason's face and put the gun into his brother's hand in one smooth movement. He nodded approvingly, sensing a perceptible difference, the slightest tightening of Jason's fingers and Wellington spoke words of encouragement, telling his sleepy brother to concentrate, to tighten his left hand, the hand he was helping Jason to grasp.

Jason tried raising his head, to see. He couldn't. Wellington stepped slightly backward, telling his brother again that he must try squeezing his fingers. Jason finally nodded, indicating he understood. Wellington breathed in deeply. His own death had always been the imperative, if peace was ever to exist between the brothers. Perhaps now he could stop hating. Time stood still and he closed his eyes too late to avoid witnessing the devastation tearing through his brother's head. The entry wound was almost completely hidden under the thick black hair, though the exit wound would be horrific if the matter blowing out and away from Jason's head was any indication.

The weapon clutched in Jason's hand fell into his lap. His head had first been blown to the side before snapping back and falling forward onto the desk at nine-fifty, after which Wellington dialled his brother's cell. The call was answered immediately, the line left open for less than a minute.

The first of those four jerry cans adequately saturated the perimeter of the carpeted office; the second completely covered all the furnishing and library he had taken so many years to acquire. He emptied the third into the space immediately surrounding Jason and his chair back. He had taken note while watching a CSI show a year earlier that the ME was able to ID the victim's body due to the fact the perpetrator hadn't used sufficient accelerant for the fire he had hoped would destroy all traces of evidence at the crime scene. Wellington wouldn't make the same mistake. He emptied half the fourth container directly onto the desk, placing the remainder to one side of the damaged head, letting the gasoline pour out from the spout onto Jason's bent-over and saturated front.

The temperature in the house was unbearable. What had begun as crackling, sizzling sounds had developed quickly into a rumbling murmur that was now a full-fledged roar.

Neither had he forgotten he had opened the two valves which fed propane from two five-hundred litre exterior tanks to the impractical fireplaces in the living room and the office he hadn't used in two years. The office went first without any need to question his work. The kitchen came next, followed by the dining room and living room where he had thrown the match while closing the inside door to the entrance way.

The work clothes came off quickly and carefully and he washed himself one last time with the hand wipes, removing all traces. Had he not worn the mask his face would have been covered with blood and he could smell burnt powder on the coveralls. He dressed in Jason's clothes just as quickly, making certain he had the house keys, Jason's car keys and that his cell phone had been re-attached to his belt. He felt for the wallet in the rear pocket and the silver billfold in the front, finding each one. He checked the cell for the call: One received, none dialled, one message.

He stepped into the garage, tried the light that didn't come on, and threw the match for much needed personal satisfaction. He hated the car as much as he hated the house and had taken the precaution of barring entry from the inside with the built-in slide bar. The heat was sudden and scorching. Both doors to the garage were fire-rated, a moot point, he thought as he stepped from the entrance without hurrying. Outside, he put down the suitcase, turned into the closed-in area to topple the last container of gasoline and threw in the final match. When he turned the key in the lock the time was nine-fifty-five.

*

Jason ran to the Escalade he had left at the foot of the driveway and swung open the driver side door. He reached for the suede jacket strewn across the passenger seat, started the motor and then pushed the release for the trunk. He shoved the suitcase as far in as he could and threw on the jacket before jumping in behind the wheel and reversing until the front wheels hit the pavement of the street, shifting into forward, driving back in, this time faster, panic-stopping farther up the driveway. He left the motor running and the door open wide open when he jumped out.

He ran to the house, ranting hysterically as he crashed into the door, searing his hands as he grabbed at the handles, breaking the skin over his knuckles as he drove his fists into the door. Smoke was making its way through parts of the roof and some of the interior blinds in the front had either fallen from their railings or melted from the heat. He dialled 911 at ten, barely able to talk rationally through the tears and the choking. He ran to the window at the front porch where all he could see was a room engulfed in flames and a body that might have once been a man.

Only his hysteria mixed with panic and the need to save his brother made him grip the handles of the door again so tightly, screaming out against the pain as much as for his failure. The door panels were stained with blood that had browned instantly from the tremendous heat on the other side, the triple-paned windows also smeared with desperation. His shoulders ached from the constant pounding and all he could hear was the sound of his own wailing. When he turned, his shock was unrehearsed.

The front yard was ablaze with the quick-flashing white, red and blue lights of Emergency Response Vehicles. The two men running at him were screaming soundless words, waving wildly. The police officer grabbed at his arm with an authority and force that should have given him no choice, but his struggle to stay at the window was real. Only when the second cop caught up with his partner was the frantic Jason pulled away.

They were silent, standing beside him, torn between consoling the sobbing man and watching the incredible inferno consume the house, accompanied by a cacophony of high-pitched sirens and men yelling above the roar of the flames. Someone in yellow, with a tank on his back and a shield over his face came to them and shouted orders from behind the acrylic-mask, telling them to move away. They pulled Jason to between the first patrol cars which had skidded to a stop beside his and the three men stood in awe as the street filled with the local curious and photo opportunists. Jason seethed, hating that he couldn't openly despise them.

Four firefighters had hurried behind the blazing inferno that had begun collapsing the upper story, keeping as much distance between them and the structure as possible. They had been out of sight mere seconds before reappearing at a pace belying the weight of their asbestos suits and breathing apparatus. The one in the front had his mask off, waving his hands frantically for everyone to clear the area. No one stayed to ask why and the human wave of yellows and reflective greys moved in a solid line toward the road.

The dual explosions converted the house into a fireball, filling the nearby sky with glowing cinders and heated ash that rained down on everyone in the immediate area. The firefighters were the only ones who didn't raise their arms for protection as the curious horde behind them broke and ran, shouting curses as they brushed their clothing and hair as though they had been forced to stand there and gawk.

Well over an hour had passed before the smoking, crumpled and charred framework began appearing even as flames continued flaring up randomly from what had once been the basement, igniting cinder bombs that exploded without notice. The house had completely collapsed and the same high winds that continued blowing life into the furious orange flames carried the incredible heat across hundreds of metres. The time was approaching twelve before the firefighters got close enough with their hoses for the sole purpose of smothering the smouldering remains.

By one o'clock, all that remained for the spectators was the yellow police tape securing the area as a possible crime scene, one cop car, the Fire Inspector's car, a Cadillac Escalade and a charcoal heap that would inspire a scene in a low-budget horror film. The fire trucks had gone, Urgence Santé technicians had cared for Jason's badly burnt fingers before leaving and the neighbourly crowd had seen enough to fuel conversation for a year.

And Jason had forgotten about Renée. She would have to hear the news, from him, and soon. What could he say, he worried aloud and how could he possibly put his brother's death into words? One of the uniformed officers offered to make the call, backing off when Jason's eyes and face filled with tears and his bandaged hands fumbled with the speed dial.

Renée was silent, listening to the tearful monologue on the other end of the phone. When she understood what he had said to her, she froze where she stood, as though the bitter wind swirling around Jason had somehow found her and gripped her. She began convulsing, both officers gaping at Jason as her scream reached them through the phone. He was with the police, he explained, when he managed to calm her. They had questions he alone could answer. A letter had been discovered, a suicide note, something about the house and they needed to know more about what Wellington had meant and for whom.

He read to her: "Tell her how much I truly I hated this house. Good-bye to all, Wellington Trystan Bartlett".

The police wanted to know about the "her" and what her involvement might be. He'd be home later, following an interview at the precinct, and "Renée, cancel our dinner reservation."
*

Everyone on the scene who had seen the note agreed that he

had, indeed, hated the house. The Medical Examiner arrived as everyone was leaving, though more for the formality of declaring a death than transporting a weightless body bag of clues and evidence to the pathology lab.

Jason accepted the coffee even though what he really wanted was a Johnnie Walker Blue. There were three of them: One detective who had arrived late on the scene and the two uniforms who had been first on the scene.

"My wife and I left two weeks ago for France, on the twenty-second." He explained. "In fact, we arrived home last night. My brother called before we left, asking that I join him this morning at precisely nine o'clock. I thought for breakfast, a birthday breakfast. Yes, we're twins, fifty-three." He sipped from the paper cup. "He wasn't one who often thought of others, or valued time, though he hadn't said for breakfast specifically. He did say nine o'clock, and I assumed. I didn't imagine he had anything else to discuss, a power play of sorts, I suppose. My brother's been out of work for two years and had certain self-image problems. He was always a dollar short and a day late. As much as he tried, he never caught up. Two years ago his wife left him after fifteen years of marriage. She had actually somehow convinced him that he should invest the balance of his inheritance into paying off the mortgage on the house, after he'd funded most of her athletic club. Then she left him and, of course, she was entitled to half the value of the house. As I said, a dollar short. He was never the same after she left. He became a recluse. He never went out, he never called and he began drinking. He had said something about business meetings in the States, though personally I believe he invented the trip to save face."

The detective asked the primary question. "He made me beneficiary of his will," was the answer. "Our father made us both take insurance policies against each other's life, until we married. Like I said, he was recluse. He had no friends. I suppose I was the logical choice. I knew he was very despondent, dejected, but I never thought he intended anything as dreadful as this. Fifty-three with no prospects and no money, not a future anyone would envy."

Jason listened intently, studying the next question.

"No. We weren't that kind of family. In fact, we were no family at all. I hadn't seen him for over a year, different circles. He would never have approached me for money, and I would never have offered: Out of sight out of mind, I'm ashamed to say." The heat emanating from the coffee cup became unbearable in his bandaged fingers and he put it down. "He'd been drinking when I arrived. In fact, I joined him for one," he smiled, tearfully, "a birthday toast, so to speak. I had no idea my words would be the last he would hear. When he said he was dying I dismissed the words as an attempt at," he paused, "I don't know what…self-pity, perhaps a search for sympathy and I didn't take him seriously. Until I saw he was serious and I asked him how, from what. The end would be soon, was all he said, but that I would see him again and I shouldn't worry. Then he asked me to leave, saying that he suddenly felt tired and apologized for disturbing my wife's day. We were supposed to dine out this evening, for my birthday. I never suspected this. Had I any clue, I never would have gone."

They asked how his hands were, and he answered they were fine. They were anything but.

"Then I left at about nine-forty and a few moments later he called me on my cell, asking me to come back. I guess I took ten, maybe fifteen minutes. That's when I phoned 911. You know the rest."

He listened intently once more.

"I have no plausible explanation beyond a disturbed mind for why he would want me to witness his death, and such a horrible one, a cruel gift at the very least and one I will never forget. This day will haunt me forever."

There was no need to identify the body which arrived at the morgue an hour after Jason began answering questions. Very little had remained to put in the bag and the note had pretty much said it all. The police would be talking with the neighbours and ex-wife, adding in the same breath that the scene was pretty much self-explanatory. Some people finally do get what they want out of life.

Jason refused the ride home, thanking them distractedly for offering. He'd be okay and would have his hands checked out later, after he made sure his wife was fine. They understood.

*

True to his word, Jason went to the walk-in clinic to have his hands examined more closely. The burns were severe, especially at the fingertips. Any scarring would be negligible, though he was to expect some. The pain would subside within a day; he was to follow the instructions on the bottle to the letter and avoid alcohol. He had called Renée, telling her where he was and why, telling her what she should expect. He suggested she take a sedative and go to bed. Five PM was still ten for her body clock and he expected he might be another few hours. He would try his best not to wake her and they would talk in the morning.

*

Not long after Jason left the clinic, Jean-François LeTuvier returned to the Delta. He dropped onto the bed, struggling to open the bottle of Johnnie Walker Black he had bought for another special occasion. He preferred the Black label over Blue, which he would certainly drink to fit any future occasion or need. The taste of Black was a little sharper, the taste fuller and more to his liking. The Red simply wasn't interesting, not anymore.

He looked at the plastic vial he had picked up at the pharmacy, tossing it aside. He poured another JW Black. The pain was still there, but he cared less about it. He would allow himself two more and then he would leave. His future was clear in his mind. Only one person could alter or destroy his dream. As for his two pasts, whatever data might be missing in the first for his long or short term needs would soon be found. What was history more than names, places and dates, which he possessed? The second past had been faultlessly created and meticulously structured At least that would be one truth. He was forty-five and at that age what was there to prove about one's past given the circumstances. Such concerns were the domain of the young, the competitive and the unsure. The need for competition or uncertainty no longer existed.

Anyone who had ever met Jean-François LeTuvier would bear witness to his being thoroughly unfamiliar with such unworldly constraints. Jason B. Bartlett was another matter.

*

That night Jason sat in the Escalade for long moments before stepping out and walking pensively towards the elevator that would carry him to the luxury condo. Wellington's death had brought several issues to the forefront of his thoughts. How would life now be with Renée? The special something they once cherished had become a comfortable lifestyle, no different from the lives of their friends. They had been so comfortable for so long. How would she react to his taking her, loving her as he had one night so many years ago, the night of their wedding, when he had filled her with his heat and a passion she had never known before or since?

He remembered the exact words she had cried out in his parents' guest room under his cupped hands for fear they would be discovered as she begged him to go deeper, harder, to hurt her so much she would remember the feeling forever, remember him forever. He had never forgotten how she grasped his head between her hands and forced her mouth against his in a deep probing kiss before whispering she loved him, that she would always love him.

He had kept the silk memento of the evening for so many years and now he wondered, more than he ever had, if she had ever really known. How many times had he thought of the evening that was mere moments away? The corridor leading to the apartment was plush and quiet for a Friday evening at eleven o'clock and his fingers holding the key were unsteady from pain as much as from the unknown. The apartment was dark and quiet. He turned a dial illuminating the foyer, then the living room, and stood there uncertain.

The carpeted stairway leading to the second-floor bedroom was dark. He made his way one step at a time, not hurrying. He stood at the door, placing the hand he'd begun favouring on the handle, trying not to make the slightest sound. He stepped inside, staring at the bed she hadn't slept in. He was less secretive in his movements, reacting as he should in his own home. He padded into the guest room, opening the door to a room perfectly prepared for any guest. He turned on more lights, returning downstairs after checking the master bathroom and his second-floor office. The condo was an open-concept and very little was hidden from view. He walked through the dining room into the kitchen, and then he saw the folded parchment on the stereo at the far side of the living room and he knew.
*

My dearest love, my one true love,

The news about Wellington was devastating. I could never adequately explain to you how much, or why, though I shall grieve for a very long time.

Our relationship has never been what we truly desired, and so many years have gone by. Yet neither one of us ever confronted the issue as honestly as we should have, my love, and you know my words are true.

I have never forgotten what we shared that one special evening, the eve of my wedding when we loved each other the way few real lovers ever could. I gazed into your eyes and whispered that I loved you, I would always love you, and I knew then you had always loved me. I will always love you for what we might have been, had our lives together begun differently. I suppose that makes me a coward. Forgive me, my love, as I forgive you for all you have done. I will always deeply believe you harbour some remnant of love for me, remembering the fleeting and passionate moment of lovemaking we shared. I know you do, though neither can I live a lie which is yours alone and not mine.

You were wrong to begin an affair with Carmelita. Yes, my love, I know her name, and I caution you to beware. She knows you as well as I do and will be much more dangerous in her demands, though you were right to begin divorce proceedings, if not somewhat craven in your candid technique. We can never recapture what we might once have had, so sadly. We will never know the precious memories we might have shared.

I have signed the papers, indicating what I expect to receive as a reasonable settlement. I doubt very much that my demands will necessitate further discussion and have enclosed the name of my attorney to whom I shall send a copy. He is authorized by me to conclude these affairs as quickly as possible.

I am returning this evening to my beloved France and will send for my personal belongings over the next few days. I have poured you one last Blue, my love, an acquired taste as you surely must know, since you always did prefer Black for special occasions. Life is only as cruel as our own design, my love, and in that design we have both excelled for there can be no greater cruelty than what we have never lived, you and I.

I love you, I always did, and I hope you will never stop loving me in your own way, irrespective of the name you may assign me.

Adieu, my love,

Signed, November 03, Renée de Thierry, wife of the late Jason B. Bartlett

*

He collapsed onto the floor, crying himself into a deep sleep, awaking at 2:00 AM, the connoisseur scotch in the heavy crystal old-fashioned still resting in his lap. He threw the glass onto the couch and went upstairs to sleep in her bed.

Transition

The weekend went by quickly. By the time Jason woke Monday morning he'd gone to the bank to withdraw sufficient funds for his weekend plans, he signed with a realty agent for the sale of the luxury condo and revamped his entire wardrobe. The two-day shopping spree included various up-scale haberdashers he'd visited before, trying for a different image, a new and fresh symbol of his new beginning. What he didn't give to the mission, he discarded, and what he hadn't brought home from the boutiques would be delivered by mid-week.

Sunday evening he realized he wouldn't be going into the office the following morning, still grief-stricken at the loss of his brother. Subconsciously he had known he wouldn't, but the events of the past few days were so overwhelming and demanding of his time that he had given the office very little thought.

When he called the company in the morning the receptionist connected him immediately. The man was old school, identifying himself with his full name when answering, which wasn't necessary. There was nothing to explain, the man insisted. The entire office was abuzz with what they had read in the weekend newspapers. Jason was to take as much time as he needed.

His boss had chosen the path of least conversation and his relief was audible when Jason responded that the funeral service would be private. What else was there to say? He was to stay in touch after two weeks, if more time was needed. Take care of yourself, regards to the wife, and the conversation was over.

For the time being, no one would be the wiser about Renée's sudden departure, especially Carmelita. Renée's warning about her was unmistakable and he had taken it to heart. He had gone to the hotel once each day and by checkout time Monday none of the contents from the suitcase he'd brought from the house remained, including the suitcase he had put into a mission box.

Flowers had been delivered from the law offices of Taylor, Lefebvre & Dunn, initiated by Mme. Jacqueline Duvernay, and from IntelSanté with a "from all of us," probably scrawled by one of the flower shop employees. By dinnertime two prospective buyers had visited, one had made an offer. He had made tentative funeral arrangements, subject to change, and he was alone for dinner once again.

He spent the evening loading the CDs into his notebook and reviewing all current and past files, both personal and corporate. By midnight he had read through all the e-mails received during his vacation and was up to speed with what was going on at the office. One message had come from Theresa, and one from Carmelita, both expressing regret and offering sympathy. He checked the company registry. Theresa was his secretary. He responded to neither.

Tuesday morning the police called, confirming an autopsy performed over the weekend had revealed the cause of death was actually a self-inflicted gunshot to the head. The lab determined Wellington had begun the fire from at least two levels of his home, if not three, and had called Jason before shooting himself once to the side of the head. The weapon used was an unregistered Berretta 92FS with one round discharged. Death had been instantaneous. The serial number had been ground off and the gun would remain in their possession for possible further examination. Though they admitted it would likely not be fired again. The fire had been secondary, for purposes the victim alone would ever know.

The autopsy had been a matter of course, they apologized. The body, effectively reduced to ashes, was too severely burned for the official determination not to read death by suicide. If his brother had intended to make a statement, he had succeeded. The body had been released by the ME and would be ready for pick-up at the convenience of the family's preferred funeral home. Please accept our condolences.

Tuesday afternoon a cleaning crew of five arrived to prepare the luxury condo for its eventual new owners. By Tuesday evening three more couples had shown interest, one had made an offer to purchase and Jason had met with the Funeral Director. Despite being morosely comical given the nature of the death, cremation had been the final decision and the director seemed to concur.

He called Geneviève who had likely monitored his name on caller ID, refusing the call. He left a voice-mail, out of respect, dialling again for something to eat. He didn't keep newspapers once he had read them. The headlines were too upsetting after everything else. Maître Gaston George Lefebvre, of his brother's law firm, had been found dead in his Montreal home late Monday night. Police were investigating clues that might link his death with another, although they had no further comment at the moment. Maître Lefebvre had been known for his ties with the underworld and was one of Montreal's most celebrated criminal lawyers. Monsieur Michel Marcotte, an executive at the pharmaceutical firm VitaVie had also been found Monday night, strangled in his Prince Arthur street apartment. Police suspected a possible tie-in to the death of Maître Lefebvre and are continuing the investigation.

Wednesday morning the service was simple, efficient, and paid for by credit card. He accepted the urn, his brother's distorted school ring, and made one stop on his way to his condo. He stood against the bitterly cold wind for thirty minutes, watching. The urn bobbed erratically as wind and current carried the ashes and ring towards the main channel of the St. Lawrence Seaway before filling completely with the murky, frigid water and sinking to the soft, muddy bed ten polluted metres below. Neither the urn nor the ring would ever be found, unless by some dredging operation in the decades to come.

As he turned to walk away he stopped, examining the fingers of his left hand still scarred and sensitive from the recent burns he sustained while attempting to save his brother, now bluish from the bitter wind. He had no real claim to the band. She'd left him for good He struggled with himself, wincing at the pain as the gold ring worked its way past his swollen knuckles and over his throbbing fingertips, instantly disappearing into the air before hitting the water.

The red light was flashing on the phone when he arrived home. Louise, the agent, had an offer he couldn't refuse. They would meet with the couple the next day, and sign. There would be no better offer, she insisted. She would bring the champagne to clinch the already done deal, a fait accompli. The second call display was the Communauté Urbaine de Montréal, the cops. The message was from Inspecteur Danny Lemieux. The third call was from Jacqueline Duvernay.

Ladies first, though he made the call with some apprehension after pouring a Blue to relax. She had called to personally express her sympathies for his loss. She had come to know Wellington well over the years and had always thought very highly of him. She would miss him dearly.

"As you know, Mr. Bartlett, I am the Executor of your brother's will. I cannot tell you how shocked I am that I must perform those duties after having seen him such a short while ago."

"I can imagine this is very difficult for you, Mme. Duvernay. He was a very likable person, though perhaps too shy for his own good, especially with women. I believe he was very lonely at the end. The service was this morning, and very private. I attended alone."

"Not your wife?"

"No, I regret to say. We have, well," he hesitated, "my brother's death has made a bad situation worse. You understand?"

"Yes, of course I do." She did. "It's all very sad. I suppose we will never know." Her pause was imperceptible. "My boss, Maître Lefebvre, as you may know, was found dead Monday night in his condominium."

Jason gasped, not believing the news. "He what?" he said, "No. I have been too busy to bother with any other news. My sincerest condolences, madame," he offered. "What was the cause? Was he ill?"

"They believed at first his death was an accident, apparently his stereo cabinet collapsed into the bathtub while he was bathing. Now they say his death might have been a suicide and he may have been involved somehow in the death of a Michel Marcotte. The police called today asking about a possible relationship between the two. The thought is ridiculous, of course. Until today I had never heard the name."

"I have also had a call from an Inspecteur Lemieux. I am supposed to call him as soon as possible. He didn't say why. I imagine they have more news about my brother's death."

"They do. They have questions as well, Mr. Bartlett."

"I can't imagine what else they would have to ask. They were very thorough last Friday."

"Your brother had sixteen thousand dollars in a desk model safe that survived the fire. The safe contained a copy of his will and a direct link to these law offices, Maître Lefebvre and me, being that I am named as the Executor."

"And they suspect what exactly, Mme. Duvernay."

"It would appear, thus far, according to the evidence, that this Michel Marcotte was killed by Maître Lefebvre who then killed himself. They have a bracelet which they say is inscribed with both their names, at least one name and a nickname of some sort."

"Nickname?" he repeated.

"Gi-Gi, of all things," she answered, sounding frustrated. "There must be hundreds of identical initials. They also found his car parked in his garage, damaged in a way consistent with several damaged vehicles in front of Marcotte's apartment last Thursday evening."

"I'm not sure I know where all this is going, Mme. Duvernay." Jason paused, as though shrugging his shoulders. "They believe my brother is somehow implicated? They believe he's gay? He isn't of course, or wasn't. The implication is entirely absurd as I'm sure you are well aware."

"Indeed, an aspect of the investigation I have already fervently insisted is without merit. I told them that in all my years of working very closely with Maître Lefebvre I have never heard him referred to as Gi-Gi. He would certainly have spurned such a ridiculous appellation and for as many years as I have known your brother their relationship was strictly business, business protected by privilege."

"Is there a supposed connection between Wellington and this so-called Marcotte?"

"Not that I am aware. However, the investigation is ongoing."

"It is all very disturbing."

Madame Duvernay hesitated. "Mr. Bartlett, may I be candid?"

"From the little I know of you, madame, I would expect nothing less."

"Your brother and Maître Lefebvre were friends, good friends."

"But you just said…"

"Mr. Bartlett, I asked for candour. Please." Her brief pause served as sufficient admonition. "I am interested in two things: The good name of my boss and the privacy of a respected client, nothing more."

"Accept my apology. Please continue."

"They were good friends, they had been for years. No more need be said about the matter. If your brother saw fit not to include you in that part of his life, nor will I. Maître Lefebvre thought very highly of your brother, very highly indeed. He made provisions for your brother in his will."

"What?" Jason's gasp wasn't theatrical.

"Your brother is named in his will, Mr. Bartlett, for a rather substantial amount. No provision had been made for your brother's death, which means the bequest, the gift, if you will, now falls to you."

"He must have family."

"Irrespective of all other assignments, monsieur, what was intended for your brother is now yours. That is how the system works."

"That is unusually generous and unexpected, Mme. Duvernay Very unexpected indeed."

"I expect so, Mr. Bartlett. You should, of course, anticipate a delay in the settlement of your brother's estate. Officially your brother's death is being considered as a suicide, which is not problematic in itself because the limitation of that particular clause in the insurance policy expired years ago. The problem is with the house. Proving the fire wasn't intentional arson will be somewhat difficult. I would think impossible, and, of course, as Executor, I am mandated to satisfy the balance of the car payments for the vehicle Well... your brother, left in the garage. The estate may also be responsible for the remaining value of the house. If you are not already aware, your brother took out a second mortgage a few years ago. I believe he did so in order to finance a divorce settlement."

"You know my brother very well, Mme. Duvernay."

Jason wanted badly to call her Jacqueline. He wanted to

do her at that very moment, wondering why he never had when she had always been so close.

She ignored the comment. "I believe I can have everything settled by Friday, the seventeenth. You will not be required to come by the office, unless you see a need. The times I have available on my schedule are the seventeenth at five-thirty or seven."

"I'm not certain of my schedule at this point, Mme. Duvernay. I may have previous commitments."

"As I said, your being here isn't necessary. I made the suggestion for your convenience, to answer any questions you might have. Why don't we leave the appointment open, if I may suggest? And, if I don't hear from you by Monday, the thirteenth, I'll assume I should forward all documentation by courier."

"Agreed, and I thank you for calling, madame, for taking so much time from your schedule to accommodate me. I also want to say how much I empathize with you for the loss of Maître Lefebvre."

"Thank you, Mr. Bartlett, à bientôt."

"Sûrement, madame, à bientôt."

He wanted the courier at his door that night, not the thirteenth or seventeenth. There was very little Jacqueline Duvernay did not know about the inner workings of her boss' secret world, both business and private, and he wondered how much she knew now. He supposed a good deal. The next call was to Danny Lemieux and he poured another Blue, confident Jacqueline Duvernay had set the stage.

"Monsieur Bartlett, when the scene investigators were examining what was left of the house all that remained, unfortunately, was a steel safety box in which they found sixteen thousand dollars and your brother's will."

"Yes, I've been speaking with my brother's law firm. I'm already aware of the discovery."

"Then you are aware, Monsieur Bartlett, that Maître Lefebvre has been found dead and possibly linked to another killing as well, a Monsieur Michel Marcotte."

"Yes, I am."

"Beyond the business nature of your brother's relationship with Gaston Lefebvre, are you aware of any other, perhaps more personal aspects of the relationship."

"Do you mean," Jason hesitated, "that my brother was Monsieur Lefebvre's lover? Don't be ridiculous."

"I meant, did he know Maître Lefebvre other than strictly for business purposes, were they friends?"

"I have no idea, not in the least. If my brother was living a secret life, I was not privy to any such proclivity. My brother and I were not close, inspector. I hardly knew him, especially over the past two years I regret to say." He paused for effect. "What I can say, and what others will attest to, is that during our time at university he was as socially active as anyone else and until his separation from his wife he was in her company exclusively, shall I say. Following that fiasco he essentially became a recluse about two years ago, worsening last year with the final divorce papers. Since then, and as far as I know, he's had no social contact. On the other hand, there was not much contact to begin with, especially with my wife and me."

"May I ask how so?"

"Simply put, we each went our own way since university. We chose to walk different roads, the high and the low so to speak."

"The expression escapes me."

"We each took separate paths, had different interests. There were a few parties, nothing more, the obligatory stuff all families have to deal with."

"When we investigated Marcotte's apartment we found irrefutable evidence he enjoyed an alternative lifestyle. Following up on that particular lead, several patrons of a bar he frequented gave statements that a man fitting the description of Lefebvre was seen talking with him on Wednesday evening. A subsequent investigation of Lefebvre's apartment revealed clothing that perfectly matched the description of those witnesses. The one curious link between your brother and the other two deaths is the will we found in the drawer."

"Inspector, with all due respect, that must be a coincidence."

"That is what we believe as well, Monsieur Bartlett. Mme. Duvernay was adamant that your brother's relationship with Lefebvre was strictly as a client of the firm. However, we are in the business of joining pieces of a puzzle so that they make sense. At this point the case is evolving into a murder-suicide, and a suicide which is unrelated. However your brother's case has not yet been officially closed. We're still waiting for results from the lab and scene investigators."

"Inspector, we were brothers by virtue of birth. I'm certain by the time your investigation is over you will know much more about my brother's past and present than I ever did."

"Your brother withdrew very large amounts from his accounts between June and September. Would you have any idea why? Did he have personal troubles, debts, gambling perhaps?"

"Inspector, you know he was unemployed for two years. He was despondent, probably at his wits end. Of course, he had problems."

"He never went to you for help?"

"No, he never did. I often wondered why not. False pride, I suppose."

"Pride can sometimes lead us towards unfortunate circumstances."

"In this case, Inspector, I can think of no greater

misfortune."

"And very regrettable, monsieur, that your brother became a needless victim of the modern age."

"I would suggest he was more likely the victim of reality, Inspector, not modern times. When brothers have drifted apart over the centuries those past times were, for them, modern, victims of the condition of the specie, not the times. Cain and Abel were the first, we won't be the last."

"Cain killed Abel because he was jealous. He felt rejected."

"And my brother killed himself for those very reasons." He took a breath. "Where does this leave us, monsieur?"

"With many unanswered questions, Monsieur Bartlett," he responded. "As I have said, officially, we have a murder-suicide with the possible complication of a second suicide. May I ask what your plans are for the near future?"

"Yes, of course, you may. I shall be returning to work on the twentieth. Until then I shall be here at home, for the most part. You may contact me whenever you wish."

"Merci, monsieur. I wish you a pleasant evening and my condolences."

He fell asleep thinking of Jacqueline Duvernay, of how she might look, of what she might be wearing and of what she might be thinking. Thursday was a new day, a new beginning. The phone had rung twice since the tragic news became known, both conversations courteously generic. They had not wanted to call too soon, whoever "they" were. Of course, he would love to come to dinner, in a week or so, when everything was settled and he and Renée could be more themselves. Yes, she was fine, though slightly medicated and resting at the moment.

The papers were signed after the overly anxious couple spent too much time admiring their soon-to-be luxury love nest and he wondered how long they would be in it together. Louise did bring the champagne, as promised, and she was as anxious for them to leave as he was. She had negotiated ten percent over market value. After deducting her commission and honouring the balance of the mortgage, Renée would receive more than one million from the sale. The sum would constitute approximately half her settlement, half of her implied condition she had attached to the less pragmatic and heartfelt letter she had left for him on Friday.

She would receive all monies arising from the sale after commissions and settlement in full of the mortgage, in addition to fifty-percent of his personal investment portfolio he had initially funded with the half million inheritance invested to his advantage over the past thirty-two years: another two million. Renée would do very well. He would keep all furnishings, her Z4, the other half his investments, his substantial personal bank accounts and their joint account, which would cover most of the current credit card and other domestic bills.

He still loved her, he always would. By now she would have resigned in absentia from her post as Professeure de la langue Française et Linguistiques, stating personal family problems, her parents' health or whatever else would seem appropriate, he thought. The meeting with the notary would be Monday morning, with Renée's attorney in attendance and Jason would have five weeks following the meeting, until the week before Christmas, to set his affairs in order. But all that was ahead of him. Louise was in the now, she was with him and Renée had written "with whatever name he assigned her." He had no cause for celebration. Renée would get everything. His sole benefit would be having Louise for the night, which was particularly fine with him.

Much of the first bottle of champagne spilled onto the carpet. She had bought the best. Why wouldn't she with an easy seventy grand as her portion of the commission? They quickly finished what was left and he broke out another that would nicely complement the first. She had been ecstatic when the buyers had signed, even more so when they had gone. As he prepared the wine, she put on a Dean Martin CD and, when he came back, she was dancing in perfect rhythm to the music. He sat fixated, fantasizing, watching her enjoy the moment, eventually making a daring suggestion intended to sound light-hearted, not serious. She didn't miss a beat, smiling, and by the end of the second song she was dancing in her bra and nylons that were attached by garters to the sexiest pair of panties he'd seen in a long week. Finally she collapsed beside him, setting the tone for the evening.

The Lejaby bra and panties were soon tossed to one side, the wine forgotten. The two were wet with sweat, dehydrated by lust and drank the first glass of the chilled wine like water. Then they giggled and covered their mouths too late.

He whispered another suggestion into her ear and she sniggered, loving the idea. Why not? She'd never be back and he'd soon be gone. So why not? The question at hand being panties or no panties, the answer: no panties. The robes were plush and cozy. The towels under them were plush, cozy and small, barely covering her breasts and the sparse hair at the apex of her legs enhanced her sensuality all the more. Cameras be damned, and by the time they arrived at the top floor with its 360° panoramic view her robe hung over his arm and Louise was pinching the top ends of her towel together between two fingers.

Two couples in the pool watched them scurry into the sauna and another saw them from the whirlpool as Jason and Louise passed by, Jason noticing their identical reactions and smiling. When he told Louise she laughed so heartily Jason thought the others must have heard. She opened her towel and suggested a whirlpool. He said no and took the towel.

The bottle of Chardonnay spilled partially onto the

heated cedar slats that were the unforgiving seats. The boards were particularly difficult for Jason, Louise barely touched them. As her heated and slippery breasts rubbed against his chest he thought of Celeste and how she had wanted the balcony doors left open, and whether the couple in the spa would be curious enough to peer in or adventurous enough to join them. Looking past Louise's gyrating body he saw the couples at the far end of the pool exchanging nods and smiles, half hoping the third couple wouldn't disappoint him, at least not the woman, he thought craning his neck, her closeness concealing the lips he wanted to see as much as feel.

They shuddered as one when he had gone as far as he could go and they hugged each other closely, spent from the heat and the drink. Freeing herself, she stood facing him. Her body glistened. She parted her legs slowly, cupping her breasts, her pink lips opening to him at eye level. He was mesmerized by the wetness, wanting more, excited by her pungent scent. He pushed himself from the bench, sliding against the dry heat of the wall, pulling her in, taking her once more with renewed ardour until she collapsed against him, quivering, held tightly in arms that kept her from falling.

Friday morning she was as vivacious as she had the night before, though she was naked and her hair was not as perfect. She was thirty-two, blonde, divorced without kids and wore lingerie all men dream about. By ten o'clock the night before that's all she had been wearing, by eleven the living room floor was strewn with romantic CDs and her ruined lingerie. By twelve they had come back from the sauna to begin all over again. They had both been pleasantly drunk for the same and different reasons. They had both made money, Louise and Renée, lots of money, and he had given her more champagne than he had served himself. She specialized in seven-figure real estate, her career was her life and she wasn't interested in a serious relationship, preferring the occasional good evening and he certainly was good. So was she. She'd been in the right place at the right time.

They would see each other on Monday at 3:00 PM, as previously agreed, and she left her latest success without her panties or bra, satisfied and satiated. By Friday morning he completed the review of personal data found in his home office, as well as all documentation stored in his and Renée's safety deposit box at the bank that he closed.

None of the information was relevant, methodically shredded by week's end, leaving very little proof that he was who he might have to say he was. Moot point, he knew. Nothing else mattered. Though he did realize that, with a little extra pressure, he was writing his signature the way he had prior to burning his hands.
*

When Jean-François LeTuvier boarded the Air France flight en route to Lyons Friday, connecting to Madrid before continuing his journey to the Mediterranean coast, he had no idea the weekend papers had been discreet regarding the official findings revolving around Maître Lefebvre's death. Marcotte had been entirely forgotten by the press. Gaston Lefebvre, one of Montreal's leading criminal lawyers, they wrote, had been found dead in his apartment the previous Monday. Although the cause of death was being officially listed as suicide, the police were not discounting the possibility of murder, a settling of accounts and the investigation would continue, or so they would say until people stopped asking.

The weekend would be arduous and, he hoped, equally fulfilling. He had gone for a detailed progress report, which he had insisted on seeing in person: the culmination of everything he had planned and he would be there to ensure perfection in every regard.

During the return flight the lead flight attendant working. in First Class, for reasons which were obvious to most passengers, noticed his ring and commented on its unique design. He thanked her, explaining that his bride was to have given him the ring, before the horrible accident which took her life: the reason he wore it on the third finger of the left hand. He arrived home later than planned on Monday morning.

*

There had been precious little time to spare, and he was thankful the red light on his phone was not flashing. Louise arrived promptly at three, the new buyers close behind, and Renée's lawyer called to say he would be thirty minutes late. The air was electrically charged to say the least. Friday morning was still fresh in their minds, Jason and Louise both relieved when the happy couple went on a tour of their new acquisition.

When the couple came back from their exploration, the pent-up tension between the seller and his agent had been released and Jason had good news for both of them. The condo would be available as of the twenty-fourth, the thirtieth at the very latest. The transfer of the deed was completed by four PM, over a polite glass of champagne Jason thought to supply, and the buyers accepted his offer of a quarter-million worth of designer furniture for pennies on the dollar. They wrote the cheque happily, the documents signed, everyone was gone by four except Louise who left at seven the following morning.

*

Jean-François boarded the Air Canada flight Tuesday at ten AM, landing landed at Toronto's Person International an hour and twenty minutes later. He stayed thirty-six hours before his return flight to Montreal, his second home, albeit no longer the second largest French-speaking city in the world. And he hated it.

Split Verdict

*

Jason must have passed the phone's flashing red band a dozen times, resisting the temptation to return Louise's call throughout the entire evening. Thursday he woke to a damp, bleak and colourless day. The wind slapped at the windows all morning long and what had begun as rain pelting the oversized thermal panes had turned to snow, which later turned to greyish slush. His coffee was strong, instantly tearing at his stomach. When he finally did go to the phone, he viewed the ID without much thought at all. He knew now what would happen, how everything would play out. He was tired, wanting the end to be near. The entire year had been gruelling, what with his brother's death, the divorce, Renée leaving him, the sale of the condo and the police investigation. The phone call from the night before was from Jacqueline Duvernay, not Louise, and he mildly admonished himself for not having listened to the message long before going to bed. When he did, he smiled and pressed re-dial.

She had received the two-point-two- million dollar insurance settlement, which she would forward by special courier the following day. And could he be at home between the hours of ten and twelve? Wellington's house, although fully ensured against fire, was not covered for criminal intent or negligence and the amount owed to the bank was one-hundred and fifty thousand, plus a charge of fifty thousand dollars the bank judged as reasonable to cover the cost of cleaning up the property, the ownership of which had reverted to them. The car destroyed in the fire was not covered by the insurer and she suggested, for the sake of nine thousand dollars owing, there was very little logic in incurring additional court costs by challenging the decision. The sixteen thousand in cash had been returned to her by the police, and the final statement from the law firm would be eighteen thousand dollars. She had taken the liberty of deducting the amount and a fully itemized fee schedule would be enclosed with the documentation. As previously mentioned, Maître Lefebvre had bequeathed an amount of five hundred thousand dollars to Wellington, which would be enclosed separately, for a total after deductions of two million two hundred and eighty-five thousand dollars.

Yes, he would be home, and he would certainly call with any questions, though he didn't anticipate any. He thanked her for all she had done and ended the call. The temptation had been overwhelming. How easy she would have been to comfort, to help through her double loss, to undress her and take her to Renée's bed, though he knew all the while she would see Wellington and inadvertently speaking inappropriately after he had come so far would be the easiest blunder of all.

*

Friday morning he called Eric J. Bloomington, his boss, advising he would arrive at the office first thing Monday morning, the 20th. He would need about two hours of his time in order to properly discuss several topics for the good of the firm.

He called his own lawyer for an up-date on the divorce proceedings, advised that the dissolution would take at least two more months. He gave Maître Bisson the address of Renée's lawyer, with instructions that all future correspondence be forwarded to his attention. He told Bisson he would be out of town for a while, explaining he had had sold the condo, and asked for an amount that would satisfy the lawyer's fee schedule. He wrote the cheque and considered himself divorced as of that moment.

Driving the Z4 for the first time, he wished he had done so before. The BMW was in Renée's name with six months remaining on the lease. He wrote the cheque, payable immediately, and left the dealer in a taxi. Hell hath no fury like a woman scorned and he saw no reason to piss her off.

He called Louise, disconnecting without leaving a message. He thought of calling Jacqueline Duvernay and walked away from the phone, cursing the self-imposed privation.

*

Jean-François LeTuvier arrived in Almería in time for a glass of wine and a light breakfast before his first appointment. The Gulf of Almería was a perfect Mediterranean blue, blending perfectly with the clear sky at the horizon. There was none of the hustle and bustle he had left six thousand kilometres behind. He had fallen in love with the seaside town during his early teens and had returned several times since, alone, always knowing one day he would call Almería home.

The meeting with the contractors and designers went extremely well. The villa would be completed by early December, at which time the final payment would be expected. His second meeting was with his decorators commissioned to furnish and decorate the villa in a way that was both masculine and neutral. He would coordinate personal touches at a later time.

Saturday evening he walked the crowded streets, enjoying the local patatas con mayonesa, a curious combination of French fries topped with mayonnaise and wrapped in newspaper. The subtropical night air was warm and he didn't miss his overcoat or the snow he had left behind. Young people were smoking "los negros," acting older than their years with glasses of wine and beer, watched by older couples who had once done the same. They weren't envious. They were enjoying the present as much as they had once enjoyed the past and Jean-François thought of the sad society awaiting his return, for however briefly, and he questioned his own reasoning.

*

The twentieth was the precursor to weather that would follow over the next four months. Rain mixed with snow fell all day and the ice forming as day became night was jagged and mixed with sand, salt and the litter of careless pedestrians and drivers who preferred the spotlessness of their coat pockets and car interiors over civic pride. Jason Bartlett drove through the horrors of pre-winter downtown traffic with a purpose in lieu of expectation. He was expected.

Eric L. Bloomington resided on the twentieth floor. He was the president and CEO of IntelSanté. When Jason was escorted through the mahogany doors leading into a cherry panelled office he stood in front of the huge cherry desk, unexpectedly preoccupied by the wine-coloured carpet. The high-back leather chairs were trimmed in cherry wood, the frames on three of the four walls had lacquered cherry frames and he again he thought of Celeste. The windows afforded a panoramic view and lined the fourth wall. The sun drapes were a pale wine-colour and heavier curtains gathered at both ends with gold ropes were a darker shade. The man was somewhere between sixty-five and seventy, and obviously controlled majority shares. His hair was pure white, his suit was dark blue and his tie was as perfect as the French cuffs protruding enough to show that his links were monogrammed and expensive.

Jason had dressed for the occasion. He would leave the company on his own terms and be at his best doing it. The best laid plans of mice and men, and however the rest of the ridiculous adage went, he thought. The office was too perfect and he wondered whether the old guy ever actually worked or just sat there, as he was now, smiling diffidently and extending a hand so that his cuffs stood out even more. He spoke flatteringly about how refreshed Jason looked, how calm he appeared considering the recent events he had experienced and how happy everyone would be that he was back.

True, Jason thought, most city boys could smell bullshit before stepping in it, unlike their country cousins, and this was bullshit reduced to its purest form. Jason smiled as though seeing Bloomington for the first time. He had one thought on his mind: Know when to close, and the time was near. Renée had ended his hard-earned career with her decision to return home to France. Had she stayed, he would have continued with his life as planned, climbing the corporate ladder towards an even more blissful existence. Now all that was as meaningless as the data he had collected over the past few weeks and not the time to play hero. The golden rules in his career had always been: know when to stop talking, know when to close, know when to walk. He had two items he would leave with Bloomington: the keys to the company Escalade and his laptop, with no need for long, drawn out good-byes.

The newspapers would likely become unkind in the reporting of certain current events. Yes, he conceded, his brother had been in a gay relationship for however long the situation had lasted. Yes, he was officially separated and the divorce would be finalized within a few months. No, he was not interested in the woman on the sixth floor. She was a diversion, a reason not to go home, nothing more. Yes, he agreed. She certainly viewed the relationship differently.

Yes. But don't they all?

The firm had as much starch in its policies as the old man had in his shirt. They would not tolerate high profile executives straying from the norm. A relatively private flirtation was one thing. Being divorced and having someone on the sixth floor possibly flaunting a victory was something else, and Jason agreed. He could leave immediately, before news travelled to anyone that he was in the building, anyone meaning Carmelita. Or he could stay and the news would quickly spread throughout the corporation and eventually to the long-standing, conventional customer base, not to mention the board. He had tenure, which meant they couldn't get rid of him without his collaboration. Then there were the headlines and Bloomington knew as well as Jason the pompous board would react badly to being even distantly associated with a suicide-murder investigation involving homosexual overtones. If he did stay, neither one doubted he would have the upper hand. He would, though ultimately not in his best interest. They agreed on both counts to mutual advantage.

He had been with the firm for twenty-five years, give or take, and he fully expected the respect and the understanding of the directors and board members. The old man listened with diminishing interest and, once Jason's intentions became clear, adamant he would not reconsider, the question of how to best handle the details took obvious precedence. Bloomington was visibly relieved Jason had taken the initiative. There were personal items in his office which he wanted to collect, suggesting security could escort him. The old man showed quiet indignation at the inference after so many years working together, proposing instead that after clearing out his office they might have lunch together in the corporate dining room once more for old-time sake.

Once more, what did that mean? Was this a father and son event, he wondered? Jason saw both sadness and expectation in Bloomington's eyes and, for a moment, he believed the man regretted his initial haste in response to the resignation. But he was old school, very obviously so, and what was done was done. He would not recant. Plan your dive, and dive your plan, or get royally fucked. What the hell. Yes, why not? Being with the old man would give them the opportunity to review and sign the separation papers as well as allowing the accounting department to prepare the final cheques that would include a severance payment of one year, as stated in his contract, and the redemption value of his stock options. Anyway, he had run out of food at home.

*

The final hour in his office had been an experience capturing once and for all the essence of self. There was no photo, no souvenir of past trips and no playful screensaver: the office of a man who feared being caught in the middle. He wondered why Renée, knowing what he now knew, had stayed, lie or no lie.

Bloomington was a man of action, or his subordinates who feared him were. By 2:00 PM lunch had concluded, they had both imbibed reasonable amounts of the best and Jason had two cheques in his possession. The one-year severance was 150K and the stock options totalled two-fifty. After taxes at source he walked out with two hundred and twenty thousand.

He had suffered two separations in two weeks. The fantasy living within him for twenty-five years had dissolved, though, to Jason, her leaving was more than the mere dissolution of a marriage. He no longer had his dream; the fantasy had been taken from him for which he could only hate himself. He shook his head, knowing the time for hating was over.

He felt no loss when he left the firm, though he did feel compassion for an old man. When he handed over the laptop he had simply said his corporate affairs were up to date, turning and walking from the cherry-coloured office. He had entertained a slight curiosity about Carmelita, very slight when weighing the pleasure of screwing his dead brother's girlfriend against life in prison, and when he strode through the revolving brass doors that part of his life ended.

By the end of the business day, Monday, November 20th, a final transfer had been made to the less conspicuous banking system allowed by the Swiss. Jason Bartholomew Bartlett ceased to exist and Jean-François LeTuvier was en route to the Trudeau Airport, booked on a flight to Toronto for a two-day sojourn after which he would travel to his home in Almeria, Spain.

Christmas Eve

The gated villa everyone would soon know as La Casa Mimada sat perched at the very edge of the rocky precipice that was the centre-piece of the town. There for everyone to see the pure white walls reflecting the constant sun and rounded, amber-coloured clay roof tiles he special-ordered to distinguish the property from the traditional and mundane burnt-orange roofing of adjoining homes.

Construction of the villa had been completed precisely in accordance with each and every specification. Nothing had been overlooked and no cost had been spared. He was the talk of the town, particularly amongst the women, young and old, who gossiped more about him than the men folk who were more interested in the villa. The tradesmen had all been hired from the local area and by the time he moved in the whole neighbourhood knew as much of the minute design details as he did himself.

The fourteen rooms were spacious. The master bedroom, guest room, salon, dining room and gourmet kitchen all led onto an expansive white stucco patio with ever-changing vistas and the blue brilliance of the Mediterranean. The infinity pool was heated, of all things, most agreed, painted in the blue tones of the sparkling sea it appeared to flow into from a waterfall at the edge of the cliff designed to duplicate the contours of the gulf.

He was eccentric, and mysterious. Imagine having three bathrooms, a gymnasium and a garage for two cars. What nonsense, they murmured, not to mention the expense. More to the point, who would be the first to invite him for dinner, or be invited by the handsome neighbour so at least one amongst them could see for themselves the contemporary and modern furnishings which had been purchased and coordinated by an exclusive and beautiful designer from Malagá? She had done much of her work while he was gone, which was most weekends, was all the men could say about her, which was completely unsatisfactory to the women.

The men spoke more about the women who chattered about him, than Jean-François, failing to see what the fuss was about. He had passed by their favourite terraza three times over the past month for a glass of wine and breakfast, twice joining them for a friendly game of backgammon. He had won both matches with humility and a warm smile, and after the second he suggested a rematch at their convenience sometime in the future. Then he left them to wonder about him at a level that was manly and intellectual, not with the flustered chattiness of the women.

He was French and spoke an educated, flawless Spanish. He was down to earth, albeit somewhat aloof, and he wasn't married. The men had instantly regretted answering their wives' probing questions with easy quickness. They had surrendered one of their own for the sake of peace at home and amongst themselves they decided they would right the wrong and warn him the next time they drank wine together and beat him at backgammon.

Pronouncing his name was troublesome. The "hota" sound of the Spanish J conflicted badly with the hard "je" sound of the French, and the cedilla in François made most of them spit. They drank to the good health and long life of the new Francisco with one, and then two glasses of vino tinto before Francisco won his third game.

He would be gone for a few days, he explained, hoping

the trip would be his last for some time to come. He wanted to enjoy his home and his neighbours. One member of the breakfast club was the cabinet maker who had installed the imported cabinetry in the villa. They shook hands and the secret deal was done. Payment was a trivia they would deal with upon his return and he would like what he would then see. When the man asked whether he had specific instructions regarding the work, Francisco simply slipped him the paper he'd been neatly folding. The man smiled widely, mimicking Francisco who put a finger to his lips

He had been part of the community for one month and was slowly fitting in. He wasn't yet one of them, that would come eventually. Neither had he moved into one of those xenophobic retirement communities designed for paranoid retirees and insecure tourists. They trusted him, they liked him and he liked them. The widows in town were few, though most hadn't been alone very long and he noticed even more side glances and open smiles as he enjoyed his mid-evening stroll through town. He must be somewhere between mid-forties and early fifties, they whispered, many insisting at the very worst that he was forty-nine. He was far too well-conditioned, his hair was pitch-black and his tanned skin was clear and smooth.

Mid-December was pleasant along the gulf shore, though at that time of year the locals would leave the beach to the Germans who freely bared their breasts, appalling British tourists who stayed to themselves and sat with their knees up against or under Shetland sweaters, convinced they were enjoying themselves. Then there were the requisite Americans, unashamedly confusing staring someone down and speaking loudly with communicating in a foreign language. Jean-François winced at the sound, raising his open hands and shrugging his shoulders in an attempt to convey he had no idea what they wanted. When the woman asked her husband to speak louder, Jean-

François smiled apologetically and walked away.

His flight to Madrid left from Malagá at 1:00 PM Wednesday, December 20th. He departed the capital at six PM, aboard a direct overnighter and according to the most recent weather information he could expect minus twelve with intermittent snow by the time he arrived.

His ETA was six PM the same day, local time.

*

He met Peter Wilson during his first trip to Toronto in November, the owner of Diplomat Limousine Service who knew his business and agreed to work exclusively for Jean-François over the next several weeks. He was fluent in French and each member of his fleet spoke at least two languages. He dressed as well as or better than most of his clients, and certainly better than most office workers who trudged their way mournfully downtown each day via the Go Train.

He'd been of tremendous assistance to Jean-François, recognized from the start as a reliable ally. Prior to ending his initial visit, Jean-François contracted Wilson to act on his behalf should a need arise. Wilson was no slouch, very much the opposite: he was erudite with regular customers who had become contacts even highly placed people would wish for. Having him to rely upon would be a great service and major convenience. Wilson accepted the short-term assignment and the two men communicated regularly.

The midnight blue Cadillac was parked outside Departures, Wilson not the least worried about parking restrictions. He was on his cell, leaning against the limo LeTuvier was hurrying towards with his suitcase trailing wildly behind. Both men were laughing at the site and, strangely, neither knowing why, they each said good-bye before snapping their phones closed to greet one another. Wilson was dressed for winter, as was his passenger, and neither would have been out of place on the glossy pages of a men's fashion magazine.

Jean-François would require his services for the next several days, excepting Christmas Day, though should his services be required Christmas Eve the agreed upon rate would triple. The hour wasn't late by the time Wilson let him off at the downtown Crowne Plaza on Front Street, albeit near three AM for Jean-François. They bid one another goodnight and the car would be waiting for him at eight AM. Jean-François suggested breakfast together and Wilson declined. That's not what he did. As much as he liked LeTuvier, he was still a client.

According to reports the weather would cooperate and Jean-François was extremely pleased winter's unpredictable hostility would not interfere with his well-choreographed objective. He wanted to look good, perfect, and winter's harsh winds had a way of disrupting such plans.

The Spanish ladies had been right, as their husband's had eagerly told him in an effort to balance the scales in his favour. "¡Los varones, juntos! ¡Sí! ¡Para siempre!" they had cried in unison, so they would be heard mostly by themselves. He was toned, he'd been working out, he was tanned from lounging by his pool and he hadn't lost one night's sleep in the last seven weeks. He slept well, which is not to say he slept without interruption, waking each morning at 2:00 AM

He felt rested and healthy, younger than ever. He had eaten almost nothing once at the hotel, limiting himself to three Blacks. He hadn't trusted the concierge with the task and had pressed the slacks to the three suits until the creases were razor sharp. His shirts had been pressed to perfection and his ties fell naturally to maintain their fullness. His links were 18kt, bought in Spain, and his shoes were tasselled mirrors.

His clock hummed at seven, room service arriving promptly at seven-fifteen. By seven-thirty he was showered, shaved, and by 7:45 he hadn't eaten, though he did drink a full carafe of coffee, brushing away the obvious signs from his teeth before donning his white shirt. He checked himself a dozen times, fussed with the pocket hanky and greeted Wilson in the lobby precisely at eight. The first-day mission was simple: Reconnoitre, make initial contact and leave. Get the hell away, fast, and Wilson understood the need. Jean-François had gone into some detail, leaving the chauffeur to imagine or formulate whatever suited his curiosity.

Jean-François could easily have walked to the appointment in a matter of minutes, had he called for an appointment, or had he been so inclined, or had he chosen June and not December. None were applicable to the day. He was ninety addresses to the west of the same street, though winter in most metropolitan centres south of the 45th parallel was anything but clean and Toronto was in the forty-third. More importantly, arriving by car was the plan and Wilson drove the eastward distance in moments.

At eight-ten Wilson pointed discreetly from behind the darkly tinted windshield and Jean-François chilled. He said nothing. Neither did Wilson who drove away without commenting when his client climbed from the backseat. Part of his service was sensing his client's need, as well as making them feel important. For the most part, those who could afford his rates were already important and LeTuvier certainly seemed to fit the bill. He was confident and not a man of many words, Peter Wilson thought. The chauffeur knew people. He had spent his life reading them and matching their words with their mannerisms. This guy was the real thing and not someone to mess with. He was a man who was about to realize a dream, or accept his fate, though Wilson saw something that made him feel both sad and cold.

Wilson was to drive to the predetermined address and meet with LeTuvier ten minutes later. When he scanned the plaza before turning into traffic, one man was conspicuous by his measured stride. The lobby was crowded with workers seemingly anxious to get to their jobs. No one pushed or shoved, neither did they give any ground in their efforts to gain first place in the daily challenge of the crowded elevator.

Two doors came together as two others slid apart and they both went in. When Pat turned she was facing into the shoulders of a man wearing a tapered, full-length black leather coat and a black felt fedora trimmed with a black leather band. His hands were gloved and he carried no briefcase. When the second-floor light twinkled and the doors began sliding apart she moved from behind as he stepped to the side, managing to touch his body against hers. She glanced behind her, too late as the doors closed. His head was facing away and she saw nothing. He had. She was gorgeous.

By the time he'd travelled to the top floor and back down, stopping once again on the second, the limo was once again parked in the yellow tow zone. When he opened the door, Jean-François' expression revealed nothing of what he was thinking. He had spent the last two months in turmoil, not for what he had done but for what he had not. Would she still love him? Had she ever loved him, or had he been her escape from a narrow reality? He was deep in thought, worried by what might happen, Wilson smiling at the man in his rear-view mirror.

They were on a first name basis. Mr. and Mr. somehow seemed inappropriate, given one's complicity with the other. The time was close to ten when Wilson climbed from the front seat and joined his short-term boss in the rear of the limo. He reached for a glass nestled securely in the fully stocked bar, then for the bottle and unscrewed the familiar black and gold cap. He filled the glass one-third full, and left the ice where it belonged for anyone who enjoyed a good scotch, extending his hand until his client gripped the glass with nervous fingers. Then he left Jean-François to steel himself against the difficult task ahead, convinced LeTuvier was the man for the job. At ten-fifteen Wilson stepped out, insisting LeTuvier stay as he was until his door was opened for him. After all, he wanted exposure for the sake of his reputation as much as LeTuvier desired anonymity. The air was still. They shook hands firmly and Jean-François was gone.

They looked completely ridiculous, Jean-François thought as he passed a group of five polyester-clad women huddled in the corner of the entrance, smoking outlawed cigarettes, desperately lighting a second with the first and littering the ground at their feet with red-stained butts. They stared at him, as he expected. Ignoring them, he turned to see Wilson at the car with his thumbs up. Turning back his reflection in the green-tinted glass of the entrance to the Toronto Municipal Library was smiling at him confidently.

He knew beforehand his destination was the second floor Administrative Services, pleased, considering the possibility he might suddenly require a hasty retreat. He also knew the 23rd of December was a full work day. They next day the offices would close at twelve, as would the library. The hallway was decorated with sparkling reds and blues, greens and golds, and Christmas music played softly from somewhere. Carols were the only music he didn't find strange in English and was pleased he could speak French with Wilson. Someone wished him Merry Christmas. He returned the greeting. Then another person passed him and said season's greetings. He smiled.
*

"Pardonnez-moi, madame," he paused until she acknowledged him. When she did, he had her full attention.

366

"Is this the office where I might find Madame Patricia Henderson?"

She looked at him as though he had two heads, he thought. "Mrs. Henderson?"

"That is correct. I understand she is the Administratrice Déléguée," he paused once more, seeming to catch himself. "I am so sorry, I meant to say the Directrice and I wish to see her on a matter of some importance."

"You have an appointment, do you?"

"I regret that I do not, madame." He shrugged, sheepishly, partly dismantling the barrier. She was clearly one of those who yelled when speaking with foreigners. "I have recently and unexpectedly arrived from out of town."

"Quebec?" she ventured.

"Madame, you injure my sensibilities. I am French." She didn't understand, nonplused. You poor woman, he thought. "Perhaps, madame, you might call her?" And then you might read one of your own books.

"I'm very sorry. Mrs. Henderson is in meetings all morning. Year-end reviews, you understand." He wondered why underlings, those with no say and no esteem, feel the need to over-explain. "I have very definite instructions. She does not want to be disturbed. Do you have a card to leave? Perhaps she can call you to arrange another appointment."

Apparently she hadn't seen the twelve long-stem roses, he thought, giving her a neutral look that would possibly not convey that she was stupid or visually impaired. "I believe that I might," and he reached into his pocket. "Please tell her that Monsieur Jean-François LeTuvier had hoped for the pleasure of her company before his departure. My business in your city was unexpected. Please tell her that I deeply apologize. Unfortunately, my current schedule is very tight, if I may say so, and dictates that I leave as unexpectedly as I arrived." He smiled, laying the flowers on the receptionist's desk. "I have taken the liberty of enclosing a note for madame. Please see that she gets these, with my card."

"She'll be available this afternoon. I'm sure she'll be in touch with you at that time."

He walked away feeling relieved, feeling sad, feeling excited, and feeling depleted. From the main doors to the gleaming limousine he nodded, smiling, Wilson responding in kind. When he was close enough the two high-fived and drove away. Mission accomplished with no casualties.

*

The morning had been nerve-racking, spending much of her time arguing the new budget cutbacks she had earlier been told would be held back for one more year, and now she was expected to select and inform one of her staff that, effective immediately, they were no longer required. Merry Christmas from the City of Toronto.

Her nerves were frayed by the time she returned to her office for a fast lunch from the typical brown bag, though hers was leather, deep green, recently purchased, and very expensive. Her co-workers and direct reports were gathered around the door to her office and she had to squeeze her way through the growing female mob that would not give way. They were the most gorgeous, long-stemmed roses she had ever seen, that they had ever seen, and they all pushed their reluctant boss towards her desk.

"Who are they from?" they asked as one anxious voice. "There's a note!" someone exclaimed. "Read it. Read it, Patty." Someone took the note from the ribbon and gave it to her.

She had no idea, none at all. Then the surround-sound of murmurs penetrated her daze. She smelled them first, and no one was leaving in search of water. They wanted to know everything, and no one was leaving until she confessed all. She broke the seal, feeling afraid, collapsing onto her desk before reading the last word. Her body shook with spasms and her eyes sobbed an unstoppable flow of tears. The closest of her staff reached for the card which had fallen to the floor and read aloud to the others: Chérie, my darling Patricia, how easily I could have written that I love you, but you must hear these words, and feel them, as I long to feel you once again and to hear your sweet voice whisper, babe, que je t'aime.

One of them dialled O on the hands-free and asked the receptionist who the man was they had seen through the glass wall partitioning them from the public. Some French guy, she responded, reaching for the card and bastardizing the name. She thought he had said he was leaving town, or something like that, whatever.

Pat wailed so loudly that even more people rushed into her crowded to see what was amiss. The receptionist stayed where she was. The ladies surrounding Pat had had no idea. How could they have known the elegant and dashing European who had delivered the flowers had come for her? God he seemed so strong, and so gorgeous, and tall, and handsome, and so tanned. They all agreed he would not leave without coming to see her once more, not after coming all the way from France, not after leaving such a romantic note. He wouldn't possibly leave. He would at least call, they all insisted. Surely he wouldn't leave so soon before Christmas. He'd be back, they assured her, and they all read the note. The members of the all-male committee decided wisely the unfinished meeting could be delayed until the next day. Cutbacks were one thing, a distraught woman was another. Get her out of here, they urged, and someone get her home.

That night one home on the quiet suburban street in Burlington stood out, perversely dark amidst the glitter and sparkle of the coloured lights and trees reflecting off the freshly covered snowbanks. She had not eaten a bite, and had not undressed. She barely knew how she had made it home from the train, and her skin was raw with salted wetness.

Had he known, he would have felt her pain, absorbed her sadness. Sadly, the two men in the blue limousine parked at the front of her house did not know the first part of his plan had become a horrible and wrenching heartbreak. When the single white light from inside the house went out, they drove off, proud of a good day's work.

*

Some things never change. Irrespective of location and the reduced workday, the day before Christmas was always a good time, even for those who hated their jobs. Conversely, for those who had a reason to hate Christmas, Christmas Eve was the second worst day of the year. The first came a day later.

Most of Pat's friends had been mutual and they had all stopped coming round. Newly single women were dangerous, especially towards wives whose husbands had lost interest in them. She was alone. The few friends she did have were nine-to-five friends who never visited. She lived in a society where having friends had become constant hard work and she had become a workload. Each one had offered to stay with her, still wondering, still curious, but with only two shopping days before Christmas they were quietly happy when she refused.

Friday morning was too alive, too cheery, and too much for her. The meeting had been called for nine and would last until twelve. The women corralled her and the men avoided her, which seemed to work perfectly well for everyone. She exchanged her gifts with her direct reports at eight-thirty, without any of her usual excitement. Then she left, letting them enjoy a little eggnog before she would return to announce which one had lost the draw, which one would spend the New Year searching for a new job, possibly the youngest of the men who could always be counted on to make the eggnog taste a little warmer.

At 8:59 she closed the door to the conference room behind her. The blue limousine pulled up in front of the building at ten. After climbing out, without assistance, he examined himself in the dark side windows and disappeared from his own view as the tinted rear window lowered. Thumbs were up once again. He looked good, very good, and they both smiled conspiratorially.
*

She still needed her job, more for the money than her mind. She would not be that stupid two consecutive days. The man was silver-haired and immaculately dressed in navy blue. His suit was expensive, and his tie was perfectly knotted. His jewellery was expensive, yet discreet, and his manner commanded attention. This time she dialled the conference room, informing the Administrative Director that a gentleman, not the same gentleman, was asking for her by name at the front reception. He gave no name, although he was insisting she would very much want to see him on behalf of his French employer.

The committee members eyed one another, and then at the empty chair, shrugging their shoulders in unison for what would be another wasted day. She ran through the office in shoes designed for style and comfort, not speed, unaware of the several dozen eyes following her through to the reception area.

Wilson could see immediately what had so captivated LeTuvier. She was indeed beautiful, though he thought she looked tired. He also thought he understood why. She was in great shape and he couldn't remember the last time he had seen a woman that well-dressed without appearing self-centred. She was not the woman LeTuvier had described to him, and much lovelier than he had seen over the past few weeks as she had been unaware he had been her silent protector for Jean-François. He now knew something LeTuvier didn't and he would play the advantage to the max, for a little while anyway. If LeTuvier had thought she was gorgeous in her suede coat and hat, what would he think to see her as she was, standing in front of him?

Her hair was longer than in the photos he had been given, styled and coloured differently, more auburn, and this woman knew how to wear her make-up more than her Kodak facsimile. Her heels were high, though not stiletto, and her dress was short, with front vents that would make any man want to stop and stare. He didn't. This was business, a matter of utmost importance to his client. Her blouse was sheer and décolleté and the camisole underneath completed a sophisticated fashion statement he was anxious to recount to LeTuvier. He smiled with sincere warmth.

"Bonjour, Madame Henderson," he tilted his head.

She responded smoothly, "Bonjour, monsieur."

He spoke slowly. "J'ai le plaisir…"

"Excuse me. I'm afraid my French is very poor. I've only recently started my lessons."

"Excuse my rudeness, madame. I intended no discomfort." She nodded, not knowing what to say. She had no words. She wanted him to talk and her visible eagerness made that clear to him. Noses were pressed against the partition and the receptionist was hoping the phone would ring. "I have been asked to deliver a letter to you, Mademoiselle Patricia, on behalf of a certain gentleman. I do believe you will understand more once you have read it." He reached into his inside coat pocket, retrieving the coloured envelope, handing it to her. "I have been asked to wait for your response, mademoiselle. Please. Take your time. My time is yours." He offered his arm. "Perhaps you would be more comfortable sitting? My time is entirely yours."

No one was working, including the Committee members straining to see from the back row.

*

My darling Patricia, how many times have I dreamt that we would be together, of seeing you at my side once again, of smelling your sweet breath, and hearing your sweet words that are meant for me alone?

Come to me my darling, if I am still in your dreams, if you have not yet given your heart to another. Come to me so that we might dream together, forever.

How I hope that you do, my darling. By the time you read this letter I will be closer to what I hope is our new home than I was to you yesterday, as I stood by your side in the elevator and cried silently because I could not reach out to you, thinking that you might reject me for having deserted you the way that I did.

If, in any small way, I can still deserve your love, then come to me.

I will love you forever,

Yours, until eternity,

Jean-François

*

She tucked the letter under her arm, opening the smaller envelope. One photo showed a beautiful Spanish-styled villa, the second showed a silver-on-gold tube dress and matching panties that lay on a bed beside a window. In the background was a huge body of blue water. Wilson waited patiently. He wanted to sweep her into his arms and rush her to the car, to LeTuvier, knowing he couldn't. The day wasn't his; the day belonged to them.

"Mademoiselle, the gentleman requests that you accept his invitation by five PM today. I can tell you, personally, that he regrets the immediacy. This is my card, mademoiselle. If you prefer, I would be pleased to contact you at an earlier hour that is convenient to you." He gave her no opportunity to answer. "He has instructed me to say that, should the answer be affirmative, a delivery will be made to your home this evening at eight PM. However, should your response not be of a positive nature, he wishes you well and trusts your future will be a happy one. Would you prefer that I call you this afternoon before five?"

Her eyes were red and her face was smudged black with running mascara. Her lips quivered, making speech impossible as the Administrative Director seemed to him at that moment more like a forlorn and innocent child.

"Mr. Wilson, please tell me he's here. Tell me he hasn't returned to his home."

"I do sincerely regret, mademoiselle, I cannot tell you what you would like to hear," he replied honestly. "At this very moment he is en route to where he feels he must be, and then, as I understand his intentions, onto his home in Spain. He has asked me to tell you that he will call you later today, should your response be positive, of course. You must have your answer by five PM, Mademoiselle Patricia. Also, the gentleman has asked that I be the one to deliver the package to your home this evening at eight PM, precisely. I trust I will not cause you any inconvenience at that late hour?"

She started sobbing, nodding her head yes, and then, no, and then yes, again, which had all been too much for her co-workers who hurried in to see what was wrong and ready to attack the blue-suited messenger in defence of one of their own, somewhat confused when she jumped up and began hugging him so tightly and spreading her tears and mascara over his cheek.

"That would be a yes, mademoiselle?" he queried.

"Yes, yes. Yes. It's a yes." And she kissed his cheek.

He eased himself from of her grip. "Thank you, mademoiselle. I believe the gentleman will be very pleased when I convey your message. And, may I say, I am as anxious as you for eight o'clock." He left, acknowledging the receptionist with the slightest tilt of his head.

Pat hugged and kissed the nearest woman, and then the second nearest, as another shamelessly read the letter aloud and they all began to kiss and hug each other, most of the men regretting not having moved as quickly. The Committee returned to the conference room to adjourn.

When Wilson arrived at the limousine his eyes were moist and the condition of his face prompted questions that turned to laughter only men would understand. As the limo began pulling away the laugher stopped abruptly as three women came running out from the building. The limo slowed smoothly as the women stopped suddenly, seeing the car. The rear smoked-glass window lowered and the man in the backseat leaned forward to peer out towards them from under his wide-brimmed hat, two of the women aware that he wasn't studying at them. They had seen him before and they told her. He was the man at the reception. They huddled close to her and watched her cry. Seeing him drive away Pat realized how very close she had been to him and strained to remember every detail.
*

She hated him with all her heart and she loved him even more. Over the past nine weeks she had changed. She knew nothing of what the future held other than her past had died and she had not died with it. She had become functional in French and paid much more attention to the way she dressed. She had taken fashion courses and had changed her hairdresser. The new one was called Henri. He spoke French to her so she would understand, and eventually she had begun answering him. She had discarded all her clothes, everything, and had put her house up for sale. She had joined a health club and she had never been in better shape. The weight gain had come with her new tone and she looked great. The neighbours talked about her, she knew they did, and they could all *foutre le camp,* or just fuck off. She certainly had changed.

She was a new woman, though missing something and she knew exactly what. Woman's intuition kicked in and the three women went shopping like flighty school girls.
*

He had known about the For Sale sign from the day she had planted the stake into the front lawn of her home. He had seen it the night before, not yet decorated with the familiar red stripe and four-letter word now boasting of the agent's success in selling the house so quickly. The night was quiet and the snow-packed street in the upscale and residential Burlington on the shores of frozen Lake Ontario was deserted. They toasted one another in the comfortable luxury of the limo, Wilson with coffee, LeTuvier with Johnnie Walker Black, as snowflakes drifted aimlessly like doilies against a glittering patchwork of flickering coloured lights and accumulated on the windshield of the limo until the automatic wipers swept them into a double arc.

Christmas had two sides, they agreed: the good and the bad. They gave pause to think of all those who would not be returning home from parties or shopping. The gentle snow falling around them was not so gentle on the highways and the news report interrupting the non-stop Christmas carols made them lower their drinks and shrug at each other, shaking their heads. Good times had abruptly ended for several families who would never forget the blood-splattered windshields of the cars whose drivers had not stopped their respective good times when they should have. The new ghosts of Christmas Present would spend the twelve days of Christmas naked and alone, enshrouded in white clinical sheets and lying in wait to greet other frigid corpses over the joyous days to come, filed away on cold steel slabs with tags on their toes. The choice had been theirs. They could have been home with loved ones, hanging lights and angel hair on trees made of wood and plastic, and the pathologists partied on. The more the merrier. They would get to each one in due course. Now was the time for family.

"A toast to your good health, good sir," Jean-François took a sip of scotch.

"And likewise to yours, good sir, though, in truth, I have already this evening imbibed sufficient quantities of this excellent elixir which has, in point of fact, killed me."

"Then, to your future, sir, that might have been."

"And to yours, sir, and might you only drink coffee on such a night as this."

Wilson was.

Jean-François put the glass down at 7:55. The time had come for Wilson to do his thing. The trunk barely made a sound as Wilson closed the lid. He arrived at the door of the bungalow two minutes later.

*

The wireless phone rang at precisely 7:57, startling Pat so much she jumped up from her sofa before realizing she had, becoming more flustered as she searched to locate the sound. She had been expecting the doorbell, not the phone, and she was now suddenly afraid Mr. Wilson would not come, that he would have been involved in one of the several accidents on the highways that were being announced on the news. She had one ring left before the message centre would take over. The receiver was in her hand, knowing her voice would betray her and she said nothing.

"Chérie," the voice was familiar and relaxed, "c'est moi, c'est Jean-François. Comment tu vas, chérie?"

She was crying and laughing. "Je vais très bien, darling, very, very well. Where are you? There is a lot of static. I have my computer opened to Earth Search, right here, and I think you must be somewhere between the Canaries and Spain, n'est pas?"

377

He chuckled. "I am pleased that you can now speak with me in French, chérie. The language does suit you very much."

"I've changed. I'm not the same person, darling."

"I know, Patricia. I have not been as far away from you as you might think. Monsieur Wilson has been a good friend to me and your guardian in my place."

"Is it true? Were you with me in the elevator yesterday?"

"Yes. It is very true indeed."

"You bastard!" she replied.

"Not a false appellation, I do admit."

"Where are you? I want to know exactly."

"You know the airlines, chérie. Regrettably I am still very much on your side of the Canaries," he created more static, "I wanted desperately to call you from where I am," he teased, "to wish you a Merry Christmas, Feliz Navidad and, of course, Joyeux Noël is now very appropriate. I heard very good news this afternoon, chérie. How do you feel about learning Spanish?"

"You heard from a man what you should have heard from me. I should hate you. I do hate you."

"That is not what Monsieur Wilson has told me, chérie. He told me that you love me still very much. You made a terrible mess of his face, also, as you did once to mine."

"That was you in the car. They said it was you. You're here, aren't you? You're horrible! Maybe I'll change my mind. What do you think about that, monsieur? Please tell me you're here."

"I do promise you that I am painfully far from you at this very moment, chérie. I wish that I could be much closer." There was silence and more static. "I have chosen a beautiful Christmas gift for you, chérie. May I tell you what?"

"No. No. No. I don't want to know."

"I see the hour has arrived, 8:00 PM. I believe you are about to answer the door, darling. I do believe Monsieur Wilson is arriving at this very moment." The doorbell chimed precisely on time. "Good-bye, chérie, et Joyeux Noël encore. I will leave now so that you might enjoy your evening."

"You stay exactly where you are, you bastard," she demanded. "You don't go anywhere. Do you understand me? You dare hang up and I will always hate you. Do you understand?"

"As you wish, darling. I will stay where I am, but, chérie, please hurry. The night air is disagreeably cold." The real cold was the chill surging along her spine, making her shudder. Cold? "Monsieur Wilson is waiting, chérie."

Jean-François held the phone away from his ear as Pat's crashed onto the hardwood floor. The door opened wide, framing Wilson perfectly with both his gloved hands cupped together and extended towards her.

"Good evening, Mademoiselle Patricia. It's very good to see you once again, and a very Merry Christmas to you." Her eyes were fixed on the tiny felt box with its single yellow bow housed securely in his black kid leather gloves. "The gentleman has asked that I deliver what I understand is a very special gift, precisely at this hour. May I be the first to offer my congratulations?"

Her hands were quivering, not from the cold stillness of the winter's eve, but the expectation of what she would see nestled in the little box. "It's a ring?"

"I do believe that's correct, mademoiselle, or might I be very presumptuous and say Madame LeTuvier." Her face became more radiant than the glow from any Christmas ornament, bringing a smile to his face as the accomplice he was, though she didn't see. "I realize you are on the phone, Mademoiselle Patricia. However, if I may, the gentleman has asked whether he might present himself in person."

She'd been half-listening to him, too intent on the box she had not yet opened. She looked up, as though in a dream. "The gentleman?"

He smiled widely. "Why, Monsieur LeTuvier, of course."

He stepped to the side, his eyes beginning to gloss over, careful not to trip over the Gucci luggage she hadn't noticed by his side, doing so in time to avoid being knocked over by the whirlwind of emerald green silk sprinting past him.

The elegant European whose heart had been hers since their first night together in the Caribbean was walking purposefully towards the beautiful snow angel flying at him in a wild flurry of green against the backdrop of winter white and flickering blues, greens, reds, and golds. The snow on his shoulders seemed like epaulettes and his hair was dusted with white. He had never been one for hats and would never wear one again.

He ran to her, sweeping her into his arms before her slippered feet had left more than a few delicate imprints in the snow, holding her the way she had dreamt each night that he would. When their lips parted their faces were wet with her tears and streaked with shades of green-blue and glossy red. She was trembling, not from the cold, and she stammered badly on the difficult "que" sound.

"Que je t'aime, babe, que je t'aime," was all Wilson heard as he leaned in, closing the door behind them.

Dreams Are Forever

Pat had not recovered her composure by the time Wilson drove the couple to the Pearson Airport the following Friday. The week hadn't existed at all for her. All she could remember was their constant lovemaking, one brief interlude melding with another.

The Committee was understandably perplexed by the sudden announcement of her immediate departure, even though a week earlier they'd been insisting she nominate one of her staff for his or her immediate departure. Her absence would create a serious shortfall in daily operations of the library, and what would they do without her? Could she stay one month longer, they pleaded? Unfortunately not, she replied demurely. Her resignation was effective immediately, or as soon as she could free her man from the ring of chattering women encircling him and as soon as she had shown all of them the photos of her new home in the south of Spain, photos of her villa.

Despite the season, setting her affairs in order was an easy matter. She hadn't wasted very much time reorganizing her life upon her return from Punta Cana, believing the charming LeTuvier had been a chance happening, a fling, a fantasy and maybe she would see him again or maybe she wouldn't. More importantly, in her mind, Patricia Henderson had gone missing along with her husband and both were presumed dead: her revival. Henderson was thought not to have left the island, though somehow he'd been linked to a monstrous killing in Savannah which had ended in a dead end. The cops in all three countries were stumped and she made clear to the detectives who had come to the house that she had no interest in her husband, his disappearance or the killing. He was vile, though probably not a killer. He was gone, he'd vanished and that was good enough for her. This was her renaissance and she savoured every new moment.

Her personal portfolio had grown very substantially with the sale of her house and the significant amounts from Henderson's insurance policies and investments. If not at par with Jean-François' wealth, she wasn't far behind and the day they boarded the Air Iberia flight en route to Madrid, they did so on equal terms. She wasn't the same woman he'd left behind in Punta Cana. She was new and improved. For so many lonely nights she had dreamt of those three days and four magical nights with him, now she felt as though he was taking her back in time to relive them.

Jean-François suggested she might enjoy spending a few days in Madrid, visiting the museums and cathedrals. Then he teased more, saying they should perhaps spend time in Malagá visiting castles, a ridiculous suggestion to which she replied with a single shake of her head as the pilot called out that Las Islas Canarias could be seen from the starboard portholes. She wasn't certain, Jean-François nodding that, indeed, they were seated on the starboard side. She hadn't slept well since Christmas Eve, and she wouldn't until she saw her Spanish villa. They had years ahead of them to visit dead kings and castles, cathedrals and vineyards.

The three-hour stopover in Madrid seemed interminable. The flight to Malagá added one hour more, though flying at eight-thousand metres allowed Pat to see much of the mountainous landscape beneath her and the bright blue lace-like border of the Mediterranean as the aircraft circled for its final approach. The Bentley CFS was waiting for them and Pat began realizing the parametres of her new life. And, yes she wanted the top down.

The drive to Almería lasted another three hours, a distance Jean-François could easily have driven in two. Though Pat had the last word, if not every word. She hadn't stopped asking questions, insisting he repeat every word in Spanish. She was on a roller coaster ride and she wasn't getting off anytime soon.

Coming into the seaport town she didn't know which way to look first, not giving him enough time to answer one question before asking another. When he finally pulled over to the curb and stopped, she thought he needed to buy something or other at the little tienda. She was wrong. He made no move to leave the vehicle. The shop owner, who stood leaning against his doorframe, waved and called out to him by name; Jean-François waved back and Pat smiled timidly. She had stepped from the plane into her new life, more questions flooding into her head as quickly as the fears. And why had the man called him Francisco? Suddenly she was scared, not for herself. She was afraid for the two of them together.

Jean-François turned away from her in his seat, pointing upward to a white façade reflecting the brilliant midday sun from the very edge of the precipice towering over the entire town. "Esa es tu casa, mí querida," he said, facing her. "Your villa awaits you, señora."

"Where, which one?" she asked, tugging anxiously at his arm.

"You cannot properly see your villa at this time of day because the sun that is reflected from the walls does blind us, chérie. The white one is yours, the whitest, the one that glares down at you."

He caught the attention once more of the man still leaning in the doorway. Jean-François waved goodbye to his neighbour, saying something that made the man smile and tap the pocket watch he'd pulled from his hip pocket. The climb up the narrow winding road was agonizingly slow and she knew he was teasing her on purpose, slowing or stopping several times along the way for no apparent reason. When he finally did come to a full stop, she sat perfectly still, wordless, peering through the tinted windshield as the three-metre wrought iron gate opened inwardly to welcome her. He allowed enough time for what she was seeing to sink in before proceeding under the arch identifying the private property as La Villa Mimada, mounted by his neighbour during his absence.

She asked what the words signified. They meant spoiled, as in pampered and, he continued, she would be both for as long as he lived. He fell quiet as he drove past the gates swinging closed behind them. To the left was the curved façade of the villa, framing the glistening pool seemingly feeding into the Mediterranean. To the right, a beautiful garden for entertaining and ahead of them two wide-panelled doors of the garage raised simultaneously. He waited for them to fully open before driving through. The Aston Martin Vantage was bright yellow with a custom midnight blue canvas roof.

"Yours," was all he said.

"The car?" she asked.

"Yes, chérie, and everything you see." He smiled. "Welcome to our new home."

*

The pool glittered with reflections from the rainbow of paper-covered lights fencing in the patio and terrace of his neighbour's luxurious villa set up as an elegant restaurant with linen-covered tables following the contours of the pool. The musicians were all dressed in shiny black blouses with wide sleeves and tight pants tucked into their riding boots that made her think of Zorro. One played the Gaita, the

384

most traditional of all Spanish instruments, and she knew by his smile he was playing the song for her. It was her the gayest, most vibrant New Year's Eve ever. Her dress, which he selected, which she thought was too provocative for a party, suited her perfectly. When she saw how her neighbours and other ladies in the town were dressed, she was glad she hadn't argued his choice.

Some of the younger women wore short pleated skirts with stilettos or knee-high boots and sheer blouses, turning their eye-catching lingerie into fashion accessories. Others wore long gowns or chic party dresses. The men dressed in black suits with white shirts opened at the collar and their shoes were highly polished. She had never seen so many beautiful women and so many handsome men in one place.

They danced and sang all evening long, together and with others, Jean-François laughing at her each time he saw her repeating the names of new acquaintances in whispers, trying to imitate the inflections of the Andalucian accent. The women stole her away several times, the men just as often. They loved her immediately, the common language one of smiles and nods with a smattering of unfamiliar words. She would learn. She had already begun to in whispers.

By twelve-thirty their excuses were reluctantly accepted with knowing smiles and giggles from the women and good-humoured joking and clapping by the men that caused the women to frown disapprovingly. For Pat the evening had been a blur. She had never been kissed so many times in her life; even the women were kissing her. She was the only one crying, though everyone understood why and they hugged her all the more affectionately.

At the villa Jean-François told her of all the invitations he'd accepted for the coming weeks and as they crossed the pool he stopped suddenly, pulling her gently towards him. They were alone under the stars, above the town that was aglow with coloured lights and alive with music, singing and laughter: her time as much as his and she didn't wait for him. The cowl neckline of the simple black evening gown highlighted the contours and fullness of her breasts, held in place with narrow silk bands across her shoulders. Her back was bare and the gown came away from her breasts teasingly before she pushed it slowly to the ceramic tiles without the slightest wriggling, keeping her legs perfectly straight from her round-toe patent leather pumps to the tiniest satin panties he could find at the finest shops in Madrid.

He stood watching as she came towards him, tugging urgently at his belt buckle and his shirt tails. They parted long enough for him to tear off his shirt, kick off his shoes and push his pants to the ground along with his much unneeded socks. She stepped back, watching as he completed the awkward process of an overly anxious male disrobing. Then, sooner than he thought possible, she was in front of him with her legs opened and one hand inside the black satin. He grabbed at one side, then the other, pulling easily in opposite directions and promising to buy her more. She had become used to the intimate silk and form-fitting apparel he wore and she pulled at them, making the same promise as she pushed them down until he could kick them free of his feet.

She came into his arms as effortlessly as though she were a mere image of herself, a fantasy. The water was warm and tantalizing against their nakedness, neither one knowing what to kiss or caress first. He let one arm drop, her body aligning with his, feeling the evidence of his insistent ardour. She laughed and hugged him closely as he lifted her around and over the obstruction, offering no apology. Her arms were wrapped around his neck, helping him as he let her down gently, and precisely. There was no difference in her feminine warmth and the warmth of the salted pool water as the immediate tightness engulfing him and her spontaneous spasms transferred to every responsive centimetre of his eager probe.

There could be no greater feeling of freedom than making passionate love in shoulder-deep heated water, being together as one under stars flickering against the absolute blackness of a universe, insignificant against the unimaginable immensity of an infinite eternity. He mused as absently as his body would allow, how different were the lives men lived in their dreams from the dreams they sought in their lives? Both could sometimes be exotic and dangerous and neither would always be safe or predictable. Was he now living a dream, or dreaming of his life?

He eased out of her, holding her close as he carried her from the depth of the pool into the cooler night air. Her body prickled against the sudden freshness, her hair sweeping across her shoulders as he raised her by her hips and brought her gently against him once again. Seeing their twisting bodies entwined in the moonlit reflection of the bedroom windows she realized for the first time what she had done, crying safely in his grasp at the peak of their ecstasy.

When he asked her why, she remained silent, letting her body tell him what she could not.

"Los sueños son para siempre, cariño, yo creo. Sweet Dreams." And she drifted off in his arms, oblivious to her passage into her now separate world.

She was right. He knew dreams were forever, that reality was not. Our pain is in living. So then, what was there to fear in death, other than the expectation of one's death?

It was 1:30 AM. By one-forty he was asleep

*

Peter Wilson stood by the open door as Jean-François ran towards her, smiling widely with the thumb of his gloved hand pointing upwards. He remembered the white snow on his shoulders like fluffy epaulettes and the white crystals coming to rest on his uncovered head were neither cold nor damp. He had never seen her so uncontrolled and wild, yet so determined, as she glided through the falling snowflakes towards him in a flurry of greens and seeming not to touch the snow. Her slippered feet seemed so small and delicate to him, and he ran all the faster to sweep her into his arms before she left no more than a few delicate imprints in the snow, holding her the way he had dreamt each night he would. She was warm, yet he felt no warmth. Her hair was soft and fragrant against his face, yet he breathed in clinical scents that were strange and unfamiliar to him. Her breath was sweet against his open mouth, yet he tasted nothing but his own dryness. She had no weight, even though she filled his arms.

She loved him. How she must have loved him. "Que je t'aime, cariño, que je t'aime, babe," were the words resounding around him. He sensed her trembling and thought she was cold, though she wasn't cold, and he felt Wilson's hand against his back as he rushed her through the door. Though when he turned Wilson had gone and when he turned to Patricia he was alone. His face was streaked with colourless tears, not the greens or blues or reds he expected to wipe away, which he had always wiped from his face.

He closed his eyes tightly, squeezing out the tears, and when they opened she was there, in front of him and far from his arms. She was trembling, though not from the cold. She quivered from fear and regret, stammering badly as she struggled to speak.

"I'm sorry, cariño, so very sorry. I love you and I hope that helps."
*

The jury had virtually been instructed by the judge to return a verdict of guilty, in which case the sentence would be death by lethal injection. The question of jurisdiction had been quickly resolved. The Dominican Republic wanted nothing to do with the murder and Canada realized the cost savings of having the Americans try him. Besides, Canada had long ago abandoned the death penalty and the Americans wanted him dead. Georgia had willingly deferred to Louisiana who had a more stringent perspective on multiple murders. They wanted him dead and a New Orleans judge was the perfect choice.

He had expected death since the first day he pencilled John Roberts' name into his agenda and his plans began taking shape. He heard the verdict read aloud, the sentence pronounced without emotion. He would be put to death by lethal injection at two AM. What did it matter which day, or which month? Living one week longer, or a month, or a year mattered to him not at all. The sooner the better, giving him less time to anticipate, less time to fear.

Pat had been the most shocked by what he had done, her revulsion the real sentence, carried out immediately and without mercy.
*

The cold of the steel table transferred through his coarse grey denim shirt, making him shiver involuntarily. He hated that he did. Patricia knowing he was unafraid was an important part of his death, because he felt no fear. Even though he had admitted to the expectation of death throughout the trial, he had never felt the fear of death. So was the close proximity of his death sheltering him from fear; or had he been wrong all along?

The thin cotton blanket barely came to his waist, his bare feet protruding from its bottom. As she watched intently, the technicians worked busily and indifferently around him, preparing the fluids that would mix together triggering his execution. He hadn't asked for a priest or minister and none had volunteered to save his soul from eternal damnation. He'd never been religious, though he found himself thinking about hell and eternity. He closed his eyes against the blinding overhead lamp, until he heard her say the needle was ready and he opened them.

The huge clock on the wall showed one-forty-five, the long red second hand announcing each one with annoyingly loud ticks. He made a tight fist, feeling the resistance of the wide leather straps securing his arm in place. His eyes met hers; he wanted to see past them into her thoughts. "Dreams are forever, chérie, aren't they? We must believe that is so. It is our eternity, our salvation. Forgive me, my darling."

She ignored him. What more could she say? The process would soon begin with nothing left for her but to walk away. She wore white surgical garb and a surgical mask with a loose-fitting cotton cap, and as she reached for the draw string he tried to think of her as she had once been for him.

By order of the court the glass panel partitioning the viewing room was not one-way. He saw them as clearly as they saw him. He knew they would be there; the judge's final seething words still real to him, and seeing them together, reunited, made him want 2:00AM to come quickly.

They were cropped and framed as though posing in a family photograph. But they were unreal. They couldn't be real, but they were right there in front of him, staring at his prostrated and strapped body. The women were dressed in white; the men were as he had last seen them, seated in two rows of six with Jacqueline Duvernay standing at one end and Geneviève standing at the other: witnesses to his eternal damnation, to his crossing into the netherworld.

Pat dropped the cord, pressing the button that would activate the intercom. "They wish to speak with you one last time, Wellington."

His real name sounded strange coming from her lips. In the front row Jacqueline stood by Celeste, and Felicity sat between Celeste and Louise. Seraphina sat between Louise and Dalila who also sat beside Renée. At the other end Geneviève stood by her lifelong social barometer. In the back row, his six appointments sat expectantly.

Jacqueline wore a white satin bra, matching embroidered high-rise panties and low-heeled pumps. She spoke first, matter-of-factly, unbothered by Wellington seeing her undressed for the first time. "I always wanted you, Wellington," she smiled. "Now you will never know how many nights I fell asleep dreaming of your fingers touching me, arousing me. Do you like seeing me so close to Celeste this way, Wellington? Watch me, Wellington. Watch her reaction to me, to my fingers and my kisses."

Jacqueline knelt down. Leaning teasingly into Celeste's parted legs her perfectly pear-shaped body blocked his view. She raised her buttocks, letting him see the tips of her glossy red fingertips probing hard under the satin material at the soft, fleshy apexes of her thighs. He had never seen her naked and knew this could not be true. He had never done anything to hurt the women. The men he could understand, but why would the women taunt him and why would they want to witness his death?

He knew dreams were forever. He believed that was true, yet so was death. But the dead don't dream, or so he thought. So was this a dream, his dream, a constant reminder of his capital sins, or the real prelude to his death tainted with haunting memories and illusions? He would never know, he could never know, never be sure. He knew that much, he thought. The clock on the wall showed 1:46.

Celeste reached forward, unclasping Jacqueline's bra, draping her legs over the other's slender back and reclining. "I'm angry with you, Wellington, very angry, indeed. You tricked me, and deceived me. You are not the gentleman I thought you were and you caused me more than a little hardship." She gulped a deep, sudden breath, moving a hand to pull at the delicate fringes of her white-laced French teddy. "The police were very unkind to me and very persistent."

He struggled to tell her he had sent Roberts' computer as proof of her innocence, but his mouth was dry and he was totally mesmerized by seeing the two women together.

"I vote for your death, Wellington, so you may never see me, see us, like this again."

She gasped unabashedly, Jacqueline easing away, letting her bra fall to the floor.

"Vote," he questioned, "I don't understand."

Jacqueline turned, leaning into Celeste's still open legs; her own spread wide, her lips glistening and pungent. She was beautiful. "Yes Wellington. We are here to vote on whether you will be condemned to the eternal peace that comes with death... or to dream forever."

Celeste turned, jerking her stained panties from John Roberts' open mouth, pulling the ribbons away from his coated face.

"A woman scorned, Wellington." She hurled them at the window. "You were right to think dead men don't dream and, because they do not, I vote for death."

"As would I," Jacqueline added, reaching behind to interlace her fingers with Celeste's, "but I don't have a vote, Wellington. I was never directly involved, as much as I wanted you, as much as I still want you after all you have done. You should have come to the office that last night, Wellington, after hours. You could have seen me, touched me, enjoyed me the way you enjoyed Celeste. The way I enjoy her now."

She turned to please Celeste, the two women caressing one another.

The voice cried out unexpectedly. "I have something to say. I need for all of you to know what I feel." Everyone's attention was on John Roberts who hadn't moved. "I loved my wife. I loved her very much. I know what you all think," he studied his own naked and greyed body scarred with sores that had once been red, and now were brown, "but this doesn't mean I didn't love her, or that she didn't love me. What you said of me that day was all true and most likely I am better off dead. Perhaps I should even thank you, if my death had been your decision to make. As much as my decision about you was arbitrary, what right did you have? No one deserves being found the way I was found by the police. I soiled myself, Wellington. My face was covered with mucous and tears. How dare you decide the world should see me that way? It is true, dead men don't dream. I shall never again dream of my sweet wife, though I wish you pleasant dreams, Wellington. You must never forget what you have done to us. You must see us as we are forever and ever."

Roberts raised a hand as Wellington strained to speak. "It's finished. You turned my death into a game." He spoke to Celeste condescendingly. She sneered. "I think that was the worst of all."

"Asshole." Henderson was next. "I should have known someone was banging the bitch."

Wellington found the strength he needed. "Fuck you! You're the one person I would gladly kill again. So do not fuck with me. If you vote for death, we will meet again and you will know death twice. I promise you. Vote for death. I challenge you. If you vote for dreams I'll be with her for eternity, my eternity, not yours. I'll be with your wife, the wife, forever."

"What a joke, the bitch is killing you. Something about that you don't understand?" Suddenly Henderson went to stand, his bloated aqua-blue face grimacing with frustration to discover long serrated spears held him fixed to his seat. His eyes were streaked with red from seawater and he spoke as though gasping for breath. "I do vote for death and I'll be at the gates of hell to welcome you. Then we'll see."

"Je vous en prie, asshole," Wellington returned. "Learn any French on the other side? Learn anything on the other side? That you're in hell is enough for me to willingly join you there."

Wellington relaxed, laying his head into soft and contoured leather headrest. The time: 1:48.

"You didn't let me say goodbye to her, Wellington." Roberts continued.

"Shut up, you squirming fool," insisted Wiernknoff, twirling a yellowed and sticky bauble in his steady fingers, "or I will pull out your little pin and stab you again. You didn't let me say goodbye to her," he whined, mimicking. "It is just as well your wife cannot see you as you are with your sticky face. You should be pleased. What would she think of your filth? You stink. Neither did I get to say goodbye to my wife. What I would give to speak a few simple and comforting words to her. She is too frail even to end her own life, though I know she has tried. I would beg her to be strong and tell her we will be together soon, and that she should not be afraid when at last she sees the light." His cold eyes pierced Wellington's. "You are right, Bartlett, believing the expectation of death is worse than death itself, yet she would not know. I miss her because of you, but I am happy. I am at peace because I know now she will soon know that same peace and walk with me once again when we are together. So, in fact, Bartlett, you have done me a service by saving me from my own eventual disgrace."

Wiernknoff stood, staring at his killer, mockingly, unaffected by the staunched hole in his cheek. "How timid you seem without your toys, Bartlett." He smiled. "Yes, I know your name." He pointed to Roberts. "His wife is better off without him, mine needed me. She still does need me, though she will do well despite my temporary exclusion from her life. You had no reason to kill me, to kill any of us.

Your own weakness drove you to the crimes, your narrow vision and interpretation of self. Nothing more. You failed in life, of course. Such was your destiny. However you failed in your eyes alone. I say so because no one else cares, or ever cared. Certainly none of us: the men you killed for no better reason than vanity or the women you helped to diminish for your own selfish pleasure. You are, if nothing else, a self-centred fool and a murderer. I vote for death, and not because of my own, because you had thought to kill my innocent wife. Your death is my revenge. I care little if we ever see one another again." He paused, scowling at Roberts. "If you truly loved your wife, you would be with her, always, and she with you."

"I did feel, and I still do feel regret for what I did to you. I would never have killed your wife. I would have found another way." Wellington stared at the acoustic ceiling. "I wanted to cut your throat or bash in your head, but I didn't know how and I didn't want to hurt you. I'm sorry. Truly, I am."

"That's a load if I ever heard any, Wellington. By the way, I love your name." Felicity had listened to the men, visibly more interested in watching Celeste and Jacqueline together. "You and I fucked like monkeys that night. I was awake when you thought I was sleeping and wanted to pull you into my bed before you left that morning. You were good."

He looked over at Pat who was working methodically at killing him. There were no secrets in death, he knew that now. He'd been Jean-François LeTuvier to her, sophisticated, charming and European. Now she had put a needle into his arm, preparing to execute him by order of the state. He wanted desperately to explain Felicity to her, unable to find the words. He knew he had disappointed her and, worse, she knew. She knew all, they knew all. So did his mother, grateful she was not there to condemn him or vote.

"Don't worry, Wellington. We all die, dying is our common destiny. We all enjoyed. You enjoyed, and I did very, very much." She was playfully provocative in her bustier and garters, taking Louise's hand in hers, guiding willing fingers between her bare thighs. "Which is not to say you won't miss out on a future that might have been. Too bad." The two women kissed hard. "I vote for dreams, Wellington. Not everyone deserves redemption, but I believe you do. I believe you're a good man. I know you're a good lover and I hope we see each other again."

Louise urged Felicity to acknowledge and respond to her ministrations. Felicity leaned over, putting a hand gently to her cheek, smiling lovingly. Her vote given, she whispered into the Louise's ear.

"Lesbians, Wellington, this is the reassurance you search for, pushing yourself into lesbians who care nothing about you? See them for what they are, they have come to mock you as you prepare to die." Wellington didn't hear. The time was 1:50. "It is the expectation of death, Wellington, don't you know? Are you afraid now, or do you fear having no soul to discover?"

The garrotte hung from Marcotte's neck like a bloodied and macabre pendant, and none of his fellow conservative jurors seemed to mind he was wearing a red leather sleeveless vest with matching chaps and a bright yellow thong. The boots and spurs could not be seen by most, though they all knew. All present were dressed for a rave or costume party, and none cared. Why would they? They were either dead or women who had loved the killer. What was of interest to each one was the manner of the others' deaths, or the women they were openly ogling apart from Marcotte.

"So I was a fag. Weren't you, Wellington? What a beautiful couple you and your boyfriend Gi-Gi would have made, if anyone had ever seen you. At least I was honest about what I was."

"Not at the office, you weren't, fagot."

"You're one of us."

"No! I am not! Ask them, ask all of them!" He struggled to point along the first row with rigid fingers.

"So what? So you did a few women, each one of them a whore in their own way. Can you not see that? That doesn't change what you are. I couldn't risk anyone finding out. I'm sorry. I was sorry. Still, you had no good reason to do this."

"Yes, I did. I wouldn't have told anyone, you know that. You helped ruin my life, along with them. I did to you what you did to me: an eye for an eye." He smiled cruelly at the German, "and a tooth for a tooth. The difference being, Marcotte, I chose a more direct and unequivocal method."

"You killed me!"

"Yes, I killed you. And who cares? What's your point? You barely made the obituaries. You fired me for no fucking good reason. Fuck you, fagot!"

"You're not wrong. I am, I was, but I did not deserve this." He held both ends of the death tool. "I mean, really, Bartlett. A gun I could understand, or a knife. But this?" He stood, clenching his fists, his front stained with blood and wine. "Lesbians are fine, fags have to die: the ultimate male hypocrisy. I vote for your death, Bartlett, your eternal damnation and I pray we meet again!"

"We won't," was the weak reply, "we won't, never again."

"And why is that, Wellington? Why is that?" he screamed.

"Because, Marcotte, I'm crossing over to a better place. I'll soon be dead. But before I go, tell me. Did he win? Do you miss him?"

"Do you miss me, Trystan?" Gaston stood with sufficient character to halt Marcotte's response. The air

397

around him was electric blue, his naked body entirely depilated and bloated. "Would you ever love me as you see me now? Did you ever love me?"

Wellington looked at Pat, devastated. Now she would know all. What was curious to him was that he was dying, being killed, yet he cared what she thought. She had once wondered what her cariño would do after leaving the island, now he wondered what she would do after he was dead.

"Yes. I miss you, Gaston. You will never know how much, though I can say nothing to you. I cannot explain myself to you or defend what I did. I acted with passion, a passion for you as much as for another whom I loved, and whom I still love. Though my love for her does not mean I loved you any less."

"But you killed me, and not her. How can you have loved me and killed me, my love."

Wellington cringed under the tightness of his constraints. "Yes. I'm sorry, very sorry. We did have some good times together."

"Yes, we did have some good times, too few and within the framework of your lie."

When would the lights go out, he wondered? The time was1:52. He was beginning to feel lifeless, or were they killing him too soon? Who would know? Who would care?

Louise laughed. "Wellington, no one will care. No one." She kissed Felicity, "Least of all us." She paused, enjoying the other's exotic caress. "Not that we didn't all enjoy you. Felicity was right. You were good, very good, and so is she...hmm. She's so tasty. But you know that."

"You know what I am thinking," he prompted, and they all laughed.

"Yes, Wellington." Louise answered, "We know all. You have no secrets. Not here, not now."

"Then, you know how I feel, how I..."

"How you repent?" she interrupted, laughing

uncontrollably while the others watched with wide grins or chuckled.

"Yes, how I repent," was his simple response.

"You don't want redemption, Wellington. You want complete absolution from all of us." She kissed Felicity, cupping her breasts. "I vote for dreams, Wellington."

"Why? Why do you vote for dreams?"

She giggled. "Because we don't hate you and we want to share ourselves with you again and again." Louise opened her fleecy white towel, letting it fall to the floor so that the women around her might openly admire her. Indeed, their eyes did linger, appraising her appreciatively. Then to him, smiling mischievously.

He ignored her, he ignored all of them. What little time remained was too important. "And you Gi-Gi, how do you vote?"

"Trystan, I vote that you dream of me forever. I do so not out of spite, my love. I do so out of love and the hope you will once again want me, this time forever. I love you, Trystan, I always have. And I will wait for you."

"Then, would you not want me to die?"

"No, my love. Death is not without pain. I will wait. I will be here for you, whenever you come."

Wellington turned away. Would his death be painful? Was the pain not in living? Wasn't pain only found in life? Hadn't he said that? Why had Pat said something so cruel? Hadn't he always loved her? He turned to the clock, searching through blurred eyes. The time was 1:55, but what did time matter? What were three lost minutes in a lifetime? What was a lifetime?

He felt no fear, for he had no time to nurture the expectation of death, only the death itself, and weren't dreams forever? Dreams were forever, he knew, and so was death, or so his father had always told him. So was this his dream, or was this his death? He would never know. How would he, for he had no fear? He knew fear existed within the expectation of death, not death itself. He did not seek redemption; he sought their acceptance of his justification. He did have valid reasons. He did.

The first three had feared for their lives, for they all had an expectation of their deaths. The others had not, for there had been no expectation. So how should he feel? How should he act? They had all died, miserably or not, so what would be so difficult for him to do the same? He was better than any of them.

The two women were laughing, though not at him and he barely recognized them. They were merely enjoying the juxtaposition of violent death and sex. After all, sex had been their life as it had been their end. Or why would they be there? One was black, with the blackest hair that seemed blue and beautiful. The other was white and girlish with the most beautiful blonde hair. They wore matching full-length gowns as white as the whitest snow and of the finest silk. They wore soft, satin slippers and had never felt so much like fine ladies. They sat holding hands, observing him as he lay on the table half covered by the thin green blanket and smiling at the bare feet protruding from under the edge trim.

"You're laughing at me," he said, not angrily, seeing the other women enjoying tender caresses or urgent responses. "I know you. Don't I? I also know I never hurt you." They nodded, no. He smiled. Time was running out. "Thank you. You're Seraphina, and you're Dalila. You showed me. I remember you showed me."

"We showed you, baby, and you showed us. It's all a two-way street."

"No," he insisted. "There was no two-way street. You showed me, the two of you, and I thank you. I should have known, I should have seen."

"You paid us, Wellington. There ain't no need to thank

us." She patted Dalila's knee. "Fact is, we fucked you for the money, not counting the tip. The tip is what helped us, and we thank you."

"Being with you was fun. I remember having fun for the first time in so long."

"Baby, what we had was business." Seraphina reached for Dalila. "This here is my fun, baby. The rest don't count for nothin', only her. But we did learn, we did learn."

"What did you learn, Seraphina? What did you learn, Dalila?"

They whispered to each other first. "We learned kindness," they both said. "We learned kindness, baby."

"And how do you vote, Seraphina? How do you vote, Dalila? Do I dream, or do I die?"

"Oh, baby, don't you see? You are dying, over and over again in an endless number of dreams or in time standing still, baby. It ain't nothin' more."

"My socks are off, Seraphina. This time my socks are off. Do you see?"

"Wellington, we're two for one. You had us together, now we'll vote together, for you, and we don't care about socks, not now, not then. We vote for your dreams, baby. Do you want to know why?"

"No. I think I know why."

"Why is that, baby?"

"Because I'm good," Wellington smiled, hoping.

"No, boy, that ain't so," Seraphina laughed as she stood, twirling in her white satin slippers, "because you treated us so good, like ladies. No one ever has, and now see what we've become, the finest ladies anyone ever did see."

"It would seem you're better off with filthy whores in a filthy green room and your cheap vacation flings in lofts and hotel rooms than with my wife, brother."

Seraphina turned abruptly, sitting quickly as the demonstrative finger told her to do so. Most of his head was missing and the charred part of his face that did remain gave him a ghoulish resemblance to the phantom of the opera.

"Fuck you, Jason."

"How you must have hated me."

"The question was never how much I hated you, rather how much I loved Renée."

"Indeed," Jason mused. "There is one aspect of death you will learn, brother. There is civility in what we do, in what we say."

"I'm not dead yet, so fuck off."

"Not yet," Jason answered. "One advantage to being dead is that we know all, we see all, past and present. It's like a Christmas story, brother dearest. I know what you did that night, Trystan, to my wife, to my blushing bride. Trystan, Trystan, mommy's favourite Trystan."

"Fuck you. So I fucked her, so what? What we shared was more than that."

"More than that," he repeated. "Like what? You loved her? No, brother. You fucked her, pure and simple. You didn't share anything, she was practically unconscious."

"Yes. I did love Renée. I always have."

"You saw her with her legs open and you pushed yourself into her, you forced yourself. Is that love to you?"

"I did love her. I do love her." He looked to Pat who was making the final check. The time was 1:57. He had gone too far. "I'll see you in hell, brother."

"No, you will not. However, I do accept your confession, as I am sure Renée does."

"I know already, but tell me."

"You have killed six needlessly, when killing one, brother, would have accomplished as much. Whether you die or live, your life dreaming of that death is irrelevant, though I do vote for death and may God…"

"Do not blaspheme, Jason!" Wellington cried out, trying to calm himself. "I'll see you burn again, in hell, if that's what it takes to rid myself of you once and for all. I will defend myself against you and Henderson and whoever else cares to join you. Goodnight."

She leaned forward. "Never say goodnight, Wellington. Never say goodnight, not to me." Her thin muslin chemise was short and see-through. Her low-heeled pumps were the same shade of pure white. "You were a fool not to know, Wellington. Do you think I would have let you touch me, ravage me the way you did, had I not known." She turned to Geneviève who took her hand and understood. "I love you, Wellington. I always have and Geneviève has always known."

"I didn't know, Renée. I'm sorry. You never told me."

"That makes you a fool, Wellington. You should have known. You should have stood to say something when the minister said "or forever hold your peace." We fucked so well together that night, you and I, the way true lovers do, and you believed I never knew. How many times have you remembered our night, Wellington? How well did we fuck, how well did we dance together at my wedding when you imagined me naked in your arms, making love to me? Yes, I know. Now see where you are. Now you truly are fucked, my darling."

They all nodded in agreement, laughing at him. Renée brought a hand around Geneviève's waist to the smooth and tanned roundness accentuated by her thong-styled one piece gym outfit. Geneviève was shaking her head, as she always had, despising him so self-righteously.

"You wasted both our lives, Wellington, thinking of her when you were doing me. What a waste, when you could have had her anytime, or the two of us." She kissed Renée. "Maybe that would have converted you...queer."

He tried reading Geneviève's taunting eyes, chilled, like peering into two arctic circles. She had always known, the frigid bitch. What was she doing there, he wondered? She was visibly so relieved her role was one of spectator, adjudicator. So content to watch him die. Who had invited her? Who would he kill in his next life for having brought her to his death? He hadn't once thought about her, save in his earthly nightmares. Even seeing her standing so close and half naked beside Renée did nothing for him. She was the real whore.

"She's the real whore, brother," he shouted. "She's the whore, the reason you're all dead."

"You were never good enough for me. As hard as you tried you were never good enough. You must feel better now, Wellington, relieved your failures and miseries are over."

"Not even my promotion to National Sales Manager was good enough for you, days before you left. Nothing less than VP would do. Trips to Spain never made you happy. You had to be in Antibes, with her." His eyes pointed to Renée. "I did nothing but good for you, bitch, and you dare to be with the woman I love, watching me die?"

"Yes." She twirled, leaning across Renée, letting him see Renée's coloured nails digging gently into her undulating flesh.

"And how do the both of you vote, Renée, you and the disgruntled whore? Are you also voting together?"

Renée spoke first. "I vote for dreams, Wellington. So you might always see me, though you will never be with me, never touch me. We know how you long for another."

She glanced through the glass at Pat.

"And you, bitch?"

Civility was not uppermost on his mind.

"You bastard," Geneviève retorted. "If it weren't for men like you there wouldn't be women like me."

"And what kind is that?"

"The kind that hate men," she said, casually, uncaring. "You should have been with Renée, and the two of you should have accepted the known consequences for what you could have done together. You never belonged to me, or with me. I know that and will always hate you for being what you are."

"At least I'm not a whore."

"You are...the worst kind. You were too cowardly to admit the original truth. You married me for success and then used me to cover up your sick perversion." She kissed Renée, ardently. "Tell me, did all these women help you forget your fagot friend?"

"I never did business on my back. Tell me, how do you vote, whore?"

"I can't vote, you fool, though I would if I could, which would mean your death. Enough said? I read the note, you bastard, we all did. The wrong brother burned."

She and Renée embraced tenderly, needing one another during the final moments.

*

Jacqueline stood in her panties and shoes, her body glistening with sexuality.

"Wellington Trystan Bartlett, alias Jean-François LeTuvier, you lay before a jury of your victims, prostrated and pathetic, to hear our sentence. Do you have anything to say that has not yet been said?"

He strained his neck. "Sentence has already been passed. That's why I'm here. Let it happen. Let me cross over to heaven or hell. Please let me go."

"The vote, Wellington... is a tie. We love you as much as we hate you. We want you dead as much as we want you to relive this moment."

"What do you mean, Jacqueline? What are you saying? Tell me!" he implored. "Tell me!"

Pat's warm and firm touch calmed him.

"You killed him as much for me as for your own reasons, cariño. I know, and I love you for what you did. How can I condemn you for loving me so much? Though neither can I condone what you did." She squeezed his shoulder. "Do not hate me for what I must do, cariño. They wanted me to vote. I'm not. I insisted I would not. I could not. I'm here to carry out your sentence with compassion. Know that I love you. I will always love you, even though you have disappointed and hurt me."

What was she saying? What was she doing? He felt the cold fluid attack his veins as a deep, sickening blackness came over him without sound, without sensation. He wanted to scream, to kick out. His body twitched and he strained to kick hard, held in place. He tried to free himself, but he couldn't. The curtain closed.

*

He stirred, not realizing at first the phone had rung. Pat lay by his side, purring; the clock behind her confirming what he already knew in a muted green glow. The phone would always ring at 2:00 AM and he cared not all that time might be told in heaven or hell.

The third ring came and he looked from the clock to his arm. The needle was gone and her warm hand was squeezing him gently, reassuring him. Behind her, under the stars, the moonlit waters of the black Mediterranean sparkled. She was adoring him with passion and love in her eyes, Jean-François not seeing the disenchantment he was searching for. He wasn't dreaming. She was real. Her warmth and her smile were real and she loved him.

He pulled her close, hugging her hard, telling her that he would love her till death would they part. He reached for the phone on the fifth ring.

"Digàme," was all he said.

"C'est Monsieur Jean-François LeTuvier?"

"Yes, this is he."

"Bon matin, Jean-François," the familiar voice answered. "It is I. C'est Jacqueline Duvernay."

Split Verdict

Other Mystery – Suspense - Thriller Novels

By Doug Booth:

Split Verdict

The 4th Man

The Madam

Family Lies

Mother of Pearl

From Inside Her Bedroom

The Feast of Tombola

Deferred Prejudice

The Hunt for Gilligan Rose

The Fatal Diners' Club

Silent Conviction

A Christmas Killer, Comfort and Joy

Pariah In the Mirror

***

No One to Tell (Creative Non-fiction)

www.ingramcontent.com/pod-product-compliance
Lightning Source LLC
Chambersburg PA
CBHW051935240626
47153CB00005B/1496